ARTIFICIAL INTENTIONS

Rosemarie A. D'Amico

iUniverse, Inc.
New York   Bloomington

Artificial Intentions

Copyright © 2010 Rosemarie A. D'Amico

This is a work of fiction. All of the characters, names, incidents, organizations, and dialogue
in this novel are either the products of the author's imagination or are used fictitiously.

iUniverse books may be ordered through booksellers or by contacting:

iUniverse
1663 Liberty Drive
Bloomington, IN 47403
www.iuniverse.com
1-800-Authors (1-800-288-4677)

Because of the dynamic nature of the Internet, any Web addresses or links contained in
this book may have changed since publication and may no longer be valid. The views
expressed in this work are solely those of the author and do not necessarily reflect the
views of the publisher, and the publisher hereby disclaims any responsibility for them.

ISBN: 978-1-4502-6729-8 (pbk)
ISBN: 978-1-4502-6730-4 (cloth)
ISBN: 978-1-4502-6731-1 (ebk)

Printed in the United States of America

iUniverse rev. date: 10/27/2010

Visit the author's website at www.rosemarie-damico.com

For my family: all of those people who individually make up the unit which provides yours truly with all the essentials of life.

Prologue

Hatred boiled within and made everything look like it had been dipped in red paint. The stalker was hidden in the shadows by the chain link fence along the back of the property. Overhead lights, protected by wire cages, cast a yellowish hue around the loading dock. Through the stalker's eyes the light appeared orange.

The hatred caused the stalker to breathe in short, gasping breaths, which didn't help with already high blood pressure.

I am here to finish this. Finish him. Make him suffer.

The stalker had let hate take over any rational thought. Hatred had ruled every waking moment, of every day, and every week, for the last month.

A car approached from the right, creeping along in the darkness. The beginning of the end, the stalker thought smugly. Just come a little closer.

The car stopped and the driver's door opened. A man stepped out of the car and stood there, looking around.

The noise of the car's engine was the only sound, except for the stalker's frantic breathing. The hatred was boiling too fast now, it was boiling to the top and was going to boil over. The stalker tried calming down, tried breathing slower, through the nose. The light around the loading dock was now deep red, blood red, furious red. Stars were flickering behind the eyelids and tympani drums beat furiously in the ears. Fast and panicked breathing was reducing the carbon dioxide in the bloodstream, causing the blood vessels to the brain to constrict. Dizziness followed, and the stalker knew that calming down was the only hope of carrying through. This thought caused the panicked breathing to increase. Just before the stalker passed out from hyperventilation, a muffled sound came from the left and the driver of the car fell to the ground.

Chapter one

THE WARMTH OF THE SUNLIGHT on my closed eyelids told me it was morning but my body wasn't responding. Today I was starting a new job at the pristine and stuck-up law firm of McCallum & Watts, and next to sticking needles in my eyes, my next favourite thing was starting a new job. At a stuck-up law firm.

Don't get me wrong, I was glad to have the job. I had been unemployed for six weeks and was starting to get desperate. In the past, I'd never gone more than a few days between jobs but this was 2002, not the early nineties, when you could quit a job in disgust, throw everyone the finger and start a new job the next morning at nine.

My last boss, Harold Didrickson, was being investigated by the Ontario Securities Commission for his participation in the manipulation of public stock prices. The company that had employed us, TechniGroup Consulting Inc. or TGC, was in the throes of being reorganized by a huge conglomerate that had purchased it for pennies a share.

My index finger gently rubbed the top of my ear where I had been shot by one of the executives of TGC in what turned out to be one of the nastiest scandals to rock the high-tech world. I'd lost the tip of my ear and my job but six weeks later, I was relatively unscathed. Glad to be starting a new job and relieved to know I'd soon have a regular paycheck, but the job itself was a few steps back in my career. Not that I was complaining, because as I had repeatedly told myself since I'd accepted the position, one couldn't be picky.

I forced my eyes open and glanced at the clock beside my bed and groaned. It was only 6:30 and I didn't have to be at my new desk until 9:00. By my standards, half the day was over by 9:00 a.m. At TGC I was in the office most days by 7:30 a.m. and if I left by 6:00 p.m., I considered it a good day. More often than not I worked weekends and in the last couple of years there, I was traveling a lot. Not a heavy workload by executive standards, but then again, I wasn't paid like an executive. I was a paralegal, with a specialization in corporate and securities law. However, compared to what paralegals made at law firms, I was well paid. *Was* being the operative word. I was taking a pay cut at McCallum & Watts but I also wasn't hired to do paralegal work. My new title was Legal Secretary.

Typing, dictaphone (yes, lawyers still dictated into those funny little machines), filing, billings, and making appointments was my new job description. And making nice-nice with the clients, especially those who paid their bills. Definitely a step backwards for me, but a job.

I turned on my back and stretched, pointing my toes and trying to reach the end of the bed. It was a game I used to play as a child, stretching every morning when I woke up to see if I'd grown overnight. Along with the standard children's prayer we said every night, *"Now I lay me down to sleep…"*, I'd add under my breath, "And please God, make me grow". It hadn't worked, but I still checked every morning. I was thirty-four years old and just under five feet tall. Four foot eleven, to be precise, but I considered it my prerogative to add an inch when anyone asked. I dreaded growing older because I'd heard that some elderly people shrink in height.

I gave up the game of trying to reach the footboard of the bed and kicked off the duvet. The warm morning air drifted through the open window and I could smell summer. It was the middle of June and the thought of summer gave me an excited feeling in my stomach. Baseball, sprinklers, firecrackers, hide and seek after dark, staying up late, and barbecues. I was thinking like a school kid, but whenever I smelled summer in the air, I was ten years old again. Summer meant the end of school and endless play. I quickly brought myself back to reality though and stumbled out of bed to the shower.

Two weeks later I was still telling myself that I couldn't be picky about the job. *It's a job, it's a job,* I chanted to the beat of the photocopier. The repetitive sound of the automatic feeder on the monstrous photocopier was becoming hypnotic. *Che-chunk, che-chunk, che-chunk.* I'd been listening to the sound now for the last three hours as I photocopied a mountain of paper for one of the lawyers in the corporate tax section. As low man on the totem pole, I had been getting all of the dog jobs. The secretaries in our group gleefully dumped the dog jobs on me and I found myself having to practice verbal restraint on a daily basis.

I pressed my back against the counter and did a couple of deep knee-bends to get the kinks out of my lower back. Along with this job being boring and mundane, it made my body ache. The photocopy job was one that I alone was tasked with doing because the lawyer in charge told me it was too confidential to send to the main photocopy room where there were oodles of lowly paid young men who would be happy to help out. As if anyone in their right mind would find anything interesting in these mounds of paper.

The room was suddenly silent which told me that the photocopier was finally done. I pushed myself away from the counter and bent over the sorter bin on the end of the copier to retrieve the copies.

"Hey," a voice greeted me.

"Hey yourself," I said over my shoulder. "I'm almost done here, you can have the machine."

When I stood up with my arms full of papers, a very young, pimply-faced person was standing at the door to the room. This was a person I didn't recognize but that wasn't surprising because I was still seeing new faces every day at McCallum & Watts. There were reportedly 350 people on staff, 145 of whom were lawyers. My sharp deductive reasoning told me that this one was definitely not a lawyer. He looked totally out of place in his dress pants, starched white shirt and thin leather tie. The fact that he wasn't wearing a suit jacket and was pushing a mail cart, told me he was one of us. Support staff.

"I don't need the machine. Are you Kate Monahan?" he asked me. I nodded.

"Ashley in Corporate asked me to tell you to get your butt back to your desk." With that he pushed off down the hall.

Ashley can go fuck herself, I thought to myself as I bundled-up three hundred pounds of paper in my arms and started the long trudge back to my workstation. Ashley had appointed herself my supervisor and if I didn't throttle her before this week was out, it would be a miracle. She had arrived at McCallum & Watts right out of legal secretarial school at the ripe age of nineteen and had been here now for three years. In our little corporate tax group she was the most senior secretary in terms of years on the premises so when I joined the group, she took it upon herself to show me the ropes. That was the first day. On the second day, and each subsequent day, she had been climbing higher on her little hill, singing, I was sure, *I'm the king of the castle.*

There were five of us legal secretaries in the bullpen, as it was affectionately called by the *all-male* team of lawyers who we supported. There were eight of *them.* One partner, supervising seven junior associates. All of whom specialized in tax law. A quick shiver went up my spine and then back down again, at the thought of tax law. Dry, boring and mind-numbing was the only way to describe tax law. It was also a pretty apt description of the eight lawyers in our group.

Ashley on the other hand was cute and perky and her voice sounded like fingernails on a chalk board. It didn't take me long to figure out that there was a high turnover in support staff in our bullpen and Ashley had assured me it was because of the boring work. Not that *she* thought it was boring. I was sure the high turnover was because of the perky Ms. Ashley. Every piece of work that came our way passed through her hands first and she doled it out. I was still getting my feet wet, she told me every day, so that was why I had to do all the photocopying and open the mail. My computer was gathering dust from lack of use and access to the files was still restricted to me, "until you understand the department," I was patronizingly told, at least two thousand times each day.

My mother would be proud of my restraint, but I had started grinding my teeth again. To keep my comments to myself I had to constantly clench my jaw and physically restrain myself. It was a job. And a paycheck.

The ton of paper I was carrying made a loud thunk when it hit my desk and I had to quickly grab it as the pile started to topple.

"Kathleen," I heard Ashley behind me. She was big on proper names and made a point of using mine.

"Yes, Ash." My voice sounded bored and I hoped she got the dig with the way I had shortened her name.

"The personnel manager wants to see you," she said excitedly. "Right away."

The little bitch, I thought. She's reported me for something and I felt like I was back in the seventh grade. I turned around and faced her.

"Is there a problem Ashley? Did I put the staples in the wrong corner on that tax return yesterday?"

Her faced flushed and she looked a little guilty.

"No." She took a deep breath and puffed out her 32 double A chest. "I have no idea why she wants to see you." There was defiance in her voice so I believed her. She was too young and stupid to lie well. Lying truthfully came with experience. I knew.

I made my way through the rabbit warren of workstations and waited patiently for the elevator, which, if I was in luck, would arrive before quitting time. The law offices occupied five floors and there was no way I was walking up five floors to the personnel manager's office. In the six weeks I had been off work, I had started an exercise regime to get myself back in shape. Religiously every day, after dinner, I would walk briskly around my neighbourhood for an hour. I did that five nights a week and took the weekends off. I hated exercise, so I refused to do any more than my nightly walk. Including walking up stairs.

I had also quit smoking which was a feat in itself. I had been a chain-smoker who would've put the Marlboro Man to shame and deep down I was quite proud of myself for successfully kicking the habit. So far. At the thought of smoking, my hands went automatically to the pockets of my skirt for a cigarette. My finger punched impatiently at the elevator button instead.

Linda Beeston was sitting primly behind her neat-as-a-pin desk when I knocked on the door frame. The lack of visible work or mounds of paper was in no way indicative of how busy I knew Linda was. She was responsible for all of the support staff in the firm and the latest numbers indicated she rode herd on over 200 people. She herself had a staff of four just to keep track of everyone. Linda had interviewed and hired me because, being the smart lady she was, she recognized my skills and experience. However, they had no need at that time for another paralegal, so she had hired me as a secretary. I was grateful, but I was close to putting Linda on my shit list for having hooked me up with the perky Ashley.

"Come on in," she invited me. "I've been expecting you. Close the door."

She had one, uncomfortable, straight-back chair in her office. Just like the ones we've all sat on outside the principal's office. I lowered my weary butt into it and smiled at her. It was a wary smile, because I wasn't sure what was on the agenda.

"So. How's it going with the great Ashley?" Her eyes were smiling at me.

"Wonderful," I joked. "I'm thinking of naming my first born after her. She's a peerless leader."

Linda laughed. "Look, I'm sorry for having to put you in that group. We know your qualifications. The firm was thrilled to get someone of your experience and as I told you when I hired you, if something came up that was more suitable for you, we'd move you." She paid me the compliment with sincerity.

"Just don't tell me you're promoting Ashley and you want me to take over her job."

Linda shook her head. "God forbid. Ashley wouldn't move out of that group. Tax is her life. So she tells me," she said with a smirk.

"That's a very telling statement, you know Linda."

We both laughed.

"McCallum & Watts has just hired a senior corporate securities lawyer from one of the rival firms and he's specifically asked for you. He's coming in as a very senior partner and when he found out you were here, he almost made it a condition of his employment. Are you interested?"

She certainly had my attention now.

"Of course. If it's corporate securities work, I'm there. And I'm flattered."

I couldn't imagine who it was but I did know most of the top guns in

Toronto. I'd either worked with them, or against, them in the job I had at Scapelli, Marks & Wilson.

"Great. We consider it quite a coup that we've lured him away from Scapelli's. John Clancy, our senior corporate partner is retiring next year and between you and me, I think they might have their eye on Mr. Johnston to replace him."

When she said Mr. Johnston, my stomach sank so I waited for the sucker punch.

"Would Mr. Johnston have a first name?" I asked.

"Cleveland. Says everyone calls him Cleve."

Well, Cleve had obviously forgiven me for my past sins or this was his way of making me pay for all those nasty things I'd said to him. My mind shot back to the last time I'd seen him and how I'd been an absolute, first-class, no doubt about it, bitch.

"Monday," I heard Linda say and I jerked my attention back to her voice. "Come on and I'll introduce you to your new workstation."

I followed her meekly down the hall. Today was Friday. I had all weekend to figure out how to apologize.

Chapter two

"Is this supposed to be good news or bad news?" I asked incredulously. My voice was raised a little and I made a conscious effort to lower it.

"Bad news for us. Good news for me," he said meekly.

To say the least, I thought. Shit, fuck and damn. We were less than three months into our relationship and Jay was telling me he had to move. Cities. Not down the block.

"Sorry," I told him. And I meant it. In my typically selfish style I was just thinking about myself. "The job. Tell me about the job. It sounds fantastic."

"Well, that remains to be seen. But it's something I can't pass up. It's only six months in New York and then I'll be back in Toronto. Like I said, they want to train me there and if everything goes well, they'll promote me back here."

His hand rubbed my shoulder distractedly and we were both silent. Jay Harmon and I had known each other all our lives but we had only taken the relationship to an intimate level in the past couple of months. He told me he was head over heels in love with me and although I hadn't admitted it out loud to him, I felt the same way. I was still having trouble with our age difference and the fact that I was six years older. We started out as best friends and even though the relationship had taken on a new twist in the last few months, we remained first and foremost, best friends.

As a friend, I was ecstatic for Jay because I knew how much his career meant to him. Like me, he had lost his job at TechniGroup Consulting. Jay had his MBA from Western and like all Western grads, he was a mover and a shaker. He had loads of potential, and I for one wasn't about to hold him back. As much as I was going to miss him, it was only six months, I told myself.

"So, can I assume you'll wait for me?" Jay said with a grin.

"You have to ask? I guess I'll have to change my long distance carrier now."

I heaved myself off the sofa where we'd been watching the ball game. "I'm going to make some coffee. Want some?"

"Any beer?"

"Sure," I said as brightly as I could.

Jay had delivered the good news/bad news to me on Friday night and here I was on Sunday night, waving good-bye at Pearson Airport. The bad news had continued to get worse when he told me, after the ball game, that he had to leave Sunday.

I stood like a lost child beside the car as I watched Jay weave through the other passengers into the terminal. Air Canada was about to whisk away the only bright spot in my dreary life and I waved pathetically at Jay's disappearing figure.

About seven years ago I had spent many Sunday nights in this same spot beside the curb, at Pearson Airport, under the yellow International Departures sign. Back then I'd been saying my farewells to my now ex-husband, on his way back to his business in Phoenix. We'd met at the law firm where I was working and he was a client. Our whirlwind romance turned into a tornado of lust that ended up in marriage. The plans were made for me to move to Phoenix, but I never got around to packing up my apartment. The team I was working with always had one more deal to close. Eventually my excuses wore thin.

Tommy and I are still good friends and he makes an effort to call me whenever he's in town. I grimly told myself that, this time, I'd make an effort. My life had become comfortable with Jay, knowing that he was in the same city, in the same neighbourhood, always there to talk to. Comfortable was good. Comfortable was, well, comforting. I was thirty-four years old, which was practically a spinster by some standards. Not that my aim in life had ever been to catch me a man and marry him. Admittedly, my first stab at marriage had turned out pretty pathetically, but with Jay I felt that we might have a chance for a life together.

My reflection in the car window made me feel sick. Sick at the sight of my morbid face, looking like a dejected puppy. Suck it up girl, I mentally yelled at myself. Get on with it. Self-pity had never been one of my strong suits so I physically pulled myself together, and loaded myself into Jay's jet-black Saab. Jay had generously offered me the use of his precious vehicle and I jumped at the chance to drive something that wasn't on the verge of breaking down and that actually had door locks that worked.

Monday morning found me full of dread, if that's still an expression used in the English language, sitting at my new desk. Cleveland Johnston was due to arrive any minute and I was still working on something cute and sassy to say to him.

Our histories together went way back and it seemed that I had known Cleve most of my professional life. He was a junior associate lawyer and I was a legal secretary at Scapelli's when we first met. Over the years Cleve gained the experience to make partner and eventually head-up their securities practice. I remained a legal secretary/paralegal. Sure, I had the fancy moniker of corporate securities paralegal, but my job remained the same. Herding the lawyers, supervising the support staff, making things happen. I had a mid-life crisis in my late twenties and quit the law firm and worked temp until I landed at TechniGroup Consulting, a high-tech, public company.

Harold Didrickson, who was the Senior Vice-President, Legal at TGC had hired me to help him set up the legal department when the business was booming. He had retained Scapelli's to do our corporate and securities work and Cleve Johnston headed up the team at Scapelli's, so we had remained in contact.

The shit hit the fan at TechniGroup Consulting when my best friend Evelyn was murdered, and Jay was fired because the chief financial officer, Rick Cox, thought Jay had something to do with it. I was privy to certain information that pretty conclusively fingered Rick Cox and when he was eventually fired, the corporate bullshit press release said that he was *resigning*. Number one rule when dealing with the press: an executive is always allowed to maintain a certain decorum when murder and mayhem happen in the high tech world. In the meantime though the fact remained that Jay had lost his job. When I asked Cleve to help Jay keep his job because the board of directors knew Rick Cox was responsible, he played lawyer with me and stood by the company's statement that Rick Cox was resigning to pursue other interests. Much yelling and breast-beating ensued, albeit one-sided. Cleve remained the consummate professional and listened calmly to my tirade but I ended up slamming down the phone on him. A few days later he had tried in a backhanded way to apologize but I cut him off, making some typically snide comment about friendship. My mother repeatedly tells me that my smart mouth will get me nowhere, but for some odd reason, I continue to ignore her.

Needless to say, the situation was about to become awkward. I had neither spoken to nor seen Cleve in several months and I believe some people would get great joy out of seeing the beads of sweat that had broken out all over my body.

"What goes around, comes around" was another of my mother's favourite sayings and when I heard Cleve's voice several offices down the hall, I knew that *it* was about to come around. I shook all thoughts of my mother from my head and put my head down and pretended to be busy.

"And this is your office and of course, you know your assistant, Kathleen Monahan," I heard Linda saying. I sucked in a deep breath and pushed my steno chair away from the desk and stood up. Cleveland Johnston stood there, towering over Linda and grinning at me. Kind of a Cheshire cat grin. I stared up at all six feet, five inches of him and grinned back.

"I'll leave you two then," Linda said. "Kate's been here long enough to be able to show you the ropes. Kate, call me if there's anything you two need."

Cleve silently gestured at the open door to his office, inviting me to lead the way. I heard the door close behind me and I turned around and looked up at him. The silence was deafening and the sweat on my upper lip was probably very visible. I surreptitiously wiped at it and said, "So, how many of the lawyers you met today were shocked to meet a white guy?"

He laughed. "All of the guys I'd met at the partners' dinner the other night figured it out quickly enough but a few of the associates I was introduced to this morning were surprised to find out that the skin colour didn't go with the name." People were always surprised to find out that Cleveland Johnston was a very tall, white man. A very tall, handsome, some would say gorgeous, white man. But I was somewhat biased, having suffered a massive crush on him, way back when.

Cleve walked over to his desk, plunked his large legal briefcase down and snapped open the two locks. He reached inside and pulled out two champagne glasses that were wrapped in navy blue, linen napkins. His massive fingers gently unfurled the napkins and he placed the glasses gingerly on the desktop. He then flourished a champagne bottle and began working the cork, all the time staring at me with a stern look. When the cork blew out of the bottle, he smiled widely and ceremoniously poured champagne into two glasses. He held one out to me and I took a few steps towards him to accept the glass.

"To new beginnings, Kate." He held his glass up and toasted me.

"To new beginnings," I repeated. I took a sip and knew that no apologies were going to be necessary.

Chapter three

OUR FIRST WEEK WORKING TOGETHER at McCallum & Watts was uneventful. Much time was spent doing up the paperwork for Cleve's clients at Scapelli's to have their files transferred to his new law firm. I think Cleve was proud of the fact that about three-quarters of his clients chose to follow him to McCallum & Watts. The twenty-five percent of his clients who refused to make the change were mostly those whose families had used the services of Scapelli's since the birth of their great-grandfathers.

And of course, the one client's name who popped out and slapped my heart was Phoenix Technologies, Inc. I had worked on the file at Scapelli's when Phoenix first went public and I remembered the frantic pace at the time. We all worked long hours, especially when the prospectus for the initial public offering of their shares was being finalized. There were all-night sessions at the commercial printers, proofreading the documents as changes were being made. I shook my head in amazement thinking about how *driven* we all were. There were several nights when we finished at the office around two in the morning and then went out to an all-night diner for something to eat. When we were finished there would be a string of limousines parked out front to chauffeur us home. Several times it was so late that I just had the driver wait while I showered and went straight back to the office. Being part of the excitement, part of the team, was what kept me going. And my desire to be around Tommy, the young president of Phoenix.

In between the time of filing the preliminary prospectus with the Ontario Securities Commission and the Securities & Exchange Commission in the U.S., and the countdown to filing the final prospectus, I went on the road with the executives from Phoenix and the underwriters while they sold the stock. I looked after the travel and meeting arrangements as they criss-crossed the country. The frenetic pace, and spending almost twenty-four hours a day with Tommy, led to the inevitable.

At the closing of the public issue, when the lawyers were manhandling all of the documents and the underwriters were breathlessly waiting to hand over their check, Tommy had sidled up to me and whispered a proposal in my ear. Our marriage lasted a couple of months but the friendship remained to this day. The last time I had heard from Tommy was a couple of months ago when my face was plastered all over the national news. He told me the picture of me being helped into an ambulance had sent waves of panic through him, but I had brushed off his concern. He had left me a couple of messages after that but I hadn't returned his calls. In hindsight, I wished I had.

As a member of the board of directors and the corporate secretary of Phoenix Technologies, Cleve had to attend all of their board meetings, and the one scheduled for the following week, in New York, was planned to be a regular, run-of-the-mill, quarterly meeting. The agenda he had prepared for the meeting contained all of the standard stuff: approval of the minutes of the last meeting; review and approval of quarterly financial statements and the 10-Q; five-year forecasts; executive bonuses, etc., etc. The meeting was scheduled for early Wednesday morning, so Cleve flew out late Tuesday night. We had booked him a hotel in Manhattan, near the Phoenix offices.

Feelings of deja vu overwhelmed me as I worked on the file before the meeting. They weren't good feelings but I brushed them aside, trying to re-establish the feelings of excitement I used to have whenever I worked on the file. All I could remember though was feeling like a failure because when my marriage fell apart, I left Scapelli's for good and had my mid-life crisis, early. I had worked temp for a while, hopping from job to job, trying to overcome the depression.

The day before he left for the board meetings in New York, Cleve had asked me to call Tommy and speak to him about the agenda and any last minute changes. Tommy was in a meeting and I ended up speaking with his secretary, Carrie.

"Tell him it's Kate Monahan at Cleve Johnston's office. Cleve needs to know if there have been any last minute changes to the agenda."

"I'll give him the message," she said. "And Kate?" She hesitated for a moment.

"Yeah."

"He'll be pleasantly surprised to find out you're working with Mr. Johnston."

"Pleasantly surprised?" It was the first time I had spoken to anyone at Phoenix since I started with Cleve.

"He speaks fondly and very highly of you." Her manner of speech was somewhat stilted, and I pictured an older woman, sitting primly at her desk with her steno pad centered on her blotter with a sharpened pencil at the ready.

"Uh, thank you. Did Mr. Johnston not mention that I was working with him?" I knew this was going to be awkward and when she had said Tommy was in a meeting, I had been glad not to have to speak with him.

"Not that I'm aware of. Thank you for calling and I'll make sure Mr. Connaught gets the message."

When I returned from lunch later, there was a message on my voicemail from Tommy. It made me blush.

"Kate, Kate, Kate. Surprise, surprise, surprise. I couldn't believe it when my secretary told me you were working with Cleve. That's great news." There was a long pause in the message and I was about to hang up when he spoke again. "Come to New York for the meeting. We could renew old acquaintances." He chuckled into the phone. "Call me back."

He'd finished the message speaking in that soft, sexy voice that I remembered so well. I quickly hung up the phone and buried my head in the filing cabinet while I waited for my face to return to its original colour. I didn't tell Cleve about the phone call because I had no intention of going to New York.

Cleve called exactly at five the next day.

"Checking up on me?" I teased him.

"Uh no," he said, sounding distracted.

"Why are you calling? You're supposed to be on a plane. Did you miss it?" I had booked him on a 4:00 p.m. flight out because the board meeting had been scheduled to finish by 2:00.

"No. I'm still at Phoenix's offices. Listen, Kate. Are there any messages for me?" I heard voices in the background.

"Nope. Want me to check your voice mail?" I offered.

"No. I already did. Tommy didn't call?"

"Tommy? Isn't he there with you?"

"Just a sec." Muffled sounds came through the phone and then he was back on the phone. "Thanks," was all he said. Then he hung up the phone.

I couldn't believe what had just happened and I stared at the receiver when the dial tone started. My fingers flew as I punched in the phone number at Phoenix's offices. I asked for Tommy's secretary.

A voice that I didn't recognize answered the phone. "Mr. Connaught's office."

"Carrie?"

"No. She's not available at the moment. May I take a message?"

"It's Kate Monahan at McCallum & Watts. Can I speak to Cleveland Johnston?"

"I'm sorry ma'am." The voice became officious. "I can't disturb the board meeting in session."

"I understand. But this is an emergency."

"I've been given strict instructions. Let me have your number and I'll give Mr. Johnston the message."

"He has it." I forgot my manners and didn't say good-bye as I quickly hung up the phone.

The next hour dragged as I waited for a return call and when my phone didn't ring, I tried calling Phoenix again. The main switchboard was on voice mail and the electronic voice told me to either dial the extension of the person I was calling, or spell their name into the phone, starting with the last name. I had no idea what Carrie's last name was so I pressed the sequence of numbers that spelled out *Connaught*. The phone rang five times and Tommy's voice mail picked up. I dialed zero hoping that it would bump me to his secretary's phone but I ended up back at the switchboard. Voice mail hell. I hung up in disgust and went home.

Chapter four

WHEN CLEVE WASN'T AT THE office the next morning by 9:15 I called his house. There was no answer.

I spent the better part of the next hour opening boxes of files that had come over from Scapelli's and putting the contents away in the four-drawer filing cabinets. Mindless work. My mouth had a metallic taste which I knew was from a nervous stomach. And I wanted a cigarette. Bad. What the *hell* was wrong with me?

When the phone finally rang at 10:30 I knew it was Cleve and a sudden feeling of foreboding came over me. As anxious as I had been to talk to him, I couldn't pick up the phone. I just stood there and *watched* it ring. Four rings and then it kicked over to voice mail. I turned my back on the phone and stood in front of the file cabinet, wondering why I had just done something so stupid. My phone rang again and I turned around to look at it. The intercom was flashing.

It was the receptionist on our floor.

"Oh Kate. You're there. Hang up and I'll put Mr. Johnston through."

My finger pushed the red release button and I disconnected her.

"Kathleen Monahan," I said into the phone, pretending I didn't know who it was.

"Hi." That was it. A simple *hi*. But that one syllable word said so much. Just the way he kind of dragged it out. I pretended to ignore the tone of his voice.

"Hello yourself. Need me to book you a flight back?"

"No. I'll be here a while. Kate, something's happened. Can you transfer this call into my office and take it there?"

Linda Beeston, the personnel manager, was standing outside Cleve's office when I opened the door. The look on her face told me that she knew about the call and that someone had forewarned her.

"We've got a driver outside, Kate, to take you home to pack a bag and take you to the Island Airport. Is there anything I can do for you here?"

Like a deaf mute I shook my head.

"Well, please call us if there's anything you need here in Toronto. And let Mr. Johnston know that we'll look after things here in his absence." She was telling me this while I rummaged in the desk drawer for my purse. I was really looking for cigarettes and remembered that I'd quit.

She escorted me down to the front of the building and over to the waiting car. It was a navy blue Lincoln Continental sedan and the driver was standing at the rear door, holding it open.

Linda gave a weak smile and patted my arm before I got in the car.

"I'm sorry Kate."

"Thanks," I whispered back to her.

The driver obviously knew my address and we didn't speak until he pulled up to the curb in front of my house.

"I'll wait here, ma'am," he said to me as he held open the back door.

"I won't be long."

My bedroom was in a shambles and most of my work clothes were in a heap on the rocking chair beside the bed, waiting to be taken to the dry cleaners. I grabbed a few outfits and jammed them into my suitcase along with my sweat pants and several pairs of socks and underwear. Most of my pantyhose were in sad shape but I managed to find a new pair, still in their package at the back of my dresser drawer. My running shoes and windbreaker were in the front hall closet and they were the last things to go in the suitcase.

I looked sadly at my latest goldfish, Beulah, and said good-bye. Probably for good. By the time I got back from New York, she would no doubt be dead, along with the other twenty or so goldfish I had managed to kill over the last couple of years. I had no luck keeping them alive and with a forced exit from the city and no one to come in and feed her, she was a goner for sure. God forbid the SPCA ever found out about me. I pinched an extra dose of fish food into her bowl and waved.

The driver was smoking a cigarette and lounging beside the car when I came out. He quickly butted it under his shoe and came towards me to take my suitcase.

"Got another one?" I asked him.

His face was a question mark.

"Cigarette."

"Oh. Yeah." He dug in his breast pocket and handed me a pack of

DuMaurier's. I greedily took one and dragged a little too deeply when he lit it for me. I held back a cough and put my hand on the side of the car to steady myself. The nicotine shot through my system and I felt my blood tingle. The second drag felt familiar, and the smoke stung my nostrils. I didn't care.

"You can smoke in the car, ma'am. If you like."

I had two more on the way to the airport and when we arrived at the private terminal after crossing a short piece of Lake Ontario on the ferry, he proffered a new package of DuMaurier's with matches. The matches had his company name stamped on them.

A small man in a dark, navy suit met me at the car and walked me through the private terminal, directly out onto the tarmac. A sleek aircraft waited for me. I wished the circumstances were different and I could pretend that I was a celebrity or just a plain old billionaire. He followed me up the staircase into the plane and stowed my suitcase for me.

I could see two people sitting in the cockpit and the man in the left-hand seat turned around when we boarded. He pried himself out of his seat and came into the cabin. He offered his hand.

"Captain Floyd, ma'am. Thanks Alfred," he said to my escort.

I watched as Alfred left the plane and manhandled the staircase up into the plane. Captain Floyd secured the door and turned back to me.

"Please. Sit."

I closed my eyes tightly and scrunched up my face to try and get my concentration back. The only words I had spoken to anyone since Cleve's phone call were to the limo driver to ask for a cigarette.

"Right. Sorry." I turned around into the cabin and looked about. There were four seats on each side of the aisle, and I took one of the seats facing the front by a window. The total seating capacity was eight, with four seats facing front and four facing back. There was a polished wood table in front of the seats which looked as wide as most boardroom tables.

"Please make yourself comfortable," the Captain said as he reached over to help me with my seatbelt.

"We're flying into Teterboro, New Jersey and our flying time is less than two hours. The co-pilot will be back as soon as we're airborne and get you some refreshments."

"Thank you. I'll be fine."

We were in the air at our cruising altitude within a few minutes and the pilot's voice came over the speaker. It was weird having him speak directly to me and I paid attention, unlike the times I travel on a commercial aircraft and I ignore all the announcements.

"Ms. Monahan. Captain Floyd speaking. We're at our cruising altitude and I've turned off the seat-belt and no-smoking signs. In case you didn't notice when you boarded, the restroom is at the rear of the aircraft."

My hand went automatically to my pocket and I lit a cigarette. As I dragged on it I thought about how easy it was to go back to the habit. No will power whatsoever. The first sign of stress and I fell back in the trap. What a weakling.

The sky was cloudless outside the window and I stared into the nothingness. My thoughts finally returned to my phone conversation with Cleve and a glance at my watch reminded me that it had only been a little over an hour since we had spoken.

"The news isn't good, Kathleen," he had started.

"What? What's happened?" I demanded.

"They found Tommy's body early this morning."

"What do you mean, Tommy's body?"

"He was missing yesterday."

"Why didn't you tell me when you called at five?"

"We didn't know there was anything wrong at that time."

"Bullshit Cleve." My blood pressure was rising and I wasn't sure if it was from fear or frustration.

"Kate. Leave it. I'm sorry, but Tommy's dead. The police won't tell us anything yet. We've sent the Phoenix corporate jet for you and it's ready to leave as soon as you are."

I didn't answer him. I couldn't. Sweet Tommy was dead and I couldn't file the information anywhere in my head.

I finally answered him. "I'm not coming."

"What?"

"I'm not coming," I repeated. My stomach was doing triple flips remembering my encounter with death a few short months ago. I looked under Cleve's desk for the recycling bin in case my breakfast decided it wasn't staying put. Death and I didn't do well together.

"Tommy and I were friends. That's all," I continued. "We've been divorced for years. You know that Cleve."

"But you're listed as his next of kin," Cleve said.

"His next of kin? I don't think so. We were *divorced* years ago."

"I know that Kate. But his papers list you as next of kin."

"Be that as it may, Cleve, I'm not coming. I can't. I'll just hang out here and look after things for you," I said helplessly. My brain felt like it was enveloped in a fog and I just wanted to be by myself, not talking to anyone.

"Thank you for calling," I said formally. Could I be called the widow? The ex-widow? The widow wanted time alone.

"Kathleen," Cleve shouted into the phone. "Are you with me?"

His shout brought me back to the present.

"Yes," I answered, suddenly feeling out of breath.

"I knew I should have had someone there with you. Now listen to me. Are you listening?"

"Yes," I breathed into the phone.

"You have to come. Tommy's will states that you are his next of kin and his life insurance policy names you as the beneficiary."

"That has to be outdated, Cleve. We're divorced."

"Kate, it's not outdated. The will was written a few months ago and the life insurance policy is less than a year old."

"I don't have to be there, Cleve. I can't do it and I think you know why. I'm no good in these situations. If there are papers to sign, send them to me."

"Kate, there's more. It's why I need you to come to New York right away."

"What is it?"

"Tommy's left you his majority shares in the company. We need a chairman of the board. Now."

Chapter five

THERE WAS ANOTHER BLUE LINCOLN to meet me at the airport in Teterboro and I was glad that the only other person in the car was the driver. The heat of the day greeted me when I stepped off the plane but I shivered nonetheless. I hadn't asked Cleve how Tommy had died and I shook my head at that. When the phone had rung and Cleve had said "Hi", I somehow knew. I was thankful the call hadn't come in the middle of the night. My feelings of foreboding were weird enough in the middle of the day but if it'd happened at night-time, I think I'd be even more spooked.

A very attractive woman, about thirty years old, met me in the reception area at the Phoenix Technologies offices, located at Lexington and East 46th. She was about six inches taller than me and she had one of those hourglass figures you read about. Some would call her too big in the hips, but the suit she was wearing showcased her magnificent hips and small waist. Her hair was a beautiful brown, if brown has ever been described as beautiful, and cut short in a bob. It suited her.

"Ms. Monahan," she greeted me quietly and put out her hand. "Carrie MacIntosh."

I was surprised. I had expected Tommy's secretary to be about my mother's age.

"Hi Carrie."

"I'm really sorry about Mr. Connaught." Her eyes were water-filled but her face was composed.

"Thank you. Is Cleve Johnston around?"

"He's back in the boardroom. Follow me."

She led the way through reception and down a long corridor. I had to trot to keep up with her. I hate women with long legs.

"Carrie," I called after her. "I'd rather see Cleve alone. That is, if he's with people in the boardroom."

"I'll put you in Mr. Connaught's office. That's no problem."

She stopped abruptly in front of a door and opened it. She waved me through and I entered into what was obviously a secretarial office.

"My place," she explained as she walked past the desk and opened yet another door. I followed her in and quickly glanced around.

"Make yourself comfortable. Coffee?"

"Please," I mumbled to the door as it closed. She seemed very efficient.

Tommy's office was huge and the two exterior walls were all glass, overlooking Manhattan. His desk was centered in the room and soft seating was dispersed around the thick, luxurious carpet. One side of the space was taken up with a large, rectangular meeting table with eight, high-backed, leather chairs. I wandered around and noticed there were very few personal touches. A bookcase held two shelves of mementos, marble and acrylic paper weights commemorating various corporate achievements, sales and marketing give-aways and such.

I heard the door open behind me and turned around to see Carrie, entering the room with a tray of coffee. She placed it on a coffee table.

"I've told Mr. Johnston that you've arrived. He'll be right in. Is there anything else you need right now?"

"Thanks. I guess I'll need a hotel room."

"Already taken care of."

I looked around for an ashtray. Tommy had loathed my smoking.

"Ashtray?"

"I'm sorry, Ms. Monahan, but smoking is not allowed in the office."

I dug my DuMaurier's out of my pocket and lit one.

"It's okay, I'll use the saucer," I said as I blew out a cloud of smoke. I knew if I could smoke, I could handle what was going to happen in the next couple of hours.

Carrie opened a drawer in the bottom of a credenza and extracted an ashtray.

"How long have you been working with Tommy?" I asked her.

"Three months."

The office door opened and Cleve walked in. Carrie's long legs took her to the door in a few steps.

"I'll be outside at my desk if you need anything."

"Thank you Carrie," Cleve and I said at the same time. The door closed quietly and Cleve looked at me for a moment.

"I thought you'd given up that nasty habit," he said, pointing at the cigarette.

"No willpower." I butted the half-smoked cigarette in the ashtray and walked over to the window. I stood there with my arms wrapped around myself and took in the view.

We were both quiet for a couple of minutes and without turning around I asked Cleve, "How did he die?"

"Gunshot to the back of the head."

Ohmigod. Ohmigod. My stomach turned and my head swam. Tommy had been murdered. It hadn't even occurred to me. Without thinking too much about it, I had assumed he had died in some sort of accident.

"Have they arrested anyone?" I finally asked.

"No."

"Any suspects?"

"No."

I turned around and faced him.

"None? Was it a mugging? Was he in the wrong place at the wrong time?"

"We don't know Kate. It's too soon for the police to be telling us anything. In the meantime, we've got a public company here. A press release has gone out but we have to do some damage control."

"Fuck damage control. Fuck the company. I don't care. I'm in the wrong place. At the wrong time. This isn't right Cleve." I was having trouble putting coherent thoughts, words and sentences together.

"Right or wrong, Kate, you were listed as his next of kin. His secretary told us that his mother and father are both dead. Did he have any brothers, sisters, aunts?"

"No." I shook my head. I remembered Tommy telling me how he felt being an orphan at twenty-three. His parents had died in a head-on collision. He had grand plans for a large family, to make up for his loss. We never even got to the planning stages.

"As his heir, you'll have some decisions to make. Hard decisions."

"Not now Cleve. I'd rather just help look after the funeral arrangements."

"That'll have to wait. The police aren't releasing the body until after the autopsy and they can't say when that'll be."

He reached inside his jacket and took out a white envelope which he held out to me. I didn't take it.

"This was found in his papers. It has your name on it and says to be opened only on his death."

"I don't think I can right now Cleve. I need to use the ladies room."

"Please Kate. Be reasonable. I can't possibly imagine how you're feeling right now. I understand though. So I'll leave the envelope here for you and when you're ready, please, read it. Have Carrie find me when you're ready to talk."

He placed the envelope in the center of Tommy's desk and left the office.

I spent the next fifteen minutes huddled in a cubicle in the ladies room. Trying to sort out my feelings. The heaviness I felt was my body and mind in mourning, that I knew. I had felt the same way when my best friend Evelyn had died earlier that year. I finally surmised that my behaviour was denial. Denial that another good friend had passed. It was too early to be discussing wills and inheritances. Tommy's body was probably still warm in the morgue and Cleve wanted me to participate in damage control.

Control of what I wondered? Phoenix Technologies was a company I knew little about. I had been involved with it over ten years ago when it was a fledgling high-tech company. What I did know was that technology ten years ago didn't even resemble technology today. I hadn't read much of the file when it came over from Scapelli's, so my only current knowledge of the company was a brief conversation the previous week with Cleve. He had told me that Phoenix Technologies stock was still listed on the TSE and NASDAQ, and that they had grown to over 1,100 employees with offices in several cities. Tommy had moved the executive offices out of Phoenix to New York a few years ago. That was the extent of what I knew of the company.

I edged Tommy's large executive chair closer to the desk and picked up the white envelope gingerly with my thumb and index finger of each hand. It was addressed to me in Tommy's handwriting. The first line read: *Kathleen Monahan*. Underneath that in small, printed capital letters it read: *TO BE OPENED BY ADDRESSEE ONLY ON THE OCCASION OF MY DEATH.* Occasion of his death? How formal. I turned the envelope over and noticed that Tommy had signed his name over the seal.

I touched the floor with the tips of my toes and swiveled the chair around to face the windows. I sat that way for a few minutes while I smoked and collected my thoughts. Sure, we'd been friends all these years. I tried to remember if Tommy had ever had another girlfriend. He had never remarried. When I asked for a divorce he'd told me very somberly that he'd never marry again. Not fucking likely, I remember thinking. Tommy was a catch. Handsome, caring, rich, funny. But after a while there wasn't any spark for me. I thought of how I felt about Jay. Jay could cause a spark.

So Tommy and I split amicably, and remained steadfast friends. Occasional dinners and frequent phone conversations. I never had an inkling that he had cared so much about me that he felt the need to name me as his beneficiary. And leave me in such a *fucking mess*.

I swung the chair back around and quickly slit open the envelope. It was dated two days after my brush with death a few months back, and was written in Tommy's handwriting.

Dearest Kate, it read. Dearest? He had never referred to me as dearest. It continued: *What I saw on television the other night made my heart stop. But just for a second because I saw you were walking into the ambulance and you were obviously all right. I'm not sure how I would deal with the news if someone came to tell me you were dead. But that's what you've just heard about me, and for that, I'm sorry. That last sentence was the hardest thing I've ever had to write.*

My eyes filled up with tears and the rest of the letter became a blur. You son-of-a-bitch, I thought. Why are you dumping this on me? I wiped my eyes angrily and continued reading.

If you're reading this letter, I'm dead. There. I said it. I've missed you all the years we've been apart but I understand why you decided our marriage couldn't work. I am truly grateful that we've remained friends. You have my utmost respect for the person you are.

Enough of the mushy stuff, he wrote. Thank God. *This letter is by way of explanation of what you will learn of the contents of my last will and testament.*

I have left to you the sum of my worldly goods. Sounds quite Victorian, doesn't it? My worldly goods include my golf clubs, my aquarium with the exotic fish (just fucking lovely, I thought, more fish to kill off), *my collection of Beatles albums, and the rest of my possessions. Including my majority ownership of Phoenix Technologies, Inc.*

Why? Because there is no one else I trust to continue the company. And yes, Kate, I've stipulated that you are to become the Chairman (or Chairperson) of the Board, immediately. Being the good little legal beagle that you are, you know that the shareholders appoint the directors and the directors appoint the officers. Being the rightful owner now of the shares, you can appoint yourself a director. And rest assured that the remaining directors will immediately approve your appointment as Chair.

You have the brains, the guts and the willpower to do this. You've just never been given the chance.

Trust Cleveland Johnston to give you the counsel you deserve. My kindest regards, with much love and affection. Tommy.

I immediately lit a cigarette just to show him I *didn't* have the willpower.

Chapter six

"CARRIE?" I CALLED HER NAME quietly through the door I had opened a crack. She quickly turned around in her steno chair.

"Yes?"

I beckoned at her with my index finger and motioned for her to come in. Being the efficient secretary, she quickly picked up her steno pad and two sharpened pencils. I asked her to sit in one of the chairs in front of Tommy's desk. I took the chair beside her.

"I need to go to my hotel," I told her.

She made a note on her steno pad.

"Right away, Ms. Monahan. I'll have Mr. Connaught's driver out front immediately." She rose from her chair to leave and I put my hand on her forearm.

"Please. Carrie. Sit down."

She reclaimed her seat and poised her pencil over the pad to take more instructions. I reached over and took the pencil and steno pad out of her hands and placed them on the desk in front of us. That made her finally look me in the eye.

"This situation is very hard for everyone," I started. "And I imagine, especially hard for you. I know Tommy, uhm, Mr. Connaught, was a very good man and I'm sure he treated you well."

"Yes. Yes he did." Her eyes were filled with water again. This time her face did not remain composed and she pursed her lips to try and control the tears. I knew the feeling.

"Good. I'm glad to hear that. Tommy was a great guy. I've just read a letter he left me and it seems he wants me to have some involvement with the company." *Some involvement.* Nothing like understating the situation.

"Yes. Yes. That's good," she whispered. "Mr. Connaught always spoke highly of you." She took a deep breath and I could see she was trying to regain control.

"If I might ask, Ms. Monahan, what is it you do in Toronto?" she asked me.

"Do? You know what I do. I work with Cleve Johnston. At the law firm."

"Yes. I know that. But are you a securities lawyer, or a tax lawyer, or a corporate lawyer? I wasn't sure since Mr. Johnston hadn't had time to fill us in on his new partners."

I was dumbfounded.

"Uh. I work in the securities and corporate field. But I'm not a lawyer Carrie. I'm a secretary. Like you. A legal secretary, but a secretary just the same. In my last job I had the high and mighty title of Corporate Securities Paralegal. But I was just a glorified secretary."

As I was telling her this her eyes got a little wider and a slight smile showed at the corners of her mouth. I waited for the inevitable bitchy response.

"I'm glad to know that," she said genuinely. "And I hope I can stay around and help you out here." She mischievously wrinkled her nose and I knew her offer was genuine.

"Thanks Carrie." I knew I had a comrade in arms. "Are all of the directors in the boardroom?"

She nodded.

"Then show me how to sneak out of here without running into any of them."

Tommy's driver, the same one who had picked me up at the airport, drove me to The New York Palace Hotel and whisked me through the reception up to the 54th floor. He assured me he had already checked in for me and that my suite was ready. I was feeling a little like a movie star.

He left me with his card and told me to page him, at any time, if I needed his services. The name on the card read "Lou Cardenello".

"Thank you, Lou," I told him. He handed me the key to my room and silently walked back down the hall. I closed the heavy door and turned around to survey the room. Or rooms. The suite was huge. And luxurious.

I threw my suitcase on the bed and proceeded to unpack. My clothes seemed seedy and worn in this room, and I wished I had taken the time to pull out some of my good outfits. Okay. One good outfit. I called the valet service from the phone beside the bed and asked how soon I could get clothes dry-cleaned.

"Immediately, Ms. Monahan. Within the hour. Just put everything in a bag you'll find in your closet on the floor by your door, and I'll send a bellman to pick them up right away."

Now that was service.

I stuffed everything I had brought with me except a clean pair of panties and sweat socks into the laundry bag and tossed it out to the front door. Then I grabbed the thick, terry cloth robe hanging in the closet, and locked myself in the bathroom for some privacy and a long, hot soak.

The bathroom was the size of a small gymnasium and the sunken bathtub could hold a family of six. While I waited for the tub to fill, I found a well stocked bar hidden in a mahogany armoire. *In the bathroom.* The height of decadence. I filled one of the large crystal glasses with Diet Coke and slid into the tub.

I dozed off for a few minutes and the electronic ringing of the telephone woke me. The buzzing sound irritated me and I thrashed around in the water for a moment, trying to get my bearings and came perilously close to going under. I made a mental note to wear a lifejacket in the tub next time I took a bath.

The phone was conveniently located on the wall beside the tub and I grabbed at it to make the buzzing stop. I had been asleep longer than I thought because the water in the tub was cool.

"Hello." I started shivering.

"Kate?" Shit. It was Cleve. My hiding was over.

"Oh. Hi. Cleve."

"Kate. You shouldn't have disappeared on us like that."

"I didn't disappear. Tommy's secretary knew where I was. I had to get out for a while."

"Okay, okay. Listen. I've a few things to say to you. First, my condolences. I never had a chance to tell you how sorry I was."

I cut him off before he became too maudlin.

"That's okay Cleve." I looked around the bathroom to see if I could manage to get out of the tub and grab a towel and still hang on to the phone. The receiver cord was very short so I continued to shiver.

"Secondly, Kate. As much as this whole situation is a shock to you, we have to move swiftly on a few business issues. That's where we need your full attention and co-operation. I've kept the members of the board here in town and I'd like to call a special meeting of the directors tonight. With your consent of course."

A special meeting of the directors. That term was very familiar to me but it had never before given me such an eerie feeling. Special meetings are those called on an urgent basis, when there isn't time to give as much notice of the meeting as is required in the company's by-laws. In those circumstances, I'm generally busy, typing up waivers for the directors to sign, consenting to the business to be transacted the meeting, etc., etc. This time though, I wouldn't have to prepare any of the documents for the meeting. Usually, before special meetings of directors, I'd run around like a meshugana getting everyone settled. Looking after grown men. I guess this time someone else would look after the documents and *I'd* sit in on the meeting. And they wanted my consent.

"Sure. What time is it now?"

"Five thirty."

"Fine. Call the meeting for nine o'clock. In the meantime, I'd like to meet with Tommy's personal lawyer and have him describe to me the terms of the will. How it relates to my inheritance of the shares. I want to know exactly where I stand before I go in that meeting."

"Uhm. I'll try and get in touch with him."

"Cleve. I'm *not* going in that meeting without knowing where I stand. You either find that lawyer or you can send all of the directors home." I wanted to finish off with: Do I make myself clear? That was one of my mother's favourite expressions, but this man had been my boss earlier in the day.

"You're right. I'll call you back, Kate."

I quickly pulled myself out of the tub and wrapped a towel around me. My clothes had all been returned to my suite and were hanging in the closet in plastic wrap. They had even ironed my sweatpants. I could learn to love this.

Chapter seven

WHILE I WAITED FOR CLEVE to call me back, I telephoned my parents to break the news about Tommy. They were upset, especially my mother who had adored him. I deliberately neglected to tell them about the will.

Then I called Jay and told him I was in New York.

"What a surprise!" he said excitedly. "Can we do something tonight?"

"No. Sorry." I stalled.

"Oh. No problem. Are you working?"

"Not exactly. Well kind of. At Phoenix Technologies."

"Oh yeah," he said slowly. "Your ex-husband's company." A slight tone of jealousy came through when he said ex-husband. That miffed me a little.

"No longer ex-husband, Jay. He died."

"Oh. Oh, Jesus. I'm sorry Kate."

"Thanks. That's why I'm here. In New York."

"What happened?"

"He was shot."

"Shit. Only in New York. Should I come over?"

"No, it's okay. There's some sort of special directors meeting tonight, which I'm involved in." Another grand understatement. "I don't know what time it'll be over. Maybe I'll call you later?"

"Of course. For sure. Anything."

"Great. I gotta go. I'll call you."

"Kate."

"Yeah."

"I'm so sorry about Tommy. I love you."

"Bye Jay."

God, we were great conversationalists. We were just out of practice, I told myself. The red light on the phone was blinking, and I stared at it. Another fucking voice mail system. The card beside the phone told me how to access my messages and I dialed a series of numbers just to hear a click. The caller hadn't bothered to leave a message. So I sat huddled on the bed waiting for the phone to ring.

The room was dark and it matched my mood. The situation I found myself in was overwhelming. I was supposedly now the major shareholder of a high technology, publicly-traded company. The responsibility was going to be tremendous. Eleven hundred employees. Probably several hundred shareholders. Offices in several cities. Products and services that I knew absolutely dick-all about. To say nothing of the Beatles' collection and the exotic fish. And what the hell was I going to do with *golf clubs*?

Lou, the driver, pulled the car up to a steel-encased skyscraper on Fifth Avenue where I could see Cleve waiting for me at the front entrance. I had the back door of the car open before Lou could get to it and he looked a little put out as I got out of the car.

"I'll wait," he told me. "But I can't park here so please call my pager when you're ready to leave."

"It's okay. We can get a cab."

"I *don't* think so, ma'am. This is my job."

"Oh. Right. Sorry." I was going to have to get used to dealing with this one.

Cleve signed us in at the security desk in the large, cavernous lobby and quickly led me to the elevator bank marked for floors 52 through 70. We were both silent as the elevator started and I sneaked a glance at Cleve's profile. There were visible lines around the corners of his eyes and the laugh lines which were normally so noticeable around his mouth had disappeared.

"Tired?" I asked him.

"Exhausted," he said without looking at me.

"I'm sorry."

"For what?"

"For your loss." He turned to face me and suddenly he looked like a little boy in a giant's body.

"I know you and Tommy were close. More than just client and attorney."

He nodded his head. "You're right. It had gone past the attorney-client relationship in the last couple of years. We golfed. You know."

The elevator doors opened and we entered directly into a darkened reception area. Cleve led me past several groups of arm chairs and sofas and through a set of large, double doors into the offices beyond. He obviously knew where he was going and he flicked the light switch on in a small, glass-enclosed meeting room. He plunked his briefcase down on the table and immediately picked up the phone and dialed a three-digit number.

"We're here," was all he said before he hung up the phone.

"Know your way around, don't you?"

"Remember? I used to work here. Not that I spent much time in the New York office," he explained. And then it hit me. We were in the New York office of Scapelli's. When Cleve had called me at the hotel to tell me that he had arranged for us to meet with Tommy's personal lawyer, he didn't mention what firm he was with. But it made sense. Most clients keep all of their work within the same law firm. The name Dennis Hillary wasn't familiar to me but he had probably not been with the firm when I was an employee years ago in the Toronto office.

I took a seat and waited. When Mr. Hillary entered the meeting room I wasn't surprised to see a man who looked like the proverbial bookworm. Guys who did wills and estates were not the most exciting types, and Dennis certainly fit the bill. He was small, not that I held that against him, although with three inch heels on I'd probably tower over him at the cotillion. Long strands of damp hair were brushed over his bald head, from one ear to the other. Little bug eyes stared at me through thick, frameless glasses, and when I stood up to shake his hand, he wouldn't look directly at me. His hand was damp and the shake was lifeless. He didn't let me down either, when he started to speak and his stutter was easily discernible.

The man immediately went up several notches in my esteem, because I knew that no worthy law firm would have such a nerd on staff, unless he was absolutely brilliant. Dennis settled himself at the table and messed with the bellows file of materials in front of him. He glanced at Cleve several times and it was obvious that Cleve's presence made him nervous.

He cleared his throat a couple of times before he spoke.

"Miss Monahan. First of all, let me express my deepest condolences." He was looking at the tabletop as he said this. I looked over at Cleve with a little grin on my face and he shrugged his shoulders.

"Thank you Mr. Hillary."

He balled up his fist which he placed in front of his mouth and coughed, clearing his throat.

"As Mr. Johnston has told you, I had the job of preparing Mr. Connaught's last will and testament." He finally looked up at me. "Which I have right here." He proudly flourished a thick document.

I would hope so, I thought.

"Before I proceed with the reading, might I ask if you would like Mr. Johnston," he coughed again behind his hand, "to uhm, leave, uhm, wait for us outside?"

31

There were little beads of sweat clearly visible on his forehead and under his lower lip. The man needed to calm down.

"No that won't be necessary. But maybe Mr. Johnston could round up some cold drinks for us?" I looked over at Cleve and gave him a look, which he clearly didn't understand, but he lumbered out of his chair and left the room.

"Mr. Hillary. I need Mr. Johnston to be here. He's Phoenix Technologies' corporate lawyer. He obviously makes you nervous, but please, calm down."

Dennis gave a high-pitched squeal, and his face broke out in a wide grin.

"No. No, no, no. Mr. Johnston and I are colleagues. It's *you* I'm a little nervous of. People around here still speak of you, and even before Mr. Connaught named you in his will, I knew of you. We have several partners here in New York who started in the Toronto office. Some of them as law students. They still quiver at the mention of your name."

I guffawed. "You're putting me on, Dennis."

He shook his head. "Oh no, Miss. Your reputation has certainly preceded you. I understand you used to run quite a tight ship there in Toronto. May I tell you one of my favourite stories, one that gets repeated most years at the firm party?"

Jesus. The man was looney-tunes.

"Sure," I agreed, glancing at the door, hoping for my knight with the Cokes to return swiftly.

"Several years after you had left Scapelli's," he started, "you returned to the law firm one night with your current boss. Scapelli's was acting for the company you worked for, doing, uhm, an acquisition, I believe."

I stared blankly at him, willing him to get to the point. So far, nothing rang a bell.

"One of the junior lawyers, who I understand you used to work with during your time at Scapelli's, was part of the team working on the acquisition. She has since left Scapelli's and is now at the Ontario Securities Commission."

That rang a bell. Missy Goodman. How could I forget. The type of woman who gave the rest of us a bad name. A chip on her shoulder the size of a large tree trunk. She had started at Scapelli's as a summer student, spent a year articling and then was hired on full-time after she was called to the Bar. Initially, she and I had become good friends. I took her under my wing and showed her the ropes. And then the little bitch had turned on me.

She was one of the few women allowed into the all-male bastion of the corporate securities department at Scapelli's. So she had something to prove. Little Missy Goodman. It was Missy when she was a summer and articling student, and then Melissa, as soon as she became a full-fledged lawyer.

32

I was naive then, and the one thing I have to thank Missy for is my wariness at making new friends. Jesus, she'd even spent a weekend with my family at my parent's place on Georgian Bay. But as soon as she was called to the bar, *I* was the secretary and *she* was the lawyer. And make no mistake about it. It was difficult working with her after that. Especially in the team environment I liked to foster in our group. She stayed at Scapelli's for four years and then made the jump to the OSC. I now remembered what the story was that Dennis was droning on about.

"So," he continued eagerly. "You showed up with your boss. Everyone was running around, doing their thing. And Melissa Goodman came up to you with some documents in her hand, and in front of everyone, asked you to make some photocopies."

I smiled widely.

"And you said, *Fuck you*," he blushed as he said fuck, "*I'm* the client now. Make your own damn copies."

He beamed. "Legend. Absolute legend."

I heard Cleve laugh behind me. "He's right Kate."

The sweat had disappeared from Dennis' face. I decided I liked him.

Chapter eight

THE ACTUAL "READING" OF TOMMY'S will took less than twenty minutes. I tried really hard to concentrate but the heretofores, henceforths and notwithstandings kept me mostly confused. My knowledge of wills and estates could fill the head of a pin so I was lost.

But, the bottom line was it was all mine. Whatever it was that Tommy had owned was now mine. Hithertofore. Henceforth. And forevermore. The true bottom line though wasn't defined in the will because, as Dennis explained, they had to present value everything in the estate and the valuation would take some time.

"However, if you're interested in a ballpark figure, for the shares alone, that I can provide you," he told me.

"How many shares are issued and outstanding in Phoenix?" I asked.

Dennis deferred to Cleve on this one.

"Almost ten million at last count."

Whew. "And the current trading price?"

Again, Cleve answered. "About seven and three-eighths."

That was $7.375 a share. My math was terrible, but already my head was swimming.

Dennis piped up. "That makes the outstanding shares worth roughly $73,750,000."

My throat tightened and I was sure I was choking. Just to make sure, I fumbled in my purse and found my cigarettes and quickly lit one. Seventy-three million dollars. Jesus, Mary and Joseph.

Now I had to know. Up until now, I hadn't thought about what this inheritance meant. In terms of dollars. Not more than a month ago, I was unemployed, and worried about whether I should spend the money for an oil change on my old clunker. I smoked my cigarette and stared at Dennis and Cleve.

I finally popped the question. "What was Tommy's percentage?"

"Thirty-three percent."

My old boss used to tell me I didn't have trouble with *math*, I had trouble with *arithmetic*. I didn't even try to make the calculation.

I thought it rude to ask the next question, but I pushed on.

"And that would be approximately what, Einstein?"

"A little over twenty-four million dollars, Kate." Dennis said this proudly. He'd probably never had a client who'd left someone so much money.

"On paper," Cleve added.

Of course, on paper. I couldn't believe Tommy had been worth so much. On paper, of course.

"And, then there's the matter of the life insurance policy," Dennis said.

"Why would Tommy have a life insurance policy when he was worth so much?" I asked.

"The stock market is never a sure thing, and as he said in his will, he wanted to make sure he provided for you," Dennis told me.

Why Tommy felt he had to provide for me was beyond my comprehension. I had never asked for, and in fact I would not have even accepted, alimony. I was too proud and besides, I was self-sufficient. My job had supported me before I met Tommy, and my job continued to provide for me. All of this wealth was overwhelming. To say nothing of the responsibility that went along with it.

I stood up and started pacing the room, chain-smoking.

"Cleve, I can't take this all in. The money, the responsibility, it's impossible. And unbelievable."

Here I was suddenly very rich, and very depressed. And I certainly didn't like the way I had inherited it all.

Dennis coughed to get my attention.

"The life insurance policy is valued at one million dollars," he quickly spit out. He'd been dying to tell me that.

"Ha. A measly million? Peanuts," I said sarcastically.

Dennis coughed again but this time it came out as a squeal.

"She's joking Dennis, joking," Cleve assured him.

I finally sat at the table and put my head down on my arms. I wanted to go to sleep now. Waves of fatigue rolled over me and I felt my eyes closing. I wanted to curl up in a ball under my duvet in my little apartment, and go to sleep. Sleep comes easiest to me when I'm stressed but I reluctantly forced myself to sit up and pay attention.

"Can I have some coffee? Is there a machine around where I can make some?"

Dennis jumped up. "I'll get it for you. Decaf?"

"No way. I need high test."

When Dennis left the room, Cleve quietly asked me, "How are you feeling about all of this, Kate?"

"How the fuck do you think I'm feeling?" I shouted. "Do you want me to jump up and down and yell, I'm going to Disney World? This is terrible, it sucks. I never asked for all of this. I've never even dreamed about winning the lottery. I have no idea what to do about all of this. I don't want it." I had a sudden thought. "I can refuse to take it, can't I?"

Cleve slowly shook his head.

"Why would you want to do that?"

"Because I *don't want it*. What part of that don't you understand?"

"Calm down."

"Don't tell me to calm down. You take the money. And the responsibility. And the eleven hundred employees. And the fucking exotic fish." At that, I burst into tears. I was so incredibly mature.

Dennis arrived at that moment with a thermos of coffee in one hand and a stack of Styrofoam cups in the other.

"Dennis," Cleve said. "Can you give us a minute?"

When Dennis had left the room, again, Cleve told me to sit down and get a grip on myself. The man was definitely the strong, sympathetic type.

"You can't change what's happened Kate."

"No I can't." I wiped my nose in a very unladylike manner on a balled-up Kleenex that I found at the bottom of my purse. "But I don't have to like it. In fact, at this moment, I'm more pissed off at Tommy then I've ever been. Didn't he have a favourite charity or something?"

"Kate, you're missing the point. Phoenix Technologies was his life. And he said in his will that he wanted it left in the capable hands of the one person he trusted implicitly. You."

"Well, Phoenix Technologies is in deep shit. Sure, I can type like a demon, transcribe dicta-tapes until the cows come home, organize a mean meeting, but I have no idea how to chair a board of directors and run a multi-million dollar company."

Cleve reached across the table and covered my hand with his huge paw.

"You'll just have to learn."

I turned up the air conditioner full blast, and stood naked under the ceiling vent. When I was chilled sufficiently I crawled under the covers on the king-size bed, curled up in a ball and tried to sleep but I could still feel the caffeine coursing through my veins. The digital alarm clock on the bedside table read 1:45 a.m. and I cursed the amount of coffee I had consumed over the past several hours.

It had been just after midnight when Lou returned me to the hotel. The lobby was quiet and I was overwhelmed with feelings of loneliness as I trudged to the elevators.

After the meeting with Dennis, Cleve and I had returned to the Phoenix offices for the emergency board meeting. Cleve introduced me to each of the directors and then he conducted the meeting because I had told him I had absolutely no intention of chairing the meeting and that the onus was on him to get through the business at hand. I had sat mute throughout most of the meeting, trying to pay attention and understand everything going on.

It was the first time in my life that I remember feeling completely intimidated and shy. Shy wasn't even a word in my vocabulary but the overwhelming enormity of what had happened to me in the last twelve hours rendered me helpless in front of these people.

The names of the directors were familiar to me when I was introduced but my mind was too full to try and remember their backgrounds. A couple of them I remembered from my dealings with the company when it had first gone public. One of the directors was a vice president of the company.

Cleve had started the meeting by introducing me formally and then explaining the terms and conditions of Tommy's will. There were no gasps of surprise so I was sure everyone had been brought up to speed before I arrived. Cleve then put forth a motion to appoint me chairperson of the board and it had been carried unanimously.

The next item for discussion was the content of the press release that would be sent out first thing in the morning. The release set out in vague verbiage how I had come to be appointed to the office of chairperson. Several directors were quoted with *bon mots* about the tragedy of the loss of life and how pleased they were that I was joining the company and that I'd be a great addition to the team.

There was a paragraph about me, outlining my illustrious career in law and high technology. I had trouble believing that what had been written was actually about me. It was all factual but it gave me an uneasy feeling. Whoever had written it made it sound too good.

I held up the draft press release and pointed to the paragraph about me.

"Is this necessary?" I asked Cleve who was sitting beside me at the boardroom table.

"Absolutely. The shareholders are going to want to know who's running the ship."

"It's too flowery. Almost unbelievable. Tone it down a little. I don't think we should oversell me."

"We'll rewrite it. But we have to put in your background."

"Fine. I'd rather we didn't have to do any damage control when someone takes a close look at it. We should be up front from the beginning. Full, true and plain disclosure," I reminded him, stating the strong, basic principle of securities law.

"Absolutely," Cleve agreed with me. I wasn't going to play any of the games with press releases that I had witnessed in my years at TechniGroup Consulting.

A short press release had gone out earlier in the day announcing the death of Tommy and the shares of the company had closed down about half a dollar. Cleve warned me that we could expect that the stock would be down again the next day and that it would be impossible to predict what the market's reaction was going to be.

We finished up the meeting quickly, covering off the approval of the financial statements because the company had a deadline for filing the various documents with the OSC and the SEC and the stock exchanges. I abstained from voting.

Before leaving the office I asked for a copy of all press releases from the last two years and the last two annual reports and 10K's. I had some serious studying to do and some fast catching-up. And I was probably going to have to hire a tutor to help me through the financial stuff.

After the meeting I made a quick exit and Cleve escorted me down in the elevator to the waiting car. In the elevator I broached the subject I had been avoiding all day.

"I want to speak to the police about Tommy's death. I need to find out what happened. Has anyone been in contact with you?"

"Yes," he responded slowly. "In fact, there've been several messages from the detective in charge. They want to meet with you as soon as possible."

"They have *no* idea who was responsible?"

Cleve didn't answer me.

"What's happening with the investigation?" I pressed him.

We were outside the building now, beside the car, and Cleve conveniently ignored my question and opened the back door for me.

"Do you realize, I know nothing about how Tommy died. Except that he was shot in the back of the head. Now, if you have some more information, I'd be grateful if you'd share it with me."

Cleve gave a visible sigh and a fatherly look came over his face.

"The investigation is continuing. Obviously. I have no hint of what's going on."

"You're patronizing me Cleve. Don't do that."

"Fine. You'll find out soon enough. I understand they're investigating Tommy's death as a homicide, as you know, and that they suspect it was someone who knew him. They have definitely told me it wasn't a random mugging."

"Thank you. What was so hard about sharing that information?"

Cleve stared at me hard, for a few moments.

"Because it seems you're the obvious suspect."

Chapter nine

SLEEP FINALLY CAME TO ME but I woke up restlessly several times in the night. I dragged myself out of bed around seven and immediately made myself a pot of coffee. While I waited for it to brew I brushed my teeth and dunked my face into a sink of cold water to try and revive myself. I wondered if this is how drug addicts felt in the morning.

The red light on my phone was blinking and I checked for the messages I had ignored last night. There was only one and it was from Jay.

I called his studio apartment and woke him up. Told him I needed to see him before he went to work and asked him to come to the hotel and have breakfast with me. When he arrived forty minutes later I gave him a long, hard hug.

"Nice digs," he said as he looked around the suite. "Certainly coming up in the world," he joked.

"Comes with the territory. That's what I need to talk to you about."

We sat at the small dining room table where room service had laid out muffins, croissants, jam in little jars, fresh fruit, juice and coffee. I poured myself another coffee and explained to Jay what had happened over the last day. He didn't speak throughout my whole explanation and when I finished, he had an amused grin on his face.

"I don't know what to say," he said.

"Yeah, well neither do I." I lit my third cigarette of the day and blew the smoke at the ceiling, away from Jay. He hadn't said anything when I first lit up in front of him and I was grateful. One doesn't need to be reminded of one's weaknesses.

"What're you going to do, Kate?"

I shrugged my shoulders.

"Are you up for this?"

"What do you mean? The challenge? The new job?"

"No, that's not what I mean," Jay said. "I know you. I've known you all my life and I've never known you to back away from a challenge. You're incredibly bright and you'll have no problem catching up with the business. I meant the wealth that comes with the challenge. Are you up for handling it?"

"I have no idea. You know me. I live from paycheck to paycheck. I barely have anything in my RRSPs. Last night I told Cleve I didn't want it. I'm still thinking that way. Do you happen to know if sudden, new-found wealth changes people?"

"No idea. We were dirt poor as kids and I'm just glad to have a job and have enough money left over each week to send my mom. I'd have no idea how to handle what you've got now. I read somewhere recently that they've done a study on people who've won large sums of money in lotteries and they all say they aren't any happier. But you're a well-adjusted person now. Are you looking to be happier? Why would all this money change you?"

"The responsibility. It's making me miserable already."

"Scared of a little responsibility?" he challenged me.

I shook my head.

"Then dive in. Have fun with it. How many years have you been telling me you could do a better job than the monkeys at the top?"

"That was fantasyland. This is reality. And reality sucks."

"Well, welcome to reality."

As much as I felt like calling in sick on my first day on the job, I thought it would be prudent to at least show up and make an effort. I had no idea what to expect and no inkling of what lay ahead of me.

Carrie was at her desk when I arrived at 9:30 and I asked her to join me in my office.

"I'll need your help with today with a few things," I told her. "I need to get the lay of the land, so to speak. So, first things first. Can you show me where the coffee room is?"

She looked a little surprised but pleased.

I followed her through a maze of corridors to a large kitchen which resembled coffee rooms in offices around the world. Microwave oven, large refrigerator with an ice-maker on the front of the door, coffee-maker with several pots on the go, bulletin boards on the walls, and several Formica-covered, round tables with chairs. The room was empty of people and after I poured myself a cup we returned to my office. We didn't bump into any staff in the hallways and I was surprised at how quiet the place was.

"The police have been calling?" I asked her.

She nodded.

"Well, let's call them back and set something up. I need to talk to them."

Two detectives arrived about half an hour later and I put aside the Wall Street Journal where I had been looking for financial news reports on Tommy's death.

To my surprise, both detectives were women. They were complete opposites but that's where the similarity to Cagney & Lacey ended. The one who introduced herself as Detective Bartlett was African-American and not much taller than me. The kindest way I can think of describing her physically would be rotund. She was round. Her face was circular and she wore her hair in a perfectly-shaped Afro. She was sporting two extra chins.

Detective Shipley was so tall I wondered if she had thought about playing professional basketball. My best guess put her at about six foot two. Her mousy brown hair was cropped short and it looked like she cut it herself. She was wearing brown, plain clothing which suited her just fine.

They were strictly business and after a fashion got right to the point.

"Thank you for seeing us so quickly Ms. Monahan," Shipley said as she rummaged around in her purse. "Ha," she finally said, and flourished a dog-eared notebook. She put her head back in the purse and I glanced at her partner who just shrugged her shoulders and rolled her eyes.

"Pen, a pen," I heard her mumble and I offered one across the desk to her.

She grabbed at it gratefully and flipped over several pages in the notebook. Shipley was not impressing me and I checked out her overcoat to see if there were any more resemblances to Peter Falk's Detective Columbo. She finally settled down with the pen poised over her notebook and looked me in the eye.

"Could you let us know your whereabouts on the night Mr. Connaught was murdered?"

Nothing like getting right to the point.

"I was in Toronto."

She noted that in the notebook.

"Exactly where?"

"In my apartment," I replied.

"Can anyone verify that?"

"No." I didn't like the direction she was heading with this line of questioning, but I wasn't surprised. When Cleve had told me that I was a suspect, my immediate reaction had been horror at the thought.

"Initially Kate, you'd be the best bet for a suspect. The ex-wife who stands to inherit."

Cleve had watched the gamut of emotions run across my face and then had done his best to calm me down.

I snorted. "What, are they nuts?" I said.

"I know it's ridiculous. We both know it. But they still have to question you."

So, when Shipley started asking me very direct questions, I had my answers ready.

"When was the last time you saw your husband?"

"My ex-husband." I stressed the *ex*.

"Your ex-husband. When was the last time you saw him?" she repeated.

"I think it was about six months ago." I had been thinking a lot about that the night before and I had remembered fondly the last time he came to town. As usual, Tommy'd been on a tight schedule but made time to call me and we went out for dinner. I couldn't remember the exact date but it had definitely been before all the trouble at TechniGroup.

"Had you spoken to him in the last few days?" Detective Shipley asked me.

I hesitated before answering because I wondered if a message on voice mail counted.

"No. But I did have a message on my answering machine at work from him the day he died."

Shipley made a long note in her book before looking up at me again. I wondered if Detective Bartlett ever spoke.

"And what was the message?"

"He said he wanted me to come to New York. My boss, Mr. Johnston was coming here for a board of directors meeting and Tommy left a message asking me to come along."

"How did he sound on the message?"

"He sounded great. Full of enthusiasm, as usual. He was surprised to learn that I was working with Mr. Johnston."

"Please describe your relationship with Mr. Connaught," she said woodenly. It sounded like a question right out of a survey.

I didn't have to think about my response. "Good. We were friends."

Detective Bartlett's eyebrows went up in disbelief at my response.

I stared at her and said, "Do you find that hard to believe Ms. Bartlett? That a divorced couple could have a good relationship?"

She blushed under her dark skin and lamely shook her head.

"Are you currently involved in a relationship with someone?" Shipley continued.

"Yes. But what's that got to do with the price of rice in China?" I demanded.

"Just trying to get the whole picture."

I'd had enough of their questions and decided to turn the tables.

"I'd like some information on how your investigation is going. Do you have any suspects?"

They both looked at each other and I was sure I saw the beginning of a grin on Bartlett's face.

"Besides me?" I snapped.

"We're not at liberty to say." Shipley closed her notebook and jammed it back in her purse. "We'd like a copy of your financial statements."

"My what?"

"Your financial statements. We can get the information by going directly to your bank and your employer, but you could help us by just handing over the information."

"That's just a waste of your time. Let's go on the record here and now," I stated emphatically. "I did *not* kill Tommy Connaught, and I did *not* have anything to do with his death. And I will *not* hand over my financial statements. You want them, go through proper channels."

Shipley had an amused look on her face at my outburst and I was sure she was thinking *I think thou doth protest too much*.

I ignored her. "And yesterday was the first I heard that Mr. Connaught was naming me as his beneficiary. I would suggest that you turn your sights on someone else because you're wasting your time investigating me."

They both stood up to leave and Shipley left her card on my desk. I felt completely frustrated and was positive I'd hear from them again.

Chapter ten

THE NEXT HOUR WAS SPENT very productively. I sat dumbly in my chair and stared out the window and chain-smoked. I felt useless and out of my comfort zone. I had trouble putting any thoughts in coherent order and repeatedly asked myself why I was here. I also thought about leaving. Packing it in and returning to Toronto. Running away from it all. Getting the hell out of Dodge.

Just before I slid completely into the black-hole of self-pity, I heard a timid knock on the office door. It was Carrie.

"You've got a call," she told me.

I looked at her standing in front of my desk and wondered where she got the money to buy her clothes. Yesterday she'd been wearing an absolute knock-out suit and today she had on an outfit that probably set her back several hundreds of dollars. Like the suit she had on yesterday, this outfit showed off her hourglass figure. The jacket was long, tapered at the waist and flared out over her hips. Without moving my head I glanced down at the pathetic suit I was wearing. Definitely not dressed for success.

"Ms. Monahan?"

I snapped my attention back to Carrie.

"Sorry. You were saying?"

"You've got a call holding. I wasn't going to interrupt but I thought you'd want this one. Someone from the morgue."

The someone at the morgue was calling to let me know that the body was ready to be released. The body. I understood that all bodies were like slabs of meat to them but they could have been a little more delicate when they were calling the next of kin.

I had no idea what to do next. So I went to find Cleve. Carrie told me he was working out of a small meeting room down the hall. I stuck my head in the door and found him surrounded by mounds of papers and books.

"Gotta minute?" I interrupted him.

"Hey." He seemed happy to see me. "I've been buried up to my neck here with paper. I need some of your time to go through all this mess with you."

"Sure Cleve. But first I need some help."

He was quick to offer to make the arrangements on my behalf.

"What kind of service do you have in mind?"

"I haven't thought about it," I told him truthfully. "Can you just get Tommy to a funeral home and then I'll decide?"

His hand reached across the table and covered mine.

"Consider it done. What else can we help you with right now?"

"Everything. Can I be absolutely honest here?"

He nodded.

"I'm completely overwhelmed. I've got no idea where to start. And I have no idea what needs to be done." I threw my hands up in the air. "Tell me what needs looking after. What's expected of me?"

He thought for a minute before replying. "First of all, there's nothing that needs your immediate attention. Maybe you should just take the next day or so and catch up on your reading. Last night you asked for all of the annual reports, press releases and financial statements. Why don't you work your way through those first? Then I can spend some time bringing you up to speed. You should meet the executive team. And the project leaders. Get to know the people. Once you know the people, they can introduce you to Phoenix's products and projects."

It sounded like a plan to me.

"What are your immediate plans, Cleve? Are you sticking around for a while?" I knew it was a lot to ask. He had a family in Toronto.

"For as long as I'm needed," he reassured me.

The financial statements were a total puzzle to me. The press releases and annual reports were a bit more helpful, and I started to gather a little understanding of the company. I was cautious though because I knew from experience how much or how little a public company was willing to share with the public. If it was mediocre news it was published with much fanfare. If it was great news they called a press conference. If it was bad news, they had a conference call with the stock analysts and tried to make it look like good news and downplayed the bad parts. Full, true and plain disclosure took on a whole new meaning when you were wading through a public company's press releases.

The last two years' releases gave me a very skimpy view of what was happening at Phoenix. There were releases announcing contract awards, financial results, appointments of directors and officers, and that was about it. The annual reports were pretty much a compilation of all the news that was fit to print in one place, setting out the company's accomplishments for the past year, their plans going forward and the yearly audited financial statements.

The financial statements, from what I could understand, indicated that the company was consistently making money. The latest annual report showed a five year history of the stock price, and it had steadily risen in small increments over the five years.

But I definitely needed a lesson on how to read the financial statements. Heated discussions I had overheard throughout the years of senior executives arguing with the auditors to sign off on different accounting treatments kept echoing in the back of my mind. I needed to know where a company could pad the statements.

I gave up in disgust at six o'clock and left the office. I was surprised to see Lou waiting for me beside the dark Lincoln in front of the building.

"Don't you have a life?" I joked.

He held the door of the car open for me and gave me a little smile.

"I was always on call until I heard from Mr. Connaught. I intend to keep at it until I hear differently from you."

He was concentrating on the traffic as we pulled away from the curb.

"Lou," I called from the back seat. His eyes met mine in the rearview mirror.

"Can I ask you a question?"

He nodded.

"Why weren't you driving Mr. Connaught on the night he was killed?"

He maneuvered around a stalled car blocking our lane and didn't answer me until his attention allowed.

"I'm not sure when he was killed, ma'am, but I didn't drive him on Wednesday. When I went to pick him up on Wednesday morning at his apartment, he never showed. I just thought he'd gone to the office early. He did that some times. But then his secretary, Miss Carrie, called me, all in a panic, around ten o'clock that morning wanting to know where he was."

This was all news to me.

"You mean he never showed up for the directors' meeting on Wednesday morning?"

"Not that I'm aware of ma'am."

"Do you know when they found his body?"

"No ma'am."

Why hadn't I asked any of these questions earlier? I grabbed the cellular phone that was mounted between the seats and dialed Cleve's cell number. I looked at my watch and hoped I got him before he got on the plane. I had insisted he go home for the weekend.

The phone wasn't through one ring before he answered.

"Cleveland Johnston."

"Hi. It's Kate. Did you report Tommy as missing when he didn't show for the board meeting?"

"Yes," he said slowly.

"What time?"

"Around six that night."

"Did the police do anything?"

"No. They said a person has to be missing more than twenty-four hours before they could consider them as missing."

"But where was he?"

"They don't know, Kate."

"I know that. I'm just thinking out loud."

"The police are looking into it."

"Sure they are. I'm their prime suspect so that means they're not looking elsewhere."

"You're not their prime suspect. They're just covering all the bases."

I needed to know. Something was burning inside me and I needed to know, now.

"Cleve, can I get into Tommy's apartment?"

"Sure. It's yours now anyway. I understand the police are done looking through it and the doorman has the key and instructions to let you in. The law firm sent over a letter today."

I told Lou we had a change of plans and we headed for Tommy's apartment.

Chapter eleven

I WAS NERVOUS AND APPREHENSIVE now that I was here, and I tried to
look casual as I stood under the awning-covered entrance to the apartment
building and looked across the busy street at Central Park. I felt at "sixes and
sevens" as my grandmother used to say, and my feet seemed cemented to the
ground. Lou had insisted on waiting for me and was lounging beside the car.
I walked back over to where he was standing several yards down the street.

"I'll take you up on your offer," I told him.

When we had pulled up in front of the building he had offered to
introduce me to the doorman who manned the desk in the lobby of the
apartment building.

"I've known him for some time now, Miss," he had said. "I often wait for
Mr. Connaught in the lobby."

In my typically independent way I had refused his offer, but was now
having second thoughts about the whole thing. I wasn't even sure in fact if I
wanted to go into the apartment. What did I expect to find?

Lou led the way through the revolving entrance door and to the marble-
encased reception desk where an elderly gentleman sat. His uniform looked
like something right out of the Wizard of Oz, with all sorts of gold braid and
tassels. I suppressed a school-girl giggle.

He stood up as we approached and a wide smile crossed his face when he
recognized Lou. The name tag on the breast of his jacket read "Ted". After
Lou had introduced us and Ted had expressed his condolences, I made my
way to the elevator, alone. Both had offered to accompany me, but I had
declined their offer.

I stepped off the elevator into a small foyer where the door to the apartment
faced the elevator. Ted had told me the apartment was on the 14th floor and
when I asked the number of the apartment, he had told me the *whole* of the
14th floor. I had tried not to look too surprised.

The lock was well-oiled and the door opened quietly. I entered the dark apartment and closed the door behind me. Silence surrounded me and I stood in the dark for a few moments while my eyes adjusted. My hand found a panel of light switches on the wall beside the door and I flicked them randomly. Pot lights came on over my head and I swiveled in a one hundred and eighty degree turn to take in the surroundings. The entrance-way was massive, by my standards anyway, and probably measured thirty feet by thirty feet. The floor was tiled in a dark green marble and the walls stretched upwards to about fifteen feet. The area was painted in a neutral earth tone and a few small pieces of art were hung randomly.

I crossed the lobby floor and entered the apartment. My random flicking of the light switches had turned on several table lamps and a quick look to the right and left took my breath away. There were no walls and the long room appeared to be the size of a football field. I stood rooted to the spot and peered about in the soft light. To the left was the living area and straight ahead of me was a long, highly polished dining table. I quickly counted twelve chairs around it and shook my head in amazement. Everything looked like it was out of *Better Homes and Gardens*. The furniture in *my* apartment can best be described as early-American, hotel lobby.

I ventured from my spot into the living area and wandered around several groupings of sofas and easy chairs. The outside walls were not walls, they were windows. Floor to ceiling, all around the room. At the center of the windows there were French doors which opened onto a terrace overlooking the street and Central Park. Wrought-iron furniture filled the balcony.

I turned and looked to the far end of the room, past the dining area where I could see a large desk with a computer and several wing-back chairs. I quickly crossed the yards and yards of plush carpet to Tommy's desk, eager now to discover some answers. Answers to what Tommy had done in his last hours. I sat in the large leather chair at his desk and looked around. The desk was neat but not overly pristine like the rest of the apartment. This was a working area and Tommy's presence was obvious. A waft of his after-shave hit my nostrils and I felt him nearby.

I sat for a moment trying to remember the brand of his after-shave, which I had never smelled on anyone else. It brought back some sweet memories and a smile played across my face.

And then I heard a door close. The noise took a few seconds to register because where I lived in my apartment in Toronto, the sound of closing doors was a regular sound, one you became used to hearing. This sound though was a quiet one, and I remembered that I had the whole floor of the building to myself, so I shouldn't be hearing doors closing. Fear shot up my back and my shoulders clenched. My eyes darted around the room and I slowly got out of the chair. There was a door in the wall to my left and I was sure the sound had come from somewhere behind that door.

I tentatively pushed on the door and it swung open into an eating area with a large kitchen behind it. Both rooms were dark and the only light came from the outside, through the large windows.

"Hello?" I called out tentatively.

My stomach was knotted with nerves but I walked through the eating area into the kitchen. I found a corridor off the kitchen to the left and I peered into complete darkness. I stupidly started down the hallway, with my arms outstretched, feeling for a light switch on either side of the wall. A sound came from behind me but before I could turn around I was sprawled on the floor. I wasn't hurt but I cried out in surprise and quickly tried to scramble to my feet.

Whoever had pushed me, shoved at my back again and this time I yelled in frustration and anger.

"Stop."

I was on my hands and knees and before I could turn around, a fistful of knuckles slammed into the side of my head. The force of the punch landed me on my side and my hands automatically covered my face. I kicked at my attacker and tried to see who it was but I could only see a large figure standing above me in the darkness.

My ears were ringing from the punch and fear screamed up and down my spine. But no screams or sounds came out of me. I was paralyzed with fright, afraid to move. All of this had happened in seconds but time seemed endless. The body above me reached down and grabbed my suit jacket at the shoulder and heaved me a few inches off the floor. I hit out at an arm and tried to push away but I should have left my hands over my face because the next blow knocked me out cold.

The patrolmen told me that the intruder had left through the door in the kitchen that led to one of the internal staircases in the building. I was nursing a wallop of a headache and holding an ice-pack to the side of my head, while they checked the perimeter. They informed me that there were two exits to two different stairways and they were sure the kitchen exit had been used because the door was unlocked. That stairwell went all the way to the basement of the building where anyone could leave the building without being seen.

Ted the doorman was standing nervously against the window, turning his hat round and round in his hands.

When I had come to and called him on the intercom I discovered on the kitchen wall, he and Lou had rushed up to the apartment.

"Shouldn't have happened," he kept mumbling, over and over. I think the poor man was in more shock than I was, and Lou had taken control of the situation and immediately called 9-1-1.

The scene was somewhat reminiscent of what had happened to me several months ago, and I felt a certain sense of deja vu. That time someone had broken into my apartment, while I slept. Afterwards my apartment had been filled with police while I sat, dazed and confused. And pissed off.

And I was pissed off again. I had sworn that I wouldn't find myself vulnerable again, after the last time, and here I had walked right into it. The promise to myself to learn how to defend myself had never been acted on.

I looked up at the patrolman standing in front me.

"We've checked, and it seems he came in the same way he left. All of the other perimeter doors are locked. Ted here tells us no one could get past him in the lobby, so we're assuming it was a professional job of lock picking. Must have come through the basement."

I nodded in agreement because I didn't know the layout of the building. It all seemed feasible to me. But why this apartment? So, I asked the question.

"A number of reasons, ma'am," the cop told me. "My best guess is that your attacker read that the man who owned this apartment died and thought the place would be an easy mark. We can't tell if anything's been stolen, but the place doesn't seem disturbed. We think you interrupted him in his tracks."

When they had left I asked Lou to take me to my hotel. I needed to get out of here, and in spite of my throbbing head, I was full of nervous energy.

It was only 8:30 when I got back to my suite and I paced the rooms, chain-smoking and thinking. I didn't believe that the person who had broken into Tommy's apartment was a cat burglar or a drug addict, looking to score. The burglar had plenty of time to steal everything while I was laid out cold on the floor, but I was sure nothing obvious had been taken. The break-in must have had something to do with Tommy's death. I made up my mind to go back to the apartment and find out what they had been looking for.

Chapter twelve

"*How* do you get yourself into these messes?"

"*Get* myself into messes? You think I plan it, Jay?"

I was standing in the small hallway outside the door of his studio apartment. He was three floors up, above a small, independent bookstore on the ground floor.

Jay had answered the door and immediately saw the swelling on the side of my face. Rather than a hello, he wanted to know how I get into *messes*.

"And besides," I continued indignantly, "messes are what a cat makes when it misses the litter box."

"Alright, already," he said soothingly. He pulled me into the apartment and into his arms. "So I reacted badly. You scared me. Have you looked in a mirror?"

"No," I said into his chest. I never look in mirrors.

"Not a pretty sight, but you're still beautiful to me." He held me back and looked at my face again. "What happened?"

"Sucker punched." I looked around Jay's apartment and smiled. His unit could fit in the bathroom of my suite at the hotel. I sat in the lone armchair and told him my story. He just sat quietly and kept shaking his head.

"What're you going to do?" he asked me when I finished.

"I'm going back to the apartment."

Jay held up his hand like a traffic cop.

"Stop it. Do you think you're ready for this?" He put his thumb and forefinger about an inch apart and said, "Last time, you came this close," his voice was getting louder. "This close to biting it. Leave it alone. Go home. The cops'll do their job. They don't need you. Go back to Toronto." He was almost yelling now.

I just sat there and watched him and waited for him to cool down. He was remembering what had happened the last time I stuck my nose in where it didn't belong. I had been attacked in my bed, knocked out cold with a gun butt, kidnapped and ended up having the tip of my ear shot off. You'd think I'd learned my lesson but something inside me kept me fighting. As a kid, my size made me a target for every bully in the neighbourhood and I became a fighter. Jay knew me because we grew up together.

"You can't ask me to leave," I said quietly.

"I'm not asking. I'm telling."

That got my blood pressure up a few notches.

"Taking charge now? Telling me what to do? Let me tell you something. I'm *not* leaving New York." I stood up. "But I am leaving this apartment, with or without you. I'm going back to Tommy's place. Are you coming?"

He stared at me and shook his head. It wasn't a negative shake of the head, it was an *I can't believe this* type of shake.

In the taxi I held on to his arm for dear life, because I realized he was only worried about me.

This time I had a more thorough tour of Tommy's apartment and I discovered the bathrooms and bedrooms off the hallway where I had been attacked. The master bedroom was about as large as one would expect after having seen the size of the other rooms. One corner held a StairMaster and rowing machine. The oversized, king-size bed seemed small in the large room. The decor and the room reeked of masculinity. The only feature that made the room cozy was the floor to ceiling, wall to wall built-in bookcase along one wall.

I walked along the length of the bookcase and looked at Tommy's selection of reading material. Several shelves held leather-bound volumes which looked like they had never been touched. The shelves at eye-level held scores of more modern books. There were hundreds of paperback novels shelved in alphabetical order. Everything from Tom Clancy to Leon Uris with John Grisham nicely in the middle. The bottom shelves held technical manuals that came with computer programs, and engineering textbooks.

All the shelves were book-lined except one, higher up where I could see a space about a foot across. I jumped a little to see if there was anything in the space but couldn't see a thing. Shit, I hate being short at times like this.

I felt Jay behind me, looking over my shoulder. "Perfect timing," I said. "Can you see if there's anything up there?" I craned my neck upwards.

Jay reached up and pulled out a small, five by seven picture frame. He handed it to me and said, "It's a picture of you."

I peered at it, trying to remember where it had been taken. I was sitting on top of a picnic table, with my feet on the bench and my arms resting on my knees, grinning at the camera. A rare photo of me smiling because normally I hate getting my picture taken. With a flash I remembered it had been taken on our honeymoon, at a dude ranch in Arizona. We had laughed at ourselves the whole time we were there. Complete idiots on horseback, trying to be cowboys. We had both grown up in the city and, for both of us, it had been our first time on horseback.

The honeymoon package included daily trail rides and the most vivid memory of my honeymoon was of a sore butt. As athletic as Tommy had been, he'd been no horseman. He just never got the hang of it and the memory made me smile.

Jay was wandering around the bedroom, opening closets and drawers. "Everything looks untouched Kate. In fact, it doesn't even look like anyone lived here. Everything is so perfect. Except this room, at least it looks a little more normal."

"I find it very eerie. Let's tackle the computer," I suggested.

Tommy's computer was the latest and greatest in technology. Jay turned it on and sat down in front of the screen. When the machine was warmed up, Jay pointed at the screen.

"All the standard stuff. What should we look for?"

"I don't know. Just check his files. Look at the Word and Excel stuff.."

Jay went to work with the mouse and surfed around in Tommy's computer. I stood beside him and tried to follow what he was doing but he was moving around too quickly for me. My knowledge of computers extends to word processing legal documents and reading emails. After about three minutes he looked up at me and shrugged his shoulders.

"Nothing."

"Don't you think I should be the judge of that?"

He laughed. "Sure. Be my guest. But there's nothing on here but the programs."

"No files of his own?" I asked.

"Nope. Nothing. Nada. Zip. Nothing but what it takes to run the computer. There are no document files, no spreadsheet files, no databases, no nothing."

"You're sure?"

"Well, nothing that sticks out. Maybe the stuff is hidden. But to find it would take some time and someone a lot more technical than I am."

I started opening desk drawers, not sure what I was looking for. The top drawer of the desk held pens, pencils, paper clips and a few balls of dust. The second and third drawers were empty and the bottom drawer, larger than the other three, was full of hanging file folders. I eagerly thumbed through them looking for something, anything that would give me a clue to what Tommy did at this desk. They were all empty too.

"Nothing. I wonder if Tommy even worked here."

"Tell me again what it is you're looking for," Jay said.

"I don't know."

I was at a loss now as to why I had started this exercise. I wandered the length of the room to the living area and plopped down in one of the oversized chairs. The few table lamps that were lit threw soft light around the room and my eyes took it all in. I had seen rooms like this in decorator magazines - several groups of beautifully upholstered furniture strategically placed to allow for conversation, matching tables with fragile lamps, oriental and silk carpets strewn casually about. Rooms like this I had only ever dreamed about and the realization hit me that I now owned this one.

I picked up a long, sleek remote control from the table beside me and looked around for the television it belonged to, but there was no evidence of anything electronic, so I held the remote at arm's length and pushed the red power button. A very large section of the wall in front of me started sliding open and I laughed out loud.

I quickly got out of the chair and walked towards the opening. The soft light coming from behind the wall was tantalizing and the colours coming from it shimmered. I placed my hand on the cool glass and stared at the hundreds of quickly darting fish. I couldn't recall ever having seen such a large aquarium.

"It's awesome," I heard Jay say behind me.

I nodded my head in agreement and was suddenly overcome with the responsibility. On average I could keep a goldfish alive for ten days. The tank held hundreds of fish, so I figured I had at least several months before I annihilated them all. I put my face up against the glass and whispered to the fish, "Start saying your prayers, boys."

Chapter thirteen

THE NEXT MORNING I WAS full of nervous energy with nowhere to channel it. I paced the hotel suite, drinking cup after cup of strong coffee. My mind whirled with everything that needed to be done, and in the back of my mind were all sorts of unanswered questions. Questions that I had no hope of finding answers to. I knew what needed to be done – arranging Tommy's funeral, gaining a true understanding of things at Phoenix Technologies, meeting with the lawyers to settle the estate. The sheer volume of things that needed my attention made me nauseous. And then there were the questions. Questions that Jay had told me the night before would be answered in time.

"The police will handle it," he'd said several times.

"But what if they're looking in the wrong places?" I'd protested.

"What's the right place then, Kate?"

This had gone back and forth, with no resolution whatsoever. I'd just confused myself even more.

"Concentrate on the things that're important, right now," Jay had said.

"Tommy's death is important. How he died is important to me."

"I know it is. And I'm not trying to trivialize it. But face it Kate, how much did you know about him? What did you know of his life, here in New York? His friends? His co-workers?"

I shrugged my shoulders in response.

"So you're starting with nothing. You might have stumbled on something already and not know it. You have nothing to compare with. Leave it to the police. Concentrate your efforts on what's important now."

I had reluctantly agreed but now in the light of day, the questions, and the elusive answers plagued me. So I got myself busy and tackled the tasks at hand.

The funeral director reminded me of Rudolph Valentino. His black hair was slicked back and the odour of Brylcreem, reminiscent of my father's favourite brand, wafted from his head. A perfectly trimmed, pencil-thin mustache adorned his upper lip and it made his solicitous smile seem supercilious. He was dressed in a jet-black suit with a gray silk tie and the overall effect was one of Hollywood. If I were the costume designer in a Mel Brooks movie parodying funerals, this is exactly how I'd dress the funeral director. To round out the effect, his voice was one octave higher than it should have been.

"Let me express my condolences, Miss...", he glanced down at the clipboard he held, "Monahan."

I had arrived unannounced, determined to get this task off my list of things to do. If I thought of it as a task, a job, then I could get through this. I had repeatedly told myself just that on the cab ride over.

He led me to his office where he sat upright and placed his hands on the desk in front of him. The nameplate on his desk read Mr. Theodore Bradley, Director.

"How may we help you?" he offered.

Which seemed like a pretty stupid opening line if you asked me, and I wondered how he'd react if I asked him where the swimwear department was.

"Well, Mr. Bradley, I think that's pretty obvious. I need to make funeral arrangements. For Mr. Connaught."

"Yes, yes. What type of arrangements did you have in mind?"

"Cremation."

His eyebrows shot up and he looked at me with a big old question mark on his face.

"Yes?" I prompted him.

He mumbled something to himself and fussed with the papers on his desk. "When would you like to have the service?"

"No service."

This time the question mark on his face was accompanied by a little squeal from somewhere at the back of his throat. I didn't feel I had to explain.

"Just let me know how soon you can arrange for the cremation."

"But..." he sputtered.

"Do you make it a habit to question your client's wishes?" I shot at him.

He cleared his throat and shook his head.

"It's just..."

"Just what?" I helped him.

"A man of Mr. Connaught's stature. Well-known in the business community. I just thought... Normally, a service..." He was truly floundering now.

"I don't believe it says anywhere I need to justify my wishes."

I stared hard at him, daring him to question me. He didn't respond. Glad we were past the simpering, condolence stage of the proceedings, I told him where I could be reached.

His weak voice reached me as I was pulling on the office door. I turned around to him.

"The body is ready for viewing," he told me. "Do you wish some time alone with Mr. Connaught?"

No answer came from me and I turned and walked swiftly down the long hall. View the body? My pace quickened as I felt the bile rising in my throat. I burst through the double doors, sucking in the fresh air and started walking.

That afternoon, I walked until my feet were numb. My eyes didn't take in much of the scenery and most of the time I had no idea where I was. Some landmarks were familiar, but Manhattan was just a blur that day.

Most of the time I tried to ignore the thoughts tumbling around in my head. Kept pushing them to the back. Decisions I knew had to be made. Typically, I'm a doer, not a thinker. I'm told what to do and I do what I'm told. When it comes to my work, I've always had someone there dictating what needs to be done. And I'm good at taking a task and seeing it through to the end. If I'm told to organize a shareholders' meeting for two hundred and fifty people, that's all I need to be told. Leave it up to Kate, and it'll get done. That's why I've always considered myself a professional support person.

I now found myself in a situation where I alone was going to be making the decisions, but I needed someone to tell me what decisions to make. As Jay had reminded me the other night, I've always bragged that I could do better than most of the idiots I'd worked for. So now I had my chance. But did I want it? Did I want to be the head of a multi-million dollar high-tech company? Did I want to be responsible for hundreds of employees? Did I want to be beholden to public shareholders?

And did I want to live in New York? Frankly, the city scared me. I knew no-one. No friends, no relatives. Could I leave everything I had in Toronto? At that thought, I snorted. And what exactly would you be leaving behind, I asked myself.

A few friends, a rundown apartment and a car that on its best days started only when I cursed at it. My only close girlfriend had died earlier that year. My parents didn't even live in the same city. So, I told myself, there wasn't much to leave behind in Toronto. And the only thing I had in New York, right now, was Jay. My best friend, my love, my family. How long his job would keep him in New York was something I didn't want to think about.

I could sell my interest in Phoenix Technologies and run away. Run away from it all. The thought was appealing, make no mistake about it. But what would Tommy think? Did I care? He was dead and I was about to set his body on fire.

The thought of cremation suddenly seemed too cruel, too thoughtless. I was angry with Tom Connaught for plunking me into the situation, but did he do it to be cruel to me? Did he know he was going to die when he wrote that will? Somehow I doubted it. Tommy was always so full of life, so sure of himself. He exuded confidence, success. That confidence is what attracted me to him in the first place.

Tommy had said in his letter to me that he trusted me. Trusted me to look after it all. It felt like too much of a burden for me but my little voice of reason reminded me of our wedding vows. Ridiculous. We were divorced, but somehow those wedding vows, until death do us part, were coming back to haunt me.

I wasn't one to back down from a challenge, I told myself. So I thought back on the many obstacles I'd faced and the realization hit me that most of my so-called challenges were ones I knew I couldn't fail at. The difficult ones I'd walked away from. The possibility of failure was what had been bothering me all along. And nothing I'd done in the past even came close to this. Failure could mean losses of millions of dollars and losses of hundreds of jobs. Once again reality reared its ugly head.

All the while I was worrying about myself, poor little me, and how Tommy's death was going to affect *me*, I was putting off thinking about Tommy's death. Typical Kate Monahan behaviour, I chided myself. Worry about yourself, to the exclusion of the suffering of others. Well, maybe I was being a *little* hard on myself, but I did admit reluctantly that I had given little thought to Tommy's murder. Every time the subject crept into my head, I pushed it aside.

I had been a pro all my life at not allowing horrible mental pictures and dreadful thoughts into my brain. If I didn't think about it, it *couldn't* have happened. If I didn't think about it, it *wouldn't* happen. Denial with a capital D about past and future awful events. Hence my strong, superstitious belief in jinxing the pitcher - if I didn't think about something awful, or God forbid, say something out loud about wicked things that could happen, then they wouldn't happen.

What did I know about Tommy's murder? That he was shot. Did I know where his body had been found? Did I know how many times he had been shot? Did I ask any of these questions of Detectives Bartlett and Shipley? I did not. And why didn't I? Because I was too damned chicken to ask.

Detective Shipley was on a day off but Bartlett agreed to see me when I telephoned.

"What exactly can I help you with?" she asked me over her shoulder as I followed her into a small interview room. She had given me directions to the 20th Precinct on West 82nd Street, on the other side of Central Park from Tommy's apartment.

We sat at a small, square table, the top of which was sticky and disgusting, so I put my hands in my lap and my purse on the floor. We faced each other across the table. The room smelled of dirty feet, body odour, and bad breath. I breathed in and out through my mouth, trying to avoid the old, stale smell.

"Well," I hesitated. What exactly *did* I want? "Is there any news? Any breaks in your case?"

Bartlett stared straight at me and shook her head. "No."

"No suspects? No ideas at all?"

"None that we're prepared to talk about at this stage of our investigation." She continued to stare at me and clearly wasn't being very helpful.

"Can you tell me where you found his body?"

"In the loading dock area, behind the Van Buren Health Centre," she said.

"Van Buren Health Centre? Is that a clinic?" I asked.

"No ma'am," she stated. "The Van Buren is one of New York's finest hospitals," she told me proudly. "I believe it was founded with money from the Van Buren family, descendents of Martin Van Buren, the eighth President of the United States."

Well, thanks for the history lesson.

"Where is it? I don't know New York City very well," I told her.

"At the corner of West 69th and West End Avenue. West of the American Museum of Natural History. Not far from here."

The American Museum of Natural History was familiar. One of the many landmarks I had discovered earlier that day on my walk around Manhattan.

"What was he doing there?" I wondered out loud.

"We're still trying to determine that," she replied.

"Was he robbed?"

"No. All of his personal belongings appeared to be intact."

I sat quietly for a moment, wondering if I wanted to ask the next logical questions. Cleve Johnston had told me that Tommy had been shot in the back of the head. But did I want more of the gory details?

I took a deep breath and pressed on. "How many times was he shot? Did it look like he was able to fight off his attackers? Do you think he suffered?" I asked my last question in a whisper. The thought of Tommy suffering through the gawdawful pain of it all was too much to bear. I hung my head and took some deep breaths to calm myself down.

"Ms. Monahan, the Medical Examiner has indicated that death occurred because of one shot in the back of his head. Death would have been instantaneous. There was no sign of any fight, or struggle."

My jaw had been clenched while she was telling me this and I tried to relax. If there was any relief in this fucking goddamn shit mess, it was relief that Tommy had not suffered.

"Do you have any idea why he was at the Van Buren Health Centre?" I asked.

"None, at this point," Bartlett told me. "We understand from the people at Phoenix Technologies that he was supposed to be at the office, in meetings."

"That's right," I agreed with her. "He was expected to be there the whole day in meetings of the board of directors. Mr. Connaught's driver told me that he never showed up on Wednesday morning when he went to pick him up."

She was nodding her head. "Yeah, we knew that. We can't seem to account for his time from Tuesday evening when he left the office until late the next night when we found his body."

"What time was the body found?" I asked.

"Late. Long after regular working hours, because the loading dock was closed. A nurse practitioner found the body. She was waiting for a delivery and was walking around, having a cigarette. In all the disruption of the police arriving and sealing off the area, we almost had a minor disaster on our hands. The locals were denied access to the area and a special delivery almost didn't get through. It was a heart, being delivered from a hospital in Brooklyn, for an urgent transplant."

She continued, "The Van Buren is known as a first-class transplant hospital and their research department is world renowned for their work on artificial organs. My great-uncle was one of the first recipients of a heart transplant back in the late sixties and he had it done at the Van Buren," she told me by way of explanation. "The place is very special to our family."

That's nice, I thought to myself. I wondered if she was going to hit me up for a donation for a fundraising campaign.

"But what was he doing there?" I demanded rhetorically.

"No idea, ma'am. We're still interviewing all the staff who were on duty that night. So far, we haven't found anyone who knew Mr. Connaught, or knew why he might be at the hospital."

I left after a few more minutes. My talk with Detective Bartlett left me with more questions and feeling more frustrated than when I had arrived.

Chapter fourteen

FIVE DAYS LATER I STILL had no answers. I had lots of questions though about my capabilities as an executive. By Thursday, I was up to my neck in the business.

My watch and the tense muscles in my neck told me it was quitting time. I swiveled around in my chair and took in the nighttime view of Manhattan. With the hours I'd been putting in at the office, it was the only view I was getting of the city.

I made a weak attempt at tidying up my desk (never one of my stronger points) and gave up in disgust. Carrie would look after it in the morning. She was a God-send and a mind-reader. Every morning the desk was miraculously neat and within a half an hour of my working at it, chaos would reign.

On Monday morning, I'd reported to the office with a gung-ho attitude. The weekend had been spent mentally whipping myself into shape for the tasks at hand. I'd decided a positive attitude would get me through the hurdles. So far, it had only managed to make me tired.

My first order of business on Monday morning was to get better acquainted with Carrie. No one had to tell me how important and essential a good secretary was. I had to find out just how good she was.

"I'm not sure where to start," I told her. I pointed at the pile of reading material I'd left on the desk on Friday night. "Probably, I'll just continue to plow through these."

"That's good. But…," she hesitated and stopped.

"What?"

"Why not just learn as you go? Mr. Connaught's in-basket is full of work that needs attention, and he had several appointments already booked for this week. You should probably not cancel all of those."

Why didn't I think of that?

"Good idea. Walk me through what's here."

She pointed out what was urgent, what could wait and what I should ignore. She was bright and organized. Tommy's first meeting that morning was with his executive team, followed by a session with the research and development boys and girls.

"Everyone assumes the meetings are canceled," Carrie said.

"Well *un*-cancel them. I've got to meet everyone at some time. Now's as good a time as any. Tell me about these meetings. Are they regularly scheduled? Or can I expect problems?"

"Mr. Connaught had regular meetings with his teams. And I'm pretty sure they don't wait for the meetings to bring up the problems. He kept in touch with them, regularly."

"Who normally attends?"

"For the executive team meeting, there would be Russell Freeson, the Chief Financial Officer, Sandra Melnick, the Vice President, Operations, Steve Holliday, Vice President, Communications, Mark Hall, Vice President of Sales, and Nat Scott, the Vice President of Research and Development. For the R and D meeting, the heads of each of the projects as well as the Vice President will be there."

"Big crowds?"

"No. Lately, the R and D meetings have been getting smaller."

"Why's that?"

Carrie shrugged her shoulders. "Less research and development?"

"Any other appointments scheduled for today?"

She shook her head. "No, but Steve Holliday wants to see you."

Steve was one of the Vice Presidents and I remembered being introduced to him at the board meeting the other night.

"Remind me who he is."

"Vice President, Communications. He does the PR stuff. Talks to the analysts. Shareholder relations."

Now I remembered. I had silently nicknamed him *Slick* when we were introduced. Tall, young, balding, more than okay-looking and dressed like a model right off the pages of GQ.

"Did he say what he wanted to meet with me about?"

"Something about damage control," she said and shrugged her shoulders. "He was pretty vague."

"Okay, set it up."

I took a moment to take in the effect of Steve Holliday and I must admit, he was like a cool drink on a hot summer day. I don't know the price of men's clothing, but if I had to guess, I'd say his suit cost him more than I pay in taxes every year. The colour was perfect on him and one that most men wouldn't wear because they wouldn't have had the guts. Kind of a toss-up between dark blue and dark green and it hung on his body like it had been painted there. And Steve had the body for showing off a great suit. He must have been about six three because he was taller than Jay and bigger. Bigger in the shoulders, bigger in the legs, bigger in the arms.

He cleared his throat to get my attention and I blushed. I had been staring a tad too long and got caught. My hand shot out quickly and we shook.

Steve shook my hand and with his left hand steered me into one of the guest chairs in front of the desk. He took the seat next to me, inched the chair closer, crossed his legs and leaned his long arm on the back of my chair. I was dumbfounded and a little claustrophobic. His aftershave was overpowering and he was so close to me I could count the hairs in his ears. *Slick and smooth.*

"Kate," he purred at me, "so good of you to see me. And so soon after your loss. You're a trooper. Yessir. I remember Tom telling me how tough you were. And he was right. Yessir."

When he referred to Tommy as Tom, I knew he wasn't part of the inner sanctum. Anyone close to my ex-husband called him Tommy.

My eyes wandered up to Steve's balding head. What hair he had left on the top of his head was cropped short and the sides were cut professionally and looked good.

But his purring was getting to me. He was droning on about how wonderful it was that I was able to do this, how he was going to make it right, right for the company, right for the press and right for the shareholders. When I felt his hand touch my back and his fingers lightly caressing it, I'd had enough. Our knees touched when I stood up and I felt I finally had the advantage because I could look down on him. My hands tugged down on my suit jacket and I gave him my ice look.

"Are you quite finished?" I said in my best Mary Poppins voice.

"Uhm, yes. I guess so."

"Good." I walked around the desk and sat in my chair. "Have you had a female boss before Mr. Holliday?"

He shook his head.

"And it shows. Patronizing doesn't work with me. Neither does unwanted body contact." He paled a little at that comment.

"Ever had a sexual harassment suit slapped on you?"

"God, no!" he blurted out.

Now I had him where I wanted him. I stood up and put my hands on the desk in front of me and leaned across at him. My voice was menacing. A number of my friends, secretaries, receptionists, law clerks and young female lawyers had been put in these awkward situations and most times were too timid about their jobs to do anything about it. This asshole probably knew I was a secretary and wanted to find out just how timid I was.

"Mr. Connaught told you I was tough. Were you trying to find out how tough?" The question was rhetorical so I didn't wait for an answer. "Don't let my size fool you Mr. Holliday."

Now he was red. The flush started in his perfect size sixteen neck and went right to the top of his bald pate. I was sorry now that I'd admired his physique and wardrobe. When I'd stared at him the look on my face was probably an admiring one, and the idiot thought I was interested. Now *my* face was red.

I sat back down, lit a cigarette and blew the smoke in his direction.

"What was it you wanted to see me about?"

Steve Holliday could barely look at me when we all sat around the table for an executive team meeting later that day. He sat at the far end of the table and busied himself with messages on his Blackberry. I stood and shook each Vice President's hand as they arrived in the room. I had met Russell Freeson, the chief financial officer, at the board meeting on Thursday night but had not met the others. Cleve had reminded me that Russell had been with Tommy since the beginning of Phoenix and I vaguely remembered him. Russell was very young looking for someone who was the chief financial officer of a public company. He was very tall and lanky with jet black hair and a shy smile. Sandra Melnick, the Vice President of Operations looked to be about the same age as Russell. She was a bit taller than me, so she was pretty short, but she looked strong. Her neck muscles were visible and her handshake was firm. She had shoulder-length, dirty blonde hair, cut in a style that probably looked fabulous when it was blow-dried by a professional, but looked ragged and uneven now. She was naturally attractive and wore very little make up.

Mark Hall, the Vice President of Sales, looked run off his feet when he arrived, without his suit jacket on and his sleeves rolled up.

"Kate," he said as he held out his hand, "is it okay to call you Kate?" He hurried on. "I'm sorry I'm late, customers have been keeping me on the phone. Damage control, you know." Mark was on the chubby side, with a very boyish face and a really full head of hair. His hair was so thick it looked like a wig.

"Yes, it's okay to call me Kate," I told him and the others in the room. "And you're not late. We're still waiting for Nat Scott." My watch said we were already five minutes late starting and I was a stickler for being on time, so I sat down in the chair at the head of the table.

"Well folks, as you know, I'm your new Chair and CEO. I'm Kathleen Monahan, uhm, but most everyone calls me Kate." I was nervous and sounded like a fisherman from Newfoundland.

A woman younger than me entered the room and stopped inside the door. She looked like a recent high school grad. Her hair was long, done in corkscrew curls and her nose was covered in freckles.

"I'm Natalie Scott. Most everyone calls me Nat," she said, imitating me. Nat Scott was listed in the company's roster as the Vice President of Research and Development. I had assumed Nat was male. And older.

"Pleased to meet you, Nat," I said, wondering if she was going to apologize for being late. She ignored me as she took her seat, placed a writing folder in front of her, and stared at Russell Freeson across the table.

There was a perceptible chill in the room and I knew I was the cause of it. I was making everyone uncomfortable, myself included. I had no idea how to chair a meeting of an executive team.

"Well," I started, "how about each of you bring me up to date on where you are with your area of responsibility." I looked at each of them around the table. A few heads nodded and Mark Hall was the only one who spoke up.

"I'll start," he offered.

The meeting went fairly well and lasted several hours. The Vice Presidents did a thorough job of explaining their department's responsibilities to me and I tried to take it all in. As the meeting progressed my level of internal panic rose. There was so much to learn and so much to take in. I sacrilegiously cursed Tommy several times.

Sales were on target but Mark was concerned. Customers had been calling him. They wanted to know what was going to happen to the company. Although Mark had been trying to reassure them, he needed more support from the executive team. I took a stab at being a chief executive officer and asked the team to work with Mark and start talking to the customers. We agreed that we should be telling them that it was business as usual, despite the loss of the company's leader and visionary.

Nat Scott snorted at this. This one was definitely rubbing me the wrong way. "Natalie?" I prompted her. Nothing. "You've got something to say?"

The silence was deafening. She was acting like a petulant twelve year old.

"Okay then," I said, trying not to look more like an idiot than Nat.

Russell Freeson gave a good financial overview and told me that the company was in sound financial shape. I warned him that I wasn't very good at reading financial statements (yet), and that I needed to know the basics. We had cash in the bank (a good thing), invested solidly, no outstanding accounts payable, and no serious accounts receivable problems. We were halfway through our financial year and our operating expenses were on budget. The analysts were happy with the company and its potential, and until Tommy's death, the shares had been trading at a steady level. Russell promised to set up some tutorial sessions with me on how to read and interpret the financial statements.

My next meeting with the research and development team and their leader Nat Scott reminded me of a bad trip to the dentist.

The sounds of chatter emanating from the room had immediately ceased when I arrived and the icy atmosphere chilled me to the bone. I was tempted to take everyone's pulse, they were so withdrawn and quiet. And to top it off, there was an undercurrent of hostility. The group obviously expected me to run the meeting and although I wasn't prepared I threw myself into it.

"Well," I started off, stupidly, "I'm glad you could all make it." Six pairs of eyes stared back at me. "As you probably know, I'm Kathleen Monahan, and I'll be…" I paused. "I'm the, uhm, new Chairman and CEO." The eyes continued to stare at me, blankly.

Someone at the other end of the table wrote something on their pad of paper. Another person coughed lightly. The woman sitting next to me lifted her coffee cup to her lips and peered at me over the rim. The silence was deafening.

"Perhaps we could go around the table and introduce ourselves. Help me put faces to names." *Help me*, I silently prayed. Ever had a dream where you're naked in front a crowd? That's exactly how I felt. Nervous and naked. I gave myself a mental shake and listened to the introductions.

I looked at the person next to me. This one was your textbook research and development type. He was small and bookish looking. His eyes were huge behind his thick glasses and he was nervously picking at a hangnail on his thumb. He was wearing a short-sleeved, white dress shirt, buttoned at the neck with no tie. The shirt pocket held a plastic pocket protector with three pens carefully and precisely clipped to it. I'm not kidding. And to top it off, he looked younger than Natalie.

"Rick Williams," he said softly, without looking at me. I looked down at the list Carrie had given me of the attendees and quickly found his name. He was listed as the team leader for the Gila River project.

Sitting next to him was an older man. Older than Rick and Nat but probably about my age.

"Derek. Derek Hutton. I'm the project team leader for the Papago project."

Across the table from Derek was another woman, who looked like Rick William's sister. The only difference to me was the obviously missing pocket protector. She was mousy looking and her blond hair needed a wash. Her resemblance to Rick ended when she opened her mouth. Rick had sounded timid and shy. This one was far from it.

"Belinda Moffat," she barked. Her voice was deep for a woman and very loud, and when she spoke, the sound vibrated around the room. I jumped slightly in my seat. My list told me she was team leader for the Fort Apache project.

Seated on Belinda's left was Dan Thornton who actually stood up from his chair and reached across the table to shake my hand.

"Dan Thornton," he said. When he stood I could tell that he was short. His body language exuded energy although he was working hard like the rest of them trying to make my life miserable. His shirtsleeves were rolled up, and his tie was loosened and he looked like a man with a mission.

"I'm heading up the Navajo project," he told me. "Glad to have you aboard." For his friendliness, I gave him a smile.

The last person was sitting directly across from me and introduced himself as Ben Tucker. Ben was so handsome, it almost took your breath away. He had curly, thick, blond hair and a square face. Ben's face was made more perfect by his straight nose, full lips and intense eyes. Individually, facial features are pretty much the same, but the way Ben's collection was put together, it was magical. He had the face of Michaelangelo's David, and Casey Kasem's voice. Deep and resonant, but without Casey's singsong way of speaking. I detected a slight, southern drawl, especially when he called me ma'am.

"Ben Tucker, ma'am," he introduced himself and held his hand out in front of him. "I'd get up," he explained, with a shrug, "but…" Ben was in a wheelchair.

I quickly stood and reached across the table. His warm hand engulfed mine and his handshake was firm.

"San Carlos," he said, nodding his head at the list in front of me. There it was. San Carlos project team leader. The project names all sounded familiar and I turned to Nat on my left.

"Are the project names code names?" I asked her.

"Yes. They're all names of Indian reservations in Arizona. Your ex-husband had an affinity for anything related to Arizona," she said knowingly.

It was news to me, but made sense. Tommy had lived in Phoenix all his life.

"Oh," I said uselessly. Once again the room was silent and the air had become thick with tension as soon as Nat made reference to Tommy. Time to take control.

"So." I lined up the papers in front of me. "The purpose of these meetings would be what? Are we here specifically to update the CEO? Or is it an exchange of information type of meeting?"

Incredibly, all six of them stared blankly at me. There wasn't one helpful face in the pack.

"Then I can assume all projects are on target?"

Silence.

Now I was pissed off.

I glared at them around the table. The look I gave them was reminiscent of my stare-down with Steve Holliday.

"In that case, consider this meeting over." I stood up and gathered my things and headed for the door. Someone snickered behind me. Actually snickered. You remember the noise that would come out of someone's nose when the teacher's back was turned to the class and he had a "kick me" sign on his back. That kind of noise. I whipped back around at them and took a deep breath.

"If this is the type of co-operation I can expect from the team members around here, I'm disgusted," I told them through clenched teeth. "I expect a certain level of professionalism from the officers of this company, Ms. Scott. And I haven't seen it exhibited here. This meeting will start again in thirty minutes. And all project team leaders will provide me with a briefing on their respective projects."

That caught their attention and now all eyes were on me.

"Thirty minutes," I repeated. "Your report will include the status of the project, costs incurred to date, expected costs for the next month, a headcount report on all staff reporting to you, including their resumes, and anything else relevant that the CEO should know. Those of you not choosing to participate in the meeting will have their resignations on my desk in twenty-five minutes."

Now the silence was golden.

Chapter fifteen

NOT SURPRISINGLY, ALL FIVE PROJECT team leaders and their Vice President were present at the meeting thirty minutes later. And every one of them was beautifully prepared. Dan Thornton, who I'd pegged as a keener, even had PowerPoint slides. The tension in the room was still unbearable, but I did my best to ignore it.

Nat Scott's presentation was last and was basically a wrap-up of the ongoing projects. She was abrupt in her presentation. There was no eye contact between the two of us and the chill factor made the room feel like we were in the Yukon on a January day. We were obviously not going to become best friends and share beauty secrets. I thanked everyone and asked her to stay at the end of the meeting.

We were sitting across the table from each other and I waited a few moments before speaking. Tension mounted and I didn't care.

"Care to explain what happened here earlier?" I asked her.

She shook her head sharply and her long curls surrounded her face.

"Then can you explain to me how it is that you became a Vice President in this organization? Your behaviour is appalling. Tommy was a team player. I'm sure he encouraged that here at Phoenix Technologies. Did you act like that when he was around?"

"How I acted when Tommy was around is none of your business," she snarled at me. Perfectly round, red spots appeared on her cheeks, highlighting her freckles.

Unbelievable. Maybe she had a career death wish.

"Fine. But your attitude here today has me concerned. You have until the end of the day to decide if Phoenix Technologies is the place you want to be. In the meantime, I'll speak to some of the other Vice Presidents and see if they can convince me to keep you on."

"You do that," she told me. "But don't forget that research and development is a large part of this company. And the shareholders of this company are counting on research and development."

"Be that as it may, Ms. Scott, if you and I can't work together…" I left the rest of the thought to her imagination.

"*I* can work with anyone." She lowered her voice and the rest came out in a hissing whisper. "But I'll be damned if I have to take orders from a *secretary.*"

In hindsight, it was funny how she said that word "secretary". But at the time, there was so much menace and disgust in her use of the word, it gave me a shiver. I pictured two people out for a walk in the park and one steps in a massive pile of dog shit. The stuff oozes up the sides of their shoe, and they say, in a panic, "Oh my God, I've got *secretary* all over me." She clearly thought of me as a pile of shit.

"Natalie, I wouldn't expect you to take orders from a secretary," I said soothingly. "Last Thursday, I was a secretary. Today's Monday. And today, I'm the chief executive officer. I'm sure a *nerd*," and I put as much disgust in my voice when I said *nerd* as she had used when spitting out the word *secretary*, "can figure it out."

I gathered up my things and left her with one parting shot. "I expect to hear from you by the end of the day."

The stalker was fuming. Angry. How dare she *come in here and question our work? Furious. That little bitch. The stalker could taste bile rising from a roiling stomach. She* knows *nothing. Nothing* about Phoenix. *Enraged. Nothing* about *the lives we have saved. Incensed. Through clenched teeth the stalker pictured her dead. Lying on the ground in the orange light.*

I motioned for Carrie to follow me as I stormed through her office area into my office.

"So what's up with Natalie Scott?" I asked her. Secretaries, the good ones anyway, always had a pulse on the personalities.

Carrie shrugged her shoulders. "Is she doing her ice queen routine?"

"Yeah. And I definitely don't like it. Is she always like this?"

"Most of the time. Not when she was around Mr. Connaught though."

"Well, that's to be expected. Most employees are usually on their best behaviour around the boss. Although she didn't show it today."

"Maybe she's having a little trouble with you being boss," Carrie offered insightfully.

"That I figured out. But I caught other undercurrents. Like I'd pissed in her Corn Flakes or something."

Carrie blushed a little at my profanity but gave me a blank look.

"Carrie, it'd be really helpful if you knew something and shared it with me. I don't encourage gossip…" Which was a bold-faced lie, because as a secretary I used to thrive on it. Not the malicious type of gossip, but the threads of information that good secretaries would sew together so they could have the complete picture. I was a student of human behaviour, because how people treated me and acted around me dictated how we worked together.

Carrie continued to give me a dumb blonde look. Wide eyes and innocence. A wall had definitely gone up.

"Come on Carrie. Spill. Share. If I'm going to have a chance, I'll need input from you. I'm a big girl and can handle it. You never gossiped with Tommy did you?"

She shook her head.

"You probably would've eventually, when you'd been together longer. We've only been at this a day. But considering the circumstances, a little help here would be appreciated. Whatever information you give me will stay between the two of us."

"They had a relationship. Mr. Connaught and Nat."

Now it was my time to snort. "You're kidding!"

"Nope." She held up a two finger salute. "Girl Scout's promise. I swear."

"Who knew?"

"Only a few people. Although Mr. Connaught never actually came out and told me. Not that it was any of my business."

I lit a cigarette and walked over to the window. Tommy and Natalie. Somehow I couldn't picture it. She was so mealy-mouthed and tight. What did he see in her? I felt Carrie's hand on my shoulder.

"But it was over, Kate." She said this to make me feel better, as if I was hurt, just because Tommy was in a relationship with someone.

"It's okay Carrie. Tommy and I were divorced. Many years ago. He was free to do what he wanted. I'm just having trouble picturing the two of them together. When did he break it off?"

"He didn't. Natalie ended the relationship. About a month and a half ago."

Somehow that made me feel a little better. When Tommy had left me the message on my machine in Toronto last week, asking me to come to New York, his voice was inviting. He wouldn't have teased me like that if he'd been involved with someone. My thoughts were interrupted by something Carrie had said.

"Pardon?"

"I said, she ended the relationship when Mr. Connaught cut off the funding to her pet project. She was livid."

Bingo. I'd just tripped over suspect number one with a motive.

Chapter sixteen

While I was thinking malicious thoughts of how well the moniker *murderess* fit Natalie Scott, Ruldolph Valentino the undertaker called. He wanted to know if I had thought any more about a memorial service for Mr. Connaught. I hadn't and I was ashamed to admit it. Tommy deserved better than a quick cremation with yours truly as the only mourner. So I lied and told him I was still calling people and he'd hear from me within the next couple of hours.

Steve Holliday was surprised and a little embarrassed when I showed up at his office door.

"Katie, come in."

The sound of his voice coupled with him calling me Katie gave me a shiver reminiscent of someone dragging their fingernails over a chalkboard.

"Kate," I told him. "Or Kathleen. Please."

"Sure." He motioned at a chair in front of his desk. I ignored the offer.

"I need your help. Arrangements have to be made for a memorial service for Tommy. I don't know any of his friends, co-workers or business acquaintances. You seemed like the best place to start."

"Let me look after it," he offered. When and where were the only two things he asked and I felt relieved to leave the whole thing in his hands.

"Tomorrow. Late in the day." And I gave him the name of the funeral parlor. "Call Mr. Theodore Bradley. He's dying to hear from us." I chuckled at my little pun but Steve didn't get it.

My next task was to get through a two-hour sales meeting pretending I understood what was being talked about. I was pleasantly surprised that the language was English and I that did understand. Status reports were given on current bids and RFPs, and the status of contract negotiations on bids we had won. The Vice President of Sales, Mark Hall, assured me that everything was on track and there were no surprises coming up. I listened closely for sounds of condescension in his voice but there were none. I decided I liked him. He wasn't flashy and didn't speak out of the side his mouth as you would expect from a sales type.

"Is there anything else you need to know at this point, Miss Monahan?" he asked me. "Any questions for any of the staff here at the meeting or anything we can get back to you on?" Mark sounded sincere.

"No. Thank you," I said gratefully. This was such a change from the marble gargoyles I'd met from research and development.

I found two memos on my desk when I returned from the sales meeting. The first one was a very short note from Natalie Scott, stating that she intended to stay on at Phoenix (as if that were her choice, I thought) and continue to lead the R and D team. No apology and no indication that she had any remorse for the way she behaved. I had no idea how to deal with Nat Scott and frankly didn't have the stomach for the stress of having to fire someone this early in the game.

The second memo was from Steve Holliday outlining the arrangements for the memorial service. It was scheduled for 3:00 p.m. the next day (Steve said in his memo we wouldn't get as big a turn-out if we held it after 5:00 p.m.), he had pulled some strings and managed to get a small notice put in the New York Times for the next day's publication, he had put all of the 'girls' (I sucked air through my teeth at the nerve of him putting *that* on paper) in the office on the phone calling all the business associates, and he had sent out an all-points-memorandum by e-mail to Phoenix employees. And I was to kindly let him know if there were any of our personal acquaintances I wished to invite.

The day was taking its toll and a low grade headache was starting to throb at the back of my head. Time to end this workday and go home. Which was a good idea until Carrie knocked on my door and announced that the police were here and needed to speak to me.

Detectives Bartlett and Shipley helped themselves to the chairs in front of my desk. If it was possible, Shipley looked even more rumpled and frumpy than the last time she was here, and not for the first time I wondered if her persona was a little bit faked. Like Columbo's. I remembered her as being sharp and abrasive in her questioning. Today though, Bartlett started off.

"Ms. Monahan, we'd like you to tell us about the last time you spoke with Mr. Connaught."

"I think I told you this already. The first time you were here to talk to me?"

They both stared back at me, not saying word, waiting.

Fuck it. "The last time I *spoke* with Mr. Connaught was about six months ago. He was in Toronto on business and we had dinner." I sat back in my chair and folded my arms across my chest.

Shipley spoke up this time but first she flipped through her notebook, snapping the pages. "Yep." She looked up at me. "We mean the last time you spoke with him on the phone."

I had no idea where they were going with this. "I *told* you, the last time I spoke with Tommy was about six months ago. The last time I spoke with him on the phone would have been around that same time when we talked about where to have dinner."

Shipley said, "Well, the Bell Canada records at McCallum & Watts show that you received a phone call from Mr. Connaught two days before he was murdered."

I inched forward in my chair, tried to put my feet on the floor and leaned towards the Detectives. "Check your notebook Mrs. Columbo, because as I told you before, Mr. Connaught left me a voice message that day. We *did not* talk."

My insides started shaking and I was angry. Angry to think that it had been less than a week ago that my life was somewhat normal. Five days ago Tommy was alive. And in the five days since Tommy had been murdered, the best they could come up with were the Bell Canada records at the law firm?

The Detectives ignored my snide remarks.

"Tell us about how life has been since you inherited all this," Shipley said as she waved her arm around the office.

I assumed that question was rhetorical and chose not to answer it. My blood pressure was rising and I realized that the Detectives were trying to get a rise out of me. And it was working. With the combination of my body language and angry retorts to their questions, I was acting defensively and just like someone who had something to hide. Several deep breaths helped bring my blood pressure back to normal, and I tried a smile on New York's finest.

"Well, it's been a tough haul," I told them. "Tom Connaught has been dead less than five days and I'm on a helluva steep learning curve. Learning about the company, learning about the staff, learning about our products, learning how to be a chief executive officer. And, learning how to get around in New York," I said with some satisfaction. "And oh yeah, learning how *not* to kill exotic fish," I added.

They both looked puzzled by the last comment but didn't go anywhere with it.

"Your personal finances are in better shape, no doubt," Shipley said.

"Just what do you mean by that?" I demanded.

"When we looked into your situation in Toronto, it was clear that you weren't as financially well off as you are now," she said. "A small retirement fund, no large debts, credit cards paid on time, no real assets except a 1990 Toyota Corolla, a small chequing account, no savings to speak of." She was reading from her notebook and each time she noted something in the realm of my personal worth, her sidekick Bartlett held up another finger as if counting off the items.

People who know me don't want to be around me when I'm pissed off and angry. Add embarrassed to the mix and I'm downright ugly. Detective Shipley had just summed up my sorry financial life in one sentence, and Detective Bartlett had added it all up on six fat fingers. Shipley carried on, in an almost apologetic tone.

"Things have changed for the better though, haven't they? You don't have to worry about the finances now, do you? I know what it's like having an old car, one that gives you heartburn every time it doesn't start. But you don't have that worry anymore. In fact," she turned to her partner, "she has a driver now doesn't she?" Bartlett grinned and nodded.

I'd had enough. These two buffoons were wasting my time. Time that should be spent trying to find Tommy's killer.

"Okay ladies." I stood up. "You may think you're going to get a rise or a reaction out of me. But it's not going to happen. Why don't you get off your asses and go and find some bad guys?"

Bartlett started to stand up but Shipley's left hand shot out and motioned for her to sit down. When she spoke this time, her tone had changed.

"Our counterpart at the Toronto Police Service told us we'd have our hands full dealing with you." She stared directly at me. "He said you have a habit of sticking your nose in where it doesn't belong."

I took a deep breath and sat back down in my chair.

Shipley flipped a few pages back in her notebook and found what she was looking for.

"Detective Leech," she continued, "told me all about you." She looked down at her notebook and read from it. "Involved in a murder, a multiple shooting, a kidnapping, a suicide, and," she turned the page of her notebook, "securities fraud. Hey Bartlett," she said turning to her partner, "are there any felonies our Ms. Monahan hasn't been involved in?"

Guilty as charged, I thought, as I rubbed the top of my ear where a bullet had grazed it. A couple of months earlier I had been an innocent, albeit involved, by-stander in all the mayhem she was describing. Detective Leech had been the lead detective on the case. To say that he and I had shared some quality time together would be an understatement.

"Listen," I started, "that's all in the past. It has nothing to do with why we're talking today."

Shipley held up her hand, interrupting me.

"In the past, yes," she agreed with me. "But there are some disturbing similarities."

"What do you mean by that?" I demanded.

"Well, let's start with the B&E and assault at Mr. Connaught's apartment last Friday. Did you even *think* to mention that to us? You had a chance on the weekend when you dropped by to visit Detective Bartlett at the precinct. You know, Detective Leech told us that you can be a royal pain in the rear end by not sharing information that may be relevant. I'm thinkin' he may be right. What do you think Bartlett?"

Her partner nodded her head in agreement and said, "To think we had to find out from my brother-in-law, who I can barely share a civil word with. We were at my mother's last night for dinner. We found it funny that we both had cases involving a Canadian." Bartlett glared at me. "Did you think you might have told us about getting hit over the head at Mr. Connaught's apartment? You let the patrol officers think that it could have been someone who broke in to steal the contents because they knew the occupant had died. We," she paused and waved her hand several times back and forth at her partner and then herself, "we're thinking it might just be related to Mr. Connaught's murder." Her sarcasm was not lost on me, and I felt like a school girl who had just been chastised by the vice principal.

Shipley said, "Ms. Monahan. We are no closer today than we were five days ago to finding out how and why Mr. Connaught was murdered. We've got a lot of ground to cover and we'd appreciate your cooperation." I nodded my head because I didn't want them accusing me of hindering their investigation.

Shipley continued. "We need some information from the company. What the company is working on, what its customers are up to, any recent sales, some information on the employees. General access to all the files. We'd like to talk to the employees, go through the files, get a general sense of the business."

It made sense to me, but I wasn't sure about the legalities of the police going through our customer files, and the files in our research and development area.

"I have no objection to that, but I'd want to check with our Legal Department first. Just to make sure we can get you the access you need."

"Sure, you do that. We'd appreciate talking to the employees sooner than later," Shipley told me. I detected a wee bit of snideness in her tone.

I stood up from my desk, hoping that they'd take the clue and get out of my office. Shipley stared at me from her chair and didn't take my hint.

"Ms. Monahan, how tall are you?"

"And just what has *that* got to do with anything?" I shot back.

"Just answer the question. How tall are you?"

"I'm four feet eleven inches." One inch taller than my grandmother and probably a good foot or more shorter than Shipley.

"We might want to confirm that by having our crime scene technicians measure you."

"Why? You'd think I'd make up the fact that I'm under five feet? What the hell is this all about anyway?"

It was Bartlett's turn to speak up. She got a tiny nod from Shipley before she spoke. "Forensics have determined that Mr. Connaught was shot from a low angle. The only thing that makes sense at this point is that the shooter was very short."

I think I blanched. Or at least that's what it felt like. In my favourite romance novels the heroine *blanches* when she's scared or about to faint.

When the detectives finally left I stuffed a stack of mail from the in-basket into my briefcase and left the office. Carrie was at her desk and I told her to call the driver and let him know I would be walking.

She shook her head. "Lou won't like that," she admonished me.

I shrugged my shoulders. "I feel like walking. See you tomorrow."

The elevators were crowded with energetic people, obviously glad to be leaving work for the day. I wondered how many of them were employees of Phoenix.

When I stumbled out of the elevator at the ground floor it took me a moment to get my bearings. I got nudged more than once on the back of my legs with the briefcases of people rushing past me, hurrying to their subways and buses. The few other nights I had left the building, the cavernous lobby was empty. I headed for the revolving doors and was surprised to see Natalie Scott push ahead of me in the crowd.

She was dressed like a lot of New York working women. Smart business suit with running shoes and white ankle socks, and a knapsack on her back. She had her head down and barreled through the crowd. Natalie was a pushy broad and it showed in the way she treated her fellow pedestrians. She gave one person a shoulder and smartly stepped in front of another to take her place in the revolving doors. I shook my head and wondered what Tommy saw in *that*.

When I was finally lucky enough to exit the building I turned right on Lexington and started towards my hotel. It was only about a six block walk but I needed the exercise. Jay would be proud of me, I thought. It wasn't too long ago that he had to coax me to walk around the block. But in the last couple of months I had started exercising. I hated it but was adult enough to admit that I enjoyed the feeling when I was finished. Like banging your head against a wall - it felt so good when you stopped. I walked fast today to make up for the fact that I'd started smoking again. If I could get through this week in one piece, I'd quit again. That was a promise.

Natalie Scott suddenly appeared in front of me again just as I reached my hotel. She still had her head down and looked like a woman on a mission. Some "devil made me do it" moment happened and I decided to follow her. There were several people between us and I was sure she hadn't seen me. On Madison she stopped abruptly in front of a shop window and I panicked momentarily and ducked in an open doorway. I peeked around, feeling totally foolish. I was only pretending to follow her and had nothing to hide. When Natalie started off again I stepped out of my hiding place and kept pace.

The street signs told me we were now on Fifth Avenue and we were heading north because I could see the trees of Central Park several blocks away. When the Plaza Hotel and Central Park came into view, I knew where I was and decided to call it a day. I could get a cab in front of the Plaza and go home and stop playing games.

I watched Natalie cross at the busy corner of Fifth Avenue and East 59th. She kept going straight up Fifth on the sidewalk across the street from Central Park. I stood and watched her for a moment and then I started after her again. I was curious now and needed to know where she was going.

I couldn't believe it when she crossed East 63rd Street and turned into a familiar, awning-covered building entrance. I was incredulous when the doorman smiled at her and held the door open. But I was dumbfounded when the doorman told me she lived there. In the same building as Tommy.

Chapter seventeen

THE DOORMAN TOLD ME THAT Miss Scott's family had lived in the building for twenty-some years. She was still living there with her widowed mother. Their apartment was on the 20th floor.

How convenient, I thought.

"Does my key to the apartment work on all the outside doors?" I asked.

"Yes ma'am. It works on all the entrances to your apartment, the front door and the two exits. It also opens the doors on the outside of the building, at the back."

I rode the elevator to the 14th floor and let myself into the apartment. I hadn't been back since my visit with Jay and realized that the poor fish were probably dead by now. I found the remote control and opened the wall displaying the aquarium and was surprised to see signs of life. With no fish food in at least a week, they had probably been eating each other.

The aquarium was built flush into the wall and I had no idea where to put the fish food I found on the shelf below the tank. I ran my hands over the wood surrounding the tank, feeling for a knob or latch to gain access to the top of the aquarium. The wood paneling had seams but there were no obvious hinges. The space below the aquarium was open shelving so I knelt down in front of it and ran my hands down the sides of the shelves, under the top, all around. Nothing.

I picked up the remote control again and stared at all the buttons. It was larger than the remote I had for my television and I think it was called a universal control. Small buttons on the bottom read "cd", "radio", "tv", "dvd". Along one side were up and down arrows for volume and the arrows on the other side said "channel". Numbers from zero to nine filled the middle of the remote control.

I pressed the red power button and the wall closed over the aquarium.

I flicked the power button again and the wall opened and the lights came back on in the aquarium. I wondered what else the remote control powered, so I pushed the button "cd" and the Beatles blasted out of hidden speakers. Ringo's nasal voice was singing one of their ridiculous ditties, the name of which escaped me. I quickly pushed the "tv" button and the music went off but nothing else happened.

I turned slowly around the room looking for a television, pointing the remote in different directions, pushing the tv button. Nothing. The same thing when I pressed the "vcr" button.

The music blared again, at the beginning of the same stupid song when I switched to "cd". The volume buttons worked and I lowered the sound to a reasonable level. There was no sign of a stereo system and the whole thing was starting to frustrate me.

I plopped down in one of the large, easy chairs and stared at the fish tank. My fingers played with the remote and I pushed the down arrow on the channel changer and heard a very soft, low, whining sound which stopped when I took my finger off the button. I pressed the button again, holding my finger on it and the sound reminded me of an electric can opener that gets stuck. A motor trying to work and getting nowhere.

The up arrow on the channel changer was what I was looking for. When I pressed it I got a happy motor sound. I held my finger on the up arrow, listening, and watched incredulously as the entire wall holding the aquarium swung slowly open.

"Cool," I said out loud, sounding like a teenager.

With the wall open at a ninety degree angle, my questions about how to feed the fish were answered. The backside of the wall revealed the workings of the aquarium and there was an inset shelf holding a variety of fish equipment, small nets, food, things to add to the tank water and such.

The lower half of the wall revealed the stereo system. Piles of cd's were jammed into the spaces around the receiver and cd player.

The opening in the wall exposed a small room, perhaps eight feet square. The hideaway held a small table with a computer along one wall, and two small filing cabinets. Halfway up the wall beside the computer were two outlets. Wires from the outlets were hooked to the back of the computer. On top of the filing cabinets was a small laser printer.

Well, well, well, I thought to myself. What have we here? I powered on the computer. Now I would get some answers. To what, I didn't know. The fact that Tommy's computer in the den held no information didn't seem so strange now. I pulled out the small chair tucked under the desk and rubbed my hands together like a concert pianist, warming up.

I stared at the screen, watching all sorts of words fly by as it booted up.

A small, colourful box appeared and disappeared just as quickly. Something about doctor somebody, the virus checker. Finally, things I recognized started appearing on the screen and the Windows logo and icons appeared.

I grabbed the mouse, ready to start exploring but a small box, centered on the screen materialized and commanded me to enter my password.

"Shit," I said out loud.

A lost cause. Tommy was technical enough to realize the worth of a solid password, and if the machine needed a password, there was definitely something to protect. My only experience with passwords for computers was at the law office where we would have to log-on to the local area network. I never changed my password if I could help it, and it was usually something as simple as my name or my mother's name. There was never much to hide on my computer, just letters, agreements and nonsense.

The computer in the den didn't require a password but then again, there was nothing on that computer except the software to run it.

I fed the fish and thought about my chances of discovering what the password might be. I had come across nothing so far, in the apartment or at Tommy's office, of a personal nature where he might have written down secret passwords.

A sudden remembrance flashed before me and I almost slapped myself for being so stupid. Tommy lived by his electronic organizer. He had one of those small, handheld, computer-type organizers that fit in the inside breast pocket of a suit. The last time we had dinner together he had whipped it out and proudly showed me. He demonstrated how it held all of his appointments, kept all of his phone numbers organized, and how he could create little memos to himself and store them on it. It had a minuscule keyboard.

I had laughed at it and told him to learn to type on a real keyboard. He had assured me he could type.

"Keyboarding, it's called nowadays, Kate," he'd said. "And remember, I'm a code-head from way back. Programmers can type faster than most secretaries."

Where was his organizer? My search of the apartment hadn't revealed it. There was no sign of it at the office. The logical and obvious answer was that he had it on him when he died.

No personal belongings had been returned to me as next of kin so the police must still have everything. I made a mental note to call them in the morning.

The two filing cabinets were locked and no amount of tugging and cajoling would open them. I had no idea where to look for keys.

The surprise and elation I'd felt at finding the room turned to dejection.

I powered off the computer and closed the magic wall. I looked around for a good hiding place for the remote control and ended up putting it in my purse. All the good hiding spots were too obvious and the apartment had already been broken into once. I wasn't taking any chances.

Chapter eighteen

I CALLED THE DETECTIVES IN the morning and asked about Tommy's things.

"I'm afraid I can't release those at the moment," Detective Shipley told me.

"Why?"

"Evidence."

"Well, can you at least tell me what there was?"

"No."

I sighed loudly through my nose. I was obviously getting nowhere.

"Okay. Let's stop playing hide the weenie. Did you find an electronic organizer?"

"A what?"

"A small black case. You can electronically store phone numbers, appointments, things like that on it."

"How big is it?"

"About four inches square."

"Small enough to fit into a pocket?"

"Yes."

"And you said it was black? Does it look like a Blackberry?"

"Yes," I said emphatically.

"Nope."

"Nope what? It's not among his personal effects?"

"Nope."

I hung up before some sarcastic remark crossed my lips about New York's finest.

The stalker was in the middle row on the left side of the chapel. Trying to be inconspicuous. Breathing had returned to normal but only after enormous effort to concentrate and to hold the hatred back. The hatred had gone away when Tom Connaught was pronounced dead. But there were times in the last couple of days when the hatred came back and got close to the surface. She *brought it back.* She *was responsible now.*

The memorial service was held at the funeral home which wasn't large enough to hold everyone who showed up. There were employees, members of the board of directors, partners from the law firms, and dozens and dozens of other people who I didn't recognize.

Hordes of people were milling around outside the entrance when I arrived in the back of Lou's car. Both sides of the street were lined with limousines with their drivers standing smartly beside them. There were no parking spots available but that didn't deter Lou who stopped in front of the funeral home, double parking the car. He quickly put the car in park and told me over his shoulder to wait until he opened the door for me. I suppose he didn't want to be seen slacking off in front of his professional brethren and I wearily assured him that I was in no rush.

My body felt heavy and my mind was numb. Lou opened the door and offered his hand to help me out.

"I'll be waiting," he said quietly.

"You're not coming in?"

"Only if it's okay with you, Miss."

"Of course it's okay. This is a service for all of Tommy's friends," I assured him. He gave me a grateful smile and led me through the throng of milling people.

Two people immediately stepped forward and snapped my picture. I was dumbfounded.

"Excuse me?" I demanded of them. They both identified themselves as photographers for two of New York's daily papers.

"And your purpose here would be what?"

One of them informed me that they were just doing their job. A press release had been sent out by Phoenix announcing the memorial service and they were there as a follow up to the murder.

A press release? I couldn't believe it. I had asked Steve Holliday to handle the arrangements but I hadn't figured on him inviting the media. I scanned the crowd and easily found him. He was looking slick as usual, trying to appear solemn, giving an interview to a television crew. I quickly pushed my way through the mass of people into the funeral home to avoid any more press. Men and women, all dressed in somber clothing lined the hallways and were talking in lowered voices. I spied Mr. Theodore Bradley standing with his hands clasped in front of him at the end of the hall and hurried towards him. Several people quietly greeted me as I passed and I shook their hands, recognizing none of them.

"Mr. Bradley," I said, offering my hand. I felt out of breath, as if I had been running.

"Ms. Monahan. How are you today?" he asked.

"Fine, just fine." I was getting nervous and my stomach was churning. I peeked into the massive room, amazed to see most of the chairs already full.

"Can we get started?" I urged him. He nodded and wandered off to round up the stragglers.

I timidly stepped through the double doors into the room and was immediately overcome. The beautifully carved coffin placed at the front of the room had a small spray of flowers centered on it. Beside it was a podium with a microphone. Unrecognizable, typically funereal music was playing softly in the background. The low murmur of voices surrounded me and I looked for a seat. Blood was pounding in my ears and my eyes were unfocussed.

I found an empty chair in the back row, way off to the side. I sat with my hands tucked under my thighs, staring at the coffin. *I will get through this,* I chanted to myself. I knew I wasn't good at funerals, having attended one very recently for a close friend. Was anyone good at funerals, I wondered silently. The whole notion of public displays of mourning just didn't sit right with me. As I watched the people pouring into the room, taking their seats, I wished I had stuck by my original plan to have a private service.

"Ms. Monahan," Mr. Bradley breathed into my ear. I stared up at his blurred image, and realized my eyes were not just unfocussed, they were tear-filled.

"But you must sit at the front. We've saved seating there for you. As the only relative of the deceased, it's only right," he told me. He took my elbow and tried to help me to stand but my hands remained firmly stuck under my thighs.

"I can't," I whispered back at him.

"I'll help," I heard a familiar voice. It was Jay. Once again, I was overwhelmed, but this time with relief. The cavalry had arrived. My knight in shining armour. Jay sat in the chair beside me and knowingly, didn't touch me. He knew when to respect my personal space and my tightly hidden hands gave him the clue.

"I'll sit with you up front," he soothingly told me. "Come on." He stood up and I reluctantly followed suit. As we walked down the side aisle towards the front row the low, murmuring voices stopped all around me. You could hear the proverbial pin drop. We took our seats and waited for the proceedings to begin.

Cleve Johnston appeared before me at the podium and started talking.

I didn't hear a word he said, or what the other speakers had to say. I played one of my childhood games in my mind, and blocked it all out. Tried to envisage myself in a happy place, playing with my favourite toys. I used to do that when I had to get a needle, or the dentist was drilling my teeth. Only this time it didn't work. All I could think about was Tommy and how much I was missing him. My one hundred and fifteen pound body felt about four hundred pounds heavier and I was feeling the tell-tale signs of an oncoming migraine behind my eyes.

I don't know how long the service lasted and when I finally refocused on the ceremony, someone who I didn't recognize was at the podium. He said his last words and the music started up again, louder this time. I felt Jay's hand in mine, and wondered when he had taken it. I looked over at him and gave him a weak smile, which he returned. I glanced over my shoulder at the people and saw them standing, waiting.

"I think they're waiting for you to leave," Jay whispered in my ear.

There was no way I was walking out in front of all these unknown people, with their sympathetic faces.

"I just want to sit here for a while. Tell them to go."

Jay motioned to Mr. Bradley who then took the podium and softly thanked everyone for attending. They started to leave but several people came forward to offer their sympathy. Every one of them felt the need to clasp my hand and murmur something soothing. The amazing thing was how few of these people I knew, and I sadly realized how much about Tommy I didn't know. They were Tommy's friends, and obviously feeling the loss as much as I.

I played the bereaved widow well, and my mother would have been proud of me. I didn't snap at anyone or yell at them to get out of my face as I so dearly wanted to do. Jay stood on one side of me and my loyal soldier, Cleve Johnston, stood on guard on the other.

When the last of them had cleared the room I looked up into Jay's friendly face and bawled like a baby.

"I want to go home," I cried.

Chapter nineteen

WEDNESDAY AND THURSDAY WERE HARD, nose to the grindstone days. In the two days since the funeral I had been mentally busier than a Ph.D. student cramming for her thesis defense. But I was learning, and several times I found myself smiling when things made sense.

I dutifully read memos, reviewed reports, answered letters of condolence, signed documents, and generally amazed myself. Overall, I understood what I was reading, reviewing and approving. When I didn't understand, I asked questions. Playing the role of CEO wasn't as hard as I had anticipated, but I didn't completely fool myself. In two days, I had barely made a decision, and the few I had made, were minor.

I lit a cigarette and swiveled my chair around to gaze at the skyline. My mind was exhausted but my body was restless. And hungry. I hadn't walked anywhere in the last two days and had had absolutely no exercise. I was quickly becoming used to having Lou at my disposal and felt guilty about how the poor man was at my beck and call twenty-four hours a day.

I paged Lou and told him to go home and then tried to track down Jay. A night off from this place was more than appealing and I wanted to eat something other than room service. Jay sounded distracted when I finally reached him and he told me he had a late meeting. He'd call me tomorrow.

The offices were dark and deserted when I left and the cavernous lobby was inhabited by a sole security guard. He reminded me it was 8:45 p.m. when I signed the exit register.

"Is there somewhere close by where I can get something decent to eat?" I asked him.

"Good food, or fancy food?"

I smiled. "Good food. I hate that fancy stuff. Never seems to be enough on the plate, and half the time it looks too pretty to eat," I joked with him.

He nodded knowingly. "My fancy pants son-in-law took me to one of those places and the prices made me sick. And the food didn't help either." He stood up and pointed out the front of the building. "Just out front, turn left and about half way up the next block is a favourite place for you young folks. Called TJ's. Food's good."

TJ's was packed. At first I couldn't quite decide if it was the music or the conversation that was the most deafening. My ears quickly adjusted to the din and I heard the hostess asking me in an exasperated tone of voice if I wanted a table. The hostess with an attitude showed me to my table by leading me through the morass of bodies like she was a guided missile, where she quickly slapped the plastic coated menu on the table and took off. I wondered if she had taken her training in Paris.

I gazed around the restaurant and found it too much to take in. Television sets hung from the ceiling every six feet and each one appeared to be tuned to a different channel. There didn't appear to be any rhyme or reason to the decor. Some of the memorabilia hanging from the walls was from the fifties, some of it had a nautical theme, the bar area was festooned with ferns, giving it a seventies, *Looking for Mr. Goodbar* feel, clusters of tables were dotted around the floor and booths lined the walls. Frank Sinatra finished belting out *My Way* and was quickly followed by a hard hitting Bob Seger tune, the title of which escaped me.

A waiter appeared and took my order. My senses slowly adjusted to the place and I relaxed and sipped my Diet Coke. A table on the far side of the restaurant erupted into loud laughter. I glanced over at the table and recognized the group as Phoenix employees. Nat Scott's employees. One of them greeted me later just as I was wrestling with a particularly single-minded piece of melted mozzarella which was stuck between my teeth, refusing to let go from its warm bed of French onion soup. I pulled at the cheese with my fingers, as daintily as I could, and looked up at my visitor. It was the handsome god in a wheelchair and I fished around my memory banks for his name.

"Ms. Monahan, what a surprise," he was saying in that yummy voice of his.

"Mr. Tucker," I replied, remembering his name just in time.

"Please, call me Ben."

"Please, call me Kate," I repeated, trance-like. I pushed my food back and got a grip on myself.

"You should join us." He pointed at my dinner. "When you're finished your meal."

"Thanks. I might. How are things going anyway?"

He smiled. I melted, again.

"In the R and D department. I meant how are things in R and D?"

He wheeled himself around and said to me, over his shoulder, "Join us after you eat, and we'll fill you in."

I finished my meal and signaled for the check, meaning to make a quick exit. I had no intention of joining Ben and his table mates, and wanted to make an unobtrusive departure but as soon as I stood up and gathered my briefcase and jacket, I saw waving arms across the room. Now I had no excuse. And just what was acceptable behaviour as CEO of these employees, I glumly wondered as I plastered a smile on my face and headed towards their table.

Everyone at the table shifted around and someone grabbed a chair for me and placed it at the head of the table. I sat down and smiled stupidly. I quickly did a mental run down and surprised myself by remembering everyone. Rick Williams, the small, nerdy engineer with thick glasses sat on my left, beside him was Belinda Moffat. Her hair still looked like it needed a wash but that didn't seem to be bothering Rick, who was practically sitting in her lap. I wondered if the two of them were an item. My other clue was the moon-eyed look Rick was giving Belinda.

Dan Thornton and Ben Tucker sat on the other side of the table.

"Where are Derek and Natalie?" I asked.

"Derek couldn't get a pass, and Nat never joins us," Dan informed me.

"A pass?" I asked.

"He's married. More often than not, he runs home to the wife. And Natalie, she's too busy with her work," Dan informed me.

I smiled at everyone again, feeling like a third wheel. They all stared at me, with weak smiles. Great, I thought, I've just ruined their evening.

"So, how're things?" I feebly asked the table in general.

"Good, great," they mumbled.

A waitress appeared and saved me. "Something from the bar?"

"No, thanks. I can't stay." She wandered off. "In fact, I'm late as it is. Good to see you all." I gathered up my stuff and gave a weak wave, like the Queen Mother.

They waved back and looked relieved.

Outside the restaurant as I was trying to get my bearings and looking for a cab, someone pulled on my jacket from behind. I turned around.

"Late for what?" Ben Tucker asked me.

"Pardon?"

"You said you had to leave because you were late. Late for what?"

"Nothing," I admitted. "I just felt totally out of place. And besides, I was making everyone else uncomfortable."

"Go on. No way," he teased. "We're used to drinking with the CEO."

"You invited me. Were you trying to set me up?" I think I was flirting with him a little bit.

"No. I was just hoping to get your attention." Now he was flirting with me. "Can I buy you a coffee?" He pointed to the Starbucks across the street.

"Sure."

Ben insisted that I get a table while he ordered. I watched in amazement as he maneuvered his wheelchair through the maze of tables with one hand and served me my coffee with a flourish. He zipped back to the counter to fetch his and arrived back with a grin. I stared at him the whole time and he knew it.

"Skiing accident."

"Pardon?"

"You're wondering how I ended up in this chair. Aren't you?"

"I'm wondering lots of things. And yeah, that was one of them."

"What else do you want to know?"

"Do you still ski?"

"Yep. And play basketball and floor hockey."

All of which would explain his incredibly fit-looking upper body. I wouldn't mind getting a look at his forearms under his nicely tailored suit jacket.

We chatted about mundane things, his family, where he went to school, where he lived in the city. Chit chat. The conversation finally got around to the one thing we had in common. Phoenix Technologies.

"How long have you been at Phoenix?" I asked him.

"Going on four years. I was with the company in Arizona and moved out here to New York two years ago."

He had started as a programmer and worked his way up to project team leader in research and development. He loved it. In fact, if it was at all possible, his face became even more animated and handsome as he talked about his baby. The San Carlos project. I just sat back and watched and listened, mesmerized by his enthusiasm and his obvious passion for his job. It was a one-sided conversation, Ben talking, me listening.

"So when her project was cancelled and funding withdrawn," he was saying, "I got some of her team members on the San Carlos project."

My ears had perked up.

"Whose project?" I asked.

"Nat's. Weren't you listening?"

I blushed a little. "Sorry. I had heard about that project being cancelled. What's Natalie working on now?"

"Who knows? As usual, it's totally top secret. Very few get into her inner circle. And since the demise of Mr. Connaught, that inner circle is even fewer." He grinned at me knowingly.

I gave him my best dumb blonde look, pretending I didn't know what he was talking about.

"Oh come on. Don't tell me you don't know."

"Know what?"

"About Nat and Mr. Connaught. Everyone knew."

That's not what Carrie had told me.

"Knew what?" I persisted. "I've been holed up in my office. And I'm not exactly best friends with Nat. What are you talking about?"

He looked at me for a few moments, probably trying to decide if he had said too much.

"I've probably said too much." I had read his mind. "Nat and Mr. Connaught were an item. He was your ex-husband, wasn't he?"

I nodded.

"You seem more his type than Nat. None of us could figure out the attraction. Nat's nickname is the Ice Queen."

I smiled. I had already given her that moniker myself.

Chapter twenty

"She strikes me as very focused. Someone who takes her work very seriously," I said.

"Her work is her life. That's one of the reasons we all found it so surprising when she and Mr. Connaught started seeing each other."

It seemed obvious that most people knew about the affair, despite what Carrie told me. I wanted to question Ben about Tommy and Nat, but I needed to do it discreetly. I was in the executive offices now, not the secretarial pool and although I was sure the upper echelons of corporations had their fair share of gossip, I wasn't sure if executives kept their juicy morsels among themselves.

"What could possibly have been the attraction?" I pondered out loud. "I can't picture those two together. Tommy was so loose and easy going. Natalie Scott strikes me as someone so uptight you could bowl with her shit."

Did I just say that out loud? I looked over at Ben and he was trying very hard not to laugh.

"She's that, I'll agree," Ben said. "They worked very closely on that project of hers. Mr. Connaught used to get right in there with his shirt sleeves rolled up. We all worked long hours and he was often there with us, programming, throwing out ideas. Part of the team. I suppose all those long hours spent together just led to the two of them hitting it off." He shrugged his shoulders and sipped his coffee. "Go figure."

"Yeah, go figure," I agreed. "What was the project all about?"

"Well, it's still top secret. I could tell you, but then I'd have to shoot you." He leaned across the table and pointed his finger at me, like he was shooting a pistol. "Bang bang."

"Very funny. Just tell me what the project was about," I insisted in an exasperated tone.

"Well, I guess now that you're the CEO, I can spill my guts. This secret's been such a burden to carry around," he said very seriously. He hung his head.

My heart raced a little. Maybe this was the break I was looking for. Some solid information. I looked around me to see who our table neighbours were, and realized we were the only ones left in Starbucks.

"So spill your guts," I urged him in a near whisper. He lifted his head and he had a huge, shit-eating grin plastered across his face.

"Gotcha!" he exclaimed.

"Ha ha," I deadpanned. Ben was turning out to be just a *little* juvenile. I was suddenly overwhelmed with fatigue and decided to pack it in for the evening.

"Thanks for the coffee. I just realized how tired I am."

Ben grabbed my hand and pulled on it.

"Come on Kate. Sit down. Joke's over. Okay?"

I sat down reluctantly.

"Just tell me about the project, will you? I've enjoyed our joking, but now I'm tired. If you don't want to tell me, I'll get the info somewhere else."

"Okay, okay. It was a subcontract for a bio-medical engineering company. We were developing an interface device for one of their projects. The company is called Global Devices. Global ended up losing too much money before they could get their product to market, so they just closed it down. It was as simple as that."

"What was their product?"

"An artificial kidney."

"An artificial kidney? You're kidding me again. I've read about artificial hearts, and there's one company up in Canada that were leading the way in that area, but artificial kidneys. Wow. Very Star Wars." A low wattage light bulb was turning on in my head.

Ben shook his head. "Nope. I'm deadly serious. There are dozens of bio-medical companies out there in the race to develop artificial organs. A couple of companies have introduced artificial hearts and others are close to animal trials on other organs. If someone can come up with a plastic heart, why not a kidney? There are more people on waiting lists for kidney transplants than heart transplants."

"But what about dialysis? Isn't that, in a sense, an artificial kidney?"

"Sure it is. But in this day and age, the medical engineers think we can do better for kidney patients. If you're a patient on dialysis, you are literally tied to the dialysis machine. Most patients have dialysis three times a week, and most of them have to go to a hospital or a clinic to receive the treatment," he explained. "Global Devices was developing a kidney that could be implanted *into* the human body."

The Van Buren Health Centre was world renowned for research and transplants. Tommy was murdered behind the Van Buren Health Centre. The light bulb in my head was functioning now but only giving off about forty watts.

"Explain to me how computers are used for this sort of thing."

Ben was in his element now and eager to teach me. "Well, because the organ is artificial, the brain and central nervous system obviously can't give the organ any signals on how to work. The organ recipient has to be hooked up to a computer, outside the body, that gives the artificial organ, in this case the kidney, the signals it needs to operate properly. These computer units are about the size of a cell phone and can be clipped on to the person's belt. It sends signals to the artificial kidney through radio waves, so there are no wire hook ups. Amazing, right?"

"Amazing," I agreed, "but a little scary. Artificial hearts, artificial kidneys. What's next? An artificial brain?"

He laughed. "Probably not impossible, but highly improbable. Today that is. Who knows where we'll be in fifty years with computers?"

"Well, I don't know if I want to live long enough to see an artificial human brain. Sounds like something out of a cheap movie." I shuddered at the thought. "So how far along were we in the software development before the plug got pulled?"

Ben shrugged. "The project was almost done. Remember, Phoenix was doing just a portion."

"Which portion?"

"The remote signaling. We were developing software to enable the computer outside the body to give the remote signals to the chips embedded with the artificial organ."

"So the company just ran out of money? Totally? Did they go tits up?" I grimaced inwardly as I said that. I made a mental note to start cleaning up my gutterisms, as my mother called them. I have to start acting more ladylike, more CEO-like.

"No, they're still around. They just ran out of funding for the development of the artificial kidney."

I was a little puzzled. "So Phoenix Technologies just gets cut out of the contract?"

"It's part of the research and development world. Happens all the time. No big deal. "

"And this was Nat Scott's pet project," I stated. "How did she react when the contract was cancelled?"

"She blew a gasket. I heard she was throwing things around her office. Mr.

Connaught was in there calming her down. She left the building and didn't come back for a week. Word was she was on a holiday. Yeah, right," he said.

Oh, the girl has a temper. "How long ago did all this happen?" I asked.

"About a month or six weeks ago, I think," Ben said. "When Nat came back from her vacation," he mimed finger quotes when he said vacation, "she and Mr. Connaught were no longer a couple."

No doubt, I thought. The Tommy I knew would *never* put up with temper tantrums or hissy fits.

Chapter twenty-one

BEN'S SHORT LESSON ON ARTIFICIAL kidneys had me intrigued and wondering if somehow the work Phoenix had been doing with Global Devices was tied to Tommy's murder.

I spent the better part of the next day finding out as much as I could about artificial organs. The internet was a great help and I was amazed to find out that not only were hearts and kidneys viable organs to implant in the body, but researchers were developing artificial livers, lungs, stomachs, pancreases and urinary bladders.

My research led me to a biography about the man the medical community had christened the "father of the artificial organ". Dr. Willem Kolff was born in Holland and is credited with inventing the first artificial kidney during the Second World War using sausage casings and orange juice cans. He and his colleague Dr. Robert Jarvik are credited as the inventors of the first artificial heart that was implanted in a human.

Dr. Kolff's early invention using the sausage casings, orange juice cans and a washing machine, led to the modern dialysis machine. In his first experiment in 1938, Dr. Kolff filled sausage casings with blood, then somehow expelled the air in the casings, added some urea (a kidney waste product), and agitated the contraption in a tub of salt water. Within minutes all the urea had moved into the salt water. The next device consisted of one hundred and forty-five feet of sausage casing wrapped around a wooden drum immersed in a salt solution. The patient's blood was drawn from the wrist artery and fed directly into the casings. The drum was constantly rotating, removing the impurities from the blood. Okay, so far so good, I was understanding the basics.

And then the story got really good. Dr. Kolff used a design copied from the water pump coupling found in Ford motor engines to get the blood safely back into the patient. Voila! The concept for dialysis was born.

Unfortunately, the first fifteen patients placed on the machine died. By

1945 Kolff had made several more modifications to the machine and was using blood thinners to prevent coagulation of the blood. The first person to survive after being on the machine was a woman, in a coma from kidney failure. The machine worked its wonders and when the patient came out of the coma, her first words were "I'm going to divorce my husband"! She lived another seven years after receiving the treatment.

Dr. Kolff sent a prototype of his machine to doctors in New York City in 1947 and eventually the machine was improved to such a level that it was used regularly by people whose kidneys had failed. Today in the United Stated, tens of thousands of people undergo dialysis treatment three times a week. Many of them are waiting for a kidney transplant. Dr. Kolff moved to the U.S. in the fifties and went on to invent membrane oxygenators for bypass surgery, which eventually became the artificial heart, and worked on artificial eyes, ears and limbs.

I called Ben Tucker and asked him how much he knew about the artificial kidney project. He told me that I knew as much as he did because he had pretty much told me everything the other night at Starbucks. I didn't press him. Carrie told me that the artificial kidney project had been code named the Arapaho Project and she gave me a list of the people who had worked on it. Nat Scott was the project leader (in addition to her role as Vice President of Research and Development) and there were fifteen employees listed as team members. Tommy's paper file was not very thick and contained very little information. When I asked if Tommy kept files on his computer at the office Carrie said she wasn't sure. We turned on his desk computer and after putting in the password (which Carrie knew) we surfed around a little and discovered nothing. Apparently Tommy used his office computer for email only and there was nothing else stored or filed on it.

"Each project office is responsible for keeping the official files for their projects," Carrie told me. "Before I worked for Mr. Connaught, I worked on one of the R and D teams as the project administrator. We had to keep really good files because a lot of the work we do is on medical devices. Our files have to be ready for audit at any time by the FDA - the Food and Drug Administration. We kept all of the research notes, results of tests and any trials, stuff like that. Do you want me to ask for the files on the Arapaho project?"

"No. No thanks Carrie." Until I understood how things worked around Phoenix I wasn't about to go upsetting any apple carts. I hadn't received the warmest of welcomes so far from the staff. Admittedly, I hadn't been expecting marching bands and group hugs, but I also hadn't expected some of the icy attitudes either. I guess I didn't know what to expect. Everything had happened so quickly. One day I was working in a law office as a legal secretary and then *poof!* the next day I was in charge of my own company. I guess if I was being fair, I should give the staff the benefit of the doubt and give them some time to get to know me and accept that Tommy was gone. But I didn't have any feelings of *fair* about Nat Scott.

Chapter twenty-two

SATURDAY MORNING I CHECKED OUT of the hotel and moved into Tommy's apartment. Correction: *my* apartment. I couldn't very well justify spending scads of the company's money on a first class hotel when I had 7,000 perfectly acceptable square feet of living space available to me on Central Park. *The Upper East Side.* The enormity of it all and the overwhelming notion that I owned property in Manhattan, *and* on Fifth Avenue was a little outside my realm of reality. Tommy had died and I was an instant millionaire. I had trouble breathing whenever I thought about how much my life had changed in such a short period of time. This was not a situation that gave me any happiness, just truckloads of daunting responsibility.

Today though was not a day for self-doubt or a pity-party. I had given myself a tough talking-to the night before and had decided to get on with what needed doing. I had been in emotional limbo since finding out about Tommy's death and had been floating through each day, barely making a dent in what needed to be done. I had to move on and make some huge decisions.

Did I want to stay on as Chair and CEO of Phoenix Technologies? Did I want to live in New York?

I had spent my entire adult life living in Toronto, which is a big city by Canadian standards. In fact it was Canada's largest city. But New York City was so huge, I wasn't sure if I could live there.

My gawd, there was so much to think about. Did I need a work visa? What would I do with my apartment in Toronto? If I moved to New York, would I have to give up saying *eh*? Could I get Ron McLean and Don Cherry on Hockey Night in Canada every Saturday night on any of the American TV networks? Could I get used to four downs in American football? How would I cope on Labour Day weekend if the Toronto Argos and Hamilton Tiger Cats game wasn't televised in New York?

And who was I fooling? Being CEO of a publicly-traded company took a lot more experience than I had or could probably learn fast enough. I was surprised that the share price of Phoenix hadn't hit rock bottom with Tommy's death and the shareholders finding out that a *secretary* was taking over.

If I stayed in New York, what would happen with Jay? He was on the fast track with his new company and although he was in New York now, he was only here for training. His full-time job was back in Toronto. Our relationship could probably not survive with us living in two cities. My past experience with Tommy in this regard was probably a good yardstick.

I loved Jay and I wanted to be with him. He had told me he loved me but did that mean he was committed to a long term relationship? There was six years difference in our ages and although Jay always told me he didn't care about that, I wondered if the upheaval in my life was going to fit in with his career and his plans.

Staying in the Big Apple, staying with Phoenix, staying with Jay - it was all eating at me. It was no wonder my stomach was constantly upset. So last night I gave myself a verbal shit-kicking and made some decisions.

I was almost positive I could give New York and Phoenix Technologies a chance. What the hell. If Tommy thought I could run the company, I'd at least try for him. New York wouldn't seem so enormous and so scary for me if I settled in for a while, so I decided to get out of the hotel, which felt so temporary, and move into the apartment.

I'll be honest. The thought of moving into the apartment scared the crap out of me. The lump on the side of my head was gone but the memory of being cold-cocked upside the head was still very fresh in my mind's eye. No one liked being scared and it made me mad to think about being vulnerable.

Feeling scared and feeling vulnerable were wasted emotions as far as I was concerned. I would have to do something about it and learn to defend myself, especially since there had been no breaks in Tommy's murder or my mugging in the apartment.

Jay was waiting under the awning of the entrance to the apartment building when Lou pulled up in the car. My heart did a couple of flips and I smiled when I saw him standing there. Jay was good looking, by my standards, standing a little over six feet. His brown hair was wavy, cut short but not too short, and he had beautiful green eyes. He smiled widely back at me when the doorman opened the car door.

We held hands in the elevator on our way up to the apartment and didn't say anything until the doorman had loaded all of our suitcases into the lobby of the apartment.

"Shall I put the suitcases in the bedroom, Miss?" he asked.

I peered at his name tag. "No thanks Albert. We can manage just fine." He nodded and backed out of the lobby, closing the door quietly behind him.

Jay took me in his arms and hugged me tightly. I hugged back, with all my might. His embrace felt so good. We hadn't seen each other in days, and when I had called him last night from my hotel, I asked him to move into the apartment with me.

"At least move in for the rest of the time you're here in New York for your training. Why stay in that little walk up apartment?"

He had hesitated for a bit, and then said, "This is a big step for us Kate. Moving in together." He hesitated again.

"I know," I said. "But I don't want to be alone here in New York." Hopefully I didn't sound like I was too needy.

"Is this just a New York decision then? If we were back in Toronto would we be in separate apartments?"

"Well," I responded honestly. "I don't know. We're in New York and so much has changed in my life in the last two weeks. I know I want to be with you. Can we just say yes for now and talk about it when we're face to face?"

Jay hesitated again and then said he would see me at the apartment in the morning. When the car pulled up and I saw he had his suitcases with him, I felt pretty good.

I stood on my tiptoes and kissed him. He snaked one hand through my hair and the other one wandered down my back. He pulled me closer and I melted into him. Leaving the suitcases in the lobby we wandered into the guest bedroom and stretched out on the large, king size bed. Jay slowly unbuttoned my blouse and helped me out of my clothes. He covered my body with kisses and kept murmuring "Kathleen, I love you".

Later, I dragged him into the shower for some more fun and games, but not before he made me scrub his back.

That afternoon Jay went to his office and I carried out a complete search of the apartment. I was looking for some very specific things, like Tommy's hand-held electronic organizer, and some clue as to the password to his computer. But I was also on the look-out for anything out of the ordinary.

Starting in the kitchen I went through every cupboard and drawer. The cupboards held all the accoutrements one would expect to find in a kitchen comparable in size to a large restaurant. There was very little evidence that the kitchen was used on a regular basis. It didn't look lived in. There were no piles of junk mail on the counters, no plants, no dish towels, and very little in the way of foodstuffs. There was no junk drawer. My kitchen and my mother's kitchen always have a junk drawer. A drawer that holds take-out menus, elastic bands, pens, pieces of string, bills, receipts, Canadian Tire money, combs, and things we generally have no use for but can't bare to throw out. Tommy's kitchen did not have a junk drawer.

In the living room, dining room, lobby and hallways, I opened every drawer in every desk, coffee table, side table, buffet and credenza. I removed every picture and painting that was hanging on a wall to look behind it for a secret safe (I was really feeling like Nancy Drew at this point). I took each one of those pictures and paintings out of their frames to see if anything was hidden under the backing.

In the living room, I removed every book from the bookcase and turned it upside down, fanning the pages, hopeful that something would fall out and give me all the answers.

In the two bedrooms, I searched through every dresser drawer. The drawers and the closet were empty in the guest bedroom. In Tommy's master bedroom I went through all his clothes hanging in his walk-in closet. I checked all the pockets of all the pants and jackets and shirts. I put my hand into each shoe, not knowing what I was looking for. I was exhausted by this point but refused to stop even when I felt the tears welling up in my eyes. Tommy's aroma was pungent in the walk-in closet, and I felt myself wanting to cry for him. There was nothing in his dresser drawers other than neatly folded T-shirts, socks, underwear, an old wallet (with nothing in it), and some work-out clothes.

I fanned all the pages of all the books in Tommy's bookcase (which contained every bestseller in paperback from the last ten years), and was surprised to find two Harlequin romance novels in amongst them. They both looked vaguely familiar and I realized that they were probably old books of mine that Tommy had kept. He used to laugh at my secret obsession with romance novels, and would grab the books from me and tease me about the women on the front covers with their bosoms partly exposed, swooning in the arms of a Fabian-like Adonis.

I had no luck with the books, so I started on the framed photos and paintings hanging on the walls of the bedroom. The sun was going down by this point and the room was getting dark, so I turned on the bedside lamps. There was no overhead lighting and the room was subdued and sexy. I hurried through my task, not expecting to find anything pertinent at this point in my search. It had been a long afternoon and I was bone tired. The ends of my fingers were sore from prying the backs off picture frames, and the back of my neck was throbbing.

I pushed my way up onto the end of the bed and sat down, with my feet swinging off the floor. Now would be a good time to stop with this nonsense,

I thought. If Tommy had left a clue, it certainly was *not* in this apartment, as far as I could see.

My eyes landed on the lone photo, sitting in the little space high up on the bookcase. It was the photo of me, taken on our honeymoon. What are the chances, I thought excitedly as I jumped down from the end of the bed. In the end I had to get a chair from the living room so I could reach the picture on the upper shelf, but the effort was worth it.

A key fell onto the floor when I took off the back of the picture frame. "Bingo," I yelled.

Chapter twenty-three

MY HEART WAS POUNDING AND I needed a cigarette to help me get my thoughts organized. *Stupid, stupid* habit I chastised myself as I dragged deeply. Pacing back and forth on the terrace, I knew I was onto something significant. If Tommy had taken the trouble to hide a key in the back of a picture frame holding a picture of me, then the key was definitely a key to something.

I was waiting anxiously for Jay to come home because I wanted him there when I inserted the key into the filing cabinets hidden in Tommy's secret place. I was certain the key would unlock one of those cabinets. It was small, brass plated and looked exactly like the key to thousands of filing cabinet keys I had handled over the years. And the fact that it had the word "Steelcase" engraved on it helped. Steelcase was one of the world's largest manufacturers of office furniture and cabinets.

"Look what I found," I said, and proudly held the small key up for Jay to see when he arrived. "I waited for you to get here before I tried opening the cabinets in the room behind the wall."

Jay grabbed the remote control from the coffee table and activated the opening in the wall. The key worked on both cabinets which were chock full of files, neatly arranged alphabetically but in a strange way. The files didn't have names or words on them, only letters of the alphabet, followed by a hyphen and a number. In the A's, there were seventeen files, labeled A-1 through A-17. The cabinet on the left held files from A through R in two drawers, and the cabinet on the right had files S through Z in the top drawer. None of the files were thicker than an inch, and several appeared to hold only one or two sheets of paper.

The bottom drawer of the right hand cabinet held a jumbled assortment of power cords, computer and printer cables, a few magazines and a strong box. I eagerly grabbed the box and held it up by its handle. Jay calmly took the strong box from me and pushed the button on the front of it and it opened.

The box contained an interesting assortment of items: mine and Tommy's marriage certificate, dated almost ten years ago, Tommy's birth certificate, his passport, a crazy love letter that I had written him on the back sheet of a draft prospectus (I remembered writing it one late night at the office as we were all working on the initial public offering of Phoenix Technologies' shares), another key (which appeared to be a safety deposit box key), and Tommy's electronic organizer. Eureka! Now we were getting somewhere.

I was convinced that the electronic organizer would hold some clues and maybe some passwords. Tommy never went anywhere without it. Well, maybe he did, if it was in this strong box and not on him when he was murdered.

I handed it to Jay, hoping he would be able to unlock untold secrets. Needless to say, he was happy to work his magic on it while I started going through the files in the cabinets.

I had no sooner pulled out file A-1 when Jay told me that the electronic organizer was locked and we needed a password to access it.

"I give up," I said dejectedly. "Could Tommy have made this any harder? What in God's name could be so important that he had everything password protected?"

"Obviously, he and his company had secrets which needed protecting. I'd guess they were pretty big and possibly damaging, and it's probably why he was murdered. The police haven't said that it was a typical mugging, have they? I think he was shot because of something in his personal or business life," Jay said.

"You're right," I agreed. "I'm just frustrated. And wanting answers. And I want them the easy way. Let's take some guesses on his password," I suggested.

"Okay shoot. I'm not sure how many tries you can have before the organizer will lock you out, but usually it's at least ten. Let's start with his birthday."

"May 6, 1959."

Jay entered 561959. And then he tried may61959. And a couple variations on my birthday, September 10, 1968.

"Any other ideas?"

"Try Phoenix."

"No, another strike-out. I'm going to try your name." He entered Kate. Then Kathleen. Neither worked. "You know, I think we might be on the right track. He left everything to you in his will. The key to the cabinets was behind a picture of you. No one in New York seemed to know about you so it's a good guess that the password is one that someone wouldn't cotton-on to, probably something to do with you." Jay was getting excited now. "So, did Tommy have any nicknames for you?"

I blushed thinking about some of the pet names Tommy had for me.

"Okay," Jay said. "Let's start with one that may not be *that* personal."

I thought about it for a moment and something niggled in the back of my mind. It had been many years since Tommy and I were together and it was difficult to recall everything but I definitely remember he used to tease me a lot about something. Then the light went on!

"My middle name," I said.

"Great. What is it?" Jay asked ready to key it in. He paused. "That's weird. I should know the middle name of the woman I'm sleeping with but I don't know if you've ever told me."

"That's because I don't make a habit of telling people my middle name."

"Oh, a little testy about it, are we?" Jay teased.

I hated being teased.

"It's my grandmother's name. Florence," I told him reluctantly.

"That's not so bad," Jay said, as he started entering Florence.

"Hold on," I said quickly. "Don't waste a try on Florence. That may be my middle name, and I'll deny it if you ever tell anyone, but that's not what Tommy used to call me. His nickname for me when he wanted to tease me was Flossie."

Jay snorted. "Yeah, that's bad." He was trying to hold back a smile, but he failed miserably and broke into a laugh. "Okay, I won't use it against you. Often," he snickered and then he entered Flossie into the electronic organizer and the thing started to chime. Then we both broke into wide smiles.

Chapter twenty-four

I turned around and booted up Tommy's computer.

"If Flossie worked on that thing, what do you think the odds are that it'll be the password to his computer?"

I could feel the excitement building and was anxious to find out as much as we could. When the password log in screen came up on the computer I typed in Flossie and the computer politely told me that it was an incorrect password and I should try again.

"Shit," I mumbled and tried Flossie in all capital letters, all lower case letters and several other variations.

"Cut it out Kate," Jay told me. "You're going to lock yourself out of the computer. Hang on a minute, I'm looking for a password file on his organizer."

I sat on my hands to keep myself away from the computer and tried to be patient. At just about the point where I was going to scream in frustration, I heard the doorbell sound through the building intercom. The noise startled me because everything about this apartment was so new. Anxious to do anything but sit on my hands, I jumped up and went through the living room to the lobby and picked up the phone on the wall.

"Yes," I said into the phone.

"Albert at the Front Desk ma'am," I heard through the handset. I would hope so, I thought. No one else should be able to call up.

"Yes, Albert, what can I do for you tonight?"

"You have a visitor, ma'am. Shall I send them up?"

"Well, would you like to tell me who the visitor is, before I agree to that?" I asked him politely, but through clenched teeth. I was starting to suspect that security wasn't one of the building's stronger suits.

"A Miss Scott. Natalie Scott. Your neighbour miss, from the twentieth floor," he drawled.

Oh really, I thought. I wondered if she was bringing me a Bundt cake to welcome me to the building.

"Send her up Albert," I told him.

I quickly ran around to the living room and told Jay that we had a visitor. He could either lock himself in the secret room or come out, and close the wall opening. He chose the latter. The wall just finished closing as the front door chimes sounded. I braced myself and opened the door with a tentative smile on my face.

Natalie Scott would be a beautiful woman if she didn't have such a pinched look about her. She had gorgeous hair, long and in corkscrew curls, but it framed her face in such a way to make her look thinner than she really was. She stood about five foot seven, a giant in my books, and she held herself ramrod straight with her arms across her chest. Such body language. God, I thought once again, what did Tommy see in her?

"Hi," I said.

"Hello," she said back. I held the door open and invited her in. I introduced her to Jay who was sitting in the living room and she barely acknowledged him. Personally, I think he's great to look at and wondered why she didn't show any more interest.

"So," I began. "What brings you by?"

"I'm here for my things. The doorman told me you had moved in today."

Again, was nothing sacred and secure in this building? Geez! And what things, I wondered. I had just carried out a search of this apartment that would have made the FBI proud. I didn't recall finding any of *her* things.

She must have assumed, or been told, that I knew about her relationship with Tommy because she wasn't shy about the implication of the meaning of "my things".

"Uh, sure," I said. "What things and where would they be?"

Nat quickly glanced at the aquarium as if she knew there was something behind that wall. I played dumb. Years of practice, you know.

"Oh some CD's, and a few files from the office," she said, a little too casually.

Yeah *right*, I thought. She wanted into those filing cabinets, or the computer behind that wall, and the only way she was getting in that room was over my dead body. I shuddered as the thought passed through my brain. Cut it out, I told myself. Stop jinxing the pitcher!

I pointed at a stack of CD's sitting on a side table. "Help yourself," I offered. "As for office files, I wouldn't know where they would be. I went through Tommy's desk and there weren't any business files." I nodded at the desk at the far end of the room.

She picked up the pile of CDs and started shuffling through them. She wasn't looking at the titles, she was only going through the motions of looking. "Nope, not here," she stated as she put the stack back on the table. I caught her glancing again at the aquarium.

"Well, the files must be at the office then," she said. "I'll check with Carrie on Monday."

She headed back to the front door, and said goodbye over her shoulder. She was making a fast exit and I was glad. The woman gave me the creeps. I stared through the peephole in the door until she got on the elevator and the doors closed.

"Okay," I said to Jay as I walked back in the living room. "Something's up and she knows about that hidden room. We've got to do something about all that stuff in there."

"Well, it's probably a little late to do something tonight, but we could move it all out of here tomorrow to a secure place." He stood in the middle of the room, with his hands in the pockets of his jeans, looking smug.

"What?" I said.

"I found his password file on the organizer. And these are serious passwords. Letters and numbers combined, upper case and lower case. Probably randomly generated by a computer program so they're harder to break. I think I have the password to the computer. Good thing you told me our visitor was arriving because I was just about to yell out that we had hit pay dirt!" He grabbed the remote and opened the wall again.

The computer opened up on Jay's first try with the password. There were thousands of files on the computer, all seemingly related to Phoenix Technologies. I recognized some of the hundreds of sub-directories that were labeled by project names but that was the extent of my knowledge.

"Oh, my, gawd," I said slowly. The enormity of what lay before me was sinking in. How was I ever going to sift through all of this information when I didn't even know what I was looking for? I felt defeated, discouraged and dead tired.

"Let's call it a day," I suggested, "and go find something to eat."

Chapter twenty-five

OVER DINNER, JAY AND I talked about my big, pending decisions. Staying in New York. Staying on as Chair and CEO of Phoenix. Jay staying in New York.

Jay was no help at all on the first two issues. He kept telling me I had to do what I thought best. He was so damn supportive! I was hoping for a little push-back but he wasn't forthcoming. He was convinced that I could succeed as the head of the company and that I would adapt to New York. Jay had a blind faith in me that on the one hand was encouraging and flattering, but on the other hand, left me a little doubtful that things would be as easy as he made out.

On the question of Jay staying in New York, I was a little wary of how to broach the subject.

"So I stay in New York. What about you?" I asked.

"What about me?" he teased.

"Well, you've only got a few months of training left here in New York. Will you be going back to Toronto when you're done? Would your company let you work out of the New York office? Could you live in this city? Both our families are in Canada and although Toronto and Ottawa aren't half way around the world, it would be difficult to go for a Sunday drive and drop in on the folks for dinner."

Jay was close with his mom and his sisters, just as I was with my folks and my brother. I knew if I decided to stay in New York, it was going to be hard.

"Yeah, I'd miss my family," he agreed. "But you're my family now too and I'd miss you more."

I felt the same as he did. Had I told him yet that I loved him? I didn't think so. I had been too hung-up on our age difference. Too hung-up on the crappy things going on in my life. Too involved in things that didn't seem to matter at that moment. I was tired and emotionally spent but hell, life was way too short. So I told him.

I dry swallowed and felt a lump in my throat. This was the hard stuff for me. "Jay Harmon. I love you. I want to spend my life with you." There. I said it.

Jay's face broke into a wide smile. A wide, loving smile. "I knew you loved me. You think I'm sexy. You really want me," he chanted and teased.

"Yes," I said back. "So will you stay in New York if I stay?"

"Well, if my company won't let me work in the New York office, I think I know someone at a local high tech company who could get me a job!" He reached across the table and took my hand. "Yes, of course, I'll stay."

We held hands across the table and I felt refreshed and a lot better. Over dessert I broached the other subject that had been bothering me.

"I need to learn how to defend myself," I told Jay. "I don't feel safe. Being in the apartment creeps me out a little, and I don't want someone sneaking up on me again. After what happened to me in Toronto, and then again when I arrived here in New York, I think it's time I learned how to defend myself. I hate feeling vulnerable and not in control."

"Well," Jay joked, "you could become an instant American and buy a gun. Start believing in your right to bear arms!"

"Yeah right! Guns scare the crap out of me."

"I know, I know. I was just joking," he said. He reached across the table and took my hand. "I have a friend in Toronto who does martial arts and some Israeli type of self-defense. Let me look into it and see if there's someone here in the area who he would recommend as a teacher. We could both learn," he said eagerly. Jay was a jock and liked all things physical. Me on the other hand, not so much. Walking at a brisk pace for a mile was enough to do me in.

"Great," I agreed, trying to show lots of enthusiasm for something I knew was going to hurt.

The next morning I woke up early, resolving to get through as many files as I could on Tommy's computer. With my coffee in a large mug, and a clean ashtray I sat down and logged on to the computer. Jay found me there a couple of hours later when he finally got out of bed.

"Anything yet?" he asked. He stood behind me and massaged my shoulders.

"Ohhh, that feels good. I'll give you five bucks to never stop. And no, nothing yet. Nothing that's jumped out at me giving me a hint as to why he was murdered. I'm going through his computer files in a methodical way, through each directory and every document or file in the directory. He's filed everything meticulously by subject matter. I'm just finishing up going through the sales stuff including bid documents and RFP's. Pretty heavy reading."

"How about we forget about Phoenix for today?" Jay suggested.

It sounded tempting. I hadn't really thought about anything else in the past ten days. "Okay. What do you think we should do instead?"

"Oh, I think you'll like what I've got planned. Throw on your runners and some work-out clothes," he told me.

"Aw," I groaned.

"No complaints," he ordered. Jay scooped me up from the chair, carried me into the bedroom and plopped me on the bed. "Hustle up, young lady. Sweats, work-out bra, runners. Come on, let's get a move on."

I gave in to Jay ordering me around. It was nice for a change to have someone else take charge and make the decisions.

Forty-five minutes later we came up the stairs from the subway onto Canal Street. The crowds were thick and tourists filled the small shops full of knock-off designer handbags and perfume. It reminded me of the Chinatown area in Toronto.

It was clear Jay knew where we were going and although he had so far refused to tell me what we were up to, I was glad that I wasn't sweating and gasping for air. So far.

He told me the neighbourhood was called Soho, short for south of Houston, one of the main streets running west to east in lower Manhattan. We climbed the stairs to the second floor of a building on one of the streets off Canal and Jay rapped on the door.

The sign on the door read "Jeet Kune Do, Keepers of the Flame". Under the sign was a picture of Bruce Lee and someone else I didn't recognize.

That someone else opened the door and welcomed Jay and I. He introduced himself as Frank Sanchez, and led us into a large, nearly empty room. There were a few racks against one wall with boxing gloves and some other equipment I didn't recognize, and up against the walls were several wooden structures with rounded, short poles sticking out of them. Frank saw me eyeing them and explained that they were called wooden dummies. Really.

By now I had figured out what we were doing, and I smiled at Jay.

"After dinner last night I called Jason in Toronto. He recommended Frank," he told me. "So I called last night and explained the situation. Frank agreed to see us this morning and give us some private lessons in the art of Jeet Kune Do, or JKD." Jay pronounced it *jeet coon dough*.

"Thanks for seeing us on such short notice, Frank," Jay said.

Frank was a middle-aged man, about five foot ten. His face had some interesting wrinkles and his hair was black sprinkled with grey. He was wearing black Nike pants with a tucked-in black t-shirt. The t-shirt had a round, orange and yellow logo on the left breast. Frank looked like everyone's father but somehow, I intuitively knew, his appearance was probably deceiving.

"So, Kate," Frank said, "tell me why you're here."

"I want to learn to defend myself. More than a few times in the past six months I've found myself in situations where I ended up on the wrong end of a fist."

"Jay mentioned that last night when we were talking. So let's start with some basics."

We spent the first hour learning some basics of JKD. We practised our footwork in our "ready stance". One foot in front of the other with the heel of our back foot slightly elevated in order to allow quick movement. Frank told us our ready stance was our power base. It was too much information for me. I was concentrating so hard on what my feet were doing, that I missed some of what he was saying. We held our fists up, out and away from our body and practised our footwork while Frank stood behind us and knocked two small bamboo sticks together. Every time we heard the loud knock of the sticks, we were to move in the position that Frank had told us. We practised moving forward, backwards, to the side. Frank told us to focus on the feet and not worry about anything else. My legs started to ache after a few minutes, and my lower back was screaming. A glance at Jay told me that he wasn't aching. At the end of the foot drills he was still bouncing on the balls of his feet, and miraculously, the aches in my legs and back had gone away. My body was tuning in and my feet were responding to the rhythm of the bamboo sticks.

When we finished the footwork drills, Frank transitioned us quickly into punching. With our feet in the proper position and our elbows tucked in, he showed us how to hold our fists and then he taught us how to punch with our front fist at an imaginary face. Frank's fists and demonstrations punches were fast, and so powerful. I watched and quickly figured out that the power behind his punches was coming from his whole body, although he barely moved as he jabbed in the air. His forearms bulged and looked like Popeye's. We practiced and tried to imitate Frank's powerful punches.

He stopped us after several minutes and offered us each a bottle of water. My shoulders were aching.

"How do you make the punches look so simple but so powerful?" I asked my new teacher.

"That punch you were doing was called the jab. Jeet Kune Do or JKD translates as the 'Way of the Intercepting Fist'," he told us. "We try to intercept what our opponent is doing quickly and efficiently, and with as few movements as possible. Simple, right? All of my power is at the end of my fist and my hand moves before my body. And that's one of the basics of JKD. Bruce Lee was the father of Jeet Kune Do and its philosophy. As we go along we'll learn about the four guiding principles."

Frank continued as be counted off on his fingers, "Simplicity. Economy of motion. Longest weapon to the nearest target. And no passive moves. Jeet Kune Do is all about skill, not how many forms or katas you know, or how many techniques you have. JKD is simple yes, but not easy. Bruce Lee used simplicity to define his art of Jeet Kune Do - to intercept your opponent's intentions quickly and efficiently, with as few moves as possible."

Frank told us that he learned the art from his teacher, Jerry Poteet, who lived in California and who was one of Bruce Lee's original students.

"Jerry often uses an analogy to illustrate the point of simplicity and economy of motion. If you want to leave your house, would you crawl out a window, shimmy down the drain pipe, jump down two stories, and hope to land in a tree? Or would you simply walk out the front door? Wouldn't that be more efficient, simple and non-complicated?" Frank smiled as he used this example.

Simple and efficient worked for me. We spent some more time on our jab and understanding the core of our power before Frank called a halt.

"Kate," he said. "Jay told me that you were attacked recently. What we've learned here today will help you in the future if you're ever attacked again, but it takes months of practice and years of commitment to be a martial artist. What I'd like to do to help you is understand the situations you were in when you were attacked, teach you some basics in understanding your reactions while you were under attack, and how to deal with them. How does that sound?"

I nodded mutely, not really wanting to re-live those moments. We walked over to the side of the room and sat side by side on a long, low bench. It helped that I didn't have to look directly at Frank or Jay as I tried to describe the attacks.

My voice was not more than a whisper as I started the re-telling. "The first time, I was asleep in my bed in my apartment. I woke up and someone was straddling my body and had his hand over my mouth. The second time, I was grabbed by the back of my blouse, and he put his arm around my neck from behind, and dragged me." I stopped for a moment and took a long drink of water, trying to make the metallic taste in my mouth go away. The sweat pouring down my back and between my breasts wasn't just from working hard on my jab. This was cold sweat, the type that smelled like fear. I blew out a few breaths and continued.

"That second time I did manage to land a punch on the side of his head, but he was a lot bigger than me. And it didn't help anyway in the end. He smacked me on the side of my head with the butt of a gun and it knocked me out." Jay's hand was lightly massaging my upper back and his touch gave me strength. I stood up, chugged the rest of the water in my bottle and turned around and faced Frank and Jay.

"The most recent attack was here in New York. Whoever it was came up behind me, pushed me down on the floor. When I turned around to face them, they grabbed the front of my jacket and hit me on the side of the head so hard it knocked me out. Again."

I took several deep breaths and then smiled a little at Frank.

"And, I'm here to tell you that I'm not taking that kind of shit anymore. Next time someone wants to mess with me, they're going to suffer too!"

"Well," Frank said. "You've got one of the critical elements of self-defense going for you. Attitude."

"Oh yeah," Jay agreed with him. "There's plenty of that!"

Frank stood up and looked straight at me. His hands were clasped in front of him and he respected my space and didn't crowd me. "Kate, you did the best you could to defend yourself in those circumstances," he told me quietly. "The first thing I want to do is teach you how to be cognizant of your surroundings. How to put your internal antenna on constant alert. Then we'll talk about how your body and mind react when you're attacked and how to deal with that."

He exuded confidence without coming across as cocky or pumped up. I liked him.

When we finished that first day, my arms were rubbery from the punching, my feet were aching from the footwork, and I had a new appreciation for my surroundings. Overall, I was spent, and hardly had the strength to make it to the subway.

Chapter twenty-six

WORKING MY WAY THROUGH THE files on Tommy's computer was not an easy job. There were thousands of them in different formats. Excel files, Word files, pdf files, pictures, videos. Everything was organized methodically and the file system on the computer matched the system in the file cabinets. Alphabetical files with numbers. Which made it a total pain in the ass to randomly search and call up a file based on its name. And the pain in my ass was exacerbated by my stiff muscles and my total lack of understanding of what I was searching for. I gave up, disgusted at myself for not having the attention span to work through it all.

That night I dreamed of Tommy but when I woke the dreams eluded me. I felt sad and think it was because I was still mourning for him. It had been eleven days since he was murdered, and although there had been a funeral and memorial service, I didn't feel the closure that's supposed to happen when we say our public good-byes. Sure he was dead, but how had he died? Why hadn't the police found his killer? Why had he died? Who shot him? I felt sure that somehow and somewhere I had the key to unlocking the answers to some of these questions. So where the fuck was the key?

I didn't have a lot of time to ponder these questions because I was due in the office early for meetings. Ah, the life of a chief executive officer.

In the coffee room at the office I was surprised to see a few early birds like myself. I longed to sit with them at the small round tables and have a good chit-chat but held myself back. Instead I shook their hands, introduced myself, and asked them a few questions about their jobs. Bit by bit I was recognizing faces and getting to know the employees.

Three coffees later, I was up-to-date on emails and determined to get through the snail mail which filled the in-basket. Most of it was garbage so I left a note telling Carrie to feel free to throw out anything that was junk. There were several envelopes addressed to Tommy from the First City Bank of

Manhattan and I wondered who should open them. I knew that technically everything that Tommy had was mine now, but I also knew that it wasn't mine until mammoth legal hurdles were overcome.

Dennis Hillary was his typically nervous self when I got him on the phone. "Dennis, I can't remember if you told me who will be the executor of Tommy's estate?" I asked him.

"I am," he squeaked. I heard him suck air through his teeth.

"So I should be sending any bank statements and stuff like that your way?"

"Yes, and anything else that you're not sure of," he offered.

I remembered the key we found in the strong box at Tommy's apartment. "Dennis do you know if Tommy had a safety deposit box at the bank?"

"No, but let me call them and find out. Did you find a key?"

"Yeah, but I'm not sure what it's for, and it has no identifiable markings on it."

Ten minutes later Dennis called back and confirmed that Tommy had a safety deposit box at First City Bank.

"And if you like," he told me, "you can go over there at any time during business hours to open it. Would you like me to accompany you?"

I declined his offer, and he gave me the bank manager's name and the branch address. The bank was closer to the Phoenix offices than to Tommy's apartment so I asked Carrie to make an appointment for me to meet the bank manager and to have Lou drive me over. I crossed my fingers that the key I had would fit the safety deposit box.

Sara Williston was the person in charge at First City Bank and she defied all preconceived notions of bank managers. She was tall, elegant, beautiful, and soft-spoken. I vaguely remembered seeing her at Tommy's memorial service. She clasped my hand in both of hers and without feeling like she was patronizing me or being overly sympathetic, she told me that she was going to miss Tom Connaught as a customer but she was looking forward to serving me and Phoenix.

"What can I help you with today?" she asked me. We were sitting in her office which was on the mezzanine floor of the bank.

"Is this a key for the safety deposit boxes here at your bank?" I held up the mystery key. It was very old-fashioned looking, very thin and longer than a normal key. The number 330 was engraved on the stem. The key manufacturer's name (Chubb) and logo were engraved on the other side. Other than those two things, there was nothing to identify it as a key to the safety deposit boxes at First City Bank.

"It sure looks like it," she said and held out her hand. I gave her the key. "Looks like one of ours, but lots of banks buy their safety deposit boxes and the keys from Chubb." She turned to her computer which was placed on the corner of her desk and started keying in some information.

"Here it is." She turned the monitor around so I could see it and pointed to a line of information. "Right there. Three thirty. That was the number of Mr. Connaught's safety deposit box." She smiled gently. "Mystery solved. Anything else?" she offered. "Do you want to access the box? Mr. Hillary from Scapelli, Marks & Wilson sent over a letter by fax a little while ago telling us that you were Mr. Connaught's heir and that we were to give you access to the safety deposit box and any information you needed."

I was nervous and anxious. Going into the safety deposit box could be the point of no return, so to speak. Searches of Tommy's computers, files, organizers, drawers, cupboards, and file cabinets had so far turned up nothing. Nothing that could be construed or interpreted as having any relevance at all to Tommy's murder.

Tommy had something hidden somewhere. The fact that he had layers of passwords protecting his electronic files and keys hidden in picture frames to protect his paper files, told me that there were secrets somewhere. I was desperate to find that something that could help me understand why my life was no longer my own. My mother always says that there is a reason for everything, and I was bound and determined to find that reason. In for a penny, in for a pound.

"Sure," I told Sara. "Let's open up the safety deposit box."

Did I have any inkling about what I was going to find? Not really. Because as street-smart as I like to think I am, the levels of human depravity that I encountered because of what was in that box, were beyond my imagination. The key to the safety deposit box ended up being the key that unlocked the end of my innocence and naiveté.

The bank manager led me into the vault at the back of the bank on the main floor. The back left-hand corner of the vault held floor-to-ceiling safety deposit boxes, each identified with a number engraved on a brass plaque on the front. Number 330 was about halfway up the wall and was one of the larger boxes. Sara removed a key chain from the pocket of her suit, chose a key, and inserted it into the top lock on the box. She held out her hand and I passed her my key which she inserted into the bottom lock. She turned both keys, removed them, and then slid the box out of its slot and handed it to me. Its weight and size surprised me.

Sara led the way and I followed her to a private booth that contained a waist-high counter and one chair.

"Ms. Watson will help you put the box back when you're finished," she told me and pointed to a woman sitting at a nearby desk. "Take your time, and please be assured of complete privacy. You can lock this door when I leave. And please let me know if you need anything else today." She shook my hand and closed the door when she left. I quietly pushed the thumb lock on the door, took a huge cleansing breath, sat down in front of the box, and reluctantly lifted the lid.

Chapter twenty-seven

JAY WAS COOKING AND I was watching him move effortlessly around the kitchen. He was barefoot, wearing his ragged jeans and a white T-shirt. The view from where I was sitting at the kitchen island was yummy and I was very appreciative. Jay placed an ice-filled glass of Diet Coke in front of me and leaned his elbows on the counter.

"Anything else, ma'am?" he teased.

"At this very moment, no, but thanks for asking."

Jay returned to the stainless steel gas stove and grabbed the handle of the large skillet that was sizzling with ambrosia-scented ingredients. He tossed the ingredients in the air and amazingly they all landed back in the skillet. Apparently he was making my favourite dinner. Call me kookie but I thought my favourite dinner, bar none, was pizza, and this sure didn't look like the makings of a meat-lover's special. However, I was not going to look a gift horse in the mouth and decided that whatever Jay was cooking was going to *become* my favourite dinner. It is possible that he had made this dish for me before and I had forgotten. And that, ladies and gentlemen, is not something I was about to own up to.

Jay was an enthusiastic cook. He had grown up in a houseful of women, the youngest child of a single mother who had five children, four of them daughters. Jay's sisters had babied him until he stopped putting up with that nonsense at age five. After that, all of the kids were treated equally, all having to share the responsibilities of the house with their mother, who worked two jobs. Each of them was expected to know how to cook, clean, do laundry, cut the grass, take out the garbage, shovel snow, wash the car, and change the linens on a bed. We had the same type of rules in our two-parent house, but I never became skilled at any of those chores because I hated doing them. To this day, I remain a reluctant housekeeper, laundress and cook. Don't get me wrong, I clean, do laundry and can make all the basic foods. But do I like it? Not really. I rush efficiently through those tasks, always knowing there is something more worthwhile that I could to be doing. Like relaxing with a good romance novel.

"Where shall we eat," Jay asked, "in here, or in the big room?"

I stopped my daydreaming and looked at Jay who was standing in front of the counter where I sat, with his hands full of cutlery, napkins and two placemats.

"Let's eat at the big dining room table. I want some room to spread out some documents."

"Okay. Let me put this stuff on the table and dinner should be ready in a few minutes. Are you going to share with me what you found out today?"

I had been holding my breath when I gently lifted the lid of the safety deposit box. As if the box contained a bomb or something. Scared to see what could be in there. Knowing that there had to be something, if Tommy had gone to all the effort he had to hide the key to the file cabinet that contained the key to the safety deposit box.

Was I a little disappointed when I found only two items in the safety deposit box? Relieved, yes, but not disappointed. In fact, I was naive enough to think that the large, legal size, buff-coloured file folder, and the large, brown envelope had to be harmless. Paper couldn't hurt you, right?

"I'm not sure what I found today," I said, finally answering Jay. "I emptied the safety deposit box into my briefcase, put the box back in the vault, and had Lou bring me straight home. I'm doing my denial thing."

Jay looked at me questioningly.

"Okay," I told him reluctantly. "I'm sure you've noted one of my personality quirks. It's called denial mode. If I think something bad is going to happen, or if I know something is going to make me sad or upset, I ignore it. Deny that it exists. I think I'm doing that with the things I found in the safety deposit box."

"Alright," he said. He put the cutlery and placemats down on the counter and came around to where I was sitting. I swiveled around on my stool and looked up at him. "I'll help you with your denial thing." He mimed quotes in the air with his fingers when he said denial thing, and then picked up both my hands. He put my right hand to his lips and kissed it lightly on the palm. "Now get off this stool and go set the table." Jay pulled me down from the stool and kissed the top of my head. "We'll figure this out together."

Jay was right. My favourite meal was now the pasta dish he prepared. Large pasta shells stuffed with mushrooms and cheese, covered in a fresh tomato sauce.

Stuffed and satisfied, we tackled the treasures from the safety deposit box together. I placed the file folder and the envelope in front of me on the large dining room table.

"Here." I shoved the envelope at him. "You go through this. I'll tackle the file folder."

Inside the file there was a stack of papers about an inch thick, all neatly punched with two holes at the top of each page, and arranged on foldable metal spikes. The sheet of paper on top was on the letterhead of the U.S. Food & Drug Administration. It was a copy of a letter from Dr. Victoria Edwards, Director of the Center for Devices & Radiological Health and was dated about three months ago. The letter was addressed to Dr. Jordan Francis, the Vice-President of Research at Global Devices. In the letter the Director denied "for a final time" Global Devices' 501(k) pre-market application for its totally implanted artificial kidney. The Director went on to say that she fully endorsed the decision of the Office of Device Evaluation (which she emphasized was part of *her* organization and which she emphasized reported to *her*) not to allow clinical trials of the artificial kidney. The Director finished the letter by advising Global Devices that *she* was the final adjudicator of this matter and that there were no other avenues of appeal available to Global Devices at this time. So there!

Several letters along the same vein but not quite as abrupt were filed behind the top letter. These letters were dated over a six month period earlier this year.

I glanced up from my file to see what Jay was doing with his envelope. He was sitting still, looking at me, waiting for me to finish. The contents of the envelope were stacked in front of him.

"What?" I said.

"Guess. Just guess what was in this envelope." He held up his hand. "No. Forget it. No guessing. You'll never get it. Are you ready for this? Your friend Miss Natalie Scott is a stalker."

"What?" I said, again.

"You heard me. This envelope is full of love letters. Really *sloppy* love letters."

Although I thought I knew the answer, I asked it anyway. "Love letters addressed to who?"

"There's no name. They all start with 'my love'."

"Are there dates on the letters?"

Jay flipped through the pile of paper in front of him.

"Some have dates and others don't. The earliest letter is dated about six months ago."

"I don't know if I want to read those."

"Hey, none of that. No 'denial mode' allowed. You've been so eager to figure this whole mess out, so here," Jay shoved the pile of letters across the table to me. "Give me your file folder and let me go through it."

There were about fifteen or twenty letters in the pile. Without reading them, I flipped through the pieces of paper to get some sense of the letters and their timing. They were written over a two month period and the last one was dated almost four months ago.

The first letter was casual, breezy, non-threatening. Natalie bearing her soul. "*I'm so shy and so scared to approach you. Can we get together for coffee? I'd love to talk to you, outside the office. I would love to be your friend. Call me on my cell or send me an email. Yours, Natalie*"

By the fifth letter, though, the letters were from a whining, desperate woman. "*Why won't you acknowledge me? Why can't we meet, have coffee, maybe dinner? Please, I only want to talk with you, be your friend.*"

The tone changed from whining and clingy, to romantic and lovesick, in the next couple of letters. They were embarrassing to read and I wondered why Tom kept them. "*I can't think of anything but you my darling. Every night my dreams are filled with the wonder of you. Our life together would be heaven on earth.*" Yuck.

Why oh why did this woman continue to work at Phoenix, and why oh why did Tommy have these creepy letters in his safety deposit box?

"*To be with you for the rest of my life is all I ask. Let me take care of you and be with you. Together we will be one.*"

I ask you, who writes like that? Even the romance novels I had been known to read once in a while did not have such love-sick dialogue in them. Did Tommy give her any encouragement? One wonders if she was getting encouragement because the letters kept coming.

The last letter sounded more like the first letter. Whining, insecure and pleading. "*I will never forget you. My love for you does not diminish, even though you won't meet me, you won't look at me. Can we ever be together?*"

Okay, I was thoroughly disgusted and totally unsympathetic. What type of woman (or man for that matter) would throw themselves so pathetically at another individual? And what type of woman couldn't take a hint? It was clear that she wasn't getting any encouragement but she kept at it.

Jay was still busily reading the file so I got up and wandered around the apartment. Something wasn't right but I couldn't quite put my finger on it. I stepped out on the balcony and lit a cigarette and leaned my elbows on the cement railing. I couldn't marry-up the image of Natalie Scott and Tommy together, and I had been having trouble with the concept of the two of them ever since I first heard mention of it at the office. Tom Connaught was a strong man, physically and mentally.

Strong men like Tommy didn't take the whining type of crap that Natalie

Scott was dishing out in those letters. That's why guys like Tommy were physically strong too - so they could run, as fast as possible, away from someone like Nat. On the one hand, Tommy wouldn't give someone like that encouragement if he wasn't interested in her, and she sure didn't help herself by letter number five when she was pleading for some companionship. On the other hand, he would have put a stop to it after letter number two if he wasn't interested in her. He would have made short-shrift of her. There's no way he would have allowed that to go on for four or five months. I was more and more convinced that those letters weren't addressed to Tommy even though everyone at the office thought they had been a couple.

Jay was at the computer in the hidey-hole behind the aquarium when I went back inside.

"What are you up to?" I asked him.

"I'm on-line trying to figure out the Food & Drug Administration. I'm not that familiar with American government organizations."

"Well, if they're anything like the Canadian government, they are one massive pile of bureaucracy. What have you found out?" I pulled a chair up and tried not to crowd him in the little space.

"The Center for Devices and Radiological Health is one of the branches of the Food and Drug Administration, which is part of the U.S. Department of Health and Human Services. The head of this unit is a Director and the Director is a Medical Doctor. There are about six or seven departments which all report to the Director." Jay was staring at the computer screen reading this information to me.

The letters in the file from the safety deposit box that I had seen were from the Director of this branch, Dr. Victoria Edwards.

"One of the departments reporting to Dr. Edwards is the Office of Device Evaluation. Hang on," he said as he scrolled through pages on the internet. "Oh," he finally said. "Now I get it. I think." He turned to me.

"The letters in that file all relate to an artificial kidney that a company called Global Devices is developing." I nodded my head because I knew that.

Jay continued. "If I understand the process from quickly looking on the internet, this department of the government authorizes clinical trials to be conducted of unapproved medical devices and they evaluate the pre-market submissions from the medical device industry. There are various classes of devices that they evaluate and if I read the file right, the artificial kidney would be a class three device - those are the ones that have the most stringent regulatory requirements."

I was quickly becoming confused, but that wasn't anything new - whenever someone talked to me about government departments my mind wandered.

I tried to keep up with Jay who amazingly had made his way through the myriad of pages on the internet and already had a basic understanding of this department.

"Class three devices are those that support or sustain life," he read from the computer screen. He looked over his shoulder at me, "I would suppose that an artificial kidney would fall into that category, huh?" I nodded in agreement.

Jay started shutting down the computer. "What else was in that file?" I asked him. The file was more than an inch thick, and more than an inch of paper equals a couple hundred of pieces of paper.

"It's basically the history of Global Device's correspondence with the Office of Device Evaluation from when they first notified them of their work on the artificial kidney. The final letter in the file, the one on top, is from the head honcho herself, denying, for the final time, their applications. In other words, Global Devices had not proven to the Director and her staff that their device was safe and ready to be tried on humans."

The date on the letter from Dr. Edwards was about three months prior. Ben Tucker at Phoenix had told me that our project was cancelled about two months ago. *And* he told me that it was cancelled due to a lack of research funds. Things were getting more confusing by the moment.

Chapter twenty-eight

THE NEXT MORNING I GOT to the office well before the earliest arrivals and fired up the big Xerox machine down the hall from my office. The behemoth copy machine might have scared off lesser beings, but I was quite intimate with this model, having spent the better part of my last job in front of one. There was one time in my illustrious career as a legal secretary that I had stood in front of a copy machine for days, making copies of documents for the closing of a huge transaction involving over eighty different interested parties. Myself and a few articling students figured out that if we stacked the equivalent amount of paper passed around on that deal, the stack would be almost as tall as One First Canadian Place, a seventy-two storey skyscraper in downtown Toronto. The mechanical sound of the automatic document feeder on the copier haunted my sleep for weeks after that deal was done.

I made two copies of the correspondence file and two copies of the love letters. I planned on returning the originals to the safety deposit box later that day.

Next on my agenda and top of my mind was doing my civic duty. I called the detectives who were investigating Tommy's death. Neither of them were available so I left a message with the clerk at the Precinct. I was certain that the contents of the safety deposit box were relevant to Tommy's murder and I was also certain that the cops would want to know.

When Carrie arrived I asked her if she had a phone number for Dr. Jordan Francis at Global Devices.

"I do," she told me. "Mr. Connaught and he talked on a daily basis for a long time, but I don't think they'd been in touch for a while. I don't remember him calling lately. Shall I get him on the line for you?"

"No, it's okay. I can dial," I told her. "Just write the number down." She looked a little hurt and I remembered that a lot of executives had their secretaries place calls for them, announcing that they were on the line. "I'm

128

not sure when I'm going to call him, so I just need to have the number." She handed me a slip of paper with the number on it.

"Anything else?" she wanted to know.

"There is actually. Can you get me the most recent file on the Global Devices project."

Carrie was busily writing this request down on the ubiquitous steno pad. She looked up at me.

"Which project? We have several contracts with them."

"Oh. I hadn't thought of that. The one where we were working with them on the artificial kidney. I think the project was cancelled a couple of months ago. Nat Scott was leading the team."

Carrie stood up from her desk. "I'll go right now and ask for the files."

"Let's not make a big deal about this. I really don't want everyone and their dog knowing I've asked for the files. Okay?"

"No one will be the wiser," she told me. "If the project is done, the files will be in the central storage area under lock and key, and I have access." She opened a door to a closet behind her desk and pulled out a large, four wheeled cart, with a wire tray on the top and one underneath. "Be back in a little bit," she said and headed down the hall.

Yikes! I was naive enough to think that "the file" would be a couple of folders. Carrie obviously knew better and I readied myself for some tough slogging through technical jargon and medical research data. Neither of which were my strong suit.

My stomach sank when Carrie arrived back with the cart full of file folders. The top and bottom trays of her cart were jammed with files, and several more were perched precariously on the top.

"Where do you want these?" she cheerily asked me.

"Why don't you just leave the cart over there beside the meeting table, and I can spread out."

"Is there anything I can help you with, Miss Monahan?" she offered.

"There is," I told her. She eagerly stood in front of the desk and waited for my instructions. "You need to call me Kate. That's a start."

She nodded her head in agreement. "But, I won't call you Kate in front of other people. Okay?"

"Okay," I agreed with her. I knew that Carrie was trained as an executive secretary and stood on formalities. "Secondly, sit down for a minute." I motioned to one of the chairs in front of my desk.

Carrie sat and smoothed her skirt. She was wearing another beautiful outfit and I was jealous as all get out that she looked so good. "Tell me about Mr. Connaught and Natalie Scott."

"Tell you what?" she asked tentatively.

"Tell me what you knew about the two of them, their relationship. What they did together." I was half-way convinced that Tommy and Natalie's relationship was no more than a figment of someone's imagination.

"Well, I never actually saw them together. And like I told you before, Mr. Connaught never came out and talked to me about the relationship. I only heard about it through the rumour mill. One of the secretaries who works with the project teams told me that Miss Scott actually told one of the team members that she was going out with Mr. Connaught. And then when the project ended, and she had her famous hissy fit, they broke up. Everyone knew that."

I still wasn't convinced but didn't let on to Carrie.

"Great, thanks for the info. So, what's on the plate for today?"

"You have no meetings booked, so far," Carrie said.

"Well, let's leave it like that, okay? Unless it's urgent, I want to keep the day clear." I looked over at the mass of files piled in the cart and felt more than a little sick at the thought of plowing through them.

The files were organized by subject matter and each subject matter had several files. The subject matters included RFP (request for proposal), Correspondence - General, Project Schedule, Client Sign-off, LED Research, FDA Approvals, PISTON Trials, etc., etc. Each of these file categories had several file folders of material and they were stuffed into what we in the legal field called bellows files. Heavy cardboard, expandable file containers. In all, there were probably close to one hundred file folders. I took a deep breath and plunged in, starting with the original request for proposal.

Global Devices had put out the RFP several years prior, and they had been looking for a technical partner to assist them in developing the interface between the implantable artificial kidney and the external energy source. The RFP had some details in the information section about how many artificial organs had failed because of high infection rates. Apparently, earlier artificial organs had to be physically connected to external energy sources and this was done through tubes connected to the device, through the patient's skin and hooked up to the energy source. There was an incredibly high rate of infection for those patients, many of whom died because of this. Other manufacturers started covering these tubes with a type of polyester fiber which the patient's skin would intertwine with, reducing the rate of infection and the germs that could get into the body.

Global Devices had come up with the bright idea of finding a company to help them develop an artificial kidney that could work with radio waves, specifically electro-magnetic waves. The external device would give power and computer commands to the internal device, without any physical hook up to the patient's body. The RFP was being sent to companies that Global

Devices thought could develop this external device. The artificial kidney was being built in-house at Global Devices.

About seventeen months after the original RFP was sent out, Phoenix Technologies was awarded the contract to partner with Global Devices. The total value of the contract was over $20 million and if the device was successful, Phoenix would be required to sign over all intellectual property rights and the source code to Global Devices. Phoenix would have no further rights to the device. Period. End of sentence.

So far, so good. I was understanding the basics of what I was reading. I spent the next four hours going through technical files, the contents of which were pretty much Greek to me. The only thing I understood was that it was four hours out of my life I would never get back.

My back was aching from sitting for so long and I was so hungry I swore I could eat the back end of a Buick. I grabbed my purse and headed out to find some food. The streets were teeming with tourists and I had no idea where to go to get some lunch. Every day I had spent at the office, Carrie had made sure my lunch was delivered. Today I felt like a kid out of school, so I wandered down East 46th towards U.N. Headquarters.

You could easily differentiate the tourists from the natives, because the New Yorkers were dressed for success, and all were carrying take out bags with their lunch. The men were wearing open necked dress shirts with no jackets, and the women looked summery in their sun dresses and lightweight suits. And apparently native New Yorkers did not sweat. Both women and men looked cool and collected whereas the tourists (yours truly included), were dripping from the humidity. I had thought Toronto summer days were brutal with humidity, but Toronto had nothing on Manhattan. The heat generated by thousands of taxis and buses, the asphalt on the roadways, the smelly, hot air coming out of the subway grates, the exhaust from the buildings and wall to wall people made it feel like a little bit of hell. Sweat was running freely down my back and chest.

I stopped to get some lunch at a sandwich shop that had a line up out the door. I marched out of the shop with my take-out lunch bag swinging, just like all the other business people in front of me.

Surprisingly there were several empty benches outside the U.N. Headquarters building so I claimed a spot and sat back to do some people watching. I smiled at the very large sculpture of a revolver with its barrel tied in a knot. Very clever. Nine busloads of tourists unloaded in front of the plaza in the time it took me to eat half my sandwich.

In spite of the throngs of people, I found it very peaceful and quiet, and my thoughts turned to Tommy and Phoenix Technologies. Was my life ever going to be as simple as it was last month? I knew that no matter what I turned up, if I kept digging to find out what happened to Tommy, it wouldn't be pleasant. If the path I was going down didn't give me any answers, I was stubborn enough that I'd find another path. Somehow, I would find the answers. At this point though, I was so confused with all the different details, I didn't even know what questions needed asking. Except of course, the big one: *who killed Tom Connaught?*

Chapter twenty-nine

I SPENT THE REST OF the afternoon reviewing the files and dealing with mundane issues that didn't require any thinking on my part. My brain was in overload, and although I have never been nominated for membership in Mensa, I proud that I was keeping up with some pretty technical stuff.

For the first year the development staff at Phoenix had worked on the "guts" of the device, and early on in the development work, the team had baptized it the PISTON system. PISTON stood for Percutaneous Intelligence System Transfer Nephrology. Needless to say, I had to look up the definitions of percutaneous and nephrology. Percutaneous is a medical term for "through the skin" or "through unbroken skin" and nephrology is the branch of internal medicine dealing with kidneys. Which makes sense (of course) because this was a device to be used outside the body, not hooked up to anything inside the body, namely, the artificial kidney. I was not just another pretty face.

At 5:00 p.m. Carrie knocked on the door and came in to ask me if I needed anything else before she headed out. I had lost complete track of time and was surprised that it was the end of the business day.

"Wow." I got up from my chair and stretched. "I can't believe it's the end of the day already. I still have to call Sara Williston at the bank to see if I can drop over and I haven't called Dr. Francis." While I was rummaging around my desk looking for their numbers, Carrie quietly picked up my phone, dialed, spoke a few words, hit the red hold button and held the receiver out to me.

"It's Sara Williston. You talk to her and I'll go get Dr. Francis on the line."

I smiled my thanks at her, took the phone and hit the button on the phone taking the line off hold. "Sara, it's Kate Monahan. I want to return some things to the safety deposit box and wanted to drop by. Is that convenient for you?"

Sara told me that I could drop by any time before 7:00 p.m. After that, she was leaving for a rock climbing class. Apparently, they have rock climbing walls inside old warehouses where people can practice the sport. I did *not* ask for further details. Rock climbing, indoors or outdoors, would rate right up there with watching golf on television. Yawn, bore.

As soon as I hung up, Carrie was back in my office looking a little disturbed.

"What's up?" I asked her.

"Dr. Francis," she said. "He's no longer working at Global Devices and they didn't have a forwarding address. I find that strange."

"Who did you talk to over there?" I asked.

"I called his old number and got someone else's voice mail. I tried the number a second time, thinking I might have dialed wrong, which I didn't. So then I called the main switchboard, which was closed for the night. Then I remembered that one of my friends who I went to secretarial school with worked there. I tracked her down through the automated directory."

"Oh. My. God. How long were you out there on the phone?"

"Just a few minutes," Carrie continued. "Lucky for me Naomi works for the head of the human resources group. Which means she has access to their internal systems. She logged on to their HR system and found out that Dr. Francis left the company about four weeks ago, and they have no forwarding address."

"You're amazing," I told her. "Go home now. We'll worry about Dr. Francis tomorrow."

"I'm off then," she said. "Just remember to page Lou when you're ready to leave."

Lou had a heck of a time navigating the streets in SoHo after my bank appointment. Cars were double-parked and two lane streets narrowed to one lane. When he finally pulled up in front of Frank Sanchez's place, I was about ten minutes late for my appointment. Jay was pacing on the sidewalk, running his hand through his hair. He almost made a move towards the car to open my door, but knew better. Lou was very possessive about his duties.

I told Lou that I didn't need him for the rest of the evening and he took the news stoically. The man had such pride in his job, and he was so over-protective of me.

"You shure, ma'am?" he asked in his thick New York accent. "Nuttin' I can do for you tonight?"

"No, Lou. Really. I have an appointment here, and then Jay and I'll go for something to eat, and then we'll catch a cab back."

When I said "cab", I swear Lou almost gasped. Like I had insulted his mother or something. "It's okay Lou," I told him as I placed a hand on his arm. "You deserve some time off. Really. Come and get me tomorrow morning at our usual time. Enjoy your evening."

"Ma'am," he said and tipped his hat at me. "Sir," he said directly to Jay. "Night." With that he got back behind the wheel of his Lincoln Town Car and left us.

"Wow," Jay piped up. "Who would have thought it would be so hard keeping the hired help happy?"

My lesson with Frank that night was all about being personally aware of my surroundings, and the effects on the body of violent or aggressive surprise. But we only got to that part of the class after Frank had put Jay and I through our paces. We spent time on our footwork drills and our punches, practicing our jab, cross and hook, and then Frank introduced us to the *qua choi* or 'back fist'. This was a punch where you used your forearm like a piston and met your target with the back of your hand. I *loved* this punch and got great satisfaction from the sound of my hand hitting the practice glove with a satisfying *thwap*. After thirty minutes I was dripping with sweat, and although Frank's dojo was air conditioned I could hardly feel the effects of it.

While I sat on the bench sipping from a bottle of water, Frank talked to me about some of the basics of self-defense.

"I don't really like to call it self-defense," he explained. "It's more self-protection. It's about being aware, sometimes hyper-aware, of your surroundings. Kate, you're responsible for your own personal security and safety." When our peripheral vision is active, he explained, our ability to detect danger increases. He talked about how to approach your car at night, why you should lock the doors as soon as you get in your car, and other different types of situations to avoid.

Frank then asked me to describe how I felt physically the first time I was attacked.

"Other than scared out of my mind?" I asked him.

"Yeah. Tell me about other things you remember."

I closed my eyes and tried to concentrate on that night, just a few months ago. Just remembering the weight of him sitting on my stomach, one of his large hands covering my mouth and the other trapping both my hands over my head, caused a metallic taste in my mouth. My stomach and bowels tightened.

I looked up at Frank standing in front me. "I remember feeling helpless," I started. "I wanted to scream but nothing would come out of my mouth. It felt like I was falling down a tunnel. It sounded like thunder in my ears." My breathing started to get short so I concentrated on taking some deep breaths. I suddenly felt like shit.

"See, even after several months, the incident still has the ability to cause physiological effects on you. You're breathing is hard." Frank sat down beside me on the bench. "Kate, look at me," he directed. "Your face is flushed and it's not from our workout. This is what I want to talk to you about."

I took a couple of deep breaths and looked at Frank. He seemed like a nice guy and even though it was only the second time I had met him, I decided I had to trust him. Jay was standing on the other side of the room, leaning on the wall, sipping from his water bottle. He was the smart one, he knew to give me my space.

"Frank, I want to forget about those incidents. I hate the way remembering them makes me feel." I stood up and starting pacing, getting myself worked up. "I can't stand not feeling in control. That son-of-a-bitch attacked me three times and then he shot me. He's fucking lucky he's in the Kingston Penitentiary because I don't know what I'd do to that sorry bastard if I ran into him. Just thinking about what he put me through makes me so angry I could spit."

"Kate. All of these feelings are totally natural. I think you're handling it well. Some women who aren't as strong as you don't cope well at all after they've been attacked. Some of them become suicidal. Let's consider your anger as some positive energy. You can picture him in your mind when you're working on your punches. Right now I want to talk to you about the effects on your body when you're under attack. Everything you described to me before is caused by a whole bunch of chemicals in your body that go haywire when you're attacked or surprised. Your muscles tense up. Right?"

I nodded in agreement.

"You suddenly can't hear certain noises and others are magnified. Right?"

I nodded again.

"You feel like you're in a tunnel. Sometimes you feel like you're falling. You have no sense of time. Everything seems totally out of your control. Right?"

Again, I nodded.

"That's the effect of the chemical cocktail. Your body goes into self-preservation mode. Your attacker counts on you being surprised and unable to help yourself. Let's learn how to keep our awareness levels high and how to defend ourselves if we're the subject of a surprise attack. Okay?"

Jay and I spent the next hour learning how to deal with unexpected surprises. Frank taught me how to take a knife away from someone who was attacking me and even though I was highly doubtful that I could do something like that, within ten minutes I was able to take the knife away from Frank and lay him out, flat on his back on the floor. Frank told me to be submissive and passive with my attacker and to never look them in the eye. That way, the attacker could feel superior and in control. I didn't need to be stronger than my attacker and I didn't need to be bigger than my attacker.

Suddenly I felt totally empowered and realized that I had found the magic I had been looking for. I had vowed to learn how to defend myself and even though I was a short little person, I was learning that size didn't mean anything in these situations, if you knew what you were doing. We practiced on Jay, the poor guy. While he pretended to attack me with a knife, I practiced taking it away from him, and dropping him to the mats that Frank had supplied. Frank ended the lesson by showing me what to do and how to escape if someone grabbed me from behind. By the end of the two hours, I was exhausted but feeling more and more in control. My thanks to Frank were heartfelt.

"Just doing my job, Kate, just doing my job," he told me. "See you in a couple of days."

Chapter thirty

JAY WOKE ME FROM A deep sleep that night. I was so physically exhausted after our class with Frank that I could barely make it through dinner. When we arrived back at the apartment I dumped my stuffed briefcase on the large dining room table.

"I have no strength to go through this shit tonight," I said to no one in particular.

Jay on the other hand, was fired up. Apparently, he gets 'juiced' after a work out and has too much energy to sleep. I highly doubt that I will *ever* feel like that.

I showed him the files I had brought home from Phoenix. He asked if he could go through them.

"Fill your boots," I told him and dragged my ass to bed. I was totally disoriented when he woke me.

"Kate," he was saying softly as he shook my shoulder. "Kate. Wake up."

"What?" I tried to push myself up with my arms into a sitting position but my forearms and shoulders ached so much they were useless. I flopped back down on the pillow. "What? This better be good Jay, or I'm telling your mom."

He threw the covers off and tugged on one of my useless arms. "Come on. I need to show you what I found in those files."

I followed him into the dark living room. A bit of light from the street below was coming through the windows and from the cubby hole in the wall behind the aquarium. The computer screen gave off a glow and a small lamp beside it was lit.

"What time is it?" I asked Jay.

"Around two," he told me. He pulled a chair up beside him and patted the seat. "Here. Sit down."

"Two?" I yawned. "Aren't you tired?"

"No. Now pay attention." He lifted up one of the files that I had brought from the office. "See here?" Jay pointed to the label on the side of the file folder.

"Yeah. I see."

"What does it say?"

I read off the name on the file folder. Global Devices. Technical Specifications. PISTON.

"Right. But look carefully. What else is on the label?"

"Oh for God's sake Jay. What? I'm barely awake." I squinted and looked at the label. "T-7," I read out loud.

"Right," Jay said. He took the file back and swiveled around on his chair to the file cabinets behind us. He pulled out the top drawer of the second cabinet and rifled through the files until he found the one he wanted. Jay pulled the file folder out with a flourish and handed it to me. "Ta da," he proudly said.

"Ta da, what?"

"These two files should be mirror images of each other. Obviously the filing system at Phoenix assigns a number to each file. I only noticed it after I had been reading the contents of the files. I remembered that the files in the cabinets were only labeled with a letter-number combination system. If this file here," he lifted up the one I had brought from the office, "is the official T-7 file, then this file," he pointed at the file I was holding, "should be a copy of the T-7 file." He took the file from me.

"But," he continued, "it's not a completely true copy." He flipped several pages to where it was marked with a small yellow Post-It note and handed it back to me. Jay then opened the file from the office to the same spot. "Remember that game we used to play when we were kids? You know, the one that came with the Saturday comics? They'd have two pictures which looked identical and you had to find the differences? Well, let's pretend we're playing that game. Do you see the differences between the two?"

The sheets of paper he was pointing to were part of a report to Global Devices detailing tests on the PISTON system. There were columns of figures, headed with symbols and letters I had never seen before. My brain was still foggy with sleep and I was having just a teensy bit of trouble with my enthusiasm level.

"Sorry, Jay. I can't see any differences."

"It's okay. Look. Here." His finger came to rest on a number on a sheet of paper in the file from the cabinet, and with his other hand he pointed out a different number, but in the same place on the page on the other file. "See? Same reports. Different numbers. And this isn't the only place where there are differences."

He turned around and faced the computer and started fiddling with the mouse. "None of this was obvious when you look at these things in isolation. If you look at Tom's computer files, nothing seems wrong. Same thing for the files in the cabinet or the files you brought from the office. It was when I had this file from your office and I saw the number on the top of the label, that I thought to look at the file in the drawer. I didn't put the Post-It notes in the file you know. They were already there, so Tom had already done his homework."

"What do you think this means?" I wondered out loud.

"That's pretty obvious to me," Jay said. "Your Mr. Connaught found some discrepancies in the reports. I think that's why he has all these files in the drawers. They seem to be a duplicate of the files from your office."

"Let me see," I said. I stood up and bent over the file cabinet and pulled a few files out randomly. When we found these files the other day, I hadn't bothered to go through them because the labels meant nothing to me. The contents of the files that I pulled out now looked familiar to me, and I said to Jay, "I think you're right. These look like the files I spent all day going through." I opened the second cabinet and pulled out the file labeled R-1. The contents were the same as the RFP file I had reviewed that afternoon.

"But where are the differences?"

"Look for the yellow Post-It notes," Jay said. "I think that's a start. And I want to look at the file from the safety deposit box - that correspondence with the FDA. Maybe that's what triggered Tom to check out the files."

"A copy of that file is in my briefcase too, but I'm too tired to go through any more papers. I'm going back to bed."

Sleep would not come and I dozed on and off for the next couple of hours. My mind kept going back over those files. How did Tommy find out about the differences in the files? What triggered him to go looking? Or who had triggered him? I wondered where Dr. Jordan Francis fit into all of this. And why wasn't he working at Global Devices anymore? When I dragged my sorry, tired ass out of bed at six o'clock, I decided to make Dr. Francis my priority for the day.

Carrie's friend Naomi said that the address they had on file at Global Devices for Dr. Francis was on the Upper West Side, near West End Avenue. She was pretty sure he wasn't living there though because when he left, he told Global Devices that he was moving. They didn't have a forwarding address.

Carrie told me all this while she stood in front of my desk. "Ask her for the name of Dr. Francis' boss. I'd like to talk to him or her."

The next time Carrie was in front of my desk, she was there to tell me that she had Dr. Bill Pritchard on the phone. "He was Dr. Francis' boss at Global." I thanked her and picked up the phone.

"Dr. Pritchard. This is Kate Monahan at Phoenix Technologies. I thought it would be a good time for me to introduce myself now that I've been here for over a week." I didn't want to get to the real reason for my call right up front. I thought I'd test the waters first.

"Yes," Dr. Pritchard replied. "What can I do for you?" He sounded like a man in a rush.

"Well, I'd like to spend some time with you folks at Global. Get to know you and the people on your team. I understand we've been partnering on some pretty important work with you guys." I knew that although the artificial kidney project was down the tubes, we still had at least two other projects on the go with Global.

"You listen here, Miss," Pritchard said. "You've got some nerve calling here. I'll tell you the same thing I told Tom Connaught." He paused for a moment and I thought I could hear him actually seething over the phone. Pritchard's reedy breathing was coming through loud and clear on the handset. "Phoenix Technologies can take a flying leap. Global Devices will never do business with you again. So stop calling here. The next time you'll hear from us will be through our lawyers." And then, not surprisingly, he hung up.

What the hell was that all about, I wondered. "Carrie," I called out. She came into the office at a trot with her ever-present steno pad, eager to help.

"I need to talk to Natalie Scott. And I need to stop bellowing for you. Sorry about that," I apologized. "I know you showed me how to use the intercom and I keep forgetting it's there. Can you ask Ms. Scott if she's available?"

But Nat Scott was nowhere to be found. Carrie came back and told me that she wasn't in the office and no one had heard from her.

"Who's her 2IC?" I asked Carrie.

"Huh?" Carrie responded.

"Sorry. I always forget that not everyone grew up in a military family. 2IC stands for second in command. They used initials for everything in the army. Used acronyms as words and had strange expressions for every-day things." When I was a kid growing up it was just like being a soldier - we were never "grounded" if we misbehaved, we were CB'd (confined to barracks). When we were learning anything new, we were in "basic". Each year when we moved on to another grade at school, we were "promoted" and we went up a rank. My dad told everyone affectionately that my mom was his 2IC (yeah, right, mom used to snort). Carrie was giving me a blank stare so I got back on the subject.

"Who looks after the R and D team when Nat isn't available?"

"I'm not sure," she told me. "But I can find out."

"Why not do this. Dig out the file from my meeting the other day with the R and D team. I was given a list of projects that they're working on. Find out who's working on the Global Devices projects and that's who I need to talk to."

She came back about ten minutes later. "There's no one working on Global Devices projects," she told me. "Apparently all work on those projects was stopped. So no one is working on them."

I felt my blood pressure rising. "That's ridiculous," I yelled. "Is that what they told you?" She nodded, mutely. "Which little geek told you that?"

"Rick Williams," she whispered.

"Get that short little shit down here, right now." Carrie started beetling out of my office. "And Carrie." She stopped and turned around with her steno pad clutched to her chest. "Sorry. I wasn't yelling at you. You know that, right?" She nodded her head. "Okay. So go find me that short little shit." I heard her giggle as she left the office.

A few minutes later Rick was sitting in one of the chairs in front of my desk. He had his legs crossed and one arm thrown back over the chair in an attempt to look casual. How a man could look casual wearing a short sleeved, white shirt, buttoned to the neck, without a tie, was beyond me. His darting eyes belied his casualness however.

"What's the status on the Global Devices projects?" I thought I'd dispense with the niceties and get right down to it. My blood pressure was still up there.

"As far as I know," he said, "there *are* no Global Devices projects."

I took a deep breath. "And *that* is contrary to what I was told in the meeting last week." I looked at the project status report I was holding in my hand. "As of last week, there were still two current projects with Global Devices. The Fort Apache project, and the San Carlos project. Those teams are supposedly headed up by Belinda Moffat and Ben Tucker. How do you explain the discrepancy?"

"And *that* is contrary to what I know." The little shit was mimicking me. "Nat told us in a staff meeting that all contracts with Global had been cancelled."

"When was that?" I asked.

"A couple of weeks ago?" He shrugged his shoulders. "I can't remember."

"Do you remember our meeting last week? When I was introduced to all of you? Do you remember that each of you gave a status on the projects you were heading?"

I wasn't sure why I was so pissed off. Maybe it was the fact that something was really wrong and I didn't know what it was. Rick had uncrossed his legs and was hunched over his knees, picking at a hangnail on his thumb. He didn't respond to me or look up as I harangued him.

"Yeah," he mumbled. He was examining his thumb now, probably looking for a good chunk of skin to chew on. The man was *really* weird. No doubt he was good at his work though. Like my estate lawyer Dennis Hillary.

"Well Belinda and Dan talked about those projects at that meeting," I reminded him. "They gave me a status report on each of them. Neither of them had the good manners to mention that they'd been cancelled. What is the matter with you people?" I demanded. "Does everyone on that team have a career death wish? Does everyone in the research and development department feel the need to lie to me?" I was really steamed.

"Here's what you're going to do for me Mr. Williams. You are going to go back to your department, and you are going to find the correspondence with Global Devices where it says that the projects have been cancelled. Then, you'll find Belinda Moffat and Ben Tucker and bring both of them back with you." I was standing up, leaning forward over my desk when I finished. I wasn't sure if I sounded like a pissed off grade school teacher or the drill sergeant that I had grown up with (also known as my dad).

Rick stood up and quickly left my office without saying a word. I lit a cigarette and stared out the windows. This was unbelievable. If it was true that Global Devices had cancelled their projects with us, then it would mean we would be showing some losses or less cash on the income statement. I'm not sure how we would account for the work already done if we hadn't been paid for it. Russell Freeson, our chief financial officer, had not mentioned to me anything about the two cancelled projects, so unless there was a big cover-up going on, someone had made a mistake somewhere on the status of these two projects. After the receptionist, the one person in a company who should be on top of all the news, and the comings and goings, is the chief financial officer.

"Miss Monahan," I heard Carrie say behind me. I stubbed out my cigarette in the small ashtray on the windowsill and turned around. Carrie was standing there with Belinda Moffat.

Chapter thirty-one

"BELINDA. HI. COME ON IN. Where are Rick and Ben?" I asked her.

"Rick's gone home with a migraine." Her voice boomed in my office and I cringed at the sound. Not that I mind *loud*, it was the sound of a fog horn in close quarters that got me. This woman had a *serious* problem and I thought of my great-aunt Irene who used to tell us to "modulate our voices" whenever we got a little rowdy.

"Really?" I said. "And what about Ben? Has he got a migraine too?"

"No ma'am, I'm not sure what his problem is, but he's not here today."

Was anybody at work today in that department? Belinda had some papers in her hand which she held out to me. I walked around the desk and took them from her and offered her a seat. The top sheet of paper was a letter from the President & CEO of Global Devices, Dr. Bill Pritchard, the lovely gentlemen I had spoken to earlier that morning.

It was basically a cease and desist letter. We were to cease and desist from doing any more work for Global. And furthermore, Dr. Pritchard demanded that we send back to his company all of the work in progress, source codes, proprietary information of Global's, working file documentation, test results, blah, blah, blah. We were to send a final invoice for work completed to date, and if we had any problem with any of his demands, we were to call his law firm. He *personally* wanted no further contact with *anyone* at Phoenix. Now I understood why he was a little pissed with me this morning.

I looked up from my reading at Belinda. Lord, if her bottom lip wasn't quivering.

I held up the letter and waved it at her. "What is this all about?" I asked her.

Then she burst into tears. Well, to be kind, burst into tears would be the dictionary definition of someone starting to cry. Belinda burst like the Hoover Dam. I swear to God liquid shot out of her nose, mouth and eyes at the same time, and gushed. Within seconds her chin and cheeks were sopping wet with fluids from her nose and her mouth. The tears were coming out of her eyes like a geyser. To top it off, the sounds coming out of her made her sound like a barnyard animal. She was crying, moaning and gasping all at the same time. At a decibel level that would put the rock band *KISS* to shame.

Carrie appeared miraculously with a box of tissues and a tall glass of water. She closed the door behind her as she exited.

Belinda grabbed at the tissue box and pulled out about six which she used to pat down her face. She ungracefully mopped her chin, grabbed several more tissues and blew her nose. Oh. My. God. The sound was fascinating and I wondered if any tug-boats on the East River thought they were hearing a mating call.

I waited while her facial orifices dried up. After a few minutes she gulped a few deep breaths and shuddered a bit. Thankfully, it was over.

"Are you okay?" I asked her.

Belinda nodded. "Yeah, I'm okay. For now. I feel so stupid." Her eyes were bloodshot and the end of her nose was a bright red.

"It's fine," I told her.

"No. It's not fine. I should have done something about this a lot sooner."

"About what?" I prodded her.

"This whole mess with Global. You know, they're good people. I'm so proud to work on their projects. They develop medical products. Not like the pharmaceutical companies. Those greedy bastards are just in business to suck out every last cent of usurious profit from sick people before their patents run out and the medicine goes generic. The group at Global are working on some leading-edge medical devices. It's absolutely breakthrough science." She had lots of enthusiasm in her voice as she talked about Global. Not so much for the pharmaceutical companies though.

"So why did we get this letter from Dr. Pritchard?" I asked her.

"I don't know. You have to believe me," she pleaded. "Nat Scott told us that we were to follow what Dr. Pritchard said in the letter, and return their stuff to them, but we were *not* to tell anyone about it. I asked her how she expected to keep this quiet." She looked at me expectantly. "You know, we have to do monthly reports on progress against the contract to be able to have invoices generated to bill them for our work. We stop producing against those contracts, no invoices go out. Which means no money coming in. Right?"

I nodded silently. I assumed that's how it worked. "So someone was bound to start asking questions sooner than later, right?" I nodded again. "You know Miss Monahan, we were doing *good* work on the Fort Apache project. It was true development work. The client had an idea and wanted to know if we

145

could help them make it work. I *love* that part of my job. When I graduated from MIT with my degree, I knew that someday I'd be working on projects that actually helped people."

She sounded genuinely distressed. I was glad though that she had stopped crying. Belinda took another deep breath and sat up straight in her chair.

"The past few weeks have been hell for me. I'm glad this is out in the open now," she told me.

"But do you know what caused Global to cancel with us?" I asked her.

She shook her head sadly. "No, and I tried asking Natalie about it. She called me a fat cow, and told me to mind my own business. I told her it *was* my business. My project. I was the team leader and I'm responsible for those staff working on the project. I told her she could call me anything she wants, but we are accountable to the shareholders of this company."

Belinda may look and sound different than most of the people working around me, but she demonstrated a clear understanding of her responsibilities. I was stymied though as to why she hadn't come forward sooner with this information.

"If you understand your responsibility to the shareholders of this company, then why did you allow this cover up to go on for as long as it did?" I demanded of her. "You should have stepped up right away with this information. You should have gone immediately to someone on the executive team and told them."

I wasn't yelling at her, just stating the facts. But then geez Louise, she started bawling again. Through the tears, the drool and the snot, she told me that she had family obligations. I leaned over the desk and pushed the box of tissues toward her. A little hint to dry herself up.

When she had composed herself, again, she told me that she had been threatened. By Nat Scott. All of the team leaders had been threatened with their jobs.

"You remember the first day we met you?" she asked me.

"How could I forget that wonderful, first meeting?" I responded with a large dose of sarcasm thrown in.

"Well, Nat had told all of us before we went into the meeting that if we breathed a word, she would fire us all. The same thing she had told us a week or two earlier when we got the original letter." Her loud voice dropped to a whisper and I had to lean over to hear her when she spoke next. "I have twin sisters who require round the clock care. I pay for their care. I couldn't afford to lose my job."

Son of a bitch. Nat Scott had not only exposed this company to liabilities I didn't even want to think about, she had ordered a cover-up of potentially material information. Covering up, or not disclosing, material information to our shareholders and the regulators was a big no-no. I swallowed hard.

Was I as afraid of the Ontario Securities Commission as I was of their U.S. counterpart, the Securities & Exchange Commission? The thought of both of those regulatory bodies gave me the willies but if the truth were told, the Ontario Securities Commission had yet to *really* punish anyone for not disclosing material information. That's because they were more into the typical "let's embarrass them" style of Canadian securities law enforcement. Unlike their U.S. brethren, who got great joy at throwing the book at crooked executives and its "let's make an example of them" style.

Our company's shares traded on the Toronto Stock Exchange and NASDAQ, so we had to abide by the rules of both the OSC and the SEC. The fact that a large customer of ours had cut off all ties with us was considered material information. Why was that material information? Because if I recalled correctly, the total worth of all the contracts in terms of revenue was around $50 million. Contracts we had already announced to the world, and revenue from those contracts that our shareholders were counting on. And that, ladies and gentlemen, is a *material* amount of money. The loss of that amount of revenue would definitely have a negative effect on our bottom line.

And securities laws say that when you are in possession of information that could affect someone's decision to buy or sell your company's shares, then you need to disclose that information. Publicly. By press release. As soon as possible after you come into possession of that information.

Fuck, fuck, fuck.

Time to call Cleve Johnston for some advice on two things. What to do about the material information now in my possession. And how to fire that manipulating bitch, Natalie Scott.

Chapter thirty-two

BEING IN CHARGE OF DAMAGE control is not something I had ever experienced first hand. Behind the scenes support was more my forte. So where to start with the whole mess was a big question mark for me, although I did know we needed to get some people involved who I could trust and who knew what they were doing. "Delegate the duty, assume the responsibility" was something my father had taught me early in life and it stuck with me.

The first person I called was *not* our in-house legal counsel. Experience told me that faced with the type of problems that I was going to throw their way, the first thing they were going to do was call *outside* counsel, at a very large law firm, who charged at least $500 an hour, and who would provide advice and opinions backed up by huge errors and omissions insurance policies.

Not that this was a problem that couldn't be fixed eventually, it was the urgency of dealing with it that was important. Bottom line was we needed to come clean with the public and the securities commissions, as soon as possible. But before we got to the bottom line, I knew I was going to have to be patient, and get the best advice for the company that I could.

Russell Freeson's secretary wasn't at her desk so I knocked on the open door to his office. Russell and three other people were sitting at his long, rectangular meeting table. Everyone was in shirtsleeves, so I assumed it was an internal meeting. Russell looked surprised to see me and stood up as I tentatively entered his office.

"I'm sorry to interrupt, but I need to speak with you on an urgent matter," I told him.

"Yes, Kate, come in." He pulled out an empty chair at the table, inviting me to sit. "We were just finishing up, weren't we guys?" He addressed the three others, and after a quick introduction to their new CEO, they swiftly gathered up their papers and made an exit.

"Okay," he said once the office was empty. "What's up?"

"I think we've got a little problem," I started out tentatively, understating things a tad. "I found out today from one of the team leaders in R and D that Global Devices pulled all of their contracts with us a couple of weeks ago. Were you aware of that?"

Russell paused for a long moment.

"No," he said. "Hell no. What do you mean when you say they pulled all their contracts?"

"Apparently they told us to cease working on all contracts and return all of their property to them." I handed him a copy of the letter from Bill Pritchard and he studied it for another long moment.

"I don't believe this. And we're just finding out now?" A rhetorical question, of course.

Red blotches were appearing on his long neck and chin and I wondered how he normally functioned under stress. Russell had been with the company since the beginning but he wasn't more than forty years old. I knew his age from reading his bio but he seriously didn't look more than thirty. Here's hoping he's weathered a few good corporate storms.

"I just found out and came straight down to see you. We need to get the lawyers involved."

"Of course, but, how did this happen? Have you spoken with Natalie Scott? What's her explanation for this? Jeez, these contracts are worth millions."

"Nat Scott isn't in the office today, so, no, I haven't spoken to her yet. I think the next time I speak with her, it'll be through our lawyers. My number one priority, after we figure out when and how we disclose this, is to fire her skinny little ass. I'm pissed Russell. Severely pissed." Now *I* was getting red blotches on my neck.

Russell and I spent the next half hour confirming with some of our own people that basically no one knew about the cancellations, except of course the heads of the teams in R and D. The accounting system showed that time was still being tracked against the projects. The current billing cycle was ending in a few days and invoices were scheduled to be issued within seven days of the end of the cycle. Just how many people were involved in perpetuating this continuing myth of having Global Devices as a revenue generating customer remained to be seen. One thing was certain though, all perpetrators would be held accountable. I had only been at the helm of Phoenix Technologies for a short while but I felt as protective of the company as a mother bear. I would track down each and every person involved, and hang them from the yard-arm at noon. Figuratively speaking, of course.

Cleve Johnston said it was good to hear my voice and he sounded genuinely happy to talk to me. Until I explained what was going on. He agreed that we had some major damage control to do and he said that he would feel better if he was in New York, directing the traffic on this.

"I'll be on the next flight," he told me. "In the meantime, let me call our New York office and get Barry Golden up to speed. Barry is our expert in all things relating to the Securities and Exchange Commission. He worked there as counsel for fifteen years and joined our New York office about three years ago."

Law firms were smart like that. They often hired lawyers who worked for government departments or agencies that they dealt with on a regular basis. Having these people on staff gave the law firm the appearance of being on the inside track. It was key though to make sure you were seen to be hiring smart people and not bureaucrats.

"Well, you and Barry can figure out what we need to do with the OSC and the SEC. Who's your best employment law expert here in New York? We're going to need them because I believe there's going to be a wholesale firing of staff in our research and development group."

"Hold your horses," Cleve advised me. He sounded like my grandpa, *hold your horses*. "One thing at a time. Don't go off half-cocked and angry."

"Angry?" I repeated. "You're damn right I'm angry."

"That's okay, Kate," Cleve interrupted me. "We just need to keep our heads level here."

I took a deep breath and decided that now was not a good time to get into a pissing match with Cleve. He was doing exactly what we paid him $500 an hour to do. He was giving me counsel. Advising me, instructing me, coaching me. I should probably shut up and get my money's worth.

Chapter thirty-three

MY STOMACH WAS SOUR FROM the three gallons of coffee I had ingested and the fact that I had not given it any real food since the night before. I was feeling more than a little overwhelmed, and my head was pounding. Sharp pains were stabbing at my skull behind my ears, a tell-tale sign of the combination of caffeine overload and low blood sugar. It was stupid of me to have gone so long without eating.

Today I decided to eat at the sandwich shop rather than take a leisurely walk and find a bench. It was mid- afternoon and downtown Manhattan had a different feel at this time of day as compared to the hustle that happened at lunch time. I took my time eating and sipped a Coke, filling up on sugar and carbs. The combination of food and two extra-strength Tylenol helped quell the sharp pains in my head.

For a while my mind wandered and I deliberately avoided thinking about the crap happening at Phoenix. I thought about other, mundane things. Tasks on my ever-present list of mental notes. Call my parents. Do some laundry. Send my brother a birthday card. Feed Tommy's fish. Practice my footwork drills and back fist. After a while I realized my headache was gone and the acid in my stomach had disappeared.

I stopped at the small plaza outside my office tower for a cigarette before heading back into the mess and saw Ben Tucker's wheelchair going through the handicapped entrance of the building.

Son of a bitch. I ground my cigarette out under my shoe and hurried into the building, hoping to catch him. I waved my hand between the closing elevator doors and they magically re-opened for me. Ben was in the elevator with three other people.

"Mr. Tucker," I said. "Good to see you. I'd like a quick word with you." I gave him my phoniest smile.

"Good to see you too Kate," he said back. He gave me one of those smiles that make most women feel fluttery down there but it wasn't working on me. I stood beside his wheelchair and focused on the electronic display of the floor numbers as the elevator moved quickly up to our offices. The doors opened at our floor and Ben held out his hand and said, "After you, Kate."

I stepped off the elevator and waited while he wheeled himself out. Once the elevator doors closed and I was sure no one else was in earshot, I said, "My office, Mr. Tucker. Now."

I turned on my heel and marched down the hall, not waiting for him. When I passed Carrie at her desk, I told her over my shoulder that Mr. Tucker and I were not to be interrupted. With my back still to Ben, who I assumed was keeping up with me, I told him to shut the door. I lit a cigarette, took a drag and got myself worked up to indignant before I turned around to look at him. He had parked his wheelchair between the two guest chairs in front of my desk.

"And just where have you been today, Mr. Tucker?" I demanded.

"Whoa. Kate." Ben held up his two hands as if he were stopping traffic. He had a big shit-eating grin on his face. "You sound like my sixth grade teacher." I decided right there that I definitely did *not* like this man.

"I asked you a question," I said.

"Since when are my absences important enough for the CEO to notice?" Ben asked. The smile was still on his face and his tone was playful and patronizing. "We've never been attendance checkers here at Phoenix Kate. We all know what we have to do and we get it done. We don't punch clocks."

He sounded like he was trying to sweet talk me. There is nothing that makes my blood boil more than being patronized *and* being talked down to.

I jammed my cigarette into the ashtray, put my hands on the desk and leaned over it towards him. "I repeat, Mr. Tucker. Where have you been today? Your absence was noted by the CEO because you were needed on an urgent matter." I think I finally got through to him because his smile disappeared.

"If you must know, I was at a medical appointment," he told me.

"Fine." I wondered what type of medical appointment kept you away from the office for most of the day.

"What's the urgent matter?" he asked me.

"Global Devices," I spit out. "What the fuck is going on?" His face paled and he looked down at his lap for a moment before answering me.

"What do you mean, what's going on?"

"Are you *kidding* me, Mr. Tucker?" I demanded. "I spent the better part of the morning with Belinda. And Rick Williams." He stared at me dumbly, and I took a deep breath before I blew up like Mount Vesuvius.

Rather than yell at him which he was probably expecting, I said in a very controlled tone, "Don't play dumb with me Ben. Tell me why Global Devices have cancelled their contracts with us. And tell me why no one in this company had the good sense to let us know that Global was no longer a client of ours."

The silence between us lasted a good thirty to forty seconds before Ben finally spoke. Thirty to forty seconds for him to formulate a good story.

"Nat Scott knew a couple of weeks ago. She was the one who had all the dealings on the contractual side with Global Devices. When they cancelled, they dealt directly with her. The people at Global who I worked with haven't returned any of my calls, so I don't know what happened."

"That doesn't explain why no one told Tommy, or me, or one of the other senior executives. Do you know what this means to the company? Do you understand our obligations as a public company? Do you have any sense at all?" I probably sounded like his school principal now, not just his sixth grade teacher. "Ben, you're one of the senior people in that group. What the hell were you thinking?"

His eyes stared through me, and his lips were pursed the whole time I was launching into him. His face was blank, expressionless and pale. I watched him noticeably shake his head and refocus his eyes on me before he spoke.

"Natalie Scott told us what had happened. She didn't tell us why. And she threatened each of us with our jobs if we said anything."

"You know Ben, I find it hard to believe that Nat Scott had that much sway over all of the team leaders. So she threatened you with your job. Why didn't one of you come forward? It makes no sense to me. I would have thought that Tom Connaught would have hired people with more common sense than what I'm seeing. This whole mess is about to become a self-fulfilling prophecy for you and your co-workers Mr. Tucker. Before the dust settles on this, each and every one of you will likely be out of a job. Now get out of my office."

Ben turned his wheelchair sharply and left without another word.

I did *not* sign up for this shit, I thought angrily, as I stomped around my office. Hmpf, I snorted, reminding myself that not only did I not sign up for this shit, it had all been dumped in my lap by the gods of irony. This is what you get Kate, I told myself, for acting so high and mighty all these years, acting like you're so special. So confident in yourself, making sarcastic remarks about everyone. The gods of irony finally had enough and said, here, you think you can do better? Think you can be a better manager? A better boss? Go ahead. Here's a little company called Phoenix just for you. Now go and lead the employees.

The irony was not lost on me.

Dr. Bill Pritchard was a gentleman. He proved this when he agreed to see me when I showed-up, unannounced, at the offices of Global Devices. Determined to get to the bottom of what had happened, I impulsively had Lou drive me to their offices located on East 29th Street in the area of the NYU Medical Center and Bellevue Hospital. The receptionist called Dr. Pritchard's office for me, even though I admitted that I didn't have an appointment.

I paced nervously and watched the receptionist pack up her desk for the day. The reception area was windowless and was furnished like the waiting room of a doctor's office. Sparsely and without too much thought of comfort. I was secretly glad to see that these folks didn't spend good money on trying to look like they had money. Like big law firms and the head offices of banks. So much money spent on furnishings that looked good and screamed *look at how much money we make.*

Dr. Pritchard was a small man, with a head full of white hair. I put him in his late seventies. He carried himself erect and although he must have been extremely pissed with Phoenix and myself, he did hold his hand out for a gentlemanly shake.

"Thank you so much for seeing me," I told him.

He stood in front of me with his hands clasped behind his back. I was hoping for an invitation into his office but we remained in the reception area.

"What can I do for you Miss Monahan? I do believe I told you that we here at Global Devices didn't want anything to do with Phoenix Technologies. Ever. I don't believe there's anything you can do to change our mind on that."

He sounded pretty adamant. For a small man, Dr. Pritchard had quite a presence and he made me feel uncertain. I stumbled over my words and suddenly felt out of my league.

"Well, Dr. Pritchard, I can't say that I blame you, however, I'm not clear on the *why*. I don't know why you terminated our contracts. I'm new to all of this, and I'm just trying to find my way." And then I felt tears stinging the back of my eyes. Oh God. I took a deep breath and willed the water in my eyes to go away. Dr. Pritchard must have noticed.

"Come with me, Miss Monahan. Let's go back to my office and have a talk." He turned and I followed. Like a good little girl.

We sat across from each other at a small working table in his office. The top of the table was the only clear space in the office. Massive stacks of papers, magazines, books, newspapers, files and God knows what else were piled around the room. On the floor, on top of what I think was his desk, on top of bursting bookcases. I looked around the room and felt just a wee bit righteous, thinking about how I used to let my filing get away from me. It was never this bad though.

Dr. Pritchard watched me looking around his office and told me, "I can't bear to get rid of anything. My wife calls it my sickness. And on top of that, she won't let me bring papers home, so it's all here. Over fifty years of medical records and research."

"But what would you do if there was ever a fire, or something got spilled on something important? Do you have copies of everything?" I was sounding like a worried secretary.

"Oh, it's not a problem," he assured me. "I've had the best secretary for the last forty years and she has copies of everything." He smiled and I realized he was a very nice gentleman. I was worried about the conversation we were about to have. I felt like a child about to tell my father something that I *knew* would disappoint him.

"Thank you again Dr. Pritchard for seeing me. After we talked this morning, I spoke with several of the staff at Phoenix. The cancellation of your contracts was news to me, and so far I haven't received any satisfactory answers as to why Global pulled the plug. This is dreadful news for us and I have to get to the bottom of it." I smiled weakly at him. "I've only been in this job for a few days, and I'm still feeling my way around. It's quite a shock to the system to find yourself promoted to president of a company."

Dr. Pritchard smiled at me. "I think I know what you're talking about. I was a practicing physician for many, many years before I joined the corporate world. It was like moving to another country where the culture was totally different and they spoke another language. I think it took me several years to acclimatize."

I nodded in agreement. Several years? Yikes. I was hoping that the culture shock would wear off in a couple of weeks.

"Where was your medical practice?" I was interested to hear how he had made the change from the medical to the corporate world.

"I was a surgeon at the Peter Bent Brigham Hospital in Boston. It's been called the Brigham and Women's Hospital since 1980. In the early nineties, there was a push for the development of artificial organs, and I was recruited to head up Global Devices. There were some venture capitalists out there who had some money to invest and I made the jump at that time." He held up his hands and wiggled his fingers. "These hands weren't getting any younger. Plus there was a history of arthritis in my family. Hands are a surgeon's life blood you know."

"How long has Global Devices had a relationship with Phoenix Technologies?" I asked him.

"Probably six or seven years," he told me. "We do business with many high tech companies. There's lots of talent out there that complements the medical talent here at Global. We spread the work around. But," he said *but* with a lot of emphasis, "we are ethical in all aspects of our work. Ethics are something we demand of our partners."

I had a feeling I was about to find out why we had been fired.

"When it was revealed that Phoenix Technologies had falsified test results which were submitted to the FDA, I immediately terminated all contracts. This type of behaviour is simply reprehensible." He was sitting up straight in his chair and I could feel his indignation across the table. "Falsifying test results for life saving medical devices is not quite the same as a small lie on your income tax return. Lives are at stake in this business, Miss, and we cannot, and will not, tolerate falsification of records. Do you have any idea how long it takes to get approvals from the Office of Device Evaluation? Years! And in the case of our artificial kidney, with Phoenix having falsified records, we have been set back at least two years in our research and our approvals."

I felt extremely sick to my stomach and craved a cigarette. Dr. Pritchard had stopped talking at this point, and it was probably time for me to say something.

"Dr. Pritchard, this is the first I have heard of these accusations," I started.

"Accusations?" he interrupted me. "These are not accusations. These are facts."

"Sorry, Dr. Pritchard. Like I said, this is the first I have heard of these, um, facts." My legal background screamed for me to at least say *allegations*, but I wasn't taking a chance on getting a further reprimand from this man.

"Can you start at the beginning and fill me in, please?"

When he was finished, I wished I had never asked the question.

Chapter thirty-four

LOU WAS STANDING BESIDE THE town car when I finally came out of the Global offices an hour later. Traffic was light and for once, Lou didn't seem to be illegally parked.

"Message for you ma'am," Lou said and he handed me a slip of paper. Although I had a company-issued cell phone in my purse, I rarely had it turned on and Carrie knew she could always get a message to me through Lou.

Lou's handwritten note said that Cleve Johnston was arriving at La Guardia on an Air Canada flight from Toronto at 7:30 p.m. I checked my watch. It was 6:30.

"How long will it take us to get to the airport?" I asked Lou.

"At this time of day, anywhere from twenty minutes to an hour. We've got lots of time," Lou said knowingly. He opened the back door of the car for me. Before he closed it though, he leaned down and told me that he had to make a quick call to his dispatcher, to cancel the other car that had been ordered by Carrie to pick up Cleve.

La Guardia Airport looks like every other godforsaken airport in North America. Steel and sterile. Airports are the loneliest places in the world in my view and my stomach cramped every time I got near one. Since the tragic events at the Twin Towers, airports are now the worst places on the earth. If you're dropping off a passenger, you barely have time to stop the car and unload them before the traffic cops are on your ass. Inside the airports, it's hell on earth thanks to Mr. Osama Bin Laden and his band of heartless murderers. So before we arrived at the airport, I told Lou that he could drop me at the arrivals area, and I would go in and meet Cleve. Lou could keep circling until we came back out.

Lou's eyes met mine in the rearview mirror and I could tell he was not happy with this plan.

"Can't we just circle and wait until he comes out? You can call him on his cell and tell him we're out here," he suggested.

"Lou, it's okay. Seriously. I will not get into any trouble inside the airport. I'll just go to the baggage area and wait for Mr. Johnston." I wanted to tell him not to be so over-protective, but that'd be like telling Joan Rivers to stop visiting the plastic surgeon.

"Okay Miss. Here. Take another one of my cards. You call me on the car phone as soon as he arrives and I'll pull up as quick as I can."

Surprisingly, the Air Canada flight was on time and it wasn't long before I saw Cleve in the surging crowd coming down the escalator to the baggage area. It wasn't hard to miss all six and a half feet of him, towering over everyone. He spotted me standing by the baggage carousel and winked. My heart melted just a little. Do we *ever* get over our crushes?

He was by my side in about six strides once he stepped off the escalator. He put his briefcase down and engulfed me in a huge bear hug. I hugged him back, my arms around his waist. There was no way I could reach his shoulders without a step stool.

"Good to see you Kate," he said. "It's a nice surprise to see you here."

"Well, I had nothing better to do," I lied. Truth be told I was desperate to talk with him. "If you're not too tired, I was hoping we could have dinner. I'm anxious to talk about all this crap."

"Sure, that's not a problem," he agreed. "Any place in particular that you want to eat?"

In the end, we had dinner at a steakhouse around the corner from his hotel. Cleve was booked into the New York Palace, the same hotel I had been staying at before I moved into Tommy's apartment.

The concierge at the hotel had assured me that we would have privacy at the restaurant when he made the reservation for us and I wasn't disappointed when the maître d' led us to our table. The lighting was subdued and all of the settings were banquettes. The restaurant wasn't overly busy.

We pushed ourselves into the banquette, both of us struggling with the seating because of our body types. Once our drink order had been given to the waiter, Cleve put his large hands in front of him on the table and said, "Okay Kate. Let's have it. What in the heck is going on?"

"I wish I knew, Cleve. Seriously. We are in deep shit and if we don't get some answers pretty soon, I'm not sure we'll recover from the potential disaster that's waiting for us." I was deadly serious, especially after my talk with Dr. Pritchard.

I brought Cleve up to speed on what had been going on. Told him about Tommy's computer and the hidey-hole in the apartment. Told him about the contents of the safety deposit box. Told him about how Jay had discovered the anomalies between the files from the office and the files in Tommy's office. Told him about the lovely Natalie Scott and her team. Gave him a very graphic description of how Belinda Moffat had shed buckets of body fluid during her crying jag. And ended by relating what Dr. Pritchard had told me that afternoon. During the course of my storytelling, our drinks had arrived, we ordered dinner, ate our meals and were now having coffee.

"Dr. Pritchard, bless his soul, is truly an amazing man. He told me that he had been a member of the team that had carried out the first successful kidney transplant in Boston in 1954. The doctor who was the head of that team, Dr. Joseph Murray, went on to win the Nobel Prize for medicine in 1990." I was getting off track. "Anyway, to put it mildly, Dr. Pritchard is some pissed with us."

"Can't blame him," Cleve said, "Assuming it's true what he says."

"He was pretty adamant that it was true. Kept insisting that what he had were facts, not allegations. I didn't argue with the man. He says that his man in charge of this project, Dr. Jordan Francis is no longer with Global Devices."

"Was he fired because of this mess?" Cleve asked.

"No, at least that's what Pritchard says. He said that he received Dr. Francis' resignation letter a few weeks ago and hasn't heard from him since. The resignation letter appeared on his desk a few days after they found out about the test results."

"What were the tests specifically for?" Cleve asked.

"They were clinical trials of the device that were carried out on a pig. They implanted the artificial kidney in the pig and our device, PISTON, the remote signaling piece, was monitored to make sure it was giving all the proper signals and data. The data that was gathered was not the data that was given to the FDA. I'm not entirely clear on how that was found out, or who discovered it, but Global Devices now have a black mark against them. Apparently, it's not considered kosher to fake results in medical tests," I said with just a tad of sarcasm.

"Dr. Pritchard said at first they were overjoyed that the tests had gone so well, that they were able to submit the devices for approval to the FDA. He said he was somewhat surprised, considering that they had run a bunch of these tests earlier and they had come up against several different problems every time. But suddenly, boom, everything's a go and everybody's happy, and the thing goes in for approval. The first Pritchard heard about this was a letter from the FDA. Addressed to Dr. Francis but it ended up on Pritchard's desk because Dr. Francis had already resigned."

"Did Pritchard say what Dr. Francis's explanation of all this was?" Cleve asked.

"He told me that he hasn't been able to talk to Dr. Francis. He's *incommunicado* so to speak. Pritchard said that a copy of an email between Dr. Francis and Tommy was found in one of Global's files dated a few days before Dr. Francis resigned. The email was vague but Dr. Pritchard said he was pretty certain that Tommy and Dr. Francis both knew what was going on."

"Does he think that Tommy was involved in this? The falsifying of records?" Cleve was indignant. He was very protective of his good friend.

"He implied as much," I told him. "The whole guilt by association. Tommy, and all of Phoenix by implication, are guilty in his mind, and hence he will not ever, ever do business with us again."

I sipped my coffee and craved a cigarette but we were in a non-smoking restaurant.

"But this doesn't explain how Natalie Scott knew and why no else found out," Cleve reminded me.

"Natalie Scott is involved with this somehow. Big time. She's responsible for research and development, and she's responsible for whatever transpired with Global. I hardly know her, but her name is stamped all over this God awful shit-pile. Her ass is so fired," I said.

"Who was the head of the team on this project?" Cleve asked.

"Nat Scott. This project was her baby, as everyone reminded me. She has every one of her team leaders shaking in their boots, afraid for their jobs. When she got the letter from Global, she threatened them all that if they mentioned it, they'd lose their jobs. That was a couple of weeks ago. Our dilemma is damage control. What do we do now Cleve?"

The stalker watched the restaurant, hidden in the shadows of a brick encased, arched doorway. Across the street from where the bitch *was having dinner. Going about her life with no worries. No problems. The* bitch *was getting in the way but the stalker would not let her stop the progress. Things that got in the way of progress were dealt with. The stalker's breathing was in control now because control was what it was going to take. Control over mind and over body. Control to see the project through to the end.*

Chapter thirty-five

WHILE WE WAITED FOR THE waiter to bring our bill, Cleve and I made a list of things that needed our focus. We agreed that he would deal with damage control with the lawyers, the regulators and the resultant press releases. I was tasked with getting in touch with the two detectives who were investigating Tommy's murder. The more we talked, the more we were convinced that Tommy's death was because of the Global Devices project. The detectives needed to be brought up to speed as soon as possible. It was two weeks to the day since Tommy was murdered and as far as I was concerned, there had been no progress on finding Tommy's killer.

"I called the detectives yesterday and left a message," I told Cleve. "I haven't heard back from them. This case clearly isn't their top priority. I'll get to them first thing tomorrow."

Which proved easier said than done. I was completely exasperated after leaving two voice messages each on the detectives' phones the next morning. So I put the phone wizard on the case. She reported back in about fifteen minutes.

"I called over to the 20th Precinct," Carrie told me. "No one was willing to give me any information on the whereabouts of either detective. So I called my dad, to get the phone number of his friend who plays first base on their softball team, who's a police officer in Brooklyn. He called the 20th Precinct for me and found out that Detective Bartlett is in the hospital with back problems. She has two herniated disks. Detective Shipley has been handling their case load on her own, and is out of town, upstate, investigating a tip they got on a three year old case." Carrie read all this information from her steno pad and when she finished she looked eagerly at me. "What else?"

"Well," I said, duly impressed with Carrie's information gathering talents. "Unless there's someone else handling Tommy's murder case, make sure that Shipley has my message to call. Say it's urgent, okay?"

Next on my list of things to do was to track down Natalie Scott and get some answers, direct from the horse's mouth, so to speak. The interoffice telephone directory gave me her phone number but when I dialed it there was no answer. No surprise there. She probably knew it was me calling and she was likely avoiding me. I decided to take the bull by the horns, and pay a visit to the research and development department.

The R and D folks were located on the floor below the executive offices. The area took up one quarter of the entire floor. In spite of all the natural light pouring in from the floor to ceiling windows, everything appeared dingy, dull and overloaded with paper, manuals, computers, printers, and pieces of equipment that were unrecognizable to me. Some desktops had two or three monitors sitting on them. It was a beehive of activity, but eerily quiet, the clicking of keyboards the only sound. Each person apparently had their own workstation, although it was difficult to discern the difference or dividing line between some areas. The amount of electronic equipment and paper was mind-boggling. I stood in the middle of the area and looked for a clue as to where Nat Scott might hang her hat. There was a lone, enclosed office on the far side of the floor, and I headed in that direction, sure that as a Vice President, Natalie would have an office with a door.

The door to the office was closed and outside, in an open area, a young woman sat at a secretarial desk which was pushed up against the wall to the office. Her back was to me as I approached the desk and she was bopping in her chair to the music which I could clearly hear coming out of earphones plugged into her ears. She was typing on her keyboard, keeping rhythm to the music. I walked around her desk and stood to the side, hoping she would pick me up in her peripheral vision, not wanting to startle her. She saw me and held up one index finger, the universal sign for *wait*. With a flourish of pretend drumming on the edge of her desk with her two index fingers, she finally looked up at me with a very big smile and removed the ear plugs.

"Hi," she said, apparently genuinely pleased to see me, judging by the smile that just didn't go away. Her short hair was jet black and cut severely, with one large mass hanging over the right side of her face. Not quite punk. She appeared to be in her late twenties.

"Hi yourself. I'm Kate Monahan." I held out my hand and she gave me a shake.

"Jenn. Jenn Ludlow. What can we do for you today Kate?"

"I'm looking for Natalie Scott. Is this her office?"

"Yep. You got it."

"Is she in?"

"Not sure."

Gawd, this was going to be painful. One question, one answer, at a time.

I thought I'd try a different angle. "Do you know if Miss Scott is in the office today?"

"Not sure," she repeated. "Door was closed when I got here and it hasn't opened. I'm not allowed to open her door when it's closed." She held up her index fingers and mimicked quotes in the air. "On pain of death, the boss tells me. Not sure if she's building something secret for NASA in there, but I'm sure not going to die finding out." She burst out laughing.

"Well, I really need to speak to her so should I just knock on the door?"

"Not supposed to do that either," Jenn said. "A door closed means no interruptions." Her voice went up an octave as she tried to imitate Nat Scott. "But, if I see her, I'll be glad to give her a message," she offered.

"Sorry," I told her. "I'm going to interrupt her." I raised my hand to knock on the door and Jenn jumped out of her chair and leaned across the desk to grab my arm.

"Please," she pleaded with me. "Don't do it."

Whoa, this was one weird set up, but I didn't want to get the girl in trouble. "Then go to the ladies room, and we'll pretend you weren't here. I'm new enough to the company, I can honestly say I didn't know the rule."

"Go right ahead then," Jenn said. "Promise though you won't tell I was here?"

"Promise," I assured her. She grabbed her purse and took off.

There was no response to my two loud raps on the door and when I tried the door knob, it wouldn't turn. It turned just fine when the security guard showed up about ten minutes later with a master key. Jenn had returned from the ladies room at this point and she was not happy that we were unlocking the door.

"A closed door means no interruptions," she told me again. "A *locked* door means don't come within ten feet of the door, even if the fire alarm is going off." Her eyes were wide and she seemed to be hyperventilating just a little as she told me this. Several employees in the area were standing up at their desks now, peering over the dividers and watching the action.

I took Jenn by the arm and led her a few feet away from the security guard who was standing there, like a bump on a log, just watching us. "It's okay Jenn. You won't get in any trouble for what I'm doing. I guarantee it," I told her.

"No one can guarantee my job," Jenn said. "That's what Nat tells all of us every day."

"Well, I can," I told her. "Seriously. Don't worry about it."

"She's right, you know." This from the security guard who was supposed to be out of earshot. "She *is* the new President."

Jenn looked at me, surprised. "You are?"

I nodded.

"Go ahead then. It's all yours." She waved me into the office with a flourish.

It ended up that Jenn was worrying for nothing. Because the office was empty. There was nothing in the office except a desk, a credenza, a two-drawer filing cabinet, a chair and a telephone. Bare, deserted, unoccupied. No trace of a human ever having inhabited the space. I stuck my head out the door and motioned to Jenn to join me. I also told the security guard that he could leave and thanked him.

Jenn stood in the center of the office with her hands on her hips and looked around. "Well, would you look at that," she said. "The rat has finally deserted the ship." She said this with a certain amount of pleasure in her voice.

"How long did you and Nat work together?" I asked her.

"Ha! Work *together*? *Together*?" she repeated. "Together implies a team. We were never a team, and she never let me, or most of the people in this department forget that. We worked for *her*." Her voice was wavering just a little bit when she finished, and she turned toward the window. I could see her taking a deep breath.

She turned back around and faced me. "Kate. Can I call you Kate?" I nodded. "Good. Kate, I hope she rots in hell. There. I said it. And I mean it. She didn't deserve to work here. And ever since she started boffing the boss, she's been worse. Gawd, what did that man see in her?"

My thoughts exactly!

"When was the last time you saw her in the office, Jenn?"

"What's today? Wednesday? Yeah? She was here on Monday morning. A regular *team* meeting. Hah! I guess I haven't seen her since."

"You didn't think it was strange that two days have gone by and you haven't talked to her or seen her?"

"Nope." Jenn shook her head. "Sometimes I'd go weeks and never see her. She worked weird hours. Heard sometimes she'd come in and work all night. I'd get emails from her time stamped three in the morning. Whee!" She jumped up a little bit and the smile I'd seen earlier was back. "She's gone. The wicked witch of the west has flown the coop. I used to think she looked just like Margaret Hamilton."

"Margaret Hamilton?" I didn't get the reference.

"The woman who played the Wicked Witch of the West in the Wizard of Oz. She and Nat Scott had the same nose."

I had to agree.

Chapter thirty-six

My next stop was a visit with our in-house security manager. His office was on the same floor as Nat Scott's but on the opposite side. Jenn Ludlow showed me the way to his office, chatting a mile a minute as she weaved her way around the maze of workstations, loads of crap on the floor, and quietly working staff members.

"What do you think it means?" she asked me. Without waiting for an answer, she kept chatting. "I think it means she's left the company." Duh. "Nothing in her office. Everything gone. What did she do with all the files in there?" Good question, I thought. "How did she get everything out of the office?" Another good question.

We had arrived at the other side of the floor, where there were several glassed-in offices along the wall. The walls of the offices were made of glass brick that obstructed the view into the offices, but allowed the light from the windows to seep through. Jenn stopped in front of one that had its door open and she poked her head inside.

"You're here Kelly? Good. Kate needs to talk to you." She put her hand on my shoulder and said in a whisper, "You need anything, you call me. Okay Kate?" I nodded to my new best friend.

"I'll do that. Thanks Jenn." She walked off, bouncing to the internal music in her head, with a wide smile plastered on her face.

Kelly was standing when I entered his office and he walked around his desk to greet me. "Hi, Ms. Monahan, I'm Kelly Northland." Kelly spoke with a soft southern drawl. I wasn't sure if it was Georgia "south" or Texas "south" because my ear wasn't attuned to American accents.

We shook hands and he offered me a chair in front of his desk. Kelly appeared to be in his late thirties, early forties and he was what you would describe as wiry. Probably no taller than five foot seven or eight, with not an extra ounce of fat on his trim body. His hair was curly, grey and cut very short on the sides. He had great posture and I guessed he was ex-military.

I made a snap decision not to trust him. Not that he gave me any initial reason for that decision, but I was finding out the hard way that not every employee at Phoenix was loyal and trustworthy. From this moment on they were all going to have to earn their way with me. The fact that we had never met but he knew who I was, was only a wee bit disconcerting, because if he was in charge of security, he would know who I was at this point in the game.

"So," Kelly started. "Are you here about the mess with Global?" He was either a mind reader or very well plugged in.

"Yes," I told him. "There are a few things I'd like to discuss with you. First off, why don't you tell me a little about yourself." I was going to sit back and get to know these people.

Kelly Northland was all business. He didn't balk at my request to talk about himself, and he didn't glorify himself in the telling.

"Been with Phoenix for almost five years now," he told me. "Before that I was a Marine. Served twenty years in the Corps as a Military Police Officer."

Ah, I thought. A meathead. At least that's what we called the MP's, or military police, in the Canadian army.

"Got interested in doing corporate security work the last few years I was with the Corps. Was stationed at headquarters in Arlington and then got promoted to Staff Sergeant and worked as an investigator at NCIS. That's the Naval Criminal Investigation Service. Some of the work we did was with the civilian authorities. So when I took retirement after twenty years, I decided I wanted to get out of policing and into protection. That's how I ended up here. I consider myself lucky, ma'am. Tom Connaught was a good man, and I'm damn sorry about what happened to him."

He finished without a flourish. Kind of reminded me of that detective in the old TV show, Dragnet. Joe Friday. Just the facts, ma'am. A man of few words.

"Tell me about security here at Phoenix, Kelly. What do we protect and how do we do it?" I asked him.

"Well, our mantra is to protect our people and our assets. On the people side of things, we make sure that everyone coming to work here has a background check done on them. Lots of our work is with government agencies, so those people need more in-depth security clearances. Government's coming out with more onerous requirements soon on background checking and security clearances, thanks to Mr. Bin Laden. On the asset side, we protect our proprietary property. That includes our patented technologies, our source codes, our software development stuff. We don't own any buildings or much of anything on the physical side, save and except for computers. But we do have a lot of money invested in our technology. So our job is to protect that technology and the designs and software work that goes into it. And with the way technology is advancing these days, it's a moving target. Our biggest threats right now are hackers and cyber terrorism."

"How many staff do you have?"

"It's me and four others. That's it. But a lot of our work is done from our desks. We're well-connected all over the world."

"Okay. Tell me what you know about the mess with Global." I sat and stared at him, with my hands on my lap.

"What I know, I heard from Russ Freeson. He called me late yesterday and filled me in. Told me that Global had cut ties with us. Told me that Natalie Scott didn't let anyone know about it. That's it."

"Did you know that Nat Scott has vacated the building?"

"Not sure what you mean. She comes and goes at very odd hours, so I'm not sure that I'd know whether she had vacated or not."

"Well, I just came from her office. And it's empty. The only thing in there is a desk, a chair and a phone."

His eyebrows went up, just a little. I'm pretty sure he was surprised to know that. He didn't say anything.

"Any idea when she packed up and left?" I asked.

"No ma'am. This is news to me." He looked a little perturbed. "Can you give me a few minutes to look into this?"

"Sure. Come and see me in my office." I stood up to leave. "And bring me the background checks on Nat Scott and all of her team leaders."

When I got back to my office I asked Carrie if Cleve Johnston had arrived. She told me he had been there for about an hour and he was working in one of the boardrooms down the hall.

He was on the phone when I opened the door but he waved me in. The round boardroom table was strewn with newspapers and files, two empty coffee cups, and a plate with half a muffin, some grapes and an apple core. The small credenza against the wall had a coffee urn and a tray of breakfast goodies. I helped myself to a coffee and waited until Cleve got off the phone.

"Morning Kate," he said as soon as he hung up.

"Morning Cleve. Looks like you got right down to work." I nodded at the mess on the table.

"Lots to do. And I brought some work from Toronto. I hadn't planned on coming to New York, so I brought some files with me. Some of my clients expect round the clock service."

We spent the next hour in a meeting. Cleve had asked Carrie to gather the executive management team for an urgent meeting. Barry Golden, the lawyer from Cleve's New York office had been asked to attend as well.

When we arrived in the main boardroom, the silence was deafening. The tension in the room was palpable. Steve Holliday and Mark Hall were doodling on papers in front of them, Sandra Melnick was staring at the wall. No one was talking and no one was looking at the person next to them or across the table from them. Needless to say, Nat Scott's absence from the table was noticeable. Barry Golden was the one face I didn't recognize so I walked over to where he was sitting and introduced myself.

"Barry, Kate Monahan." He stood up and we shook hands. Barry was medium-sized, with a bit of age on him. Part of the age was showing in his middle, which was thick and he had a bit of a paunch. He hid it well though in a tailored, double-breasted suit. His hair was snow white and well cut. "Thanks for joining us. I'm sure Cleve has filled you in and I think you'll get the flavour of the problem shortly." Barry nodded and sat back down quietly.

Sitting beside him was Terry-Lynn Jacobsen, our in-house counsel. Although she wasn't a member of the executive management team, Cleve thought it was important that she be at the meeting. Terry-Lynn was sitting hunched in her chair, staring with her head down at her notebook. Her face was covered by her thin, stringy, badly permed, chin-length hair. I had never met her but Carrie had told me a couple of days ago to be quiet around her. Apparently she scared easily and was very self-conscious of a large strawberry-coloured birthmark that covered her left eye and part of her left cheek. She didn't look up at me so I decided not to introduce myself. If she scared easily, she wouldn't want to be around me. Apparently she was a wizard at patent law (yawn, bore) and that's why Tommy had hired her. The types of problems we were about to talk about fell outside her area of expertise, but still, she was in-house counsel.

I sat at the head of the table and looked around. No one was watching me and all heads were down. A sign of guilt perhaps? I hoped to hell not. One bad apple in the barrel was enough for me. I took a deep breath and told myself to remain professional, remain calm, and above all, remain in control.

"So, as you may have heard, we've got some problems we need to deal with a-sap. You all know Cleve Johnston. He's brought his partner Barry Golden with him. Barry works at the New York office of McCallum and Watts." I took another deep breath. "You all know that Nat Scott isn't here. I just came from her office downstairs, which has been cleared out. There's not a sign of her in R and D." With that revelation, everyone was now looking at me. Even Terry-Lynn.

"We're trying to ascertain when it was that she left. Anyone here got any idea?" No takers. "When was the last time any of you talked to her?"

Sandra Melnick, our VP of Operations offered that she hadn't seen Natalie for days. That pretty much jived with everyone else's memory as well.

"Well, apparently, several weeks ago, Nat Scott received notice from Global Devices that we were to cease and desist all work on their products. Was anyone aware of that?"

Every head around the table shook in the negative. Mark Hall, the Vice President of Sales put his head in hands and I was pretty sure I heard him moan.

"Mark, you okay?"

He looked up at me, closed his eyes and nodded. Grim. I took this as a yes, and pressed on.

"So, we need to do some damage control. That's why Cleve and Barry Golden are here. Barry's got some familiarity with the SEC and hopefully we'll be able to finesse the fact that we haven't disclosed this information. Yet."

Barry spoke up. "First off Kate, this is for everyone in the room," he glanced around the table. All eyes immediately focused on Barry and everyone was paying attention now, because having the riot act read to you by a high-priced securities lawyer was the same thing as having your grandmother grab you by the earlobe. You listened. It might be painful, but you listened.

Barry had a voice that commanded attention and he continued, "As of right now, everyone in this room refrains from trading in any shares of Phoenix. We're all in possession of material information and until that information is disclosed to the public, any trades would be considered illegal."

All heads around the table were nodding, some in acknowledgement and one nodding as if to say, "tell me something I don't know".

"I'll need a record of any shares you, or anyone in your immediate family, may have bought or sold since the date the company was put on notice by Global Devices. I'd like that information right after this meeting." Everyone nodded. "Normally, you file your insider trading reports on EDGAR at the end of each month." EDGAR was the SEC's electronic document filing system that public companies used to submit reports and filings. "We'll need to let the SEC know if there have been any trades in this period. They'll look favourably on us if we put all our cards on the table."

"Okay so far?" he asked the room.

There was a chorus of yeps, yeahs, and okays around the table.

"Next thing we need to do Kate, is get a press release out on the wire. I'll work with your communications people on the drafting. We should have something worked up this morning. As soon as we get it drafted, and ready to release, I'll call over to the Enforcement Division at the SEC. Cleve and I'll go over there and fill them in on what's happened. It should be no big deal, as far as they're concerned. The law says we have an obligation to disclose to the public on a rapid and current basis. This'll be rapid because we'll send out the release as soon as the markets close today. As for it being current, well, we'll have to take the position that we have only just found out. Which is true."

Cleve jumped in at this point. "One of our partners in Toronto will be visiting the Ontario Securities Commission Enforcement Branch at the same time as Barry and I are visiting the SEC."

Cleve and Barry's plans made me feel a little more at ease. "Sounds like a plan," I told them. "Thanks. Barry, you and Steve Holliday might want to get started on that release." Steve stood up to leave and Barry was right behind him. Cleve left to make some phone calls and I was left alone with the others.

It was a pretty small executive team when you boiled it down. With Nat Scott out of the picture and Steve off drafting press releases, I was left with Russ Freeson, our chief financial officer, Mark Hall, our VP of Sales, and Sandra Melnick, our VP of Operations. Terry-Lynn was looking forlorn and lonely so I thanked her and sent her on her way.

"So. Here we are." I clasped my hands together on the table and looked at the three of them. "What a fucking mess." Mark audibly moaned again and I knew then that I wasn't going to be able to count on him when the chips were down.

"Mark, are you okay?" I demanded.

He nodded. "I guess I'm just tired. Been putting in some long hours ever since Tommy passed." He held up his hand. "But I'm okay. Really. Just gotta tough it out and look on the positive side." There was a catch in his voice and I wondered if he was going to break down. This was not a good time for one of the executives to curl up in a fetal position under his desk.

"Good," I told him in my cheeriest voice. "Right now we've got to do some *major* damage control."

"First off," I announced, "we need someone to take over R and D for the interim. That's a lot of staff without a boss, and a few of the team leaders are pretty ineffectual, I've been finding out. So they're rudderless. Any volunteers?"

I watched Sandra look pointedly at both Russ and Mark. "I'm in," she told me. "Russ has enough to do with counting the beans, and Mark needs a nap." Mark's head snapped up at this snarky remark but I gave Sandra credit. "Besides, I know more about the R and D side of things."

"Thanks," I told her. "We need to sit down and figure out what we're going to tell the staff. We probably need Steve's help with that too. We should send something out to the staff at the same time as we let the press release go."

"Russ, what are the numbers on this?"

"Not good," he said. "The total loss of revenue will be close to $40 million. We'd already billed and been paid for about $60 million worth of work over the last couple of years. And that's not counting the potential other work we could've got from Global."

"Okay team. Let's divide and conquer. There's plenty of work to go around. And Mark." He looked at me. "There's no time for a nap." This time his moan could be heard all around the room.

Chapter thirty-seven

CARRIE TOLD ME THAT KELLY Northland was waiting for me in my office and sure enough there he was, sitting ramrod straight in one of the guest chairs, with a stack of files on his lap.

"Let's sit at the working table," I said, "and you can show me what you've got."

It was early in the day but I was feeling tired and familiar feelings of being overwhelmed hovered. I was determined to keep those feelings under control. Before joining Kelly at the large work table, I walked around my desk and shrugged off my suit jacket, hanging it on the back of my chair. I ignored an urge to light a cigarette and got focused on the job at hand.

"Okay, Kelly, sit rep," I ordered. His eyebrows shot up at the familiar, military talk, and a little smile played on his stern face. My dad would demand a sit rep anytime he needed information on what was going on. Sit rep for situation report, gimme the details, don't leave anything out, and make it quick.

"Your dad was military," he said.

I looked at him, not sure if he was asking a question or stating a fact.

"Career infantry soldier," Kelly continued. "Served with NATO in Germany and the U.N. in the Sinai. Finished up his career with the Airborne." Kelly rattled off these facts easily and now my eyebrows shot up. I guess it would be easy to check my background and Kelly was proving that he was doing his job. So I nodded to let him know he had the correct facts on my father.

"I followed up on Natalie Scott's move out of the office. Security cameras show that she moved out of here two nights ago," Kelly said.

"Two nights ago, and all of this was on security cameras? Did anyone think to say something?"

"No ma'am. We don't monitor what our cameras see. They're only there to record what's going on and if there's an incident, we can play back the tapes. We're only a tenant in this building, so we rely on the building landlord's CCTV system, which is monitored. They have a security office on the second floor, where guards monitor the cameras. Their tapes say the same as ours. Two nights ago, around four in the morning. Natalie Scott is on tape, leaving our offices and going to the parking garage in the basement of this building. She made three trips, each time carrying a large banker's box. Once she had those boxes loaded in her car, she left the building."

"And security didn't think this was unusual, someone making repeated trips to their car, loading it up with boxes?"

"Not at all, ma'am. Miss Scott was known to come and go at odd hours. Security didn't think anything of it. You see, they would have done something if they knew she had left Phoenix. When someone leaves, whether they're fired or they quit, we take away their access pass which gets them into the building and into our offices. And we let the building security know so they can keep an eye out. Miss Scott was not terminated and did not quit, as far as building security was concerned, so she had carte blanche to come and go as she pleased."

"But those boxes contained company property," I protested.

"That's right, ma'am," Kelly agreed with me. "But employees take company property out of the office everyday. Lots of them work at home or at client's work sites. And, as far as I'm concerned, Natalie Scott is still an employee of the company. Isn't she?"

Jesus Christ this was frustrating. Cleve had advised me at dinner last night to hold off doing anything about Natalie until more facts were known. He told me that I needed to talk to her and get her side of the story before I ran off, half-cocked. That's why I ended up at her office this morning and why I was having this conversation with Kelly.

"Yes. She is." I wanted to stamp my feet like an eight year old who wasn't getting her way. I pushed back my chair from the table and fetched a cigarette from the bottom drawer of my desk.

As I smoked I stared at the traffic on the street below. Total gridlock. Typical at lunchtime in Manhattan as I was finding out. A sea of yellow cabs as far as I could see. I turned around and looked at Kelly who was still sitting, ramrod straight, at the work table.

"Well, I guess I'll just have to track Ms. Scott down at home and pay her a visit," I said.

"I wouldn't advise that ma'am."

"And why not, Mr. Northland? She hasn't returned any calls or emails. I think the next thing to do would be to go to her home and talk to her."

"Like I said," Kelly drawled, "not recommended. I don't trust the woman. Allow me to try and contact her."

"I'm quite capable you know Kelly." He was being just a little patronizing in my view and this whole conversation was getting me no-where.

"Yes, ma'am."

"And stop calling me ma'am," I demanded.

"Yes, ma'am," he smiled. "I know you're capable. But you've also been known to barge into situations and put yourself at risk. You're damn lucky that bullet only grazed the top of your ear. And you're damn *unlucky* to be living in a posh building right now that has an eighty year old man as its only security."

Okay, so Kelly had done more that a little bit of background checking on me. He knew about my run-in with that demented pile of shit in Toronto who shot me. And somehow, he knew about the security set-up at Tommy's, correct that, *my* apartment.

"What do you mean, the only security in my building is an eighty year old man?" I asked. "There's got to be more than that."

"Really? And after you got knocked out on one of your first visits to Mr. Connaught's apartment, did the building management offer to check security tapes to see if anyone had accessed the service entrance? Did they say they could check their logs to see who was in and out of the building? If they had logs, they'd have known if your friendly neighbour, Natalie Scott, was at home when you got hit over the head. The security in that building is non-existent."

Mr. Northland had been doing his homework and had not missed the fact that Natalie Scott lived in the same apartment building. But why was I only meeting him now? If Phoenix had security staff who were on the ball, maybe I wouldn't be sitting here right now. Maybe Tom Connaught would be sitting here, in his chair, at his desk, running his company.

"Where the hell have you been the last two weeks?" I demanded. "Were you going to point *any* of this out to me or just sit on your tight little Marine ass in your office downstairs?" My voice was raised by the time I finished.

"Ma'am, with all due respect," he started but I cut him off.

"Don't *ma'am* me," I shouted. "I'm running around like a crazy woman, trying to find out what happened to Tommy, and you've got information that may be relevant and you're sitting on it?"

Get a grip, Kate, I told myself. I butted my cigarette angrily in the ashtray on the windowsill, turned my back to Kelly and stared at my reflection in the window. In through the nose, out through the mouth. Deep breaths. Calming breaths. I have to stop losing my temper so easily, I thought.

I turned back around with my arms wrapped around myself and faced Kelly.

""Sorry," I said. Kind of. "Sorry for yelling. But seriously, why haven't you come forward before this?"

"With all due respect, Ms. Monahan, Mr. Connaught did not allow me to provide any sort of executive protection. He didn't let us do any snooping on the industrial espionage side of things either. He never asked more of us than to do background checks on employees and make sure the technology was safe. In my view, he was pretty naive about some things. You don't know why he was murdered, and the police have no clue either. I can't help but think he got himself into a situation that could have been avoided, had he thought it through. If he had come to me, maybe I could have helped." He paused. "With all due respect, *ma'am*, I'm not about to allow anything like that to happen again on my watch."

Kelly Northland was a military man, through and through. Just like any good soldier, he reverted to his training, even when given certain latitudes. All women who ranked above him in a traditional and military sense, were to be addressed as "ma'am". I was his superior in this situation and would henceforth and forevermore be known as ma'am. I'd have to live with it.

Chapter thirty-eight

"SO WHEN WERE YOU GOING to come and talk to me?" I demanded.

"When I felt you were in danger, or when I had any news that I felt was important."

When he felt I was in danger? What the fuck did that mean? How would he know if I was in danger? The only way he would know that I *hadn't* been in danger was if he had been watching me. For the last two weeks. I pointed at the door to my office.

"Out," I demanded. "Get out of my office. You've been following me and watching me. That not only creeps me out, it's a little whacked." Kelly stood up and headed for the door. My head was spinning and I was a little freaked out.

He quietly closed the door when he left and I knew what I had to do.

Mom wanted to chat but I was too distracted to fill her in on any news. I needed to talk to my dad.

When my father came on the phone I explained that I needed him to check into someone for me. Even though he was retired from the Canadian military, he was still connected and could make things happen.

"Kelly Northland. Says he was in the Marines, retired five years ago. Worked at their headquarters near the end of his career and then transferred to NCIS. He was a meathead."

"Got it. You stand by and I'll get back to you asap." I loved the way he said that. Not A-S-A-P. A-sap.

"I don't trust this guy dad," I told him.

"Okay Kathleen. I understand. I'll call my sources. Might take a couple of hours."

A little tit for tat, I figured. The checkee is going to do a little checking on the checker.

"You sure everything's okay there?" he asked. "What's this all about anyway?"

"Dad, everything's fine. Just make those calls, okay?" I made sure he had my office number before we hung up.

When Kelly had left my office, the files he had brought with him stayed behind. They were in a pile on my work table and while I waited for my lunch, I took a look. There was a file for Natalie Scott and each of her team leaders.

Papers were clipped to both sides of the files when you opened them up. On the left side was a copy of a form, several pages long. The form had the Phoenix logo on the top left side and the logo of INTELLI-Guide on the right side. INTELLI-Guide must be the company we used to carry out the background checks. On the right side of the file were copies of the employee's offer letter, resume, letters of reference, and a couple had hand-written note summaries of reference checks carried out by telephone.

The INTELLI-Guide forms asked for employee information going back fifteen years for residential addresses, twenty years (if applicable) for employment history, all educational institutions attended (even if a degree or diploma was not granted), birth, death and marriage/divorce dates for all immediate relatives (mother, father, children, brothers, sisters, grandparents, grandchildren, brothers-in-law, sisters-in-law). The form had more boxes on it than an income tax return and went on for pages.

I started reviewing the files of each of the R and D team leaders. Mr. Tight Ass Marine had piled them in alphabetical order so the first one I checked was Derek Hutton. I remembered him as the quiet one from that first, dreadful meeting with the R and D team. His file told me that he was four years older than me, he had been working at Phoenix for the last seven years, and he had *two* Masters degrees, one in computer science and one in biomedical engineering from the University of Arizona. Very impressive. Derek was married, had three children, and lived in Brooklyn. He had moved to New York four years ago from Phoenix, where he had worked for the company. The file said he joined the company right out of University.

Belinda Moffat's file contained a lot of the same type of information, but just to up the ante in my catalogue of *impressive*, Belinda had a Ph.D in medical engineering from MIT, the Massachusetts Institute of Technology. Wow. She had worked for us for three years. Her father and mother were both deceased, she had twin sisters who were ten years younger than her, and three brothers, all older. I remembered her telling me about the twin sisters and how she was responsible for their care. Belinda lived in Queens.

Nat Scott's file gave me all the basic information and nothing extra. I was hoping to find something buried which would lead me to an *ah ha* moment but I was out of luck. She was another highly educated member of our team, with a Masters degree in Biochemistry from the University of North Carolina Wilmington, and a Ph.D in the same thing from the City University of New York. I knew where she lived and wasn't at all surprised to see that she had been at the same address for most of her life. Her father died over twenty years ago and her mother was apparently still alive when Nat filled out the application form four years ago. She was an only child, which explained why she acted like a spoiled brat, and had only ever worked for our company. Four years with the company, right out of graduate school and already she's a Vice President?

I was just opening Dan Thornton's file when Carrie stuck her head in the door and told me that my dad was on the phone. Singing to her.

"Yeah, sorry about that Carrie," I apologized. "He can't help himself."

"I loved it. He asked me if I knew the song Stardust and I told him I did so he sang it to me." She was smiling as she left the office.

"Dad, stop harassing the staff," I teased him when I answered the phone.

"Harassing the staff? I doubt that. Everyone loves my singing." He was chuckling.

"So? Do you have anything for me?" I asked him.

"I do. Your Mr. Northland is okay. He checks out." I felt a little bit better at that news. "Trusted by the brass, even though he was a meathead. Worked his way up, retired as a staff sergeant. My guys tell me he was known as a hard worker who always got the job done. Thorough. Didn't cut corners. Did everything by the book."

"That's good to hear," I told him.

"You in some sort of hot water?" dad asked me.

"Not at all," I lied. "Just getting to know the people here. He manages our security department."

"Did Tommy hire him?"

"As far as I know he did."

"Then he's got to be okay." Dad had always been head over heels in admiration of Tommy and never quite got over the fact that our marriage didn't work. "Tommy would never have hired someone he didn't trust." Dad sounded so sure of himself.

"You call me then if you need anything else," he said, hanging up abruptly. Dad was not one for long phone conversations. Unless he was in the mood to sing a medley of Perry Como songs to you.

Kelly Northland was sitting in a guest chair outside my office when I went to ask Carrie to call him.

"Have you been sitting here for the past hour?" I asked him.

"Yes ma'am. Figured I wouldn't go far because you'd be wanting to talk to me sooner than later." He stood up.

"Well come on back in."

We sat in the same places at the table and Kelly couldn't help but notice that I had been going through the files. They were strewn about the table, not in a neat alphabetical pile, Marine-style. With hospital corners.

His eyes met mine, square on, across the table and he waited for me to speak first.

"Apparently, you are trustworthy. I have it on good authority," I told him. He nodded. "I needed to find out about you for myself, by myself," I explained.

"No need to explain. You did the right thing."

"You're not off the hook yet, Staff Sergeant." He smiled at my mention of his previous rank. "I want to know what you've been up to the past two weeks." I sat back and waited for his explanation.

"I've been watching out for you ma'am. Lou, your driver, keeps me posted on your whereabouts as best he can. He sure doesn't like it when you go off on your own." That explained why Lou had conniption fits every time I sent him home early.

Kelly continued. "After I heard about you getting mugged at Mr. Connaught's apartment, I made sure your back was covered at all times." I wasn't sure how I felt about this explanation. In fact, I found myself getting angry again.

"Did you have me followed?" I demanded. Kelly nodded his head. Son of a bitch. What else had he done?

"Did you put bugs or listening devices in my apartment?"

"No ma'am!" he said, quite indignantly. "I'm just watching your back. I would never invade your privacy by listening in on conversations or anything like that. It's my job to protect our employees and you are our number one employee."

"Okay," I told him reluctantly. "I don't know whether I should be grateful or not."

I leaned over the table a little towards him and whispered, "Do you carry a gun?" You know, being a Canadian in the country where every four year old can cite the Second Amendment to the Constitution, was a little intimidating. And I'll admit to being a teensy bit tainted by Hollywood and all those gun-toting 'Mericans.

"Yes ma'am, I do," he told me.

"Okay, Kelly." I sat for a few moments and thought about the whole situation. There were only two people who knew everything that I did about Tommy, Global Devices, and where we stood today - Jay and Cleve. I wondered if it was time I brought someone else into the picture. If I did that I would have to open my kimono for someone I had only met that morning. Someone who allegedly was 'looking out for my back'. How was I to know if he was trustworthy? Based on my dad's recommendation and report, I should be good to go, but I was a little gun shy these days, excuse the pun. Admittedly, I was finding it hard to trust people ever since the murder of my best friend Evelyn, and the events that happened after that.

I made up my mind quickly then to push on. I needed all the help I could get. It had been two weeks since Tommy's murder and our company was in a crisis.

"We need to start working together on this mess," I told Kelly. "You said you were an investigator at NCIS?"

He nodded.

"Good. Time to dust off those skills."

Chapter thirty-nine

THE NEXT WHILE WAS SPENT bringing Kelly up to speed. Just like I had with Cleve the night before. Only this time, Kelly interrupted and asked questions. And, he took copious notes. When I finished my narrative covering the last two weeks, we sat in silence for a few minutes. I had no idea what Kelly was thinking about, but I was a little relieved to be sharing the burden of all this information with him. If he had experience in law enforcement and was trained as an investigator, maybe now we'd start tying up all the loose ends of information we had.

I broke the silence. "So Kelly. What do you think?"

"I think this is a lot of information all at once. I'd like a couple of hours to think this through."

He gathered up the R and D team leader's files. "First thing I'm going to do is pass these off to one of my team. Have them do some deep background checking. I'll also pull the files on all staff who've worked on the Global Devices projects. Do some checking there too. Then I'm going to touch base with some of my contacts at NYPD."

I asked him if he knew Detectives Bartlett and Shipley.

"No ma'am." He shook his head. "But I did ask around about them. They're both supposedly solid cops."

This didn't make me feel any better about the lack of progress on Tommy's case. They may be solid but they weren't getting any results.

Carrie stuck her head in the door and interrupted us. "Ms. Monahan, there's a call on your line that I think you may want to take."

"Who is it Carrie?"

"Dr. Pritchard," she told me. "From Global Devices."

Well colour me surprised.

Kelly stood up. "I'll go then. I'll stay in touch."

I nodded my head but I wasn't really listening. Dr. Pritchard was on the phone, calling me. As nice as he was to me yesterday when I visited him unannounced, I was pretty certain I wouldn't be talking to him again, anytime soon.

I picked up the phone and hit the flashing light on the console.

"Kate Monahan."

"Miss Monahan," he said. "Bill Pritchard here."

"Yes, Dr. Pritchard. How are you today?" I asked.

"Confused, worried, and frankly, just a little overwrought," he told me.

His use of the old-fashioned word overwrought had me a little puzzled. As far as I knew it meant really upset, but his tone of voice was fairly calm.

"Well, I'm sorry to hear that, Dr. Pritchard," I told him.

"Not your place to be sorry, Miss Monahan. Although I have stated that Global Devices will have nothing more to do with your company, I seem to be plagued with some lingering after-effects."

You and me both, Mister, I thought. Like a shortage of about $50 million in revenues. I bit my tongue.

"Some disturbing news has come to my attention since we last talked Miss Monahan," he continued, "and I wish to speak with you about it."

"That's fine Dr. Pritchard. What can I do for you?"

"I don't wish to discuss it over the telephone. Would you be available at the end of the day?"

"I am. Shall I come to your office?" I offered.

"No, this is a subject to be discussed over a fortifying beverage. Can you meet me at the Blue Square Tavern?"

We agreed on six o'clock. Apparently, the Blue Square Tavern was close to his office and Dr. Pritchard was sure I would have no trouble finding it.

I spent the next couple of hours doing things that apparently keep chief executive officers busy. Answering emails. Returning phone calls to bankers. Ignoring phone calls from analysts. Reading internal progress reports on projects and contracts. Trying to decipher government bulletins on taxation issues. Learning how to understand our internal financial statements. Sometime around four o'clock, I looked up from the monthly income statement to find Cleve Johnston standing in front of my desk, smiling at me.

"What? Geez, you scared me."

"Ah, you make me proud," he said.

"Oh shut up," I shot back.

"Look at you," he teased. "Working like a big shot executive." He helped himself to one of the chairs in front of my desk.

"Yeah, some big shot executive. I'm sure it's taking me ten times longer to get through this stuff than an experienced executive."

"Don't sell yourself short, Kate," he told me.

"So, what are you here to tell me?" I asked him.

"That all's well. The folks at the SEC tell us that so long as we issue the press release today when the markets close, we should be okay. Barry gave them the background and it helped that we produced the information on all insider stock trades for the past month or so. I've heard basically the same thing from our guy in Toronto." He smiled. "Although he did tell me that the people he met at the OSC were not very friendly, and that he felt the temperature drop in the room when your name was mentioned."

My stomach dropped. "Don't tell me. Missy?"

He nodded. "The one and only."

Missy Goodman, or Melissa as she preferred to be called, was the lawyer I had worked with many years ago at Scapelli's, who had eventually left the private practice of law and gone to work at the Ontario Securities Commission. The one who I had told to fuck off one day in front of lots of people. I had totally forgotten that she was at the OSC when Cleve told me someone from his office would be meeting with them.

"Tell me that everything's okay with the OSC and Missy isn't holding a grudge against me." For embarrassing her in front of all those people. Not that she didn't deserve it.

"We got the same reaction from them as we did from the SEC. You've seen the press release?" Cleve asked me.

I nodded. "Signed off on it a little while ago and sent it back to Steve Holliday. It's supposed to be released when the stock markets close today." I looked at my watch which told me it was past 4:15 p.m. "Which should be any time now."

The press release was a dry piece of work, stating that our business relationship with Global Devices had been terminated by Global, with an estimate of the loss of revenues. I fully expected that our share price would take a shit-kicking in the morning when the markets opened. I also expected that Steve Holliday was going to be busy taking calls from the financial press and pissed-off shareholders. He had been advised on what he was allowed to say, and that wasn't much. I was hoping that the press release would go unnoticed but that was probably naive thinking on my part. The last two weeks had seen enough upheaval at this company that anything coming over the wire on Phoenix would be picked up and picked at by a good financial reporter. It's not often they get to report on things other than price earnings ratios and cash flows. Although, all the heat in the press these days on Bernie Ebbers and the boys at WorldCom gave me faint hope that the reporters might be so busy chasing down another whistleblowing accountant that our news would go unnoticed.

The Blue Square Tavern was located on a side street near Bellevue Hospital, and Lou had no trouble finding it.

The Blue Square Tavern certainly lived up to its name. It was a tavern in the traditional sense, it was painted blue inside and out, and the interior was a large, square room. The only thing non-traditional about it was the large, no-smoking signs pasted everywhere. I found Dr. Pritchard sitting by himself in a large booth along the left wall. The right wall was taken up by a massive bar. Bar stools in front of the bar were full, as were most of the tables and booths. Surprisingly, the noise level was relatively low and the atmosphere was subdued.

Dr. Pritchard stood and offered his hand, and waited while I sat down before he took his seat again. We ordered a Diet Coke for me and he asked the waitress for a refill of whatever it was he was drinking. Idle chit chat took up the time while we waited for our drinks. He told me that the Blue Square Tavern was a favourite hang-out for the medical staff of the two nearby hospitals. Which would account for the non-smoking signs.

I looked around the room. "It's a pretty quiet place for a tavern," I said.

"It's suppertime for the doctors so most of them will be going back to work after they eat," he explained.

Dr. Pritchard got down to business as soon as the waitress brought our drinks. He plopped a large, brown envelope on the table and slapped the top of it with his hand. The slap contained a lot of emotion from a man who up until now had been the epitome of reserved, polite and in control of himself.

He took a long sip of his drink and placed the glass in front of him. The silence between us was deafening, and I could feel the blood pounding in my ears. I was waiting for a tongue-lashing even though I had no idea what this was all about. The man just had that type of persona. His presence alone made you sit up and pay attention. I wasn't sure if he was expecting me to say anything, so as hard as it was, I stayed silent.

After what seemed like an eternity, he said, "This envelope contains some disturbing material. I'm hoping that you'll be able to explain some of it." His tone was icy.

I kept my hands wrapped around my Diet Coke to keep them from grabbing the envelope and ripping it open. Dr. Pritchard had called this meeting which meant he got to say how things would unwind. I waited while he took a few deep breaths through his nose. Finally, he slid the envelope across the table towards me but I resisted touching it for the moment. I glanced at it quickly and saw that there was nothing written on the outside of the envelope.

"Why do you think I would know anything about the contents of the envelope?" I asked him in an even tone. I reserved snarky and bitchy for other folks who didn't make me feel eight years old.

"Open it," he demanded. "Open it and then we'll talk. I'll be back." He marched off towards the back of the tavern to the men's room, I presumed.

The envelope was a large one. Probably measuring fourteen by sixteen inches. I used one finger to slide it in front of me and I stared at it, willing it to disappear. Knowing it wasn't going away, and knowing that Dr. Pritchard would be back soon, I flipped the envelope over and tore at the flap, opening it. Inside was another large, brown envelope, with a white label pasted in the middle, addressed to Dr. Jordan Francis on West 97th Street in New York. There was no return address on the front of the envelope but in the upper right hand corner there was about three dollars worth of U.S. postal stamps. I couldn't read the date on the U.S. postal service stamp which was inked over top of the stamps. The envelope was cleanly slit open along the top. The materials inside the envelope were neatly ordered and clipped at the top with a black fold-back clip. A sense of relief and deja vu washed over me when I pulled out the papers and saw what they were.

Chapter forty

WHEN I REMOVED THE LARGE, black clip holding the stack of papers together, two distinct packages of papers were revealed. The smaller of the two was a copy of the "love letters" written by Nat Scott and the thicker pile was the same correspondence with the FDA that was in the file folder I found in Tommy's safety deposit box. My stomach stopped flipping with fright and I willed myself to calm down. These documents were no surprise to me, although why they were in an envelope addressed to Dr. Francis was a big question.

Dr. Pritchard slid back into the booth and took a quick sip of his drink. "You'll remember what we talked about yesterday," he said. I nodded. Of course I remembered. Dr. Pritchard had laid out for me the sequence of events that led to his team discovering that test results had been falsified. By Phoenix people. I was still disgusted at the thought and couldn't imagine how Tommy would be feeling.

Dr. Pritchard had some funny business going on at his place as well, because apparently work continued on the artificial kidney project for some time after the date of the letter from the FDA denying the pre-market application. Someone at Global had hidden or covered up this wee bit of news. That someone was obviously Dr. Jordan Francis, the head of the project. And that someone had stolen away into the night about four weeks ago. Dr. Pritchard had told me that he came to work one morning and found Dr. Francis' resignation letter on his desk. The resignation was totally out of the blue and Dr. Pritchard was shocked at the time. Until he uncovered what had been going on. It took him a couple of weeks, but he eventually found out that the reason the FDA had denied their applications was because of the falsification of test records. By Phoenix people. Global had immediately cancelled all work with Phoenix.

"Like many in my profession," Dr. Pritchard had told me yesterday, "I'm litigation adverse. Global Devices could have sued Phoenix over this, but I thought the most efficient way to deal with it was to cancel everything with Phoenix and to try and recoup our losses with another company."

"After you left last evening," he told me, "I found myself in Jordan's office. Nothing has really been touched since he left. He hasn't returned any phone calls and his resignation letter said that he was moving and that he didn't have a forwarding address." He sipped from his drink. "What's the word to describe all of this?" He looked at me, but I wasn't sure if he was expecting an answer, so I kept quiet. "We were such good work friends. We'd been together for so many years. This whole thing was out of the blue and so unexpected." He swirled the liquid in his glass and appeared lost in his thoughts.

"Surreal. That's it. Is that the right word?" he asked. I nodded my head, still silent.

"This whole thing is surreal," he continued. "Really, to think that Jordan could be involved with falsifying records. What happened to him?" Another question which I didn't believe I was expected to answer.

Dr. Pritchard hung his head and slowly shook it back and forth.

I felt horrible for Dr. Pritchard. "Had you known Dr. Francis long?" I asked him.

He raised his head and looked at me. "Known him? We had worked together for the last twenty-seven years. We were surgeons together and then moved to Global Devices together." He sighed. "I thought I *knew* him. But really, how much do we really understand and know each other? When something like this happens, all notion of your understanding of another human being goes out the window."

Dr. Pritchard looked around the tavern, held up his empty glass when he caught the waitress' eye and motioned for another one. He shook the ice around in the bottom of his glass and looked at me.

"You know, when I got Jordan's resignation letter I thought it was some sort of joke. When I realized it wasn't a joke, I was confused. But when I found out later on the reason for his resignation, it felt like I had been hammered in the stomach by a battering ram. I literally felt faint and like I had the wind knocked out of me."

The waitress arrived and exchanged his empty glass for a full one. He grabbed it and drank half of it, fortifying himself.

"I'm over the shock now. Meeting with you last night gave me renewed strength to get to the bottom of this." He put his glass down sharply on the table.

"I found this," he pointed at the envelope, "in Jordan's office last night. Taped to the underside of one of the drawers in his desk."

"It's not the first time I've seen these documents," I told him. "The exact same letters were in Tom Connaught's safety deposit box. Except, the love letters," I mimed quotes in the air when I said love, "were the originals." Dr. Pritchard looked a little surprised at this news.

"You've described this as surreal," I went on. "And I agree. I've known Tom Connaught for years and when I first arrived in New York two weeks ago after he was killed, someone told me that he and this Natalie Scott were a couple. I could hardly believe it, based on the few times I met her. She wasn't his type. When I found the letters in the safety deposit box it got me thinking that maybe they weren't meant for Tom. There is no way that Tom Connaught would be in a relationship with the person who wrote those letters. They're not addressed to anyone. Do you think they were meant for Dr. Francis?"

"Perhaps," he said. "Jordan has been a bachelor all these years. Never married, never had a serious girlfriend. Nothing makes sense to me anymore. The tone of the letters don't sound like the Miss Scott I've met and worked with. But you should know that I carefully went through all the letters to and from the FDA. I matched them to our files. And I'm almost certain some of the ones supposedly originating from Global Devices are forged. Those ones do not appear in our files."

My stomach sank at this news.

"Along with falsifying data, apparently your people felt it was okay to forge signatures on our letterhead." Dr. Pritchard's voice was slightly raised and I was surprised. Up until now he had been the picture-perfect gentleman.

My insides started boiling and I felt myself getting angrier by the minute. I gathered the papers sitting in front me, re-clipped them together, slid them back into the envelope and held the package in my hands.

"Dr. Pritchard, I *will* get to the bottom of this," I promised him. "Whatever is going on is affecting both of our companies." I pushed the envelope across the table towards him and stood up. "Thanks for the Diet Coke." I left him staring into the bottom of his glass.

Kelly Northland answered his cell phone before the first ring finished.

"Northland," he answered.

"It's Kate. Where are you?"

"At the office. What do you need?"

"I need to punch someone but that won't solve my problems. Can we meet? In an hour or so? At my apartment?"

"On my way," he said.

I told Lou to take me home. It had been a long fucking day and I was sure the evening wasn't going to be much better.

Dinner was on the stove, the fish were fed and there was a stack of clean laundry sitting on the end of the bed. Life on the home-front was blissful. Too bad I couldn't say it was the same at the office.

Jay was coming out of the shower as I was stripping off my office clothes, my gut wrenching control top pantyhose and cross your heart bra. Jesus, Mary and Joseph it was fucking uncomfortable being dressed for work. It felt almost sinful to put on an oversized pair of Jay's sweat socks, my sweat pants, and an extra large T-shirt. In fact, I felt practically naked with hardly a piece of polyester or cotton touching my skin.

I stuck my head in the open door of the ensuite bathroom and watched Jay towel dry his hair.

"We're having company," I told him. "Did you make enough dinner for an extra person?"

He dropped his towel and grabbed me in a tight bear hug. "Hello Kathleen," he said. "How was your day?" I slapped his bare ass and pushed him away, laughing. "I'll tell you all about my day as soon as you get dressed."

In the kitchen I checked our stock of beer in the fridge. Kelly Northland struck me as a beer drinker. There were several bottles of Canadian beer on the top shelf and I smiled, thinking about Americans drinking Canadian beer, and commenting that it tasted 'thick'. I remembered the old joke: what do making love in a canoe and American beer have in common? They're both fucking close to water.

We Canadians can be a little snobbish about our beer.

Chapter forty-one

KELLY WAS A GOOD SPORT and having Jay around while we talked business didn't faze him in the least. Of course, as I suspected, the Canadian beer helped. Kelly allowed himself one while we ate dinner at the breakfast bar in the kitchen. I had the feeling that he was a very controlled person, which you probably had to be if you had been a tight-ass Marine for twenty years.

After we finished eating, I got right down to business.

"Are your staff working on the background checks?" I asked him.

"Yeah," he said. "They're still at the office, doing a lot of phone work and digging deep. I'll have a report for you first thing in the morning on anything we might have dug up."

"Okay, I've got something I need you to do."

Kelly whipped out a pen and a small pad of paper from the inside breast pocket of his sports jacket. Ready to take notes like a good Staff Sergeant. I put my hand over the pad and pushed it away. "No notes," I told him. He clicked his pen shut and laid it neatly on the counter beside the pad.

"I want you to find Dr. Jordan Francis. He's the doctor who was involved with the artificial kidney project at Global. I think I told you that he had resigned his position and no one has heard from him since. I met with Dr. Pritchard today and he showed me an envelope full of documents that he found taped to the underside of a drawer in Dr. Francis' office."

I looked at Jay who was standing on the other side of the breakfast bar loading dirty dishes into the dishwasher.

"Guess what was in the envelope?" I challenged Jay.

"Oh that's an easy one," Jay said. He reached over the counter to take away my dirty plate and Kelly's. "The same thing that was in Tom Connaught's safety deposit box."

"Right you are Mr. Harmon. The envelope had copies of the letters from Nat Scott, which by the way I am no longer referring to as love letters. From now on they will be called stalker letters." Jay smiled at me. "The envelope also had copies of the letters from the FDA, denying Global Devices the pre-market applications. Dr. Pritchard told me that he had compared that stack of letters to his files and several appear to be forged. They don't exist in his files. So now we're not only accused of falsifying test data, we're forgers too."

I turned to Kelly. "Dr. Francis resigned over four weeks ago and no one has heard from him. His apartment is over on West 97th Street." I gave him the address. "Although in his resignation letter he said he was moving. I think we need to do a little checking on him. Do you have someone who can find him?"

"Let me make a call." He walked out of the kitchen into the living area.

"I think I might like him," I told Jay. "Although I wasn't too sure this morning when I met him. I had my dad check him out."

"Oh yeah? And what did he have to say?" Jay asked.

"Kelly checks out. Apparently a good guy. My dad said his sources gave him the thumbs up. I'm more comfortable with him now. Though he strikes me as a bit of a tight-ass."

Kelly picked that moment to walk back in the kitchen and I wondered if he'd overheard us. Before I could find out though, his cell phone started ringing. Kelly quickly grabbed it from where it was clipped on his belt. Kind of like a little gun. He flipped it open and answered it in one movement. "Northland." He listened for a moment and turned and walked back out of the kitchen into the living area.

"What's his military background?" Jay asked.

"He was a marine staff sergeant who retired a few years back. He was military police and spent some time at NCIS." Jay's eyebrows rose in a question mark so I clarified it for him. "Naval Criminal Investigation Service. Kelly was an investigator for them."

Kelly was sliding his cell phone into its holster when he came back into the kitchen.

"That was one of my guys who's been doing the background checks. Apparently there's more to the story on Ben Tucker than we thought."

"What do you mean?" I asked him.

"My guys have been going through the background histories of the people in R and D and checking the facts themselves. We're not relying on the facts in the INTELLI-Guide background information. He's come up against a few walls as he's been checking out Mr. Tucker's story. The first time he thought it was just a fluke. But the second, third and fourth time the facts didn't check out, the red flags were wavin'. So far, his education and work history are lies. He apparently had several previous jobs listed and none of them are true."

"How can that be?" I demanded. "How much do we pay this company to do background checks? Has anyone checked *their* background? Did your guys find discrepancies in any of the other files?"

"Not that I've heard so far," Kelly said. "I'll give INTELL-Guide the benefit of the doubt here, but if we find any more discrepancies, I have a feeling we'll be using another company after this to do our background checking."

"You're fucking right we will be."

"So my guy has stopped checking what Mr. Tucker put down on the file, and we're now starting a trace on him with other sources. It shouldn't be too long before we find out Mr. Tucker's true identity. Apparently his social security number is fake too."

"You have *got* to be kidding me," I fumed. Kelly's cell phone rang again and he disappeared into the living room to answer it.

"Well, he seems to be getting things done," Jay observed. He closed the dishwasher door and started wiping down the counters. I didn't understand how he could appear so calm. My insides were roiling and I was royally pissed. I grabbed my cigarettes and headed for the balcony. Mr. Chisel Jaw, Drop Dead Gorgeous Tucker was a phony and I couldn't even begin to fathom why he was employed at Phoenix. I wondered who had hired him and how much damage he had done since he'd been with the company.

Kelly joined me on the balcony before I was halfway through my cigarette. He referred to his notebook and told me, "His real name is Donald McLean. He spent time in one of the state prisons in Arizona. And he's a registered sex offender."

In spite of the humid evening air, I felt a little chilled, pacing up and back on the balcony. I cupped my hands against the windows and peered inside, where Kelly was sitting at the dining room table, at the far end of the apartment. The chandelier above the dining room table was the only light coming from that end of the apartment and straight ahead of where I was on the balcony, the apartment was in darkness except for a soft glow coming from inside the cubby-hole in the wall, where Jay was working on the computer. Even though I lived on one of the main streets of Manhattan, there was little sound coming from Fifth Avenue below me.

Kelly had been working the phones ever since he broke the news to me about Donald McLean, a.k.a. Ben Tucker. Jay was somehow helping out and doing some digging on different computer databases. Me, I felt useless, so I stayed out of the way, and chain-smoked on the balcony.

Things were spinning out of control as far as I was concerned. Nat Scott had vacated the premises, left her job and the company without a word to anyone. She might as well have sent a one-word email to everyone in the company: GUILTY. But what is she guilty of, I wondered. Tucker, one of our senior people in R and D turns out to be a felon. Was he involved with Nat Scott? Jordan Francis disappears. What did he do that was so bad he had to resign his position? Was he falsifying records? Was Natalie Scott guilty of the same thing? Did Ben Tucker - or Donald McLean, dammit - help Nat Scott? Did they kill Tommy because he figured it all out?

I was suddenly very conscious of the fact that Natalie Scott lived in the same apartment building. Was she not worried about running into me, seeing me in the lobby? She left Phoenix without so much as an email, a phone call or a kiss-my-ass. One could surmise that she had no desire to have any contact with anyone from Phoenix. Too fucking bad, I thought, as I stormed into the apartment and headed for the elevator. The front door to the apartment closed quietly behind me and I punched the button on the wall to call for the elevator.

The ride to go up six floors took less than a minute, hardly enough time for me to figure out what I was going to do or say when I confronted Nat. I was surprised when the elevator doors opened to see four apartment doors, each with a solid brass plaque mounted on the door with the apartment number. All the floors in the building were apparently not like mine, containing only one apartment. I stood and stared at the four doors and tried my Amazing Kreskin routine, trying to conjure up Nat Scott's image behind one of the doors. When that didn't work, I did the next best thing. I knocked on the door closest to me. And waited. When there was no response to my knock, I went to the door next to it and rapped.

I didn't have to wait long before the door opened a crack and I heard a voice.

"Hello?" The voice was elderly.

"Hello," I answered back. "I'm Kate Monahan, from the fourteenth floor." The door opened another half inch or so but I still couldn't see who was there.

"You don't live on the fourteenth floor, Miss, and I'm calling building security right now. Mr. Connaught lives on that floor."

"Oh, please, don't call security," I quickly pleaded with her. "Mr. Connaught is my ex-husband. I'm living in the apartment now."

The door opened about six inches and a little white head peered out. The little white head was on a tiny body, one that was actually shorter than me. She was stooped over, and held onto a cane with both hands.

"Tom never spoke of an ex-wife," she told me. I wasn't surprised at this and told her so.

"Kathleen Monahan, ma'am." I held out my hand and she offered hers. It was delicate and her skin felt like silk.

"Constance Everwood," she said.

"Pleased to meet you Miss Everwood."

"Allow me to say how sorry I am about the loss of Tom Connaught. He was a good man, a solid man. And a gentleman. There aren't many of those around these days," she said. I agreed with her. "What can I do for you tonight, Miss Monahan?"

"I'm looking for Natalie Scott's apartment," I told her.

"Well, why didn't you just ask at the Front Desk?" she asked.

"I came straight up on the elevator. I just thought all floors had one apartment, like mine."

"Ha," she half-laughed. "Yours and the nineteenth floor are the only ones with single apartments. The rest of us live four apartments to the floor." She made it sound like she was living in a tenement building when in fact she was living at a very exclusive, Fifth Avenue address.

"Yes, that's too bad. Can you tell me which apartment Miss Scott lives in?"

Miss Everwood pointed at the apartment two doors over from hers. "Whatever business would you have with that one?" she asked.

"Oh, we work together," I told her, making it sound like we were girlfriends who were getting together to paint our toenails.

"Well, she's turned out as sour as that mother of hers. Do you work at Tom's company? You must, because she," Miss Everwood poked her nose in the direction of Natalie Scott's apartment, "works there too. Tom told me."

"Did you see Tom often?" I asked her.

"Often enough. At least once a week," she told me. "In the lobby. We'd ride the elevator together. He'd help me with my packages. Such a nice man. Have they found out what happened to him?"

I shook my head. "Thanks Miss Everwood." I took a step back, letting her know I needed to move on. "I hope to see you in the lobby or the elevator," I told her.

"Don't waste your time going to her apartment," she nodded again in the direction of the Scott's door. "No one answers the door after eight o'clock at night. Been that way since they moved in. You can bang on that door, you can yell that you're with the police. No one will come."

"Oh, okay," I said reluctantly. "Do you know if Miss Scott is at home? She wasn't at work today and I wondered if she was okay," I lied. I didn't give a tiny rat's ass if she was okay.

"She's home. Came in around five this morning and hasn't gone out." Constance picked up her cane and pointed it at a small peephole in her door which was placed at about the four foot mark. "I keep track," she bragged. "Can't sleep so I pace. And when I hear the elevator, I check to see who's on it." I wondered if she had ever applied to work the Front Desk of the building as a security guard. This was Neighbourhood Watch at its best, although admittedly she was only keeping track of three other families.

"Although I must admit, it's strange," she said.

"What's strange?" I asked.

"That I haven't seen her mother in six months. Good night Miss Monahan." She turned around and shuffled back into her apartment.

"Good night Miss Everwood," I answered.

Six months? That *was* strange.

Chapter forty-two

I joined Kelly and Jay at the dining room table when I got back from my jaunt upstairs. The two of them hadn't even noticed that I was gone.

"The watchdog on the twentieth floor says that Nat Scott is at home and has been since five this morning," I reported to them.

Kelly's face was a large question mark.

"I went up to Nat Scott's floor," I told him. "I'm so pissed right now. I wanted to talk to her. Get to the bottom of this."

Kelly ran his hand over his face and his fingers pulled at the sides of his mouth. The shake of his head was imperceptible, but it was there. Jay saw it too.

"Kate," Jay said, "I don't think you should be running around, checking things out by yourself. It's not safe." Kelly's slight nod, agreeing with Jay, did not go unnoticed by me. I impressed myself by deciding not to argue with either of them.

"Any news?" I asked, changing the subject.

"Yeah, on two fronts," Kelly told me. "First on Dr. Francis. There's been no sign of him for about a month at his apartment building. No one has seen him coming or going. His apartment is still full of his belongings and the food in his refrigerator has gone bad. "

"So your people were in his apartment?" I asked.

Kelly nodded. I didn't ask how they got in.

"Does it look like he packed a couple of suitcases and took off?"

Kelly shook his head. "Nope. Toothbrush is still in the bathroom, a set of suitcases are sitting in the bedroom closet. Neighbours haven't seen him."

"This is not good," I said, stating the obvious. "Dr. Pritchard and the staff at Global Devices think that he moved away. His resignation letter said that he was moving and he didn't leave a forwarding address. What the hell is going on?"

Jay and Kelly looked at me, silently. I took a deep breath and let it out slowly. Everything was out of control and I felt like Alice in Wonderland, falling and falling. What the hell had I got myself into? What the fuck had Tom Connaught been thinking when he left this shit fucking mess to me? I slammed the palms of my hands on the table and stood up, shoving the chair backwards with my legs.

"We need to call the police and report the poor man missing. Can you find out if he has any family Kelly? Maybe he's not missing. Maybe he's scared and is hiding out with them." I tried to calm myself down, breathing through my nose. I was ready to pack it in, lock, stock and barrel, right now, right here. Kate Monahan was scared and starting to panic. Slow breaths through the nose, I told myself.

Jay was starting to look concerned but knew to keep his distance. He knew that when I was scared I would lash out at anything or anyone near me.

I put my hands on the table and leaned forward a bit. "I'm okay," I told the both of them. Liar, I told myself. "I'm going to make some coffee. Who wants a cup?"

Ten minutes later we were all back at the dining room table, with our coffee. "So," I said. "Let's get back to where we were before I panicked. Sorry about that."

Kelly held up his right hand and shook his head. I took this to mean, no apology necessary.

"You said there was news on two fronts," I reminded him.

Kelly looked over at Jay and they shared a glance that went something like this: if you think she panicked over the news on Dr. Francis, wait until she hears this.

"What?" I demanded of them.

"It's about Donald McLean. We found out why he spent time in the state prison." Jay was delivering the news on this one.

"He's a sex offender. I'm not sure I want to know the gory details," I told them.

Jay ignored my wish and told me anyway. "He was convicted of sexually fondling his patients."

"What patients?" I asked.

"Well, apparently our Mr. McLean was a surgical resident at the Flagstaff Memorial Hospital. Donald McLean is a medical doctor with a specialty in surgery. Although the Arizona Medical Board doesn't agree. They revoked his license when he was convicted."

I sat there and let that news sink in. Disgusted was a good word to describe how I felt. And a little more than slightly sick to my stomach. Disgusted with myself, to think that I had found that man attractive. Disgusted with myself to think that I had flirted with him.

Jay looked at me and I had a sudden urge to crawl onto his lap and cuddle up.

"Shall I finish the story on Mr. McLean?" he offered. I nodded.

"Well, the police records that we were able to access, reported that after he was convicted, but before he was sentenced and sent to the state prison, Mr. McLean ran his car into a tree at full speed. The police report indicated that the weather was good, and there were no skid marks to indicate that he tried to avoid the tree. The report speculated that it was an attempted suicide."

Not a nice way to go, I thought, but maybe preferable to life in a prison and a sexual predator label.

"That's how he ended up in the wheelchair," Jay continued. "Spent several weeks in the hospital, and when he was released, he went straight from there to the Arizona State Prison at Winslow."

"So what's he doing out of prison?" I asked.

"He did his time," Kelly said. "Sentenced to ten years, served four, got out early because he was a model prisoner. Was a teacher at the prison, helped his fellow inmates get their high school diplomas." I detected a slight sneer in Kelly's voice, but his face didn't betray any such emotion. Maybe I was just misreading his drawl.

"One wonders how the *hell* he ended up at Phoenix Technologies," I ventured, mostly to myself. Nausea was pushing at the back of my throat and sharp, shooting pains were throbbing in my temples. Usually, these were some of the first signs of a migraine. When I got a migraine, I usually ended up flat on my back, in a dark room, for many hours and I groaned inwardly, knowing that I couldn't afford to be out of the loop for that long.

"Kate, you need a break," Jay was saying. "Where are your painkillers?" The man was a mind reader.

The nausea hit me like a wave and I had to get away from the overhead lights in the dining room and the talking, and the freaking crap that was my life at this moment.

My friend sleep arrived about fifteen minutes after I took my prescription medication and lay like a mummy on my bed, with no covers touching me and my arms crossed over my chest. Tommy came to me in my sleep and he held me and told me how sorry he was and he swore he never meant to put me into such a mess and he told me over and over and over again how much he loved me. I tried to ask him who murdered him but Tommy was holding me so tight I couldn't speak and I struggled with him. Let me go, let me go, I begged him, let me go because I needed to ask him the question. Let me go.

When I woke up I slowly rolled my eyes behind my closed lids, testing for the tell-tale pain. There was a lingering smidge so I gingerly opened my eyes and turned my head sideways and saw Jay sitting up against the headboard on his side of the bed. He was reading a book and holding a small penlight over the pages. The bedroom was dark except for this little bit of light. I rolled over and made my way across the bed until I was lying beside Jay. He quietly put his hand on my head and I fell back to sleep.

Chapter forty-three

THE NEXT MORNING I WOKE up craving coffee and feeling somewhat refreshed. I set the showerhead to massage and enjoyed the water pounding on the back of my neck. I felt a little foolish about the way our evening had ended so abruptly the night before, but I'm sure Kelly understood. I loathed appearing weak in front of others, but trying to function normally while in the grips of a migraine just isn't an option for me.

After my shower I made my way to the kitchen and was happy to see Jay sitting on one of the barstools at the breakfast counter. I came up behind him and wrapped my arms around his waist and rested my head on his back.

"Good morning," I mumbled into his T-shirt. He turned around and wrapped me in a big hug, lifting me off the floor. "Good morning yourself," he said.

"Put me down," I laughed. My feet were swinging in the air.

"Gimme a kiss first," he teased. Which I did. Which lasted way longer than a good morning kiss normally did. Which led to all sorts of delicious fun back in our bedroom. Which is why I had two showers that morning.

I finally got my coffee an hour later, which I was enjoying while I watched Jay cook us some breakfast.

"After I so gracefully ended our discussion last night, what did you and Kelly do?" I asked Jay.

"Nothing." The smell of bacon filled the kitchen. "Kelly left as soon as you went to bed. He said for you to call him today if you were feeling better. And he gave me his cell phone number. I told him I was going to continue digging for information." Jay reached under the counter while he was telling me this and pulled out some sort of appliance contraption that I had never seen before. He set it on the counter and plugged it in.

"I have to tell you," he continued, "helping out last night was great fun." Jay grabbed several large oranges from the wire basket on the counter and skillfully sliced each in half. "Digging into the police databases, accessing the Arizona State Prison records, and the Arizona Medical Board records was a little weird." Jay grabbed two glasses from the cupboard and placed one under a little spout on the appliance, which he magically flipped down. He then lifted a clear cone shaped gizmo on the appliance and placed half an orange on top of a small protrusion, put the cone back in place, and pressed a button. "It almost felt like I was hacking into computers," he was saying. "I can't believe how so much information is available on the internet." Fresh orange juice was pouring out of the little spout into the glass.

He turned around to the stove, flipped some bacon, grabbed another frying pan from the rack hanging over the counter, placed it on the stove, turned on the burner under it, and placed a dab of butter in the middle of the pan. He was then back at the juicer, quickly feeding it the orange halves. The two glasses of juice were placed side by side on the counter in front of me and in one graceful motion he was back at the stove cracking eggs (one handed) into the frying pan. I sighed a little and wondered if life got any better than this? Jay was my own private dancer, doing his choreographed footwork in the kitchen, cooking for me.

I forced my mind back to reality and gave Jay a very big smile when he placed my plate full of eggs, bacon and toast in front of me. Jay sat beside me on the matching barstool.

"Thank you for breakfast, and thank you for helping out last night." I leaned over a bit and wrapped my arm around Jay's waist and rested my head on his arm.

"You are welcome," he replied. "Now eat your breakfast."

The stalker's breathing was controlled. Deep breaths originating in the diaphragm allowed more control and the stalker concentrated on the air expanding the abdomen, not the chest. The stalker felt omniscient with all the extra oxygen the diaphragmatic breathing provided. There were no obstacles to success. Nothing could stand in the way now. Expand the abdomen, not the chest. Extra oxygen meant that sight was improved, hearing was sharper, food tasted so much better. The stalker was constantly sexually aroused. Oxygen meant power. Power meant control. The stalker peered at the medical monitor and nodded silently. Blood oxygen reading was good. Blood pressure slightly low. Heart rate normal. The stalker gloated, just a little, and smiled. Omniscient and omnipotent.

Jay was between my legs with his hands around my throat, and I didn't like it a bit. In fact, I hated it, which Frank said was a good thing. I lay there on the floor of Frank's dojo, with a tingling scalp and stinging wrists, and I was supposed to writhe out of Jay's death grip. I was feeling really pooped out but Frank was having none of that.

"Cross your arms over his and grab his wrists," he commanded me. When my hands had a good grasp on Jay's wrists, Frank told me to start moving, and to bring my knees, legs and feet up, under Jay's body. "Kick at him, throw him off balance," Frank said. When I had done that, Frank told me to roll to the side, using my shoulder, hip and foot to throw Jay off me. I rolled to the left, grunted, and pushed with my right foot. Miraculously, I ended up between Jays legs, on top of him.

Frank was urging me to strike his groin and get up and run. Embarrassed at how spent I was, I stayed on my hands and knees for a few moments and watched great globs of my sweat drop on the floor. I gulped at the air. "Fuck, fuck, fuck," I gasped. How pathetic, I thought. An hour working out and my joints were like Jell-O. I finally stood up and turned around to face Frank and Jay who were patiently waiting for me to come back to life.

After breakfast I had told Jay that I was going to play hooky from the office. Jay just laughed.

"What?"

"You're the boss so it's not called hooky." Jay paused and a big smile played around his mouth. "What are we going to do today?"

"You're playing hooky too?" He nodded. I put my arms around his waist and looked up at him. Gawd, he makes my heart go pitter-patter, I thought.

"Let's do something together that'll take my mind off everything at Phoenix for at least an hour or so." I gave him a bit of a suggestive leer which didn't work because we had ended up at Frank Sanchez's place for another self-defence class.

"Okay," Frank said. "Good." He walked over and clapped me on the back. "Good work today Kate. Let's review what we went over. You worked on what to do if someone comes up behind you and grabs you by your hair." I nodded and rubbed my scalp. Christ that hurt, getting your hair pulled. Hurt is good, said Frank. It focuses your attention. Reach up, put your hands over theirs, bend down, step back and get out of the grab. "You and Jay worked on how to disarm someone if they come at you with a gun." I rubbed my wrist, and thought about whether or not I'd be able to remember any of what I had learned today.

Frank said to act submissive when confronted by someone with a gun. I don't think I'd have any trouble with that part, short of peeing my pants, I'd have my hands up in the air, begging for my mommy. Put your hands up, hang your head, make them think they've got the upper hand. And never lose your focus, Frank demanded. When they come at you with that gun, he showed us how to put them to their knees and take the weapon from them. Admittedly, it felt good.

"And lastly," Frank was saying, "you learned what to do if someone has you on the ground. I know it's a lot of information in one session, but you need to practice. When can you come back?"

I looked at Jay and he shrugged his shoulders. This was my call. "Tomorrow?" I asked Frank. We agreed on a time and while I gathered up my stuff, Jay called Lou to tell him we were finished and coming downstairs to the car.

Apparently, Jay and Kelly had a little chat last night after I fell asleep. Kelly had a "come to Jesus talk" with Jay and today Lou the driver was Jay's new best friend. Kelly was concerned about my safety and now Jay had taken on the job of being my personal bodyguard. Which was kind of funny, considering that he had absolutely no training, which Jay didn't find funny when I pointed that out to him. I decided to go along with whatever Kelly and Jay wanted me to do, for now at least. One thing that Jay made clear to me right away was that we wouldn't be going anywhere unless it was in Lou's car. Security of my person was top of mind for Jay, Lou and Kelly. I felt so special.

At the doorway to the street, Jay stood in front of me and looked for Lou's car. When he saw it pulling up, he took me by the arm and scooted me into the back of the car. Quickly. Somehow I didn't feel like a movie star.

Chapter forty-four

Lou handed me two message slips when I slid into the back of the car. Call Carrie and call Kelly. When I called the office Carrie told me that Cleve Johnston needed to talk me, so I asked her to transfer me to his line.

"Kate, there are a few things we should talk about before I head back to Toronto. I'm hoping to catch the five thirty out of LaGuardia. When can we meet?"

The small digital clock mounted on the back of the front seat of the car told me it was 10:30. Cleve and I agreed to meet for lunch at a small Italian restaurant on East 57th, practically around the corner from my apartment. I had time to take a shower and walk to the restaurant, although Jay and Lou both told me that I would be driven over.

I called Kelly as soon as I got back in the apartment.

"Northland," he said as soon as he answered the phone.

"Sit rep," I barked at him and fancied him tightening his butt cheeks and standing at attention.

There was a bit of a pause and I think he actually figured out that I was joshing with him.

"Ma'am," he drawled. "How are you feeling today?"

"Much better Staff Sergeant, thanks for asking. What's up?

"Better we talk in person," he said guardedly.

"I'm at my apartment, and have to leave in about fifty minutes for a lunch meeting," I told him.

"I'll be there in twenty."

He was actually there in eighteen. I had taken my shower and was just finished dressing when I heard the intercom announcing his arrival. Jay and he were comfortably ensconced at the dining room table, chatting like two long lost friends when I came out of the bedroom.

"So, Kelly, what's up?" I pulled out a chair across the table from him and sat down. He flipped open his little notebook which was sitting on the table in front of him.

"Natalie Scott."

"Okay. You've got my attention. Fire away."

"Well, most of what is on her background check has been verified. What struck my investigator as a little odd were some slight time differences from what she put on the application. It didn't add up, so we went off on our own and did a deep dive check on her."

I was getting that oh-oh feeling in the pit of my gut and I didn't like it.

Kelly continued. "Seems that our Miss Scott spent some time in Arizona." He paused but I don't think it was for effect. And then he swallowed before continuing. "Flagstaff specifically."

Flagstaff was the city that had hosted our own sexual predator, Mr. Donald McLean.

"Oh really?" I said.

"Really," he replied. "Although it's not mentioned on the employment background check, apparently Miss Scott did a placement at the Flagstaff Memorial Hospital as part of her Ph.D studies in biochemistry. She spent four months working in one of their research labs. Ben Tucker, or Donald McLean, was doing his surgical residency there at the same time."

I had my hands clasped together, in front of me, resting on the table. With this news, my hands clenched and my knuckles turned white.

"What else do we know about her time in Flagstaff?" I asked.

"Nothing yet. My guy was on a flight this morning to Phoenix, connecting to Flagstaff. He'll be there early afternoon."

I looked over at Jay and then at Kelly.

"This just keeps getting worse, doesn't it?"

They both nodded.

"We have to speak to the police. To the detectives who are investigating Tommy's murder."

"Agreed," Kelly said. "Although I'd like to wait until my guy calls with something. The detectives will likely find it interesting that Ben Tucker and Nat Scott were both in Flagstaff, at the same time, but this information isn't going to help them solve the case."

"I'm getting closer to believing that both of them had something to do with Tommy's murder." I stood up and walked over to the windows and stared across at the tree tops of Central Park. "We have to tell them about Dr. Francis, too," I said to the window. My watch said I had ten minutes to get to the restaurant to meet Cleve.

Kelly told Jay he didn't have to go with me. He patted his side, under his left arm. "I'm on the case," he assured Jay. I think he had a gun under his jacket.

Cleve was waiting for me inside the small entrance to the restaurant. The building was very old and the ceilings were very low and Cleve looked like the Friendly Giant. He stood in front of the maitre 'd with his shoulders hunched and his head bent over. I gave him a small smile in greeting and then a waiter led us to our table.

I ordered a sparkling mineral water with lime and lots of ice and Cleve said he would have the same. Nothing on the menu appealed to me because I was sick just thinking about the shit going on. Silence surrounded me and I could hear the blood pounding in my ears. I stared mutely at the menu and felt spent. Sure I was tired because of my hour with Frank Sanchez, but my body always tried to shut down on me when I was stressed. Knowing I was only into the first part of the marathon of what Phoenix Technologies was going to be to me, I mentally slapped myself and girded myself for a long race. My eyes were full of tears when I finally looked up at Cleve.

He put his menu down on the table and looked across at me with concern on his face. I held up my hand, stopping him from speaking and took a sip of my sparkling water. "Sometimes, it's a little much," I told him by way of explanation. "I'm okay, though," I reassured him. I adjusted myself in the chair and sat up straighter and looked him in the eye, all business now.

"So, what do we need to discuss counsellor?"

"A couple of things. First off, I want to go back to Toronto for the weekend, but I can be back early next week. That is if you need me. You know I'm only a phone call away." I nodded. It was true. I knew I could count on Cleve for whatever I needed.

I smiled a bit. "Funny isn't it? A couple of weeks ago, you were the boss. Now I get to say who comes and goes," I joked. "Unless something comes up, I don't see why you would need to be here next week." He was listening intently to what I was saying. As if I had something important to say, which was a crock if you thought about it. What could Kate Monahan possibly have to say that a man so educated, so well respected, would listen to so intently? I reached across the table and put my hand over his.

"Mr. Johnston, do you know how much I value your friendship? How much I appreciate that you were Tommy's friend? And how much I appreciate your advice and counsel now? This is hard for me, and I know I've been a royal shit to you in the past. I'm sorry for that. I'm just glad you're here now." That was one big speech for me, a little on the bare emotional side, but it needed to be said.

Cleve's big hand engulfed mine and he squeezed lightly. "Enough said. I'm glad to be here and to be of help."

The waiter appeared and took our orders. While we waited for our food Cleve gave me some more kick-you-in-the-gut news.

"I've been thinking about the company and this mess with Global Devices," he started. "So far, we've come clean with the shareholders and the Securities Commissions about the contract cancellation. But what we haven't done is address the fact that the company is accused of falsifying records. When the FDA finds out about that, it's not going to be pretty for Phoenix."

Great. Just what I needed. More good news. And the fact that I hadn't even thought about this made me even more angry. I was the president of a company for gawd's sake. I should have thought about this. Fuck. Pay more attention Monahan, I chastised myself.

"So what do we do about this?" I asked Cleve.

"I'm going to do some research into it. See if there's any precedent out there on this. Look into what sanctions the FDA can put on companies for this type of screw-up. This is preliminary so I don't want you worried about it. But we need to be ready."

"Okay. Let's get ready. But also let's remember that right now these are only accusations and haven't been proven. This is all tied in to Tommy's murder. I'm sure of it." And then I filled him in on what Kelly and Jay had come up with last night and today. The good news on our exemplary employees, Ben Tucker and Nat Scott.

When I finished we both sat quietly for a while, sipping our coffee and waiting for the bill.

"Wow," Cleve finally said, softly. Not a word normally in Cleve's dictionary so it sounded weird coming from him. "Tommy had it all figured out, and it got him killed. Poor son of a bitch."

I couldn't agree more. Now *I* just had to figure it all out. And not get myself killed.

Chapter forty-five

THE 20TH PRECINCT LOOKED THE same as it did when I had visited it almost two weeks ago. A deceptively modern-looking building, it could have been a bank or an upscale jewellery store except for the large brass words mounted on the brick wall beside the door - 20th Precinct, The City of New York Police Department.

It was hard to believe the things that had happened in those two weeks - it seemed like a lifetime. It took me a few minutes to recall that it was only yesterday morning that Carrie had tracked down the two detectives for me. Assuming that Detective Bartlett was still in the hospital with her back problems and that Detective Shipley was back in town, Kelly and I asked for Detective Shipley at the Precinct.

When Kelly and Lou picked me up at the restaurant after my lunch with Cleve, I insisted that we speak with the police as soon as possible. Kelly instructed Lou to head over to the 20th Precinct on West 82nd Street. On the drive over, we discussed what we needed to tell the police. Kelly was adamant that we give them everything we knew. "In order for them to do their job, they have to have all the facts." I didn't disagree with him.

Shipley's clothes looked like she had slept in them and if her hair had met a hairbrush in the last week I would've been surprised. To be fair though, she was probably a little overworked with her partner off sick. She stood in front of us and held her hands together, not offering to shake. Before she spoke, her body shuddered with a very deep sigh which seemed to have started somewhere deep inside her, down near her ankles.

She nodded her head slightly at me and spoke in a soft voice. "Miss Monahan. What can I do for you?"

I introduced Kelly as the head of security for our company and left it at that. "We'd like to speak to you about a few things we think may be relevant to the murder of Tom Connaught."

She chewed a little bit on her lower lip and shook her head, just a little. "I have nothing to report on the case, I'm sorry. There is no news since the last time we spoke."

"I understand," I told her. "But there are some things that we think the police should be aware of."

"Okay," she agreed grudgingly. She turned and walked away and I assumed we were to follow her. We walked up two flights of stairs and down a narrow hallway to a small room, similar to the one that Bartlett had taken me to. Notably and thankfully, this one did not smell like the inside of my brother's hockey equipment bag.

Detective Shipley sat across the table from us and placed a small, spiral-bound notebook in front of her. Surprisingly, she actually had a pen and once she had it in her right hand, she looked up at us expectantly.

"So you said you've got some news," she said.

"Yes," I told her. "We've come across some things at the company that we think you should be aware of. Some things involving some of our employees. And we're finding out more information by the minute."

Detective Shipley was looking down at her notepad and doodling in the upper right hand corner of the page. I stopped speaking and it was a good five seconds before she looked up at me. Glad to see that I had her attention.

"I'm not sure how much you know about our company and what it does," I continued. She nodded at me. At least she was awake.

"We are in the development business. We have clients that we partner with who need high tech components developed and built. They contract us to develop and build things that haven't been done before." She was still with me. "One of our biggest partners over the last couple of years has been a company called Global Devices. They're in the medical research business. I found out recently that they had cancelled all contracts with us and demanded all of their property back."

Shipley shrugged and gave me a *so what?* look.

"Well, I've been talking to the President of Global Devices about why they cancelled with us and apparently it was because research results were being falsified. Which is not very kosher, considering that we partnered with them to build an artificial kidney for humans."

Shipley sat up just a little bit at this news.

"But, apparently, only a few people at our company knew that the contracts were cancelled, and didn't tell anyone, and have kept up a phoney pretense that everything was A-okay."

Shipley looked a little confused.

"I'm still confused about the whole thing myself," I acknowledged. "But to top it off, our Vice President of Research and Development has moved out of her office and not given any notice to the company."

"How long ago was this?" Shipley asked.

"Yesterday," I told her. Shit this was sounding so lame.

"Let me back up a little bit. A couple of days ago, I found out that Mr. Connaught had a safety deposit box." Shipley definitely perked up at this news and starting writing in her notepad. "I found papers inside the box that were copies of correspondence with the Food and Drug Administration, and originals of letters which looked to be love letters." Shipley stopped writing and looked up at me, puzzled.

"I know, it doesn't make much sense," I said lamely.

"Maybe I can help out," Kelly offered.

"Please." Before Shipley thinks I'm a complete moron.

"Miss Monahan spoke with the President of Global Devices," Kelly told her. "Apparently one of their Vice Presidents, a Doctor Jordan Francis, resigned his position at Global and hasn't been heard from in a month. There is no evidence that he's been at his apartment either. The same papers that were found in Mr. Connaught's safety deposit box were found taped to the underside of Dr. Francis' desk drawer."

The story sounded so much better coming from Kelly. "The Vice President of Research and Development who works at our company, Natalie Scott, vacated the premises and cleaned out her office on Wednesday night. On Miss Monahan's instructions, my staff have been checking the backgrounds of each of the employees in our research and development group."

Shipley interrupted at this point. "You're only *now* checking backgrounds? In this day and age?"

Kelly held up his right hand. "Of course we check backgrounds," he said indignantly. "Very thoroughly. But people lie, as we've found out. One of our employees falsified his application and we've found out that he has spent time in a state prison for sexual offences. He didn't tell us on his application that he was a qualified surgeon or that Miss Scott, our Vice President, the one who disappeared into the night, apparently worked at the same hospital as he did in Arizona several years ago. Miss Scott failed to mention any of that on her background documentation."

Kelly stopped at this point and we waited while Shipley wrote some more in her notepad. When she finally looked up at us, she asked, "What do you want me to do with this?"

"Question Miss Scott and the other employee. Find out if they know where Dr. Francis is. Look into his disappearance."

Shipley made some noise in the back of her throat, that little tiny noise that could make a mockery of whatever you had just said. The noise meant, "as if". Really. There was a collective pause among the three of us. Kelly turned a wee bit red in the face and I think Shipley was wishing she could take it back.

I stood up and looked down at Detective Shipley. "Here's something you can do," I started to tell her. Kelly stood up and took me by the elbow, putting a little pressure on it. I understood the pressure to mean *cool it*. So I took a little breath and realized that pissing off this woman would get me nowhere. "Have a nice day," I finished the thought and left the room. I must be growing up, I thought. Under similar circumstances I probably would have told the woman to rub her knuckles in shit, so I was pretty proud of myself. I made a mental note to call my mom and let her know.

I thought Kelly was right behind me but I arrived in the lobby alone. While I waited I looked around and realized the Precinct looked like the inside of my old high school. The walls were tiled and the place had an institutional feel to it. Institutional buildings like these gave me the creeps and I wondered what the hell the designers were thinking when they put tiles on the walls. As if it were a shower or a bathroom. Yuck. They were probably thinking *efficiency* and how easy it would be to clean. I wondered if they actually mopped the walls. Double yuck.

Kelly appeared in about ten minutes and we didn't stop to talk in the lobby. When we were sitting in the back of Lou's car, he told me that he had hung back for a few minutes to talk with her.

"I wanted to cut her some slack," he said. "You can't imagine how overworked some of these detectives are. Their caseloads are huge and with her partner out on sick leave, she's managing it all on her own. I asked her to give some thought to what we had told her. I wouldn't hold my breath though that she's going to do anything about it at this point. She's barely keeping her head above water."

I sat in silence and looked out the window of the car, admiring the green space of Central Park. Lou had turned into the Park on West 86th and I watched the dozens of joggers on the path near the Reservoir.

I turned to Kelly who was lost in his own thoughts.

"This is pretty hopeless isn't it?" I asked him.

"It may seem like it, at this point. But something'll break." He was trying to sound reassuring. "I've only been at this for a day or so. We will get to the bottom of this. Don't you worry, Miss Monahan."

Chapter forty-six

KELLY'S CELL PHONE RANG WHILE Lou was driving south on Fifth Avenue right past the Metropolitan Museum of Art. Another place I wanted to visit and hadn't had the time yet.

"Northland," he said into the phone, and then he listened for a few seconds. "Let me call you back in fifteen." He snapped the cover shut on his phone and shoved it back into his belt holster. Lou pulled up in front of my apartment building a few minutes later.

I exited the car onto the sidewalk and thanked Lou who was holding open the car door for me. Our doorman was standing nearby under the awning of the entrance to the building. Kelly exited the car on the sidewalk side as well, and told me he would see me to the apartment.

I got close to both he and Lou and asked them, *sotto voce*, if they thought all this extra togetherness was necessary. Lou took umbrage with that and drew in a deep breath, stuck out his seemingly fifty-two inch chest and said, not so *sotto voce*, "If anything were to happen to you, like what happened to Mr. Connaught," (he pronounced it Keh-nott), "I could nevah live wid myself."

I patted his arm and told him I appreciated his attention and his driving and that I was only joking (kind of). Kelly's cell phone rang again as we were walking into the apartment building. I gave the doorman a smile, feeling like royalty, and headed towards the back of the lobby and the elevators. Kelly was talking quietly into the phone when the elevator doors opened. We waited while three people exited, one of whom was my favourite nosy neighbour, Miss Constance Everwood from the 20th floor. I motioned to Kelly to wait for a minute and stepped up to say hello.

"Miss Everwood," I said, "Good afternoon."

She stopped and placed both hands on her cane and peered up at me.

"Miss Monahan. How nice to see you," she said.

"Likewise," I said. We walked, or rather shuffled, over to the side of the elevator lobby for a little chat. Miss Everwood was dressed in a beautiful off-white, cashmere coat, sensible chocolate brown walking shoes, and a jaunty hat right out of the thirties. It even had a little feather on the side. The whole outfit looked a little warm for the temperature outside, but some older folks are apparently cold all the time. She had a mesh shopping bag hanging from the same arm as her purse.

"Off to do some shopping?" I inquired.

"Yes. I'm just picking up a few Friday night treats. Thought I'd rent a video, get a bag of popcorn and maybe a chocolate bar. Seen any good movies lately?" she asked me.

I was a little taken aback. Her Friday night sounded like one of mine, not what you would expect of an eighty-year old woman.

"Depends," I told her. "What type of movies do you like? Chick flicks? Action?"

"I love movies with lots of sex and gratuitous violence," she said. With a straight face.

"Really?"

She slapped me on the arm. "No, I was just joshing with you. I do like movies with some action."

"Then watch Pearl Harbour. It's really good."

"No, I don't think so. Thanks anyway, but when you've lived through the horror of something like that, you don't necessarily want to see it on the big screen."

I imagine she had a point.

"Not to worry," she told me. "Part of the fun is browsing at the video store and watching people's reaction when I ask where the porno flicks are." She laughed at this and so did I. Our Miss Everwood was quite a joker.

"So," I nudged her. "Any action at the apartment of my co-worker?"

She shook her head. "Nope. Although I did get a few hours of sleep last night so I can't guarantee there wasn't some coming and going. But I doubt it. Nobody's allowed in or out of that place after eight at night. I think I told you that didn't I?"

"Yes. Yes you did Miss Everwood. Thanks for the information. Enjoy your movie and your Friday evening." She gave me a little wave and shuffled off.

Kelly was standing in the same spot, still talking on the phone. He finally hung up as I was putting my key in the apartment door.

"My guy's on the ground in Flagstaff," Kelly said. "If you've got a minute, I can come in and fill you in."

"Absolutely," I told him. "Gimme a minute to change into my jeans. Help yourself to anything you want in the kitchen."

Kelly was sitting at the breakfast bar and Jay was serving coffee when I joined them in the kitchen. As soon as I climbed up on my barstool, Jay served me a hot, black coffee.

"Thank you," I told him and then turned to Kelly, who was sitting beside me. "So, give us a report."

"Okay. Jerry Rigley, my guy, has been in Flagstaff for about two hours now. He headed straight for the hospital because he wanted to see if he could get any information from them before the administration types close up shop for the weekend. The hospital confirmed that both Miss Scott and Mr. Tucker were employed at the hospital at the same time. That's about all they would share. Jerry did manage to buy the secretary in the personnel department a coffee and she was so grateful she gave him the home addresses they had on file for both Scott and Tucker. Checking out both of those addresses are next on his list of things to do. Hopefully, he'll find someone who can recollect something about the two them."

Kelly sipped his coffee and I had a hunch he had more news so I sipped my coffee too, and waited. Jay was leaning against the opposite counter, with his arms folded across his chest.

A couple of silent moments passed and I finally broke it. "So, anything else to report Kelly?"

"Well, there is some news a little closer to home," he offered. "Apparently Mr. Ben Tucker has been seeing a nephrologist here in New York."

"Excuse my ignorance, but what's a nephrologist?" Jay asked.

"A kidney specialist," I told him. "I learned that the other day when I was doing all my reading of the Global Devices files and our PISTON project."

"Well that's interesting," I said to Kelly. "What are they treating him for? Is it an infection?"

"No, I'd say it's a little more serious than that. It seems our Ben Tucker, or Donald MacLean, is on dialysis. Three times a week."

"That would explain why he was nowhere to be found when I went looking for him the other day. Can people on dialysis hold full time jobs?" I wondered out loud. "How long does dialysis take?" I wasn't sure who I was asking these questions of, but it was definitely an interesting subject. And, it seemed that Kelly had the answers.

"Dialysis is different for each person. Each session can take anywhere from an hour to overnight. Lots of people keep their jobs while on dialysis. In Tucker's case, the dialysis appointments last three hours each time."

It suddenly struck me that at every turn we were running into kidneys. Real ones or artificial ones. I had heard more and learned more about kidneys in the last two weeks than I really cared to know. I mused about that for a while before Kelly interrupted my thoughts.

"Mr. Tucker is in dire straights though," Kelly told us. "He has kidney damage because of his paraplegia. He's losing his kidney function and is close to renal failure." Kelly reached inside his jacket and pulled out his little notebook. He flipped to a page near the middle and read from it. "Apparently he has neurogenic lower urinary tract dysfunction." He looked up at me. "He needs a kidney transplant. Soon."

"That's not all he needs," I said. "A kidney transplant. And a job. His ass is fired for lying on his job application." I felt only a wee bit of satisfaction when I said that out loud. It would have been better if I could have said it to his face.

Although it seemed like a lifetime ago, it was just yesterday that I had confronted Ben in my office about the Global Devices contract. He had denied any knowledge of what was going on. If asked, I wondered how well he would be able to deny knowing Nat Scott before working at Phoenix. The man was a convicted sexual offender, which in all likelihood put him in the category of psychopath. I think that's the right term to describe people convicted of sex crimes. Just to make sure I wandered into the bedroom and grabbed the dictionary off the shelf. *Psychopath: a person affected with antisocial personality disorder.* Well, one could argue that sexual offenders fit into the category *antisocial.* The internet gave me more insight into antisocial personality disorder. *Psychopaths use charm, manipulation, intimidation, sex and violence to control others and satisfy their needs. They have no conscience or empathy. Psychopaths are pathological liars, have grandiose self-images and use glibness and superficial charm to get what they want.* I felt like ice water had been poured over me and I shuddered.

Jesus, Mary and Joseph. What had I gotten into this time?

Chapter forty-seven

CARRIE AND I SPENT AT least an hour on the phone going over a list of things I had missed that day at the office. There were a dozen phone calls to return, none of which couldn't be put off until Monday. At least that's what I thought as she went down the list of calls.

Russ Freeson had asked that we meet as soon as possible to go over updated financial statements. He and the auditors had apparently re-worked all the numbers after he got the news about Global. The quarterly financial statements that we had filed about two weeks ago with the Securities Commissions would have to be restated and refiled. *Fuck, fuck, fuck.* Not good. More fucking damage control and I wasn't confident that we would be lucky enough to get this done with little fanfare or scrutiny. So far there had been no coverage of the release we had issued on the cancellation of the Global Devices contracts. Let's keep our fingers crossed.

Sandra Melnick, our VP Operations who had agreed to take over R and D, had called. She had spent the day with the team and wanted to report back to me. Call her on Monday.

Mark Hall, our whining VP of Sales who had made such an indelible impression on us yesterday, had called. Hoped I didn't mind, but he was going to take some time, take a few days off, maybe head over to Bermuda with his wife. Get away from it all.

"Was he kidding?" I asked Carrie.

"No Kate, he wasn't."

"Remind me to deal with that on Monday," I instructed her. Mental note to self to fire that whining wimp. Unbelievable how a good crisis brings out the finest in some people.

"Get Russ Freeson in to see me first thing on Monday. Ask him if there are copies of the financial statements that he could fax to the apartment now.

Do you have the fax number here?" She did and she would call Mr. Freeson right away.

Sara Williston from the bank had called. Twice.

"Did she say what it was about?"

"No, but the second time she called she sounded a little disappointed that you weren't here."

My watch said it was 4:30. By some standards, that would be way past quitting time for some bankers. Not Sara though. She answered on the second ring.

"Sara, it's Kate Monahan. My office said you called today."

"Hi. Thanks for calling back. I hope I didn't get you at a bad time."

"No, I'm at home, just finishing up for the day. What's up?"

"I'm not sure," she started tentatively. "Do you know if Tom was acquainted with a Dr. Jordan Francis?"

"Yes he was. Why?"

"Well, one of our branches on the Upper West Side called me today. Very strange." She paused.

"And?"

"They were doing a routine audit at the bank, and one of the auditors was checking that all the safety deposit boxes had been paid for and she recognized a name on the list of box holders."

"Whose? Dr. Francis'?"

"Yes, but she recognized the other name from recent news reports. Tom Connaught. He's a co-owner of the box. The auditor looked up Tom in the bank records and saw that he was a customer at my branch. And called."

We both paused for a minute.

"I want into that safety deposit box," I told her.

"You can't Kate. Tom was only a co-owner. We'd need Dr. Francis' permission."

"Well, that's not likely in the near future. He hasn't been heard from in almost a month."

"Is there some way to contact him?" Sara asked.

"Not that I know of. He hasn't been seen at his home or his office for over a month."

"Are NYPD looking for him?"

I snorted at this. "They didn't seem too interested today when I tried to talk to them about it. Dr. Francis was a client of our company and from talking to people at his place of work it seems he resigned his job and said he was moving away. That doesn't sound like a missing person to most people. It sounds like someone who doesn't want to be contacted."

"Well, I'm sorry but until Dr. Francis turns up, we can't access the box.

I didn't mean to upset you with this news Kate, I just thought you'd want to know."

"Yeah, thanks Sara. I'm not upset. Just another dead end in a day of dead ends. Not very encouraging but interesting."

So what the hell could be in that safety deposit box? What were Tommy and the impossible to find Dr. Francis up to?

It was Friday night, and I was glad to see the end of the work week. If I had been at my apartment in Toronto I would be doing some housework, some laundry, ordering a pizza for delivery, and hunkering down with a good Harlequin romance novel. A normal, boring, Friday evening. But nothing that had happened over the last couple of weeks resembled normal, and I longed for it. The traffic below on Fifth Avenue was heavy, and the fumes from the cabs and buses, and Lincoln Town Cars wafted up to where I was sitting on the balcony with my Diet Coke. My feet were up on a cushioned ottoman and my drink was sitting on a glass-topped table beside me. You could fit one small kitchen chair on my balcony in Toronto so I was feeling pretty special sitting in this very comfortable outdoor chair, enjoying the exhaust filled air. The smoke from my cigarette just added to the whole ambience. Jay would be back soon with our pizza and I had a good book to get into. I might even take a long bath and get into bed really early.

As things turned out, it would be a long time before I felt this relaxed again.

Chapter forty-eight

IT WAS A GOOD THING that I fell asleep so early the night before. We had a seven a.m. appointment with Frank Sanchez so I didn't whine too much when Jay had me up and at 'em at six. Jay had woken me the night before from a deliciously cozy couch in the living room where I had fallen asleep reading restated financial statements. Before I dozed off I remember thinking that I had found the cure for insomnia - financial statements - and for especially bad cases I would recommend reading the notes to the financial statements. Honest to God, did people actually read that babble?

Manhattan was beautifully quiet early on a Saturday morning and Lou was on hand to drive us to Frank's place.

I settled into the back seat of the car and thought about how quickly I was getting used to being driven around. "Lou, there is no way you are working seven days a week," I told him. "I don't care if you're driving the President of the United States."

"It's okay, ma'am," he assured me as we pulled away from our building, heading south on Fifth Avenue. "I'm off at noon today and Mr. Northland has arranged for one of our other drivers to be available."

Traffic was light this early in the morning and we made good time driving to Soho. Lou got lucky with the lights and I counted twenty consecutive blocks before we hit a red. As we drove, Jay and I discussed our weekend plans. Although I had absolutely zero desire to go to the office, I knew I had to. One of the reasons that presidents and chief executive officers were in the office seven days a week was because of the endless stream of paper, documents to be reviewed, requests to be turned down, opinions to be given, advice to be doled out, phone calls to be returned, emails to be answered, studies to be studied, research to verify, and proposals to be vetted. I wasn't complaining - well maybe a little bit - but my problem wasn't just the amount of work, it was the continual learning curve. Some of the research papers that crossed my desk were absolutely mind boggling. The fact that Tommy had degrees in biology, engineering, and software design probably made it a little easier for him to understand the mounds of paper. Yours truly had a solid high school education and two years of community college where I'd trained as a paralegal. None of my education had prepared me for the highly technical, financial, and scientific issues that crossed my desk on a daily basis. I was learning though how to fake it well.

Frank's lesson was pretty much a repeat of the day before. "We need you to practice what we went over yesterday," he told us. "Repetition and more repetition will make it second nature, so we need to train not just your body but your brain too."

Knife and gun disarms, how to get out of choke holds, what to do when someone grabs you from behind. We practiced, and then practiced some more. And then just to be sure, we practiced one more time. Jay would attack me and then I would reciprocate. How to handle the situations was almost becoming second nature to me and as Jay and I went through the motions I allowed my mind to zone out and my body to take over. The hour flew by and when Frank suggested we take a few minutes to practice our jabs and low line kicks, I was all for it. I do believe I actually got a second wind and wasn't half as exhausted as I was the day before. Could I actually be getting in shape?

The three of us stood around chugging from bottles of water when we finally finished up about an hour and a half later.

"So Kate, what do you think about all this training?" Frank asked me. "Do you feel like you're getting the hang of it?"

I mopped the sweat from my face before answering. "I think I'm getting it. I'm starting to understand it better. Today was good though because I was able to react to Jay's attacks without too much thinking. I'm actually liking it and enjoying the physical side of it. Especially the punching and kicking."

"Good to hear. But remember, there's no substitute for awareness. Keep your mind sharp and always be aware of your situation. Don't let your guard down. Don't get into stupid situations." Jay nodded his head in agreement with Frank.

"Understood Frank," I assured him.

I was at my desk by ten o'clock. I had a quick shower at home after our workout with Frank where I changed into presentable jeans, T-shirt and running shoes. If I had to work, I was going to be comfortable.

The office was expectedly quiet - it was after all a Saturday morning in the summer. When I had signed in with the security guard in the lobby of the office tower, I noticed that there were only a few signatures of Phoenix staff on the list. Not that I recognized any of them. I was only a couple of weeks into the job and most of the employees were still strangers to me.

The mound of papers in my in-basket made me groan and I decided to make some coffee before tackling the pile. The hallways were dark, with the only light coming through glass panels built into the walls next to the doors of offices that had windows to the outside. There was an eerie greenish glow coming from one open doorway and I smiled when I realized it was coming from the photocopier. The coffee room was pitch black but I found the light switch right where it should have been. The door to the coffee room closed behind me quietly.

There were two large coffee machines on the long counter. One which made a whole pot of coffee at a time and the other which dispensed caffeinated or decaffeinated coffee by the cup. I fetched a large china mug from the cupboard and placed it under the spout on the one-cup machine, pushed the button for caffeinated, and watched in fascination through the clear glass front of the machine as it measured up a goodly amount of coffee beans, ground them, placed the coffee grounds in a funny looking gizmo, shot a large amount of boiling water through it which drained into my cup, and then disposed of the used coffee grounds into another container. Very cool.

Back at my desk I worked through my in-basket, dealing with each item as best I could. The things I couldn't manage without some advice were put into a separate pile. Mundane crap was put into another pile for Carrie to deal with.

Sandra Melnick had left three technical proposals, each in its own file folder, and all three held together with a large rubber band. A large, yellow Post-it note was stuck on the top with a handwritten note from Sandra. She thought I might want to be in the loop on what was going on in the R and D group, and these three proposals were the largest projects for which we were preparing bids. Each file had a template form stapled on the inside cover of the file folder with some basic information. At the bottom of each form there was a section for financial information. Each of these proposals was worth over $10 million, if we were to be the successful bidder. Successful would be nice, I thought, and a couple of these projects could help with the dent in our financials that the loss of the Global Devices work had caused.

The next couple of hours were spent reading and devouring the contents of these three files. I made copious notes to myself and stuck dozens of little, yellow Post-it notes in the margins of the documents highlighting areas where I had questions. Each file contained a bundle of spreadsheets, which were created by our internal financial staff, setting out what we estimated it would cost the company to carry out the work. Some of the spreadsheets had so many columns and rows I could barely read them.

During the time I'd been at the office, Jay had called me twice and Kelly Northland had called me once. Jay was not happy that I was going to the office and I had refused to let him come with me. He tried, unsuccessfully, to talk me out of it. The two phone calls from him were his way of checking up on me.

"I don't understand why you couldn't just bring the work home with you," he'd said the first time he'd called.

Kelly pretty much echoed what Jay had said and told me that he was on his way to the office, he'd see me shortly. Jay must have called him and told on me. I wondered if he was going to call my mom too.

"Kelly, I'm fine. The place is quiet. I'm getting some work done." I was talking to a dead phone.

I felt comfortable at the office, and Jay and Kelly were probably over-reacting. To what I wasn't sure. They both were being over-protective, which I reluctantly acknowledged and appreciated, but, in my typical, hard headed fashion, I ignored.

When I finished with the three proposals, I swiveled in my chair to the computer and fired it up. I would finish up by going through my emails and seeing if there was anything urgent. Then, home, and a leisurely afternoon with Jay. Maybe I could convince him to go with me to one of the art museums or for a walk in Central Park. Maybe we could visit the zoo which was right across the street from the apartment and which I was dying to visit.

Microsoft Outlook took a while to boot up and by the time it was running I knew why it had taken so long. My in-basket had over two hundred unread messages. For gawd's sake, I thought, I was out of the office for one day. I either had to get a Blackberry so I could stay on top of the emails or give Carrie access so she could deal with them.

The message on the top of the list was the most recently received one so I scrolled down several screens to get to the first unread message, so I could go through them in order. The first eighteen messages were spam and by the time I had opened and deleted the eighteenth I was disgusted. Disgusted with the content of the spam messages and disgusted that there were people out there who spent their days sending shit like this. The next dozen messages were legitimate business emails, which I read. They could be dealt with on Monday so I left them where they were in the in-basket. Anxious to finish up, I started scanning the sender's name and subject line to see if there was anything that needed my attention that couldn't wait until Monday. I scanned and scrolled, scanned and scrolled. Dozens of the emails were internal, from the Vice Presidents, or bulletins to the employees, some of them automatically generated, like the financial update which was issued every forty-eight hours to the executive team. I scrolled over those and dozens more spam.

My finger froze on the mouse when I caught the subject line of an email I thought at first glance was spam. It read *You Don't Control It All Bitch.* This was the first spam message I had seen with a word like *bitch* in it. I clicked on the message, purely out of curiosity, and quickly wished I had ignored it.

Chapter forty-nine

It turns out that the subject line was only mildly offensive. The text of the message turned my stomach.

"You do not control the life of others, you do not control the universe. You do not control who lives and dies. The one who sat where you do today thought they were in control. You are a tiny microcosm who has no worth, no meaning, no value to this world. Like the one before you, you will cease to exist in the macrocosm. Snuffed out, extinct and no longer believing that you are in control. Bitch. Goodbye."

My breathing was shallow and my face felt flushed. I quickly pushed my chair back, separating myself from the computer. The message remained on the screen and I stared at it from a distance. *The one who sat where you do today...* Did the message mean Tommy? I quickly lit a cigarette and paced in front of the windows. Who had sent that email? The sender's email address was gobbledy-gook: ie78amaielr@nyu.edu and the message had been sent in the middle of the night.

The email was threatening and admittedly scared the crap out of me. I closed the offending message and scrolled carefully through the rest of my emails to see if there were any similar messages. Seeing none, I clicked on the large X in the top, right-hand corner of my screen, shutting down Outlook. Out of sight, out of mind, I thought.

The stalker smiled and admired the reflection in the computer screen. The calm visage reflecting back made the stalker feel powerful. The calm was not faked but as a result of biofeedback, which was a learned technique, easy for someone of the stalker's power to master. The stalker was finally in control of breathing and blood pressure. The bitch had just read the email. Untraceable email. Time to turn up the heat.

The scream caught in my throat and I couldn't get it out because I swear to God that was where my heart was. With my heart pounding at about three hundred beats a minute, I closed my eyes and took a couple of quick breaths.

"Jesus," I breathed out slowly. "You scared me."

Kelly was less than eighteen inches in front of me and he stood stock still in the exact position he was in when I had opened my office door. As soon as I closed down my computer I had phoned the driver and gathered up my things. I was spooked by the email and wanted to get out of the office.

"I was just about to knock," he explained. "Didn't mean to scare you."

"It's okay," I said. "I was just leaving."

"You look upset," he said. "What happened?"

"Besides you scaring the bejeezus out of me?" I shot back.

"Yeah, besides that."

"Just an email I got. It kind of spooked me."

Kelly pushed past me into my office and headed over towards my computer. "Show me."

While I booted up the computer, Kelly gave me another gentle lecture about not venturing out on my own. I was spooked enough by the eerie email that I paid attention.

"Until this case is settled, you can't afford to be alone outside of your apartment."

"But I can't ask you to spend your time following me around."

"I don't plan on it. That's why we've arranged for a bodyguard. Lou is officially on holidays for a few days. We'll have a professional driver and guard with you at all times."

"Isn't that a bit much?" I ventured. Kelly didn't respond so I imagine my question was rhetorical in his mind.

The computer screen asked for my log-in and password so I typed them in and waited while the computer continued. At long last the computer stopped its grinding and calmly waited for me to tell it what to do so I clicked on the email icon and my in-box popped right up. I scrolled down until I got to the email, where it sat amongst the hundreds of others.

I offered Kelly my chair and pointed at the message, leaving it unopened so he could see the subject line. He sat down, pulled his notebook out of his jacket pocket and made a few notes as he peered at the computer screen. He finally reached for the mouse and clicked on the message, opening it.

"Where's your printer?" he asked and clicked on the little printer icon at the top of the page.

"At Carrie's desk," I told him and headed to the outer office to pick up the printed copy. When I came back in the office he was on the phone, talking quietly. I sat in one of the guest chairs in front of my desk and waited for him. Again, my thoughts took me to that angry place where I cursed Tommy. Which on reflection was a waste of time. Cursing Tommy, poor Tom, wasn't getting me any closer to finding out who and what caused this shit storm.

Kelly and I didn't talk on our elevator ride to the lobby and I could literally feel heat emanating from him. The car was waiting by the curb outside the building but before we crossed the sidewalk to it, I grabbed Kelly's arm.

"Why are you so pissed off?" There was no mistaking that the heat coming from him was anger.

"I'm not pis... angry," he told me. I noted that like most old-style military guys, he didn't use 'foul' words in front of the opposite sex.

"Well, you could have fooled me."

"Let's get you home and settled," he said in his calm southern drawl, and tried to take me by the arm and lead me to the car. I shook off his hand.

"Home? And settled? What do you think I am? An invalid? Or a doddering old fool? Don't you patronize me!" Now the heat was coming off of me.

Kelly stood quietly in front of me, while I ranted, with his hands clasped in front of him. He didn't say anything. Passive aggressive son-of-a-bitch! I stormed over to the car and grabbed the handle on the back door. Which only caused me to break a fingernail because the back door was locked. So I kicked the bottom of the door, just like a spoiled fourteen year old brat. Embarrassed now by my behaviour, I took a deep breath and turned around to find Kelly standing close by.

"Sorry," I mumbled. "But I can't stand being patronized and treated like a child," I told him. To give him credit, he'd only really known me for a few days, so it was likely he hadn't caught on to Kate's quirks and temperament.

"Listen," he said. "I'm sorry if that came across as patronizing. It wasn't meant to be. But I'm worried about your safety. And that email has me as jumpy as spit on a hot skillet." That made me smile a little. "I'm worried about your safety and worried about the investigation. That's why I'm handing you over to a team of guards. They'll be with you twenty-four seven." That didn't make me smile.

"Day and night? Is that really necessary?"

"Do you want me on the case?"

I nodded.

"Then ma'am, we do it my way."

With that, he opened the back door of the sedan, and we both slid in the back seat. I was surprised to see two guys up front, neither of whom was Lou.

"Lou's taking a few days off," Kelly reminded me. "Meet some of the members of your new team."

From behind they looked like scary statues. Both had wide, muscular shoulders, and their hair was buzzed short, military style. Both had earphones jammed into their right ears with a curly cord snaking down the back of their neck and disappearing out of sight. Both were wearing aviator-style sunglasses and when they turned around in their seats to meet me, I could see my reflection in their sunglasses.

I smiled at them even though their presence made me nervous. "You guys look like commandos," I joked. Neither of them smiled at that and the one in the passenger seat said, "Pleased to meet you ma'am." The one in the driver's seat put the car in gear and we drove off.

Chapter fifty

KELLY AND JAY HAD THEIR heads together at the dining room table, planning out exactly what they needed to do to put a trace on the email.

"Hey, we're a high tech company. I know we've got a few geeks on the payroll. Why don't we use one of them to help us figure this out?" I offered.

"That's absolutely true, ma'am, but I have a little-bitty problem with that plan. I'm not sure who we can trust at this point."

"Well," Jay said. "We're going to have to pick one person to trust, because you'll need to get into the email system at Phoenix and I'm guessing that the only way to do that would be with a Phoenix employee."

I left them to figure it all out and wandered into the kitchen to make some lunch and some coffee. The Navy Seal sitting at the round table in the kitchen startled me. I had forgotten about him.

"Making yourself at home?" He sat as still as a stone statue and nodded his head, mutely. I pulled out a chair and sat across the table from him.

"Do you do this often?" I asked him.

"Often enough, ma'am."

Ah, definitely military. Being called ma'am makes me feel as old as Methuselah.

"Ex-military?" I asked rhetorically. Anything to get a conversation going. I figured him to be in his mid-thirties, but with his hair cut so short, he looked about fifteen.

"Yes ma'am. Retired last year."

I laughed and he looked a little confused.

"Sorry. I wasn't laughing at you," I said by way of explanation. "It just sounds so funny, coming from someone as young as you to be saying you're retired."

He nodded. "I guess. Had twenty years in. Thought I'd get out while the gettin' was good." And then he smiled, and that made him a little more human.

"What's your first name again?"

"Chris."

"Well, Chris, welcome to my home. Make yourself comfortable. Help yourself to anything you need. I mean it." I leaned over the table and pointed at the earplug in his ear. "Were you a Navy Seal?"

"No ma'am. Marine Corps. Military police. I worked with Mr. Northland for years."

"Can I interest you in some coffee?"

"Maybe in a bit, ma'am. I was waiting for Mr. Northland so we can do a perimeter check."

Jesus, this was sounding like being back home with my dad.

While Chris and Kelly secured the perimeter, whatever the hell that meant because there were only three entrances to the apartment - not counting the balcony - and seriously that was fourteen floors up - Jay and I ate some lunch at the counter in the kitchen. That's when he told me.

"I have to go to Toronto. I'll be gone a couple of days. I know it's not a good time, but I couldn't very well argue with them."

True. Jay was in a job that he was thankful to have. After the mess with our previous employer when Jay was fired, he was grateful for his job and he worked hard at it. There was little I could do or say except let him know it was okay.

"It's okay. Really. And don't worry about what's going on here. Apparently I now have trained commandos at my beck and call, watching over me. When are you leaving?"

His flight was in the morning. We decided to spend the rest of the day together, not talking or thinking about Phoenix Technologies or Tommy, or anything related to either of them. It was easier said than done, though, especially with Chris trailing two feet behind us at the Wildlife Centre and the Central Park Zoo. The zoo was quaint and overcrowded with lots of moms and dads and screaming, squealing little kids.

"What do you suppose the protocol is," I asked Jay, "if we stop for an ice cream? Do we offer Chris one? Are we supposed to ignore him, pretend he's not there?"

Jay wrapped his arm around my waist and pulled me close to him, in an uncharacteristic public embrace. "Ignore him, pay attention to me," he whispered into my ear. Which was easier said than done. Especially with Chris the bodyguard hovering nearby and a family of four staring at us.

Jay's flight was early the next morning and I didn't hear him leave for the airport. It took me a few seconds to remember that I was by myself in the large, king size bed and when I realized that Jay was gone, I moved over to his side of the bed and wrapped the duvet around me. I hugged his pillow and breathed in his scent. Being with Jay and living with him felt right - as corny as that sounded - and I tried to recall if I had ever felt so content. We had only shared this apartment for a week but we were already acting like a couple who had been together forever. It was strange being alone in the apartment but I relished the thought. As much as I wanted - and needed - to share my life and share my living space with Jay, being alone at times and having my space was important too. Living alone for most of my adult life had made me self-sufficient and self-reliant. And just because I had lived alone didn't mean I was a lonely person.

The digital clock on the beside table told me it was only 7:19. I kicked off the duvet and stretched and started making a mental list of things I would do today. There was laundry to be done. Some personal phone calls to make. I owed my parents a call and I hadn't spoken with my brother in over a week. I thought about going out and exploring the neighbourhood. Scout out the local grocery stores. See if I could find a newsstand that sold The Toronto Star, my favourite Sunday newspaper. I wiggled my toes and smiled in anticipation of the perfect day ahead of me.

The smile didn't last long though when the phone rang and I heard Kelly's drawl. As usual, I was avoiding the unpleasant and had not even thought about Phoenix in the five minutes I had been awake.

"Morning, ma'am."

"Kelly. How are you today?" The last thing I wanted to do today was deal with company shit. I sat up and swung my legs over the side of the bed.

"Not so good. I'd like to give you a briefing. We've had some developments over night and I need to bring you up to speed."

Kelly's developments were no doubt bad news.

"Where are you?"

"Outside your building."

"I'll buzz you up and you can make the coffee while I take a shower."

"Yes ma'am."

I wanted to crawl back under the duvet but instead I threw on some sweats and a T-shirt and waited at the front door for my daily dose of crap to be delivered.

Kelly placed a steaming mug of coffee in front of me when I climbed up on the stool at the kitchen bar. He had spent plenty of time in the apartment the last forty-eight hours and knew his way around the kitchen. It felt familiar, sitting at the bar with a coffee but Kelly was standing where Jay usually did - on the other side.

"Help yourself to some food, if you like," I offered.

Kelly shook his head. "Not hungry."

I agreed. I'd lost my appetite when the phone rang twenty minutes ago.

"So, Staff Sergeant," I gently teased him. He looked so damn serious all the time. "What's going on?"

"Well, for starters, we've lost touch with our guy on the ground in Flagstaff."

"What's his name? Jerry?"

"Right. Jerry Rigley. We haven't heard from him since Friday night."

Fuck.

"He was supposed to be checking out those addresses for Natalie and Ben. What happened with that? Is he the type of guy to stop calling in?"

"No," Kelly said. "He's usually very reliable. Most of my guys are." Kelly's face was grim - more so than usual.

"You said 'my guys', Kelly. Is he one of our employees? Should I be thinking the worst?"

"No," Kelly said. He reached his hand across the counter, as if to touch me, but he pulled it back quickly. "No, he's not an employee. He's just one of my guys." Kelly sipped at his coffee.

"How so?"

"One of the guys in my network. There're dozens of us. We all knew each other in the military, in one capacity or the other. We're all retired now and a lot of the guys freelance. They do contract security work. I needed someone to investigate in Flagstaff, so I called up one of my guys."

"My escort yesterday, Chris, and the gentleman driving? Your guys?"

Kelly nodded. "Of course. It's all about trust. When you serve in the military and see some action, you trust the guys who have your back. We've all stayed in touch and we all help each other out, from time to time."

"So, not hearing from Jerry is unlike him?"

"Very." Kelly put his empty coffee mug in the dishwasher. What a good man.

"Frankly, it's totally unlike him. He did call me later Friday afternoon and let me know that he was still working on tracking down some individuals who might have known those two out in Flagstaff. That was the last contact. He's not answering his cell phone. We checked all the motels and hotels and he hasn't registered at one of those."

"Does he have family that he might have called?"

"Just his mom and dad, and when I spoke with them last night, they said they haven't heard from him in while." Kelly put both hands on the counter top and leaned forward a bit. "That's just one of the things we needed to talk about," he informed me.

"There's more?" I shook my head. "Jesus Christ, Kelly, what the hell is going on?" I slid off the stool and rummaged through my purse that was sitting on the counter. "That poor man's parents must be worried sick. He's out doing work for us and he disappears and you're standing here, all business, not worried at all." I found my pack of cigarettes and greedily lit one. "Just standing there, listing off the bad news, as if you're reading a newscast." That was nasty, and I knew it as soon as I said it. "Sorry," I quickly offered. I had to stop acting like a spoiled child.

"Fine," he said in a low voice. "But please keep in mind that one of the reasons I'm good at what I do is I try to keep it *all business*. But don't think for one minute that this is just business for me. I'm a professional but I care about the people I work with. Jerry's a friend. Yeah, I'm worried. But Jerry's a big boy. He's been known to be able to look after himself. Do you see me screaming and crying and making a huge fuss about it? No. 'Cause I'm all business. And I'll find him."

I felt chagrined and looked down at my feet. When was I going to learn to keep my trap shut?

"I'm sorry," I told him again. "I didn't mean to imply that you didn't care." He nodded in acknowledgement of my lame apology.

"What're we doing to try and find him?"

"Two guys drove up from Phoenix yesterday afternoon. They haven't found him yet. I'm expecting to hear from them this morning."

This couldn't be good. Someone reliable who hadn't checked-in and hadn't been heard from in over twenty-four hours. "Did we check the hospitals? Call the local police? Maybe he was in an accident or had a heart attack or something."

Kelly's head nodded as I talked. "Yeah. We've checked with local authorities. No one matching his description has turned up."

"What's the other bad news?" I reluctantly asked.

"There's no trace of Natalie Scott or Ben Tucker."

That sounded like good news to me, and I said so. Kelly didn't agree with me.

"No, it's not good news. We'd rather know where they are. In fact, I *want* to know where they are because it's time they answered a few questions. We spent most of yesterday afternoon and evening trying to track them down. Neither of them are answering at their apartments."

Well, call me kooky, but if I didn't want to be found, the last thing I'd do is answer the door. Kelly and his guys were not the police so it wasn't as if they were going to force the door open.

"Did you call at Nat's apartment before eight at night?" I told him what Miss Everwood had shared with me about no one being allowed in or out after eight.

"Yeah, we tried during the afternoon. The front desk here can't remember the last time they saw her. Or her mother for that matter."

Chapter fifty-one

KELLY'S PHONE RANG AND I could tell by the look on his face that he was not receiving good news from whoever was on the other end. The apartment phone started ringing and I was reluctant to answer it, wanting to hear from Kelly as soon as he hung up. As it turned out, I should have ignored it. The caller identified herself as a business reporter from The Wall Street Journal. By the name of Portia Wellington. I wondered out loud how she got my phone number.

"From Tom Connaught. We used to talk often. I put two and two together and thought I'd try this number to see if you were at his apartment," she explained.

"Well, you found me," I said, making a mental note to change the phone number. "What can I do for you?" I probably sounded a little curt with her but reporters should be used to that.

"I'm calling about the press release your company issued on Thursday. About the loss of the Global Devices contracts."

That crisis seemed like a lifetime ago but in reality the press release in question was probably less than seventy-two hours old. And what the hell was I going to tell a reporter? This was not something I wanted to deal with. Hell, it was something I didn't know *how* to deal with. At the last company I worked for there were authorized company spokespersons who were up to speed on the issues and knew what and what not to say. As the CEO, I was likely an authorized spokesperson for the company, but having had no experience with reporters, I was a little wary about saying anything. But how do you put off a reporter from The Wall Street Journal who could knowingly do more damage to your company and your share price than if you admitted that Arthur Andersen were your auditors?

"Yes, what can I help you with?"

"I'm trying to understand why the contracts with Global Devices were cancelled."

"Well," I told her, "this happens in business. Contracts are terminated. The reasons remain between the parties. That's about all I can say on the matter."

"I suppose your lawyers have warned you not to speak about the reasons, in case of future litigation?" My silence was probably answer enough for her, so she pressed on. "Is there any connection between Tom Connaught's death and the cancellation of the contracts?" Well, it's certainly looking like it from my point of view, but I wasn't going to say anything on that issue.

"Hardly," I lied, in a slightly indignant tone. "Is there anything else?"

"Have the police got any leads at all on Tom's murder? Do they have any idea what happened?" Miss Wellington was getting into the type of news that The Wall Street Journal never covered.

"You'd have to ask the police. I'm sure they have their theories. Is that all Miss Wellington?"

"I guess that's all for now, Miss Monahan. Although I would love the opportunity to have an in-depth interview with you. About the company, your job, your background. I'm sure our readers would love to hear more about you."

"Well, that's certainly flattering, but I don't think there's much about me that's newsworthy," I said with a modicum of modesty. I just wanted to end this conversation.

"Oh come on," she laughed. "Don't sell yourself short. That picture of you on the front page of The Toronto Sun, climbing into the back of an ambulance. That picture alone must be worth a story."

That fucking Toronto Sun photo was going to haunt me for a very long time. The cover photo she was talking about was of me climbing into the back of an ambulance after I was terrorized by that madman. The photo was payback for me refusing to let the paramedics put me on a stretcher. It was very unflattering and showed more of my ass than I cared to share with the world. And there wasn't any story, any more. That was past history, and something I'd rather forget about. Although it wasn't surprising that a reporter had gone digging. There was a lot of press coverage of the murders, suicide, and company failure that I was involved in several months ago. So I fake-laughed right back at her and we ended the call.

I wasn't laughing though when I saw Kelly's face. He was still talking on the phone, and jotting notes in his little notebook. His face was all business. "When we know anything at all," he was saying into the phone, "we'll call you. Count on it. Yeah. Bye." He flipped the phone shut and tossed it on the counter top. "Shit," he muttered under his breath.

"What? What's going on?"

They had found Jerry's car in a neighbourhood on the outskirts of Flagstaff. But no sign of Jerry. Kelly's guys were knocking on doors. So far, nothing.

"The good news is it's early in the morning out there and they're likely to find lots of people at home. That was Jerry's mom I was talking to. She's waiting to hear from us. She's a soldier's mom and she's spent lots of time over the years waiting to hear about her son."

I hugged myself and thought about Jerry's mom, and wondered why I felt so bad about someone I didn't even know. The enormity of being responsible for so many people hit me. Our company employed hundreds of people, and those hundreds had relatives who cared for them. And then there were the men and women who were only peripherally involved in our company. Like Kelly's "guys". My head reeled. I actually felt a little faint. My insulated world that three weeks ago had included little ol' me, Jay, my family, his family and a few acquaintances, had grown exponentially. How could I possibly care about people I didn't even know? Hadn't even met? Yet my heart was pounding, my breath was short, and deep inside me I knew that Tommy had cared for these people. Employees yes, but Tommy would have cared for them and their families like they were his own. I resolved to do the same.

"I can help. I can't sit around and do nothing. I'll go out of my mind." Kelly and I were arguing, and I was losing.

"There's too much that we don't know at this stage. I can't allow it." I almost let him get away with it, but I was born argumentative.

"Allow it?"

He interrupted me before I went any further.

"Yes, allow it. You've put your trust in me. Stop being so pigheaded. You're getting in the way. I know you're the boss and I know you want to be in charge. But I have to insist."

"Fine." I gave in reluctantly.

"She's all yours, Chris." He smiled at Chris, my bodyguard, who had arrived about ten minutes ago. The silent behemoth just nodded his head and stood like a stone statue in the living room, his hands clasped in front of him.

Chris made sure the door was locked behind Kelly when he left and I wandered out to the balcony for a cigarette. The air was feeling muggy and sticky, and it reminded me of Toronto on a humid, July afternoon. There was no breeze and the smoke from my cigarette just hung in the air. The day loomed ahead of me. I was a virtual prisoner in my apartment with a bodyguard for company. I knew I had to keep busy or go out of my mind, worrying and wondering what Kelly was up to. He had told me there were several avenues he needed to explore but first he needed to go back to the 20th Precinct. See if he could enlist some assistance from New York's finest in uncovering the whereabouts of Natalie Scott, Ben Tucker and Dr. Francis.

It took me all of three minutes to do a thorough job of feeding the fish in the magical aquarium built into the wall. I killed another fifteen minutes making the bed, throwing dirty clothes into the hamper, re-hanging the bath towels and emptying the dishwasher. The mundane tasks did nothing to slow down my thoughts and of course I just made myself more frustrated and pissed off. Locked inside my home. Unable to do anything to help.

But how could you help Kate, I asked myself. Always wanting to stick your nose in where it doesn't belong, I chided myself. But it *is* my business, the voice inside my head argued. Miss Busybody, who can't stand it when she's not in control and isn't being kept up to date on progress. I shook my head and instead of fighting with myself, I sat quietly in a dining room chair, and tried to be an adult about all of this. Worked at calming down my pea brain. Reasoned with myself. I rubbed the top of my right ear and reminded myself what happened the last time I just couldn't help myself and got involved in a situation that was *way* over my head.

My brain had taken enough self-arguing and before I drove myself completely crazy, I decided to go for a walk. Chris the bodyguard wasn't happy with me, but he did agree that he could protect me sufficiently if push came to shove, on the streets of Manhattan.

The air felt muggier at street level but it felt good to be outside. Standing under the canopy at the front of the apartment building, I looked right and then left, trying to decide which way to go. Across the street was Central Park which Jay and I had explored the day before. If I turned right, I would walk north. For no specific reason, I turned left and when I reached Central Park South, I crossed Fifth Avenue and walked across the southernmost part of the Park. The street vendors were out in full force, their makeshift stalls tucked into the shade of the trees up against the low stone wall which surrounded the Park. Nine horses with their buggies and drivers lined the street. The area teemed with tourists. Chris dogged my heels as I walked and I did my best to ignore him.

When I reached Central Park West, I crossed Columbus Circle and Broadway and kept walking west, down West 60th Street. The area was a mix of residential and businesses, populated with apartment and office buildings. I walked for blocks, randomly turning up different streets. I passed the Julliard School and the Metropolitan Opera House. Tenth Avenue appealed to me so I turned onto it and continued my walk. Within a couple of blocks, I could see ambulances turning into a large complex. A large, white sign with black lettering identified the complex as the Van Buren Health Centre. Underneath several clinics were identified, and at the very bottom, in smaller letters it read "Deliveries Accepted Only From West 79th St., Monday to Friday, 7 am to 5 pm ONLY".

I pointed at the Deliveries Only part of the sign and asked Chris, "Where's West 79th?" He pointed up the street. "The next block," he said. I headed in that direction, knowing that my wanderings had not been random after all. Another large, white sign appeared with huge red letters reading "Deliveries" and under that in smaller black letters "Van Buren Health Centre".

A paved road about five hundred feet long and two lanes wide went off to the left. There was no sidewalk but I turned in anyway and headed down the road to the back of the Health Centre.

"Ma'am," Chris called out to me.

Without turning around I waved him on and said, "Come on. I just want to explore back here."

I didn't tell him this was where Tommy's body had been found and that some sort of magnet was pulling me down the road. Grass lined the road and there were some trees planted on the right side. I could see a chain link fence behind the trees, running along the hospital's property and disappearing in the distance. After walking a couple of minutes I came to the back of the hospital where there were six delivery bays, each with its own industrial size garage door. Large, cement dividers separated each delivery bay and I imagined that the trucks would back in to a bay and offload their cargo through the garage door. It being the weekend, the area was deserted, with only a white panel van parked off to the side.

I stood quietly and breathed in my surroundings, wondering where Tommy had been shot. Past the asphalt delivery area there was grass, some sad looking shrubs, and the chain link fence. Beyond the fence there were tall, brick buildings, most likely apartments. I turned slowly in a circle, taking it all in.

The back of the hospital building was solid brick with the delivery doors the only obvious way in. Above each of the large doors, yellow light bulbs encased in round wire cages protruded from the walls. West 79th Street seemed quite a distance away, down the long driveway.

Where did they find his body? I crossed a huge expanse of asphalt towards the fence, scanning the ground, picturing his lifeless corpse, lying unattended. Did he lie on the cold ground, alive, hoping for someone, anyone to help him? Did he lie on the cold ground feeling his life draining away? My breath caught in my throat and I sobbed out loud. When I reached the fence, I laced my fingers through the chain links and stared at the buildings on the other side.

And thought about the sick son-of-a-bitch who had shot Tommy and left him here, on the asphalt. Did the killer stand over Tommy and watch him die?

Anger took the place of grief and I wanted to scream. I turned on my heel and started back towards the main street. Chris, who had been standing by the loading docks watching me, followed along.

Chapter fifty-two

A FAMILIAR-LOOKING LINCOLN TOWN CAR was idling at the end of the long roadway leading out of the hospital loading area. As we approached the car, the front passenger door opened and Kelly got out and waited for us. No words were spoken and I put up no fight when he opened the back door of the car. I slid across the seat and he joined me.

"Have you been following me?" I asked.

"No ma'am. Chris was watching out for you."

"Then what are you doing here now?"

The car was still parked and I noticed that the driver and Chris were standing on the sidewalk, talking. Kelly turned sideways in his seat to face me and laid his left arm along the back of the leather seat.

"After I left you this morning, I had a call from Detective Shipley," he started. This didn't sound like it was going to be joyous news. "A body was found two days ago and they've just made a preliminary identification. Had been dead about a week which hampered their efforts to find out who it is. Shipley said the prelim ID says it's Dr. Francis."

I didn't have anything to say to that and turned my head to the left and stared out the window. Traffic was light and there wasn't much going on outside the car. Kelly let the silence hang between us.

Dr. Francis. I'd never met the man, never laid eyes on him. I knew of him for less than a week. So why did I feel so sad? So helpless and hopeless?

"Did she say how he died?" I asked.

Kelly shook his head. "No, they're still doing the autopsy. But the body showed signs of mutilation."

My stomach turned.

"What?" My voice was barely a whisper.

"Both kidneys had been removed."

Oh. My. God.

"I need to go home. Now. Please."

I sat at Tommy's desk in the formal office space adjacent to the dining room. Besides a telephone, the only thing on the desk was a pad of white, blue-lined paper, on the top of which I had written TO DO. Each item on my to do list took up a line on the sheet and I was three-quarters of the way down the page.

On the ride home from the Van Buren Health Centre which took less than fifteen minutes, I quickly went from horrified and sickened about the news of the death of Dr. Francis, to my old Sergeant-Major mode. There were things that needed to be done, and done quickly, and correctly. For a brief moment during my horrified and sickened period, I envisioned myself going back to the apartment, packing my suitcase, and heading out to the airport to fly home to Toronto. But I didn't need my mother's voice in my head to tell me that there were too many people, employees, and families of employees at Phoenix, who were depending on me. Well, not *me*, per se. They were depending on the company for their wages and well-being. If they actually *knew* who was at the helm, many would probably run screaming into the streets. Whether the employees and shareholders liked it or not, they were stuck with me, for the immediate future.

The first thing on my list that needed to be done was to talk to Cleve. Things were getting to a stage that the board of directors needed to be informed. They had been given a report a couple of days ago on the status of the Global Devices contracts and the course of action being taken by management with the SEC and the OSC. I needed advice from Cleve. On what, I wasn't sure.

He sounded relaxed when he answered the phone. It was Sunday and I hated to call him at home, but being accessible to your clients twenty-four seven is one of the reasons these guys earn an hourly rate that is close to the GDP of Romania.

"Kate, I hope everything's okay," he said.

"Not really, Cleve. That's why I'm calling." I told him about the police finding the body of Dr. Francis.

"Oh. That poor man. Was it suicide?"

"Not likely," I snorted. "Although we don't know the cause of death officially, both of his kidneys had been removed."

There was a very long pause from Cleve's end of the phone. I finally had to say something.

"Cleve. Are you there?"

"Yeah." Another long pause. I wasn't about to interrupt one of the finest minds I knew so I waited. "Look, Kate, this has *got* to be related to Tommy's murder. What are the police saying?"

"No idea, because I haven't heard from them. I'm sure you remember the two detectives assigned to Tommy's case. One of them is off sick and the other one is so overwhelmed with cases that I don't know if she knows what day it is. She called Kelly Northland, our head of security, to tell him about the body. We went to see her on Friday after you and I met for lunch and we brought up the fact that Dr. Francis was missing. She at least paid attention to that fact because that's how they were able to make a tentative ID on the body."

There was so much more to tell him but I wasn't even sure where to start. Like the fact that Nat Scott and Ben Tucker were nowhere to be found. Or the fact that Ben Tucker and Nat Scott had spent time together in Flagstaff. Or that Ben Tucker wasn't Ben Tucker and he had served time in a state prison. For crimes I didn't even want to think about. I needed to tell him about Kelly's missing guy out in Flagstaff. And the little fact about the threatening email I had received. Altogether these *facts*, along with two murders, added up to one humongous mess.

Cleve interrupted my thoughts. "I'm going to make some calls Kate. And then I'm on the next plane down there."

"We need to do some more firefighting with the board and the shareholders," I added.

"Yep. That's a given. Let me call you when I've got my flights arranged and we can figure out where to meet when I get there."

"Fly private. I'll arrange for the company plane to meet you at the Island Airport and bring you into Teterboro. It's a lot faster." Hell, we'd just lost about $50 million in revenues. I didn't think it would seem excessive to spend another several thousand dollars to fire up the company jet.

With Cleve here in the City, I would be able to cross off ninety percent of the items on my to do list. Most of the items were things I had to do for the company. Things to protect our company.

Like its reputation.

As soon as the newshounds got wind of Dr. Francis' death and put two and two together, the proverbial shit was going to hit the fan. There is nothing worse for a company than having its name bandied about in the newspaper for things out of the ordinary.

Ordinary would normally include reports on the financial condition of a company, remarks made at a shareholders meeting, a good news report on a new product. Out of the ordinary would include things like the murder of the CEO and founder of the company, the cancellation of millions of dollars worth of contracts with a major customer, the murder of a senior researcher employed by that customer, or convicted felons working as employees, under assumed names. Out of the ordinary would *not* be good for our share price. Speculation in the news always leads to a roller coaster ride for the shareholders.

Fuck, fuck, fuck.

Kelly was talking on his cell phone, and Chris the bodyguard was making coffee when I came into the kitchen. I stood by the door and watched them, and realized I was getting used to having these guys around all the time. Weird, because up until a while ago I considered myself a loner, treasuring my alone time. Admittedly I felt safe with the two of them here in my apartment.

Kelly's voice was low and he was making notes in his spiral bound notebook. The conversation ended and he flipped his phone shut. He seemed so very tired when he looked up and saw me leaning against the doorframe.

I gave him a weary smile, letting him know we were in this together.

"News?" I asked.

"Nothing much," he reported. "My geek was able to trace the source of the email you received. But we weren't able to put a name or identity to it. Seems it was sent on a server at New York University, and it was an NYU email account. Opened just before the email was sent, and closed as soon as the email hit cyberspace. Seems you need to be a registered student at the University to be able to open an email account, but they aren't willing to share any information with us. They have close to forty thousand students, so it would be like searching for the proverbial needle in a haystack."

I joined him at the breakfast counter and heaved myself up onto one of the stools. Chris wordlessly held up a mug, offering me coffee, and I nodded.

"Any news on our guy in Flagstaff?"

Kelly shook his head. "Nothing. It's like he disappeared into thin air."

Chapter fifty-three

THE STALKER RE-READ THE NOTE and smiled in smug satisfaction. The bitch would not get in the way of finishing what was started. Started so long ago. The beginning of this had felt like the end, so long ago. But time was all the stalker had for so very, very long. Time which resulted in getting one's perspective back. Now that the end was so clearly in sight, the stalker was not about to let anyone get in the way of the finish line. No one. Especially Tom Connaught's bitch.

Cleve had a little surprise up his sleeve when he arrived at the apartment, shortly after dinner. My sidekicks and I had Chinese take-out, which on a good night would have been fabulous, but on this night, did little to settle my nervous stomach.

I was waiting at the apartment door for Cleve to get off the elevator and imagined getting lost in one of his bear hugs. Which would probably put me over the edge and the last thing I needed to be doing was bawling like a baby. So instead of offering myself up for a hug, I greeted him with my hands clasped in front of me.

"Good flight?"

"Yeah. That's the way to travel between Toronto and New York. This time of day, everything would be backed up and most flights are probably late. Coming in on a private plane, having the U.S. Customs Agents meet you, and then jumping into a car right on the tarmac is almost heaven."

Cleve settled into one of the wing back chairs and I curled up on one of the sofas in the living room.

"You need to be brought up to speed on everything else that's been going on," I started. "This is one major cluster fuck, with disaster written all over it." Cleve gave me a distasteful look, and I remembered that he was not fond of my foul mouth. "Sorry."

I launched into the long list of events that had happened in the last forty-eight hours. While I talked, Cleve sat quietly, not interrupting, but taking notes on a yellow legal pad which was balanced on his thigh. When I finished he glanced up at me from his note taking, then wrote a few more things before he put the pad and pen on the table beside the chair.

"Okay, I think I have everything," he said. "Before I flew down today, I contacted some people, and I've arranged for us to meet with the Police Commissioner."

"The who?"

"The Police Commissioner. The chief of police for the New York Police Department."

"Yeah, I heard you the first time, Cleve. How did you arrange that? And why would he want to see us?"

"I called the Prime Minister's office." He stated this matter of factly.

"You called the Prime Minister's office," I repeated.

"Yes. And asked him if he had any connections here in New York."

"You called the Prime Minister's office, and he answered the phone?"

Cleve chuckled. "I can see you're obviously easily impressed, Kate. No, I called his office, and his assistant connected me with the Prime Minister, who I believe was at his summer house in Meech Lake. You'll remember that the Prime Minister used to practice law before he went into politics? He was a partner at our former law firm and we've known each for a long time. He told me that his only connection here in New York was with the former mayor, who he had met last year during the September 11th crisis."

"Interesting," I said. "I guess I forgot about that connection." The Prime Minister *had* been a lawyer at the law firm where I first met Cleve, but at that time he was just another snotty, senior partner.

"So, he called the ex-mayor, who put me in touch with the Police Commissioner." Cleve looked at his watch. "We have a meeting with him in an hour."

This was welcome news. Maybe meeting with the Police Commissioner would kick-start some action on the part of NYPD.

"I'd like Kelly to come along," I said.

Cleve was nodding. "Sure, no problem. Did you want to change?" He was staring pointedly at my sweat pants and bare feet.

"That would probably be for the best."

The Commissioner's office was massive. Like a cliché out of an early Edward G. Robinson movie, the Commissioner was squat, a little on the heavy side, with a barrel chest. He filled out the cliché with a top o' the morning to ya, Irish lilt. Desmond Patrick Murphy is how he introduced himself and I wondered if people on a first name basis with him called him Desmond Patrick. The only thing missing was a stub of a cigar in the side of his mouth.

Desmond Patrick took me by the arm and introduced me to the others in the room. Chief of Detectives, Roland Hill. Lieutenant Linda Derek from the 20th Precinct, the precinct having jurisdiction for Tommy's case. Two other detectives from the 20th Precinct whose names I forgot as soon as we were introduced, and, Detective Shipley, who I acknowledged as having already met. Shipley gave me one of those looks that could kill when Desmond Patrick led me to the table. I'm sure she wasn't too happy being called to this meeting.

We were seated around a large conference table. All eyes turned to the Commissioner who was seated at the head of the table, on my right.

"So, Miss Monahan, I understand you're a little disappointed with NYPD and how we're handling this case."

Shit. Salvo fired off the poop deck.

"No, Mr. Murphy. Not at all." Watch Kate balance on one foot. I did not want to piss anyone off, at least not yet. "We appreciate the time you and your staff are taking for us tonight." I pointedly looked across the table at Cleve, hoping for some help, but he wasn't even looking my way. "It's been two and a half weeks since Mr. Connaught was murdered. We understand that the Detectives don't have a lot of leads. We asked for some assistance tonight so we could share all the facts as we know them."

"Well," Desmond Patrick interrupted. "My friend the ex-mayor called me this afternoon and asked that we give you some help. That's why we're here. So let's get started." I guess he wasn't as insulted as I thought. "Lieutenant Derek," he barked down the conference table. "What's the status?"

"I'll admit, sir, that we're not much further along than we were two weeks ago. One of the detectives assigned to the case is on sick leave, and Detective Shipley is working the case alone."

"Well, excuse my French but that's bullshit and the bullshit stops right here." Desmond Patrick gave everyone a fierce look. "What have you got for us, Miss Monahan?"

"I'll defer to Mr. Northland. He's head of our security detail at Phoenix." I gave them a quick primer on Kelly's background so everyone understood they weren't dealing with Nancy Drew and the Hardy Boys here.

"Before Mr. Northland starts though, I'd just like to ask that you respect the confidentiality of some of the information relating to our company."

The words were barely out my mouth and I heard Shipley snort a few seats away.

"Yes?" I looked at her.

"You can't ask that we keep information confidential when we're investigating a murder. Are you asking us to ignore facts? This is just typical of you rich and uppity business types." Roger that. *Confirmed* that she was pissed with me.

Cleve jumped in at this point and put on his best *we take umbrage with those remarks* personage. "We are *not* asking that you ignore facts. We are just asking that the confidentiality of certain things we are going to disclose to you be kept confidential, if you can manage that."

"Understood," Mr. Murphy barked again and this time his fierce look was directed at Shipley.

Kelly proceeded to fill them in, just as we'd discussed in the car on the ride over. I watched the crowd around the table as he gave them the run down. His note book was open in front of him and occasionally he would flip a page, but he didn't read from it. He was politically correct and addressed most of his remarks directly at Shipley. Not that she hadn't heard some of this before, I reminded myself. The Commissioner appeared a bit bored, picking at his cuticles. Shipley's boss Linda Derek took notes but she was outpaced by the Commissioner's assistant who sat at the far end of the table. He was a young man, probably not yet thirty, of Asian descent, who seemed to be taking down everything that was said verbatim.

I chastised myself for daydreaming and brought my attention back to Kelly.

"So, in a nutshell, that's what we know. We'd like NYPD's assistance in locating Ben Tucker and Natalie Scott." I looked at Detective Shipley who was grim-faced and unmoving. She nodded at Kelly.

"Anything else?" the Commissioner asked. Without waiting for any responses, he slapped both hands down on the table and stood up. I looked at my watch. We'd been here less than fifteen minutes and it appeared that we were being given the bum's rush.

"Miss Monahan. Nice meeting you." He held out his hand and I stood up and gave him a shake. "I've got another meeting but please, use my office. The detectives here are tasked with solving this case." Another fierce look in their direction. "The City of New York takes crime seriously. The murder of one of this city's citizens is serious business." He put his hand on my shoulder. "And, we're sorry for your loss." In spite of his bluster, I think he meant it.

We spent the next ninety minutes at his conference table, rehashing the last two weeks. The detectives fired questions at us, and we answered the best we could.

Who would want to kill Dr. Francis?

We had no idea.

Why did he suddenly leave his job at Global Devices?

We had no idea.

How well did Mr. Connaught know Dr. Francis?

Again, no idea. I told them they should talk with Dr. Bill Pritchard. Get his take on things. Shipley nodded.

I gave them Sara Williston's phone number. One of them mentioned that they'd work on a search warrant to access the safety deposit box shared by Tommy and Dr. Francis.

Were we aware of any relationship between Ben Tucker and Natalie Scott?

None, other than their reporting relationship at work and the fact that they had worked together at the hospital in Flagstaff.

Shipley riled me a little with some of her questions. Like were the lawyers any further along in figuring out the value of the deceased's estate? Before I could answer that she rephrased the question and wanted to know just how much I was inheriting. And before I could answer *that*, she looked at the other detectives with a smug, knowing look. I didn't bother to answer her because she was clearly giving me a dig and besides, Cleve shot me a look across the table, which said, keep your mouth shut.

I wanted to counter with some questions of my own. Like what the hell had they been doing the last two weeks to get to the bottom of this? What had Shipley done with the information that Kelly and I shared with her on Friday? Sweet fuck all would be the answer I was going to get. The only reason we were getting anywhere at this point, late on a Sunday night was because the Commissioner had called this meeting. I was pissed, but I was tired too, so I kept the bitchiness in check.

Had the FDA been informed of the reasons for the contract cancellation by Global? This was from one of the detectives whose name I forgot, but it was a good question.

What was the latest report from Flagstaff? Was there any news on our missing investigator?

We wrapped up with handshakes all around and fake smiles on my behalf. I didn't think for a minute that my smile fooled anyone but the detectives and their boss were civil with us, promising to keep us informed.

Chapter fifty-four

MY EYES LOCKED ON THE object and my body went rigid. I was breathing yes, but not moving. I stood there for what seemed like an eternity, staring at it, trying to get my heart pumping at the hysterical rate rather than the panicked rate. My eyes shot around the bedroom. The digital clock read 11:27. The door to the ensuite bathroom was ajar and some light was filtering out. Did I leave the light on in the bathroom?

The corners of the large room were dark and my heart rate shot back up to hysterical as I willed my eyes to adjust to see if there was anything, anybody in the shadows. Just like a kid playing the game of statues, my body was frozen in a ridiculous pose.

As I usually did when I came in the bedroom, I had walked to the side of the bed where I slept and turned on the lamp on the bedside table. Light illuminated the top half of the massive, king size bed. In the split second that I was thinking about sinking into the crisp sheets and pulling the duvet over me, I spied the white envelope sitting squarely in the middle of my pillow.

I let my eyes focus on the envelope and I whimpered just a little when I saw that it was addressed to *BITCH*.

Not entirely convinced that I was alone, I nonetheless made myself, no correct that, willed myself, to leave the room. Hyper-aware now, just like Frank Sanchez had drilled into me. My peripheral vision kicked in, my back straightened up and my fists clenched. The envelope lay untouched on the pillow and as I backed out of the bedroom into the hall, I knew that the pillow was going in the garbage and I would never let it touch me again.

When I came out of the hallway into the main area of the apartment, I was relieved to see my ever-present bodyguard, Chris, sitting at the dining room table reading a newspaper. He must have known by the look on my face that something was wrong because he was quickly out of his chair, coming around the table towards me with a gun in his hand. I stupidly wondered where the gun came from and at the same time told him that there was something on my bed. He grabbed me by the wrist and pulled me into the foyer of the apartment where we both stood against the wall while he made some calls on his cell phone.

While I stood rigidly in the foyer, unable to relax my body, my brain was running wild. Someone had been in the apartment while we were at the Police Commissioner's office. How had they got in? Besides putting what looked like a harmless envelope on my bed, what else had they done? Were they still in the apartment? When was this all going to end?

An eternity later the intercom on the wall chimed and Kelly and the cavalry arrived. The cavalry were really the two other bodyguards whom I had met over the past couple of days. They and Kelly fanned out in the apartment, with their guns out and up, clasped in both hands, just like the cops in the TV shows. Chris stayed with me in the foyer. When we got the all clear, I felt my body relax a bit, but the adrenaline was still pumping. My brain was screaming for a cigarette and my heart was aching for Jay.

I ignored the nicotine need and pow-wowed with Kelly, Chris and the cavalry in the kitchen.

I could tell Kelly was livid. "I'm sorry this happened, ma'am," he told me through clenched teeth. He shot a look at Chris and then pointed to the reason why we were all standing around the round table in the kitchen. The offensive object was now inside a plastic bag and I let my eyes rest on it for a moment.

"The apartment was breached. How, we're not sure at this point, but we will find out. As of now, you'll have three men in the apartment with you at all times. We think it's easier to protect you here than in a hotel or another place."

I nodded, suddenly very tired. I thrust my chin towards the envelope. "Are we going to see what the note inside says?"

"Later. Right now it's evidence."

Satisfied with the telephone call, the stalker smiled and gently placed the handset on the telephone base, ending the long distance call to Flagstaff. The long reach of Tom Connaught's bitch and her 'soldiers' was effectively cut off. Not caring to know the name of the person sent by the bitch, the stalker had abruptly interrupted the caller. Just tell me there is no link from us to him.

My sleep was interrupted by an urgent hand, shaking my shoulder.

"Ma'am."

"Yunh." I mumbled something and willed my brain to wake up from a deep sleep. I was under some blankets on one of the couches in the living room, where I had fallen asleep in the early morning hours.

I struggled to sit up, totally disoriented because it was still dark with only a little light coming from the lamp on the side table. Kelly was crouched down in front of the couch, waiting for my eyes to focus. I ran my hands through my hair, and then rubbed them over my face.

"What time is it?" I whispered.

"Three thirty. I'm sorry to wake you but we've got a situation."

I took a deep breath, not sure if I was ready for more bad news. With my feet on the floor and the blanket wrapped around my shoulders, I looked at Kelly sitting on his heels in front of me. Looked in his eyes and couldn't stand what I saw there. My stomach flipped and my brain willed it to stay still. Stay strong. Stay tough. *Strong* and *tough* - two of my personality traits that had been seeping out of me with each passing hour, dealing with this shit-mess.

"I'm awake. What's going on?"

"They've found our guy in Flagstaff."

Jerry. The man who had a mom and dad waiting for him. The man who was working for us. Oh my God. I nodded my head, silently telling Kelly to go on.

"There's a fire right now in the administration offices at the hospital in Flagstaff. It's the middle of the night out there, so thank God no staff were there. But they found a man's body. Unconscious, suffering from smoke inhalation they think."

I put my hand on Kelly's shoulder, which felt like a piece of granite. "Is he going to be okay?"

"We hope." He placed his hands on his knees and stood up. All business now. "My other guys out there will call again soon with an update report." He reached over to turn off the lamp and I stopped him.

"Leave it on. I'm getting up." If Kelly and his guys could work around the clock for me and for our company, I could too. As helpless as I felt at this moment, I was sure I could at least make some coffee.

"I'm coming back on the next plane," Jay said when I finished describing what had happened in the twenty-four hours since he had gone back to Toronto.

"No," I told him. My voice was hoarse from lack of sleep and too many cigarettes. "It's alright. As much as I miss you and want to see you, you need to stay there. For your job. It's important."

There was a long silence and I wondered if Jay was thinking about my close call a few months ago, when that madman had shot at me, point blank.

"It's okay, really Jay. Kelly and his gang of guys are here. I promise I won't do anything to put myself out there. Kelly wouldn't let me anyway."

"I just can't understand what all of this is about. Who's doing this? And I can't believe that Dr. Francis is dead. I never met the man but I felt like I knew him just a little bit."

I agreed with Jay and we talked about that for a little while longer, theorizing but getting nowhere. We promised to call each other again, later that day.

It was early Monday morning and I was at my desk, at the Phoenix offices. A different bodyguard, Michael, was at my beck and call, sitting in the outside office in a guest chair beside Carrie's desk. It was awkward all around but I was appreciative of his presence.

I started off the day meeting with Sandra Melnick and going through the piles of files that she had left me on Friday. I swear to God that I tried to pay attention because this was important stuff for our company. But my mind kept wandering. Wondering about Jerry's parents, worried about their son. A son who had survived military service but was now unconscious, in a hospital. Left for dead because of some private investigating work on behalf of a company they had never heard of, never had anything to do with. From there my thoughts segued to Dr. Jordan Francis' family. Who were they? They would be reconciling the death of their son, their brother, their uncle. I couldn't recall a time when my heart hurt as much as it did right now. My nose started to sting, signaling the start of tears, so I sniffed hard and brought my attention back to what Sandra was telling me.

Cleve came through the office door as soon as Sandra left and he joined me at the work table. A large carafe of coffee sat in the middle of the table, with cream and sugar, china mugs, and silver spoons on a large tray. Cleve poured himself a mug before he sat down across from me. I was smoking but put the cigarette out in an overflowing ashtray.

"I just spoke with Kelly," he told me. "He brought me up to speed on what's happening in Flagstaff. In addition to the smoke inhalation, the doctors report that Mr. Rigley has some severe lacerations on his head. He was most likely knocked out and left to die. The fire chief has confirmed that the fire was deliberately set. Thankfully, there was more smoke damage than anything else."

We both sat quietly, lost in our thoughts. There wasn't much to say except the obvious. Cleve appeared to be as weary as I was so I poured both of us another coffee. I was wired with caffeine and adrenaline and it was only ten in the morning.

Chapter fifty-five

THE CAFFEINE LOAD COMBINED WITH a lack of sleep made me feel like a cat on a hot tin roof. I couldn't concentrate on any of the work staring at me from the overloaded in-basket on my desk. I had paced out my office and if my mother were here she'd be asking me if I had ants in my pants. Bothered and bitchy best described how I was feeling. And caged in. So I decided to take a walk down to the R and D floor. Have a look at Ben Tucker's place of work. Michael jumped up from his chair when I opened the door to my office.

"I'm going down to R and D," I told Carrie and the bodyguard. Michael discreetly followed along behind me, down the hallway and the inner staircase. When I came out through the fire door on the floor, I stood for a moment, getting my bearings. Off to the far right was Nat Scott's former office, and on the left of the floor were the glass brick enclosed offices, where Kelly and his security team were housed. I headed towards Nat Scott's area and was happy to see my new best friend Jenn Ludlow at her desk, surrounded with piles of paper and file folders. Her face was intent with concentration and she was humming along to music pulsing through her earphones.

She beamed me one of her gorgeous smiles when she noticed me standing in front of her desk. She pulled out her earphones and stood up.

"Hey Kate. What's shaking?" She peered around me and looked at Michael and then back at me. "Who's your shadow?" she asked with a sly smile.

I introduced them. "Jenn this is Michael. Michael, Jenn." Jenn came out from behind her desk and held out her hand like she was the Pope, expecting him to kiss her ring. She dipped her head slightly and the large swath of hair over the right side of her face swished sexily, revealing both of her eyes. Clearly smitten, Michael was unable to speak. His eighteen inch neck turned bright pink and he let Jenn's hand rest in the palm of his. I was witnessing love - or lust - at first sight. I cleared my throat trying to interrupt them as they stared at each other, mesmerized.

"Jenn," I finally said, after about ten seconds.

"Yep." She broke the eye lock and turned her head towards me.

"Where is Ben Tucker's office?"

She pointed and said, "Four workstations that a way. But I don't think he's here. Haven't seen him today."

"Thanks Jenn. I'll go over anyway."

I counted off four workstations in the direction that she had indicated and found what was definitely Ben's place. His was a wheelchair accessible workstation, with a lower than normal work surface and no desk chair. The workstation was neat and organized and everything was in its place, on low shelves, reachable by someone confined to their wheelchair. There was no sign of Ben. But did I really expect to find him sitting at his desk, working away? It took me a minute to realize that there was no computer on the desk.

Michael dutifully trailed behind me as I abruptly left the workstation and headed across the large floor to Kelly's office, where he was standing in the doorway, clearly waiting for me. He nodded at Michael and wordlessly used his head to point at the office next door, directing him there. Kelly ushered me into his office and quietly closed the door.

I didn't sit down because the caffeine continued to course through my system and the ants in my pants were still there. Kelly stood in front of his closed door and I faced him, with my hands clasped in front of me.

Kelly spoke first.

"How're you holding up?"

"Good," I lied.

Then I sucked in a deep breath and felt my body shudder, just a little. Signs of adrenaline leaving my system. "How about you Kelly? You're running on less sleep than me."

"I'm used to it. I only need a couple of hours each night."

"I was just over at Ben Tucker's desk."

"Yeah, I know. Michael's keeping me informed."

"There's no computer at his desk."

"Yep. We know that too. He has a laptop like most of the R and D staff. He must have it with him. We're checking his accounts on the network, his email account, things like that. Shipley called saying they wanted to search his workstation area, I told her that would be fine with us. They'll be over here soon."

"Can they at least be discreet about it? Can we pack everything up and give it to them? I don't want to upset the employees any more than we have to."

Kelly nodded his head. "I'll see what we can do." He walked over behind his desk, sat down and took a piece of paper out of a file folder. He slid it across the desk towards me. "The contents of the note," he offered.

I continued to stand near the door, admittedly a little reluctant to read it, acknowledge it or touch it, even though I knew it wasn't the original.

"I am in control. I hold your fate in my hands. You have no power over me. You have no power period. Lay your head on this pillow and sleep soundly."

By lunchtime I was exhausted, frustrated and close to tears. Exhausted because the caffeine was no longer doing its job. Frustrated because there didn't appear to be anything worthwhile I could do to help Kelly or the police bring an end to this shit-storm. And close to tears because I was exhausted and frustrated. So I decided to do something totally out of character. Exercise. Admittedly the idea was not mine. Frank Sanchez apparently called the office after talking to Jay who informed him of the events of the last couple of days and how the bodyguard contingent was rising exponentially. Frank called Carrie who obligingly cleared my calendar.

The tears finally overflowed as I was telling Frank about finding the envelope on my bed. I was able to do the telling without any accompanying sobs but the tears poured. Frank was a saint. He didn't do any of the patronizing *there-there it'll be okay* shit typical of men who don't know how to deal with a woman in tears. When I was done he artfully took my story and turned it into a lesson in personal security awareness. Then we worked out for over an hour and when we were done I had a new understanding of the meaning of exhausted.

Keeping one's pulse under control was extremely difficult. But extremely difficult did not mean impossible. Conquering adversity made you stronger. More powerful. Omnipotent. Because there was no challenge that could not be overcome. Oxygen-laced, deep breaths calmed the pulse and focused the mind. The hardest challenge was about to be surmounted. The bitch was about to be conquered.

When Frank called an end to the drills, I thanked him and collapsed on one of the benches up against the wall of the Dojo. With my elbows on my knees, I worked at getting my breathing back in order and watched my sweat drip on the floor. The exhaustion gave me a feeling of powerfulness, as crazy as that sounded to me. I felt powerful and strong even though my knees were weak and my arms were trembling. They say that knowledge is power, and knowing that I had worked out and trained when I was beyond exhausted made me proud of myself. I grinned inwardly and gave myself a mental pat on the back.

Michael was dutifully waiting for me in the small waiting room outside Frank's Dojo. He gave me a quiet smile and a hardly noticeable nod, acknowledging the sweat which was still beading on my face. With my gym bag slung over my shoulder I followed Michael through the door, onto the landing and then down the steep set of stairs. The hallway and staircase were well lit but the area felt dark because the walls and the stairs were painted a deep chocolate brown. At the bottom of the staircase there was a small lobby and then the door to the street.

I paid no attention to our descent, as I had gone down this stairway many times now. Like a good girl, I held on to the banister, and kept my eyes focused on Michael's back who was about four steps ahead of me. Michael crossed the small lobby in two giant steps and had the door to the street open while I was still descending the stairs.

I saw him look both ways as he stood in the doorway and then he was on the ground. He just crumpled and silently fell. My foot was on the lobby floor and I dropped my gym bag, readying myself to run the few steps to him. I looked down at the threshold of the doorway, thinking that he must have tripped and fallen, and in that split second the area around the doorway darkened. When I looked up a body was filling the doorway and there was a gun pointed at my chest.

My first thoughts were for Michael.

He must have been shot by this person and I frantically wondered why I hadn't heard any shot.

Adrenaline coursed through my veins and my breath came in short gasps.

Blood pounded so hard in my ears I could hear nothing and I tried mightily to focus on the person standing in front of me. It felt like I was looking at them through the wrong ends of a pair of binoculars and I realized that I had tunnel vision.

Tunnel vision, tunnel vision. Frank had drilled into me all the things I could expect if I found myself in a situation where my life was threatened. Tunnel vision was one of them.

And adrenaline.

And blood pounding in my ears obscuring my hearing.

And shortened breath.

I had to focus. Focus.

And be docile.

And non-threatening.

And hyper-aware.

I raised my hands in the air and looked at the ground, trying to be as non-threatening as I could.

"Please don't hurt me," I whimpered. Just like Frank taught me. "Please," I repeated.

Still looking at the floor, I was hyper-aware of this person's smell, and it was sour and fearful. Or was that me?

The gunman was standing so close to me I could feel his breath coming out of his mouth in short gasps, just like mine and I peered up at him, keeping my head bowed. The gun was held in both of his hands and his hands were shaking, and the gun was jerking up and down. He had both arms straight out in front of him and his feet were planted about shoulder width apart. I was fucking lucky that he was hesitating. That he didn't shoot me right away. It felt like a lifetime had passed since Michael had fallen to the ground. In reality it was probably less than thirty seconds.

In one smooth motion, just like I had been taught and Jay and I had drilled for hours, my left hand shot out, grabbing his wrist hard, deflecting the gun barrel away from me. The gun was now pointed at the wall and away from my chest. My right hand came down on top of the gun and I twisted with all my might. Twisted the gun barrel back towards him. Heard the snap of his finger breaking that he'd stupidly held on the trigger. He squealed. The pressure of my left hand on his wrist, and the pressure from my right hand twisting the gun caused him to let go of it.

I backed up a step, aiming his gun at him. I held the gun close to me. Saw him hesitate. Making a decision.

His decision was probably the right one. He guessed that I wouldn't shoot him because he turned and jack-rabbited over Michael's prone body and he took off running. I was right behind him, yelling like a fool.

I saw him a few storefronts up where he was dodging between two parked cars to cross the street. I ran into the street after him. My hearing was back and I clearly heard squealing tires, horns honking, and screams. The screams were mine.

Chapter fifty-six

THE VOICES WERE ALL AROUND me and I only caught snippets of what was being said. None of it made sense.

"Ran right into the street."

"... lucky she wasn't killed."

"Who is she?"

Then hands were touching me. I kicked and mumbled.

"Ma'am, it's all right."

"Ma'am, stay still."

In and out of consciousness. I finally stopped fighting and gave into it.

The bitch's body was loaded into an ambulance. The useless, goddamn stupid piece of garbage had botched it. The bitch was holding the idiot's *gun when she chased him out of the building. Seeing red. Breathing fire. Angry. So angry.*

"Kathleen." The voice was determined to wake me up. And the bright beam of light into my eye helped.

I turned my head away from the light and clamped my eyes shut. It pissed me off when I was woken up from a nap.

"Leave me alone," I mumbled, and tried to roll over on my side. The movement caused pain to wash over me so swiftly it took my breath away. I couldn't focus on just one area of pain because it enveloped my whole body. My entire being. As consciousness regained a toe hold on my brain, I took an inventory of myself and my beloved body parts. A head to foot mental inventory quickly confirmed that I must be in one piece because every body part on that inventory hurt. Throbbed. Pounded.

I opened my eyes slowly and the bright lights above me caused me to wince. Someone put their hand on my shoulder and I cried out. And then a wave of nausea that started at my feet hit me and I knew I was going to be sick to my stomach. It wasn't pretty and I didn't care. Not sure that it was possible, but I felt worse after throwing up.

By this time I figured out that I was in a hospital. Why I was there was the sixty-four thousand dollar question. I had been at Frank's Dojo training and the next thing I knew I was lying on a gurney in the most amount of pain I had ever experienced.

"Kate," someone whispered. "Everything is okay. You've got two broken ribs but everything else is fine." I opened my eyes and Kelly was standing beside me, bent over a little, talking quietly to me.

"What happened?" I asked him. My voice was hoarse and my throat hurt, but I think that was from throwing up.

"You ran into the street and got hit by a car," he told me. And then I remembered everything that had happened. Oh my Christ. Michael. Someone else to add to the list of souls damaged by me and our godforsaken company.

"Michael. How's Michael?" I asked and begged him with my eyes to tell me the truth.

Kelly paused and I could see him taking a deep breath. "He's going to be okay." He seemed relieved to tell me and I was relieved too. "He was shot in the upper thigh, and was bleeding from an artery but the medics got to him in time."

Michael was badly injured but at least he was alive. I got little comfort from that - if not for me, he wouldn't have been shot. Guilt tore inside me and made my body ache even more.

"He told me what happened," Kelly said. "How you disarmed that guy and took off after him." Kelly grinned a little. "You did good, ma'am."

Personally I didn't think so, considering where I was at the moment. I tried to give him a wee smile back but it hurt too much. I couldn't believe that even my face was aching.

"Did anyone catch the guy?"

Kelly shook his head. "No. Some witnesses at the scene said he took off running down one of the side streets. He never stopped, never looked back. Did you get a good look at him?"

"Yeah. I won't forget his face for a long time."

"Was he someone you know?"

"No. Never seen him before."

There was some activity behind Kelly and a nurse stepped around and stood beside him.

"Sir, we're moving her to a room so we'll have to ask you to step outside for a bit."

I looked around me for the first time. The paraphernalia around me belonged to an emergency department in a hospital. I was lying on a narrow stretcher, there was an IV in my left hand, and the small area was enclosed with curtains, giving me a modicum of privacy. I tuned in to the surrounding noises and could hear voices, moans, and the public address system.

"When you're settled in," Kelly told me, "the police need to get your statement." He backed away and disappeared through the curtains.

"Do I really need to stay in the hospital?" I asked the nurse.

"You sure do, dear. We need to keep an eye on you. You've got a nasty concussion. You'll be here at least twenty-four hours." While she was talking she covered me with a warm blanket which felt divine and made me realize how cold I was feeling. She fussed around the gurney, efficiently raising up the sides, hooking the IV bag to a pole on the end of the stretcher, and releasing the brakes with a clang. She threw back the curtain and pushed me through the emergency ward, out into a hallway and onto an elevator. Whatever was in the IV bag was working its magic, because I was asleep as soon as they helped me into a real bed.

It was dark outside when I woke up, disoriented and having to pee badly. Gingerly lifting my head from the pillow, I peered around the room. Frank Sanchez was sitting in a chair at the foot of the bed and Jay was in a chair beside me. Pain shot through my neck to the top of my head so I lowered it back on the pillow, and lifted my hand in a small wave.

"Hey," I croaked out. Jay took my hand and gave it a little squeeze.

"Hey yourself," he said. "How're you doing?"

"Gotta pee. Badly."

"Let me get the nurse," he offered, and then he was gone.

Twenty minutes later I was feeling a little more human. A visit to the bathroom, teeth brushed and two very large pain pills helped. Which was good because the nurse told me there was a crowd of people waiting to see me.

My headache came back in style as soon as I saw that Detective Shipley was the first one through the door. Another detective who I had met at the meeting with the Chief trailed behind her. I couldn't remember his name.

"Good evening Ms. Monahan."

"Hi, Detectives."

"We're sorry to hear about your injuries," Shipley intoned disingenuously.

Sure, I thought.

She didn't look at me as she dug around in her bag and I wondered if she'd been forced to come here. They asked me some questions about my attacker. Did I recognize him? No. Would I recognize him if saw him again? Definitely yes. Describe him. White, about five foot eight, in his late twenties or early thirties, dark brown hair, nervous type.

How did I get the gun away from him? My description caused Shipley to snort in disbelief, so I looked at her partner who just rolled his eyes. They finished up after that and left me in peace for about eight seconds.

Jay and Frank came back through the door, followed by Kelly and one of the bodyguards whose name escaped me. Hopefully all this name forgetting wasn't a side effect of the concussion. One of the nurses was on the heels of the bodyguard, tsking and harumphing in stereotypical fashion.

"Gentlemen, it's past visiting hours. Our girl needs her rest. I'll give you a few minutes," she told them, and then took me by the shoulders, sat me up, fluffed my pillows and gently helped me lay back down again. She glared at all of them and said, "Ten minutes." Then she efficiently tucked me in so tight I wasn't sure I could get out of bed if I had to.

Frank told me he was sorry for what happened but that he was proud of me for how I handled the situation. Kelly told me that he was sorry for what happened and that Jason, the bodyguard whose name I remembered as soon as Kelly said it, would be sitting outside my door, guarding me. Jason nodded in my direction and then they left. Jay pulled up a chair beside my bed, sat down and took my hand in both of his.

"When did you get back in the City?" I asked him.

"Around four o'clock. After we talked this morning, I decided to catch the first flight I could. When I landed and called you at the office, Carrie told me what happened. I came straight to the hospital."

I turned my head on the pillow and looked at him. His face had aged ten years. His hair stood straight up because of his nervous habit of running his hands through it. His eyes locked with mine and I felt more guilt because he was suffering. Because of me.

"What are we going to do Kate?" he asked me quietly.

I was suddenly very pissed. Not at Jay. At whoever was behind all of this. Pissed that some madman, or madwoman, had thoroughly taken over our lives. Feelings of rage boiled inside me, causing my head to ache and my broken ribs to throb.

"We're going to find this fucker and kick his ass, royally." I said it like I meant it.

Jay smiled. "Good plan."

Chapter fifty-seven

It was likely the drugs they gave me. I was loopy, in and out of wakefulness, with restless legs and dreams that wouldn't stop. The nurses woke me regularly to do those things they go to nursing school for. At least they kept the lights low in my room. My whole body ached and every few seconds I would get stabbing, shooting pains in a different part of my body. I could hear moaning and realized it was me. At one point in the middle of the longest night of my life, as the nurse was mindlessly taking my blood pressure with a cuff that squeezed the life out of my arm, I remember wryly thinking to myself, so this is what it feels like to get hit by a Mack truck.

Around four a.m. I woke with a start. All of my limbs had jerked me awake. I felt claustrophobic and wanted to be free of the sheets and blanket that I had been tucked into. Try as I might I couldn't lift either of my hands to move the bed sheets and although I signaled my feet with my brain to kick off the covers my body wouldn't react. When I realized that I couldn't move my head, I started to panic. Bright light was shone in each of my eyes, blinding me momentarily. My voice was useless because I couldn't open my mouth to make a sound. My body was totally paralyzed.

What was the matter with me? Were my injuries worse than the doctors thought? Did I damage my spine? Did I have a stroke? All of these thoughts screamed inside my head. Who was there? Why weren't they talking to me? Had I gone deaf too?

The bedcovers were removed and my brain was working well enough for me to realize that I could still *feel* - I just couldn't move. What the fuck was going on? Somebody!

I felt hands under my legs and two hands on my shoulders and those hands lifted me and put me on a stretcher. Thank God, I thought. Somebody realizes something is wrong. *Somebody say something* my mind pleaded. We were rolling out of my hospital room and into an elevator. My eyes darted back and forth but all I could see was the ceiling and walls of the hospital hallway, and then the ceiling of the elevator. Whoever was wheeling me away was not within my vision. After the elevator ride we went down a long, dark, tunnel-like hallway. The dim lights were spaced far apart in the ceiling which was bare cement. And then the end of my stretcher was banged hard against a door, which opened to the outside.

Where was I going? We were outside the hospital now. Something was really wrong and it just wasn't the fact that my body was paralyzed. The stretcher started moving faster and whoever was pushing it must have started to run. Just as quickly we stopped, and for the first time I heard some mumbled voices. Vehicle doors were opened and the stretcher was lifted up and wheeled inside the back of a truck. Doors were slammed, the engine turned over and we started moving. Tears were pouring out of my eyes now and draining into my ears.

My ears were wet from my tears. Unbelievable. What the fuck was going on and why was I worried about wet ears?

Lights were turned on in the back of the truck and my eyes darted left and right and I realized that I must be inside an ambulance. On both walls small cubbyholes were jammed with medical supplies, blood pressure cups and bags of intravenous fluids. A stethoscope hung from a nearby hook.

Something was tightened around my knees and then my chest. They now had me strapped to the stretcher. Who were *they*? What were they doing? I felt so helpless.

My bowels loosened and my mouth went dry when a face finally came into my vision.

The face belonged to the big cry baby Belinda Moffat.

Why was she here? She had a stethoscope plugged into her ears and she was listening to my heart which thankfully was still beating.

Why, why, why my brain screamed? What is happening? Belinda smiled at me and my eyes pleaded with her. *Why are you doing this*? She just continued to smile.

When she was done listening to my heart, she fitted me with a blood pressure cuff and took my blood pressure. While she worked, she had the same stupid smile plastered on her fat, ugly face. She didn't speak. My brain tried to compute her presence and to figure out what part she was playing in this evil game. But overriding my internal computer was a voice in my head screaming a constant stream of *why, why, why*.

The ambulance continued in motion and eventually went down a steep slope, a sensation I could feel because I felt my body shift on the stretcher. A few moments later we stopped and I heard the engine turn off. My stomach roiled. Belinda and another person - who I couldn't see or hear - unstrapped me from the gurney and I was lifted up and carried out of the ambulance. Belinda had me under the arms and my body shifted up as I was carried down the steps of the ambulance. I could see the back of a man between my feet, holding me by my legs which he had tight against his body. Still unable to move any part of my body except my eyes, I frantically looked around, taking in my surroundings, looking for something recognizable.

And then at last, I heard a voice.

"Over here. Easy. Easy."

I was being lowered down.

"Thank God she's small," the voice said.

Why? Why is it good that I'm small?

I could see Belinda's face above me as she lowered me to the ground. She gently tucked my arms close to my body and turned me on my side. Less than two inches away from my face I could see black, satiny fabric.

What is it?

Oh my God. Is it a coffin?

I needed to scream. Screaming will make me feel better.

Pain came back swiftly in my midsection as my legs were bent and my knees jammed into my chest. They were bending me like a pretzel and mother of God, the stabbing pain in my ribs left me breathless.

And then everything went black.

Something had been put over me and everything was dark, and black, and smelled like men's aftershave. I could hear a vehicle start up and the sound of it was gone in a few moments. The voices hadn't spoken again and my ears were desperate for human voices. Even Belinda's, the fucking gargoyle. Why was she doing this to me?

I heard a long, ripping noise, and couldn't calm my brain down enough to determine what it was. And then I was lifted again and the container I was in was rolling.

I was in a suitcase. The ripping noise was a zipper. A fucking suitcase. Now I was sure I must be dreaming. Why in God's name would I be in a suitcase?

I needed to get out of here.

Started to panic.

Just fucking lovely, I thought. I'm going to end up claustrophobic after all this. You stupid bitch, Kate, focus, focus.

And then I felt my hand move. Ever so slightly.

And then my big toe on my right foot started to move. Maybe my paralysis wasn't permanent. I tried pushing on the side of the suitcase with my hand, but it was useless. My toe had stopped moving but I could feel sensation in it. I pushed down with the toe but nothing happened. I probably had the sum total strength of a two-hour old baby.

The suitcase with its Kate Monahan load stopped rolling and after a few seconds I heard a distinct *ping* and then we started rising. In an elevator. Another *ping*, then more rolling for a few feet, stopping, and then rolling to a final stop, where I was laid back down on the floor. Muffled voices came to me from a distance.

My body parts were not responding the way I wanted them to but my knees were starting to ache from being jammed into my chest. I tried moving my fingers and was thrilled when I realized I could make fists. The paralysis was leaving my body. My jaw was working and I was able to open my mouth. I couldn't really tell though what else was working and what wasn't because being packed into the suitcase didn't leave much room for movement. There might have been room for a small, travel size shampoo but nothing else.

The voices were closer now and both were female. The louder of the two was definitely Belinda. I would recognize that foghorn timbre from a mile away.

The ripping noise started again and in a few moments the lid of the suitcase was moved aside.

"She's fine," Belinda was saying. "Her heart rate and BP were all within the normal range. Her blood-ox and respirations were fine. Nothing to worry about. She should be back to normal in a few minutes."

The light was dim and I could see very little. As tempted as I was to start moving my limbs and get myself out of the suitcase, I played possum and stayed jammed-in like a street vendor's pretzel.

"So long as the bitch stays alive for a little while longer, I could care less," a very familiar voice was saying.

Rough hands grabbed me from behind and rolled me out of the suitcase onto the floor. From my new vantage point, I wasn't surprised to see Nat Scott standing over me.

When we first met, I think I might have thought Natalie had attractive traits. Standing over me now, though, with her hands on her skinny hips, I took back my first impressions. Ugly, demented eyes glared at me. Her face was so taut with evil and hatred that her lips were virtually non-existent. Her hair was greasy, unkempt and matted.

I felt some relief in my ribcage as my legs straightened out, although pins and needles were stabbing at my feet as the circulation started coming back. I lay as feeble as a baby on the floor, looking up at Nat, meeting her eyes, daring her to do something.

"Put her on the table," she ordered and I was picked up under my armpits and dragged across the room by Belinda. I made it as hard as possible on her, willing my body to be deadweight and uncooperative.

"Hurry up," Natalie barked out. "We haven't got all day." Her voice faded and I was pretty sure she had left the room.

Belinda scooped me up like a toddler and plunked me on a table like a bag of groceries. We were in a room painted white, with a light coming from an old, overhead fixture. I darted my eyes around without moving my head, trying to get a fix on my surroundings.

"Don't roll off," Belinda told me in a distracted voice and she walked out of my vision.

Don't worry, I thought, taking advantage of the situation and looking around.

What I saw scared me to the depths of my soul and made me more frantic.

Like a scene out of a Frankenstein movie.

On a table up against the wall, where Belinda stood with her back to me, surgical instruments were lined up.

Four large lamps with stainless steel shades stood against the other wall.

White linens were stacked on a cart.

I was in a fucking operating room.

They were *not* keeping me here, I quickly decided.

I was *not* waiting around.

Belinda stood about four feet away from me, sorting through the instruments on the table with her back to me.

The pins and needles sensation was now in my arms but I ignored the pain from that and pushed myself up on my elbows, trying to sit up.

My body protested but I ignored it, drawing on the strength I had gained working out with Frank and Jay.

I worked myself up, and swung my near useless legs over the side of the table.

My head swam.

My breath was short.

My vision was slightly blurred.

Belinda turned around and gasped.

Even through blurred vision, Belinda was just as ugly.

She started to open her mouth but I cut her off.

"You *fucking* traitor."

Chapter fifty-eight

BELINDA STARED AT ME. MOMENTARILY speechless.

"Don't you *fucking* come near me," I told her as I slid off the table.

She opened her mouth again and yelled for Nat. I took that opportunity to close the gap between us.

And then I hit her. Hard. With the heel of my hand. At the bottom of her nose where I knew it would hurt the most.

Just like a couple of days ago when she sat in my office and spewed tears, now she was spewing blood. And she started to choke on it as she hyperventilated.

And I didn't give a shit, hoping she died.

And just to make sure, I hit her again. This time with a jab. My fist connected with her jaw and the force of the punch knocked her back into the table of surgical instruments and she crumpled to the floor. Pain reverberated from my fist to my shoulder, and I gasped. My first time hitting flesh with a properly formed fist was a little different than hitting a sparring mitt.

Belinda was moaning like a tug boat in distress. Blood continued to pour from her nose.

Now what? I wondered. I was barefoot, in a stylish hospital gown which was gaping open in the back, completely nude underneath.

From outside the room, I heard a voice which made me turn around and back up against the wall. Belinda continued to moan and spit blood on the floor beside me.

Nat Scott hurried into the room.

She glanced at Belinda on the floor and then drilled her eyes on me where I had backed up against the wall. Getting as much distance between the two of us as possible.

Nat's hands hung by her sides, clenched in fists. Her body shook with rage. I didn't wait for her to find a weapon, or for her to attack me. With

Belinda out of the game for the moment, I knew I had to make a move and make it fast. Frank had drilled into me that if I found myself in a life threatening situation, act as quickly as possible to save myself.

Nat Scott had about six inches on me in height and she probably weighed thirty pounds more than me, but I wasn't going to let that stop me. My body was still whacky and pins and needles were shooting all over my legs. My brain was screaming about survival. So I let my instincts kick in.

My useless body stumbled towards her, as quickly as I could make it move. She stood about twelve feet away from me but I closed the distance between us.

I put my hands out in front of me and I pushed her. As hard as I could. She screamed in anger and stumbled backwards, hitting the door frame.

As soon as her back hit the door frame, my body prepared itself instinctively. My right foot was slightly forward, my left foot back a bit. My weight was forward, my back heel off the ground. My right fist was up, in front of my face, my left fist up as well, closer to my jaw. I was in my fighting stance, and Frank would be proud. My body was screaming in pain but I used the pain to keep me focused.

Belinda cried out from the floor.

Nat bounced off the door frame, screaming like a banshee. She came right back at me. Screaming. Screaming from the depths of her soul. She was out of her mind. I swear her eyes turned red.

My hours of practising foot drills paid off as I sidestepped her and slammed my fist up into her chin. My fist shut her up and stunned her. But she was still standing and I wasn't finished. I stepped behind her and put my right arm around her neck. Standing on my tiptoes, I tried to squeeze the life out of her. Now who was enraged? I felt her body going limp and I threw her on the floor.

Nat lay there for a moment and looked up at me. Surprisingly, she appeared just as angry. I shook my head in disgust and stomped. On her head.

I would have kicked her but I was barefoot and didn't want to break a toe. She lay there, motionless, unconscious, and I didn't give a shit whether she was dead or alive.

My brain hadn't had time to compute what her presence here meant, but my gut told me she was definitely a player in all the mayhem that had been going on.

Belinda was still crying and moaning in the corner.

"Who else is here?" I demanded of her.

She coughed and spit more blood on the floor and didn't answer me. I nudged her not too gently with my foot and she looked up at me, with pain-filled eyes. While she decided whether or not she was going to answer me, I hog-tied her with a large roll of gauze bandage. I wrapped it around her ankles and her hands which were behind her back.

I was panting and gulping air, and every muscle and bone in my body was on fire.

For good measure, in case she came to, I tied up Nat Scott as well. And then I tried to find my way out of this hell-hole.

I cautiously peered out of the doorway into a small hall, with several doors. The hallway was wallpapered in a flowered, old fashioned print. There were crown moldings around the high ceiling, foot high baseboards, and ornate, glass knobs on the doors. The only sounds I could hear were coming from Belinda. I crept out of the room I was in, down the short hallway and into a large, sparsely furnished, living room. An old fashioned Princess phone sat on one of the end tables and I dashed for it.

It was dead. No dial tone.

Where the hell am I?

A three-sixty review of the room gave me no clues. An old sofa, with saggy, threadbare cushions sat under three heavily draped windows. In front of the sofa was a coffee table, laden with prescription pill bottles, old National Geographic magazines, pens, balled-up Kleenexes. A door on the left side of the room led to a closet, holding musty-smelling coats and dirt covered shoes.

I need to get out of here!

Another door on the far side of the room led into a kitchen. There didn't appear to be an exit from there either. I headed back down the hallway and opened the first door that I came to. Inside the door was total darkness. I groped for a light switch on the wall and flooded the room with light.

The sights in that room sickened me. My eyes saw things that my brain could not compute. My nose was scorched with the rotten smell of death and putrefaction. The cadaver of an old woman, curled on her side, lay on a steel table. What used to be her back was now a gaping hole, full of black, dried blood. Her gray hair hung stringy and limp, pieces covering her face. Wrinkled, saggy skin hung from her buttocks, her calves and her arms. Thank God her eyes were closed. My breath came in short gasps and with each outward breath I bawled and with each inward breath I gasped.

Who is she?

I turned around and ran to the next door which opened to a small bedroom, with a neatly made single bed pushed up against the wall. The last door in the hall was my salvation. I opened it and stood amazed, in an area that looked familiar.

I stumbled across the carpeted floor and banged on a door. And the sweetest face I had seen in a while peered up at me when the door opened.

Constance Everwood leaned on her cane and craned her neck up at me.

"Miss Monahan," she said. "*Why* are we in our nightdress?"

"It's not my nightdress, it's a hospital gown, and I need to call the police."

"Then step in, young lady. You'll find the telephone on a small table in my living room. That way," she motioned with her head.

Chapter fifty-nine

A WEEK LATER, I WATCHED the sun rise on Georgian Bay. My parent's cottage was on a point in the Bay facing south, so we were graced with beautiful sunrises and sunsets. A light, early morning mist covered the still water, which at this time of day was dark green, almost black. The temperature was cool and I was cocooned inside a quilt on my Muskoka chair. The heat would come in a few hours and it would be sweltering by noon, and likely humid and muggy by mid-afternoon. Early mornings were my favourite time at the cottage.

Peace and quiet and time alone. Time to think and sort things through.

I wasn't missing Manhattan in the least and was so thankful when the police had finally wrapped things up.

A couple of days later I was on a flight from LaGuardia to Toronto. Three hours after landing I arrived in my rental car at my parent's cottage. The key to the front door of the cottage was in its usual place, hung on a nail inside the unlocked shed. I took my time unloading the groceries I had picked up at the IGA in Orillia. As soon as they were unpacked and put away, I opened all the windows, loaded my few clothes into a dresser, put on my bathing suit and wandered down to the dock. I opted not to take my usual running dive off the end of the dock, in deference to my still broken ribs. Rather, I lowered myself into the lake from the wooden ladder nailed to the end of the dock. And then I floated on my back for an eternity and pretended I was ten years old again.

The police had come quickly, within minutes it seemed. By the time they had arrived, I was presentable in one of Miss Everwood's chenille bathrobes and a pair of fake fur slippers.

About two cups of tea and a half an hour later, Jay and Kelly had arrived from the hospital, where they had been frantically trying to find me.

Jay sat beside me on the divan - that's what Miss Everwood called it -

271

holding my hand. I had given him a bit of smile when he arrived but hadn't said much. Frankly, I was shell-shocked. Not one normally at a loss for words, I just plain had nothing to say. I had directed the police to Nat Scott's apartment, warning them what they would find.

"I want to go home," I finally whispered to Jay. The clock on the wall read six thirty. I was bone tired and wanted to go to bed. Jay got up and said he'd find Kelly and clear it with the police.

Miss Everwood, who had been pacing up and down the hallway, peering through the peephole, watching all the action next door came into the room when Jay went out.

"Tell me again how you escaped," she urged me. "It's thrilling. Absolutely thrilling, better than any action movie with Bruce Willis." She was loving this and I was hating it. I hadn't told her about the cadaver, who I was pretty sure was Nat Scott's mother.

We got the okay from the police and I thanked Miss Everwood profusely before I let Jay take me home. Kelly rode down in the elevator with us.

"I'll stay with you until one of the bodyguards arrives," he advised us. "Until we close this up and until we find Ben Tucker, we're still going to be guarding you twenty-four seven."

Kelly was feeling overly protective and responsible for me since I had been kidnapped while under the protection of one of his guys. The hospital security staff had found Jason, drugged and unconscious, on the floor under my hospital bed.

I was asleep before my head hit the pillow.

While I was sleeping, they found Ben Tucker. Or, as his mama christened him, Don McLean. Crying Belinda was taken to the Emergency department where she had surgery to remove six of her front teeth and her broken jaw wired up. Miss Natalie Scott refused medical treatment when she came to, so she was taken directly to the Precinct for booking. Everett McLean was arrested in Flagstaff and charged with arson and attempted murder.

"Who is Everett McLean?" I asked.

Kelly and Jay and I were in the kitchen, in what were becoming our 'usual' spots at the counter. Jay was cooking and Kelly and I were on stools, drinking coffee. I looked better than the two of them because I had slept for about six hours. Jay said he caught a few hours, and Kelly, the ever-tough, ever-rough Marine claimed he was fine, didn't need sleep.

"He's Don McLean's brother," Kelly said. "And he's singing like a canary on speed right now to the Flagstaff police. Seems poor Everett was terrorized by his brother all his life and has always done what his brother demanded. A friend of Everett's girlfriend is an employee in the administration department at the hospital. That's how he found out there was someone snooping around, asking about Everett's brother and his ex-girlfriend."

Kelly sipped from his coffee. Jay picked up the story.

"Everett called his brother, his brother told him to look after it. Which we think he understood to mean burn down the hospital and kill that guy who's snooping around."

It was too sick to think about.

"Where is Ben now?" I wanted to know so I could go and kick the shit out of him.

"Being booked right now at the Precinct," Kelly said. "They found Ben and his van on the side of the freeway on the Jersey side. His van was fried and he was wheeling himself along the shoulder of the road. Patrolman didn't know who he was when he picked him up, but being a good Samaritan, he put him in the back seat of the cruiser and loaded his wheelchair into the trunk. Our Miss Scott had already squealed on him so an APB was in the system. The Jersey cop was pretty happy to find out he had a live one locked in his back seat."

Jay laid a plate in front of each of us, laden with toast slices, scrambled eggs, bacon and tomato wedges. Not much was said for the next few minutes as we dug in. I was surprised to have an appetite.

When we were loading dirty plates into the dishwasher, Kelly's cell phone rang and he excused himself to take the call. Jay was at the kitchen sink with his hands in soapy water, scrubbing the frying pan. I stood behind him, wrapped my arms around his waist and pressed my cheek against his back. I winced at the sharp pains in my rib cage. My legs were stiff and my upper back throbbed with pulsating pain. But, regardless of the aches and pains, I'd be happy if I could stay right here, forever. Being here in the kitchen, with Jay, was uncomplicated, simple and pure. The way things should always be. I gave him a squeeze which hurt me more than him, and grabbed the dish towel and got back to reality.

Kelly came back into the kitchen and told us, "That was Detective Shipley on the phone. Natalie Scott has herself an attorney."

"Yippee for her," I sniped.

Kelly ignored me. Like the professional he was.

"She's apparently wantin' to tell her story. Detective Shipley asked if we wanted to come down and listen."

Jay and Kelly looked at me.

"Hell yeah," I said in my best Texan drawl. "Count me in."

Chapter sixty

DETECTIVE SHIPLEY MET US IN the lobby of the 20th Precinct on West 82nd Street and escorted us up the staircase to the second floor. The main area of the floor was populated with desks where a few people sat, working. Along one wall were several enclosed rooms. Shipley opened the door to one of these rooms and waved us in.

A small table was pushed up against the far wall and four folding chairs were stacked against the end of the table. An inside wall, adjoining the next enclosed room, had a large window. Shipley pointed at it.

"We'll be in the next room. Keep the lights off in here so you can see. That switch there," she pointed at a knob on the wall, "is the audio. I'll be back later." She stared at me for a moment and I was thinking she wanted to say something to me but she turned and left.

We waited silently in the darkness for about five minutes and I stared into the next room, looking at the table, the chairs, the video camera set up in the corner. It had been almost three weeks to the day since Tommy had been murdered. Senselessly.

The door in the next room opened and Natalie Scott was ushered in by a female police officer. She was wearing a white jumpsuit that looked like it was made out of paper. Her feet were shackled. Around her waist she was sporting a wide, leather belt to which her hands were cuffed. The police officer pulled out one of the chairs, sat Natalie in it, and then stood on the opposite side of the room, guarding her.

Her skin had a greenish tinge under the harsh florescent lights and her hair hadn't improved since she and I had seen each other the night before. It remained matted and greasy. She sat quietly, her chin resting on her chest. Resigned.

The bitch is near. Her smell is in the air. So close to being victorious. So close to snuffing out her vile being. So close to finally having it all under control.

A few minutes after Natalie Scott was seated in the room, the door opened again and several people entered and took seats around the table. Detective Shipley and Lieutenant Linda Derek took chairs across from Natalie. A very tall, heavy-set woman took the place next to Natalie. She heaved a large briefcase onto the table, took out a pad of paper and several pens, and then stowed it under the table. Two others, an older man and a middle-aged woman took seats at opposite ends of the table.

Detective Shipley turned on a tape-recorder in the middle of the table and the police officer standing by the wall turned on the video camera.

"For the record," Shipley started. "I am Detective Shipley." She recited her badge number, the case number, the date, and the names of the people present. The large woman beside Natalie was her lawyer, and her name was given as Anne Nicholas. The other two people were Assistant District Attorney's - Webster Purcell and Sheila Miller.

Out of control. No longer in charge of one's destiny. Caged like an animal. The rage was back. No control. You make me sick. You cannot do anything right. The bitch was free. You are not. You cannot live like this. This is not living. Rage was boiling again.

Shipley: For the record, Natalie Scott, represented here by Anne Nicholas, has indicated that she is willing to make a statement about the events of last night.

Nicholas: For the record, this statement is against counsel's advice and my client understands that what she says here will be used against her.

Purcell: For the record, the DA's office is not offering any deals for Miss Scott's statement.

Shipley: Miss Scott. Please tell us what transpired at your mother's apartment last night.

Natalie Scott looked up for the first time. She stared at Detective Shipley for a long moment and then began talking. Her voice was a monotone and sounded almost robotic.

Scott: It didn't work.

Shipley: What didn't work?

Scott: The way we planned it.

Natalie kept her head bowed, and her handcuffed hands on her lap.

Plans that don't work out are not plans. It was fucking bullshit. The stalker was angry, riled. The serenity and control were gone.

"This is bullshit," I stated. "She's acting like she's been beaten down. Bullshit. Last night she was a maniac. She would have killed me." I felt the tops of my ears turning red and I craved a cigarette.

Jay knew better than to tell me to calm down, but he did take a chance and gently laid his hand on my upper arm. He rubbed it a bit.

"She's acting," Kelly said. "I agree with you. Let's just see how this plays out."

I started pacing in the small room. Bullshit.

Shipley: Can you be a little more specific? What did you plan?

This time Nat took an extra long time without answering and several minutes of silence ensued. Lieutenant Derek lost patience. She slammed her hand down on the table. Everyone jumped. Except Natalie Scott. It was as if she were drugged.

Nicholas: Was that really necessary, Lieutenant?

Derek: This is bullshit.

Exactly!

Derek: If your client has a statement to make or something to tell us, I suggest she gets on with it.

The stalker's heart was beating so fast and so hard, it hurt. But pain was the least of the worries now. This was going to end now. *Breathing was becoming more and more difficult. It would be alright, soon.*

Scott: We needed one more healthy body. It was going to work. We had run the diagnostics and conducted several simulations. It was perfect. The piston.

Everyone in the room was looking at Nat Scott in disbelief.

Shipley: Did you say piston?

Scott: Yes.

Shipley: Can you explain? What piston?

Nat paused again for a long time. The Lieutenant was losing patience, and the two Assistant DA's were rolling their eyes at each other. Me? I knew we were being hoodwinked. The bitch was playing with us.

I turned around to Jay who was standing behind me. "Piston. Percutaneous intelligence system transfer nephrology. It's the name of the Phoenix interface that we developed with the Global Devices artificial kidney."

Jay nodded.

The air surrounding his head was orange. It was swirling. He was hot and sweat poured down out of his hair, down his back, between his legs. Everything was orange. The colour of his rage. He stared at the damp, cement wall and watched it turn red before his eyes. The jail-issued orange coveralls were drenched now in his rage, his sweat, his life.

Scott: Piston is the name of the prototype interface we developed to power an artificial kidney.

The Lieutenant sighed and shook her head in disgust. Twenty minutes had passed and we were no further along.

Shipley: Thank you. You said you needed one more healthy body. Can you tell us about that?

Scott: It had to be Monahan. We had tried and failed with the others. But Monahan stood in the way of it ever working. So we took her. Took her from the hospital. We were going to take her kidneys and give her an artificial one.

I wanted to throw up. I turned around from the glass. I couldn't look at her. Jay put his arms around me and I buried my head in his chest.

The stalker was strong. His mind was strong but his body was stronger. Breathing hard but under control he pulled himself up the bars and threaded the coveralls through the cross bar. Hanging on with one hand. Biceps and triceps screaming. His brain screaming. He used his free hand and his teeth to secure the overalls and then knowing that blissful peace would be with him soon, he slipped the knotted legs of the coveralls over his head and gratefully *let go.*

I heard a wail from the room next door and turned around to the window and saw Natalie Scott slump to the side, and fall off her chair. She was moaning loudly and lay on the floor in a fetal position.

The Lieutenant stood up. "We're done here people. Officer, call the medics."

The police officer was attending to Natalie on the floor, and everyone else was standing up, watching her.

The door to the room opened half way and someone motioned at Shipley, who left the room. She was back very quickly and whispered something to her Lieutenant. They both left as a medic from the jail arrived.

The door to our room opened and Shipley stuck her head in.

"Ben Tucker, or Don McLean, just committed suicide in his cell. We'll talk later," she told us, and quickly left.

It had rained while we were in the Precinct and the air was heavy with moisture. The sun was coming out and the temperature was just below blistering. The three of us stood on the sidewalk for a moment, adjusting our eyes and bodies to being outside again. We used the sunshine as an excuse to stand still for a while, all of us stunned by the news of Ben, or Donald's, suicide.

"Kelly," I said.

"Yes, ma'am."

"Take the rest of the day off. That's an order."

"Thank you ma'am. But I'll respectfully decline."

"Come on. Tucker slash McLean is dead. Nat Scott is locked up and probably comatose. And Belinda Moffat is under police guard at the hospital."

"Yes, ma'am," Kelly agreed with me, nodding his head. "But are we sure they are the *only* ones responsible? Until I'm convinced, we'll be watching you."

Chapter sixty-one

THIS STATEMENT IS OF MY free will. It is being written without coercion and without promise of any leniency by the District Attorney's office. My name is Belinda Moffat. I am 33 years old and I live in the Borough of Queens. I have a Ph.D in Bio-medical Engineering. I am employed by Phoenix Technologies where I have worked for approximately three years as a project manager in the research and development department. About six months ago, my boss, Natalie Scott, came to me and told me that she had a top-secret project that I was to work on with Ben Tucker. I didn't object. I did as I was asked by my bosses at Phoenix. It was certainly more workload but I was glad for the opportunity. Several months later, though, when it became clear to me that this top-secret project was all about falsifying records and test results, I objected. That's when Miss Scott threatened to fire me. I make no excuses for my behavior, but I could not afford to lose my job. It costs me close to $6,000 a month to pay for round the clock care for my twin sisters, both of whom suffer from cerebral palsy.

Again, making no excuses, I participated in the falsification of records which were submitted to the FDA by Global Devices for their artificial kidney project. You see, Ben Tucker was desperate for an artificial kidney to be approved. Because of his paraplegia, he is in renal failure and must take dialysis several times a week.

Dr. Jordan Francis, the vice president in charge of the project at Global Devices suspected that the test results were being falsified and he shared this information with Mr. Connaught, who was the president of Phoenix. How do I know this? Because Jordan Francis was my fiance. He told me of his suspicions. I didn't have the courage to tell him that I knew, and that I was participating in the fake tests. Natalie Scott and Ben Tucker suspected that they might be found out when Dr. Francis and Mr. Connaught invited them to a meeting and started to question their test methods and the results. I was at that meeting as a member of the team. Three days later Jordan stopped calling me. I was desperate to talk to him, to see him, but the people at Global said he had resigned from his job and moved away. Several days later, Mr. Connaught was murdered. I don't know for a fact that Natalie Scott or Ben Tucker killed Mr. Connaught, but I do know for a fact that they killed Jordan. They told me that they kidnapped him, drugged him, took his kidneys out and used him as a human guinea pig to test the artificial kidney. He lasted seven days. They made me help them get rid of his body.

Jordan Francis was the only man who truly loved me. In the beginning he thought it was Nat Scott who wanted him, but it was me. I got him to love me. The letters weren't from her, they were mine. Everyone thought Natalie was beautiful. Natalie didn't love him. She loved Ben.

Natalie Scott and Ben Tucker are evil. When the artificial kidney didn't work on Jordan, they tried it on Natalie's mother. The poor woman was in her nineties.

Ben Tucker was a surgeon before he came to work at Phoenix Technologies. He was in love with Natalie and she adored him. Until he operated on her mother. After that, Ben had to make Natalie take pills and that way she still adored him.

My job was to help them kill Kate Monahan. She was a bitch and she was getting in the way of Ben getting well.

I hired Bill Collins to shoot her. Bill went to high school with me but lately he's been out of work and needed money. I offered him $500. He shot her bodyguard but missed her. So then we had to get her out of the hospital because Ben thought it would be a good idea to take out her kidneys and make her suffer.

I put the paralytic drug in her IV and Bill and I took her out of the hospital. I must have not given her enough because it wore off too soon and then she hit me and knocked out my teeth.

There was more but it wasn't relevant. Stuff about her sisters and how they needed a bath every Thursday night. Belinda had clearly gone over the edge, into the deep end.

It was good to know that Dr. Francis was not in on the fixing of the test results, and I know Dr. Pritchard would be happy to hear this. At least the reputation of Global Devices would be intact.

Nat Scott was more clear-headed the day after her original try at confession. Apparently, Tucker/McLean had been doping her. It took a good twenty-four hours for the drugs to leave her system. I wondered what type of cocktail he was feeding her if she could be so full of rage, and then be practically catatonic ten hours later.

Scott: I shot Tom Connaught.

Shipley: Why?

Scott: Because he and Dr. Francis found out about the test results. At first we denied it and we tried to hide it but I knew that Tom had copied the hard drive of my computer. He had all the test result files from the Piston trials. It wasn't as if we reported huge variations in the readings on the external system. We changed some numbers by fractions. Fractions only. Ben knew this version of the artificial kidney could work. It would save his life. And my mother's. You have to understand. My mother had been ill for so many years and Ben was so dependent on dialysis. He was determined to make it work. But Tom Connaught was going to expose us. Ben couldn't go back to prison. He'd die there. So I called Tom Connaught and told him that I would give him all the faked test results. I told him to meet me behind the Van Buren Medical Center. When he came I was too scared at first to shoot him. But Ben would have been furious with me if I didn't do it. Just before Tom showed up, I got down on my knees and prayed for forgiveness for what I was about to do.

Shipley: Were you praying when you shot Mr. Connaught? Were you on your knees? Please answer the question out loud, Miss. Nodding your head can't be picked up on the tape recorder.

Scott: Yes. I was kneeling when I shot Tom.

Shipley: And what happened after that?

Scott: Kate Monahan showed up and made things worse. I knew Tom had documents from my hard drive in his apartment and I had to get them. I used an old building key and got in. Kate Monahan was there, but I only hit her. Hit her hard. I should have killed her too, right then.

Shipley: Did you help Mr. Tucker?

Scott: *Doctor* Tucker. And yes, I helped him. I loved him. I would do anything for him. When you love someone, you help them. No one ever helped me.

Shipley: How did you help Doctor Tucker?

Scott: I gave them the drugs. I helped Ben operate. But it didn't work. They both died.

Shipley: Who died?

Scott: Dr. Francis and my mother. Ben decided it would help with the research if we used the artificial kidney on a healthy patient and an aging, ill one. Dr. Francis stayed alive for seven days. My mother died on the operating table.

Shipley: Were you going to help operate on Kate Monahan?

Scott: Yes. It was my job to keep her paralyzed and wait for Ben. He was late coming. I couldn't keep her on the table and she got away. Ben never came. And now he's dead.

Before I left New York, Cleve and I, and the senior management team spent several days on more damage control. Big time damage control this time. We talked to analysts, bankers, clients, and employees.

Sandra Melnick, our VP Operations stepped up to the plate for us. I admired her skill and level thinking in times of a crisis. She spent time with the big honchos at the FDA. Explaining what had happened. Trying to clear our company's name.

We talked with analysts until we were blue in the face. I stopped returning their calls on Friday, sick of their unrelated questions and demands for information. We owned up to the criminal activity that had happened. We explained that those guilty were no longer with the company. We hoped that shareholders could see their way to trusting the board of directors and senior management when we committed to coming clean on everything. But analysts were like gossip columnists. They wanted information that couldn't possibly relate to their making a recommendation on whether or not someone should buy, hold or sell our shares.

Our stock took a shit-kicking. It started in a nose-dive after Portia Wellington wrote a somewhat speculative story in the Wall Street Journal on Monday, after talking to me on the day before. The headline went something like this: Can a Company Survive Murder and the Loss of its Visionary? That little story cost us a dollar per share. So by close of business on Monday, the shares were trading around $6.00. By Wednesday, when news hit the street that the 'Visionary's' replacement had survived an attempt on her life, *and* one of the company's vice-presidents was charged by New York's finest with attempted murder of the said replacement, the shares dropped another two dollars.

When the market opened on Thursday morning, there were only sell orders out there and we watched in horror during the day as the shares went from $4.00 and closed at $2.85. In four days the shares had lost about $4.15 in value. Three weeks ago, the ten million outstanding shares of Phoenix were worth, on paper, $73,500,000. Now they were worth $28,500,000. My thirty-three percent was now around $9,000,000.

Numbers that made me gasp.

By Friday morning, there was a little reprieve, and the shares opened at $3.50. There were more buy orders than the day before, and one of the major analysts came out with a *hold* recommendation. Meaning don't sell. Thank you very much.

And then Dr. Bill Pritchard, bless him, helped. He had called me on

Wednesday and we chatted quietly for about half an hour. I filled him in on what I knew at that point. He was very concerned about me. I assured him that I was no worse for the wear, so to speak. He called me again on Thursday afternoon.

"Kate." We were on a first name basis now. I liked it.

"Bill. How are you?"

"I'm doing fine for an old fella. Meet me for a beverage at the Blue Square Tavern?"

"Okay." I could do with a change of scenery.

"And bring your lawyer." Uh-oh.

"All right…"

"Not to worry dear. I have something I want to run by you."

Cleve was impressed with the Blue Square Tavern. Said it reminded him of a pub he used to frequent off Queen Street when he was at Osgoode Law School.

Dr. Pritchard was waiting for us at a table near the back. A middle-aged woman sat with him. I introduced Cleve, and Bill introduced Christina Dickson, his corporate counsel from a Wall Street law firm. Christina was tall, probably close to six feet, with beautiful auburn hair that fell in waves to her shoulders.

We sat and made small talk while we waited for our drinks. Christina, please call me Tina, was drinking scotch, straight up, with a twist of lemon. Bill ordered bourbon and an extra glass of ice. Cleve asked the waitress for a large draft beer, and I ordered my usual, Diet Coke. After we each had an obligatory sip of our drinks, Bill placed his hands on the table.

"Let's get down to business. I wanted to let you know that I'm going to be putting out a buy order for your shares."

I looked at Cleve, and he nodded.

"What your company has been through in the last month because of a couple of no good criminals, is, well, criminal." Bill smiled a little.

"I know you might think that I was rash in what I did. Cancelling the contracts with Phoenix. But based on the information I had at the time, it was a good business decision."

In hindsight, I agreed with him. About it being a business decision.

"But I've been doing a lot of thinking in the last few days. Before all of this happened, Global Devices had a good working relationship with Phoenix. Tom Connaught was a man who I admired. God rest his soul."

We all nodded.

"And Jordan Francis. We're going to miss him. I admit to being so relieved when I found out he wasn't in the middle of this mess that I cried." Bill paused and sipped his drink. "I spoke with the FDA today. We've got a long way to go to get back in their good books, but with the help of some of our clients, I think we can restore their confidence."

"We're talking to them too," I put in.

"For Global Devices to be successful, we need successful partners. Like Phoenix. We want to do business with you, again. So, I'm going to put my money where my mouth is. We'll buy up a truckload of your shares." He smiled a little. "You must admit, they're selling at a good price right now."

"How many shares are you thinking of buying up?" Cleve asked.

"Whatever five million dollars will get me." So more than a million shares.

"Thanks for the vote of confidence," I said. And I meant it.

We went on to discuss what we needed to do to reinstate our business relationship. The next morning, Bill held a small press conference and announced his intentions about acquiring the shares and talked about his confidence in Phoenix Technologies. Within the hour, our shares were up a dollar, trading at $4.50. When the markets closed at the end of the day, the shares were at about $4.75. There were more buy orders out there than sell orders, which was a good sign.

Chapter sixty-two

WE DID A LOT OF hand-holding with the employees and shareholders. The senior management team had a communication plan drafted before the sun came up on Wednesday. The plan called for an all-employee meeting at noon on Thursday. Before that meeting though Steve set up conference calls and one-on-one meetings for myself and our chief financial officer with analysts and bankers.

On the employee side, Sandra and I talked to everyone in person, by video conference or by webcast about the situation: what we knew as fact, what were rumours, and how the Company planned on weathering this storm.

After the first employee meeting held in our large boardroom, Jenn Ludlow sought me out. I saw her pushing her way through the crowd of people who were standing four deep around the large table. Her jet black hair covered half her face and she had about fifteen studs in the one ear that was not covered by her hair. She was smiling, as usual.

She stood in front of me and said my name. "Kate."

"Jenn," I answered her. We both smiled. She held out her arms and made a 'come here' motion with her hands. I didn't move quick enough for her so she stepped up to me and wrapped me in a big hug. I winced and groaned inwardly, wondering how long broken ribs take to heal. I hugged her back.

"I am so glad that *dickhead* is dead," she said quietly in my ear. We broke the hug and stood apart. "You know, Mr. Shit for Brains. Ben Tucker. What an asshole."

I couldn't disagree.

"And," she said in a low voice, "I *always* knew there was something wrong with Natalie Scott. I just couldn't pinpoint it." She clapped her hands once, loudly. "So, are you okay? Do you need me to kick some ass?" She laughed, and leaned closer. "And, have you *seen* that gorgeous hunk of bodyguard, Michael? I mean, take a good look, because he's about to come off the market, if you know what I mean! Who would have thought I'd fall for a straight-as-an-arrow type?"

I shrugged my shoulders. Who would have thought?

"Call me if you need *anything*," she told me, again. "Catch you on the flip side." And she was gone, into the crowd.

Muskoka chairs are built for one person, but I'm small so two of us fit just nicely into one. I was curled up on Jay's lap and we were watching the sun go down over Georgian Bay. My ribs were healing and the other aches and pains had gradually left. Daily swims and hour long back floats in the lake had helped. Jay joined me today after a long week of separation. His job had kept him in New York and I had needed some time. To myself. To think.

And now I didn't want to think any more. For a while anyway. It felt so good to be held by Jay and to feel his body next to mine.

"I've made some decisions," I said, "but I need your input before they become official decisions."

I was pretty proud of myself, thinking of someone other than myself, for once. I needed Jay to be okay with what I wanted to do.

"Sure. Fire away. I'd be glad to offer input, at no charge."

"I think I want to stay at Phoenix. It's a good company. And good people. I think Tommy would want me to stay."

"I agree. It's your company. You need to do whatever you think is necessary."

"Why are you always so agreeable?" I smiled up at him.

"Because lately, you make it easy." He smiled back. I knew he was teasing. "What other decisions have you made?"

"Well, if I stay at Phoenix, it'll have to be in New York." Jay nodded. "I want to sell Tommy's apartment and get our own."

"Agreed."

"So, this living together is something you want to continue?"

"No. Not necessarily."

My stomach sank. And here I thought everything was close to perfect. I gulped.

"No?"

"I'm okay with the way things have been the last couple of weeks," Jay said. "But…"

I sat up from where I had been curled against his chest and turned to him.

"But what?" I asked indignantly.

"Hey, easy girl," he teased. "Let me finish. I was going to say that I'm okay with the way things have been but it would be better if we were married."

The long pause that followed was Kate Monahan, finally speechless.

Thank-you

There are tons of people usually thanked at the end of a novel. In my case, there will be less than a dozen, so bear with me. First of all, I think it only appropriate that I thank my parents, Isabel and Bill Buckle, without whom I wouldn't have half the smart-aleck things to say that I do. May they rest in peace. I miss them both desperately.

My readers/proofreaders are the same three wonderful women who helped me with my first book OPTIONS. Roxanne D'Amico, Deborah Cathcart and Sheila Purcell. Thank-you Roxanne, thank-you Deborah, thank-you Sheila. Your eagle-eyes and perceptive ideas were blessings. (Any typos, mistakes or down-right stupid things in this book are the author's fault, so please don't blame Roxanne, Deborah or Sheila!)

Thank you Sifu Jerry Poteet for allowing me to quote you in my book. The wisdom and guidance you have provided to Sifu Darryl D'Amico and his students is humbly and gratefully acknowledged. Thank you Sifu Darryl, for sharing your art with me, and patiently explaining the best way to knock someone out with the heel of your hand!

Thank you to Jordan D'Amico, number one (and only) son for his insight and artful ways, and to Kate D'Amico for being a model for so many different things. Thank you (again) to my husband, Darryl, for helping me keep my sense of humour all these years.

And I owe tons of gratitude to everyone who read my first book OPTIONS and who have been urging me on with this second Kate Monahan mystery! Merci, gracias, danke, much obliged!

Rosemarie D'Amico
September 2010

ROSEMARIE D'AMICO
was a law clerk/paralegal for over 20 years, working at some of Canada's largest law firms and high tech companies. *Artificial Intentions* is her second Kate Monahan novel. She lives in Ottawa, Ontario with her husband Darryl. Visit her website at www.rosemarie-damico.com and follow her blog at www.roses-space.blogspot.com.